'You don't think she's changed her mind then?' Momentarily Jeff looked like a young boy, and again Ellie envied Charlotte for having so much of him.

She shook her head. 'She loves you,' she said.

Before they got in the car to go back to Wales, Olivia pulled her aside. 'It's very wicked of you darling. But I think I can understand it.'

Ellie felt almost disgusted by her mother – by the easy acceptance of what should have been sordid.

In that moment Ellie knew that childhood was over.

About the author

Jan Henley is a successful writer of feature articles and short stories for the women's magazine market. She is currently studying for a B.A. degree with the Open University. *Other Summers* is her first full-length novel. She lives in West Sussex with her husband and three children.

Other Summers

Jan Henley

CORONET BOOKS
Hodder and Stoughton

First published in Great Britain in 1995
by Hodder and Stoughton
A division of Hodder Headline PLC

First published in paperback in 1995
by Hodder and Stoughton

A Coronet Paperback

10 9 8 7 6 5 4 3 2 1

All characters in this publication are fictitious and any resemblance to real persons, living or dead, is purely coincidental.

British Library Cataloguing in Publication Data

Henley, Jan
Other Summers
I. Title
823 [F]

ISBN 0 340 62465 5

Typeset by Keyboard Services, Luton, Beds

Printed and bound in Great Britain by
Cox and Wyman Ltd, Reading, Berks

Hodder and Stoughton
A division of Hodder Headline PLC
338 Euston Road
London NW1 3BH

To my parents,
for their love and support

With special thanks to Wendy Tomlins, Linda Green
and Elizabeth Roy

Prologue

The fire began with a stutter. A tall, dark young woman clutching an open box of matches stood motionless and transfixed in front of the paper pyramid that she'd just built. The small flame was still wrapped in its folds.

Screwed-up papers from thirty-one years of a screwed-up life. Carefully constructed and easily destroyed. Charlotte felt the nudge of hysteria. And why not? She was alone here with all the useless pieces of paper that made up her past. So who would know – or care – if she found it funny?

She waited. The flame rested in the heart of the bonfire. Had it caught? Then the first photograph began to toast. Slowly the edges browned. The crisp, black line curled and spread, and so did Charlotte's triumphant smile.

'From small beginnings,' she murmured. Her hazel eyes were dense and unfathomable.

Now she could hardly wait for it to get going – for the destruction to let rip. The tension was tight inside her, she wanted release.

She laughed, louder than she'd laughed for a long time. Louder than she needed to. She should have done this when she first found out. It should have been her first gesture of retaliation.

Another photograph caught light, then another. The bonfire teased her. Quick, quick, slow, quick, quick, slow – it gathered momentum and then seemed to go out, until she was panting, needing to be finished.

'Burn, you bastard,' she whispered. 'Go on. Keep going.'

Another licking flame appeared. It stroked a loose-leafed bookful of childish poetry, and then the precious scribbled pages from her diary.

With a whoop, Charlotte grabbed more from the wheelbarrow, and threw them on, haphazard and wild – the pyramid becoming redundant. Before long the ground by the bonfire was littered with papers and books. She kicked them closer. Over thirty years of memories. Burned to ashes in only seconds.

She recognised one of Ellie's old school photographs, moments before it was consumed. Navy uniform, gappy smile, open eyes.

'Bitch—' Her voice was soft and controlled. She closed her eyes. Waiting for the pain. 'Even you,' she whispered. 'You have to go too. Especially you.' She could hardly believe the glimpse she'd had of that photograph. Had Ellie ever been that untouched? Even in the days before they lived at Pencraig?

At last the wheelbarrow was empty. And the fire was a raging monster, all right, fiercer than the bogey man had ever been – flames jostling for undevoured air, darting into unclaimed spaces, fighting for fabric, hungry for more. Hungry for anything – fire was like that, fire took it all. Charlotte winced. The arrows of flame had banded into one. There was only one purpose now.

She stood as close as she could, feeling the rush of heat scorching her face, reddening her bare arms and bare legs – still damp from the effort of carting the barrow from the house to the wood. Her flesh was steaming.

It was a blisteringly hot summer's day. She'd chosen it specially. The power of the heat made her faint, the sting of the smoke was in her eyes, in her throat, in her nostrils. She was choking on it. She breathed still deeper. She could feel it coming all over her.

It was a funeral pyre – she could step up and do a passable Joan of Arc. It wouldn't be impossible. She reached up her arms. She could understand sacrifice – but they weren't getting any more sacrifice out of her now.

'You can't touch me.' The words were parched and grating. 'Neither of you can.'

She stared at the sparks flying beyond the outspread branches, on and up into the hazy sky, disappearing into the muted glare of the sun. The molten core of the bonfire mesmerised her, fuelling her anger, joining with it, erupting into climax.

'Why?' she screamed. Her arms flailed uselessly, frantically reaching out for something that wasn't there, or had gone a long time ago. 'Tell me, for God's sake. Why?'

But there was no one to answer her. The flames rose higher, and as they rose the white ashes fell, weightless, on to her bare feet. All that remained was an insidious crackling, as each memory was separately awoken and collectively destroyed.

Some time passed. It was over. Charlotte stood, waiting for the fire to die down. Her sleeveless red shirt was scorched and blackened with smuts from the fire. Her knees were grazed. She felt empty. But the ritual was complete.

Taking a stick, she awkwardly poked the charred remains of the letters, the photographs, the wedding souvenirs and the red leather-bound diary. The sun was still shining, but Charlotte was shivering. Cautiously, as if they could hurt her still, she dispersed the ashes and the memories, kicking them with one dirty, sandalled foot, into the dust that they'd come from.

'Never anything else. Just ashes. Just bloody useless ashes—' she said

Sinking to her knees, she took a handful of the blackened dust, letting it fall between her fingers. And then she wept.

The tears were so strong and potent that she could feel herself losing control. And as the control slipped away, so did the hatred. The need for revenge. Charlotte was left with nothing but a growing sense of relief.

She closed her eyes. The pictures were fading—

It was eighteen years ago. Charlotte Morgan was thirteen. Her sister Ellie was nine. The red family car – with them all inside – was moving slowly down a Welsh country lane. Gradually it pulled to a halt outside the house that was to be their new home.

Part I

1

'Come on, Ellie. We're here,' Charlotte said.

Ellie Morgan rubbed at her eyes and stumbled as she climbed out of the car. But it wasn't sleep that was disorientating her. It was just that the house she could see beyond the white gate and sloping lawn was so different from what she'd expected. She stared open-mouthed. It was the kind of house that had secrets clamped behind the grey-white stone. Secrets that were beckoning to her, and beckoning to Charlotte too.

As Mother and Dad went through the white gate the two girls hung back, one so delicate and fair, the other dark and loose-limbed. They moved closer together. Ellie's eyes followed the path. It ran from the garden, past the gate, and up a slope – vanishing intriguingly into a dark wood, through the door-frame of some trees.

She felt it tugging at her. Wales was alien country to a city girl, and it had to be explored. Soon. Then Charlotte squeezed her arm, and Ellie didn't need to look at her to confirm that she felt it too. Because Charlotte always felt it too.

They followed their parents towards the new home.

'I can hear the water!' Mother's full red lips parted as she smiled her breathless smile of pleasure. Already she seemed different, and her fair hair was windblown in a careless way that Ellie had never noticed before. It made her more beautiful, but kept her even further away.

'You must have had such heavenly summers here when you were a child. If I'd known it was this wonderful, I would have let you bring me here before.' Mother's white hands fluttered, in an appealing gesture that embraced her surroundings.

Charlotte looked away in disgust.

'I did tell you how much it meant to me.' There was hardly a trace of regret in his kind eyes. He would never blame Mother for anything. 'It meant a lot to the old man too – that's why he decided to retire here.'

'And die here.' Olivia nodded sadly.

Ellie had seen her grandfather a few times when he'd come to London. But she'd never been here before, and she was glad. She wouldn't have liked to see this house before now. Now that it was theirs. And now that Dad had persuaded Mother to live here.

Dad, tall but stooping slightly as if he'd never quite learned to stand up to things, led the way to the front door. In one hand he carried a hold-all, while the other arm was slung across Mother's slim shoulders as if he could keep her down to earth. She carried only a white, wispy handkerchief. Mother was never concerned with the practical. Someone else would bring the bags in later.

Dad dumped the hold-all and ran his fingers along the grey stone. Some letters were etched into a name-plate on the wooden porch.

'Pencraig,' he said softly. Then he smiled, as if some distant memory was nudging him with pleasure. 'Top of the cliff. It's good to be back.'

Top of the cliff? Ellie couldn't see any cliff. She squinted at the unfamiliar word that made Wales seem still stranger, while Dad and Mother exchanged the kind of look that made her squirm. She recognised it at once, although she hadn't seen it for a while.

'It's going back for you, darling. But for us, it's a new beginning,' Mother breathed.

They could have been alone. They should have been alone. They'd never been like friends' parents, who asked if you wanted drinks and made you hamburgers. No, Olivia and Rolf (this was how she thought of them) were too interested in each other. Or at least Dad was interested in Mother, and she was interested in— What? Ellie wasn't sure.

She glanced at Charlotte, who rolled her dark eyes. Ellie giggled. As usual they didn't need words. Olivia and Rolf were smiling at each other again. Everything was going to be all right.

After tea they headed in unspoken agreement for the path. Charlotte went first, raking thin fingers through her mass of brown hair, long legs striding ahead to show who was boss. Ellie didn't mind. But she had to run to keep up. It was never easy, keeping up with Charlotte.

'Is this part of our garden?' she panted. Back home, which wasn't home any longer, they'd only had window-boxes and a patio.

'Land,' Charlotte corrected. 'Course not. But who's going to stop us?' She spun round to throw Ellie a challenging look, then walked backwards for a few steps. 'Keep up! We've only got an hour.'

'Grandfather could have told us if we were allowed.' Ellie couldn't take it in. In London they only went out with a grown-up in tow. Everything was brick and you had to go to the park to see much in the way of green.

'Grandfather's dead. Otherwise we wouldn't be here, dummy. He left it to Dad in his will.'

Abruptly, Charlotte thrust out an arm for her to stop, and Ellie almost cannoned into her. They walked on side by side, and hand in hand. All discoveries had to be made together.

Once inside the ring of trees they stopped at a blackened clearing where there must have been a bonfire. Charlotte kicked up the ashes with her toe. Ellie coughed, and Charlotte bashed her on the back.

'Someone's been here,' she stated importantly.

Ellie looked around with big eyes. Everything was quiet. Unnaturally quiet. Deathly quiet. She couldn't even hear the water.

'Grandfather?' she enquired in a hopeful but wavering voice.

'I told you. He's dead. He was cremated three weeks ago. Burnt.'

They both stared at the ashes. Ellie's face crumpled.

'Don't be silly.' Charlotte hugged her briskly as a mother might. 'Let's go on.'

Ellie was scared, but she had no choice. She couldn't go back. She always had to follow Charlotte.

Gradually the trees began to clear, and as the path passed through the ring it opened out on to a patch of sand-stained grass. The way ahead unfolded in glorious invitation.

'Wow!' Charlotte gasped. She pushed her hair from her forehead with the back of a dirty hand.

Ellie's fears were forgotten. She clutched Charlotte's arm. It was like the theatre Mother took them to sometimes, and just as unreal. There was a clear view from the gorse and bracken-coated cliff down to a pear-shaped bay. The evening sun was a spotlight, focused on the water, sequinning waves that lunged against the rocks.

Charlotte laughed. 'We can go rock-hopping,' she whispered. 'Come on!'

So this was why the house was called 'Pencraig'. Because

the path through the wood led to the top of the cliff.

Ellie allowed herself to be pulled towards the steep path and they began to clamber down backwards, clutching at clumps of weed for balance, scrabbling with their sandals for footholds. Ellie forgot to be scared. She hardly noticed the boulders scraping at her shins and tearing her thin summer dress. She reached the bottom only seconds after Charlotte, bruised, dirty and proud.

Turning to face each other, they grinned, and then ran hand in hand into the sea.

Even before it was over, Ellie decided that it was her best summer ever, and she made herself forget what would be at the end of it. They were so close that separation seemed impossible. Surely something must happen to save them?

The warm days fell lazily into a predictable pattern. They always got up early to swim in Dragon Bay. It was deserted, and with each day became more their own. Then they'd go to the wood. They discovered a hideout, built out of bracken, small branches and mud, against the massive trunk of an old tree.

'It's called a bivouac,' Charlotte said. 'Exciting, huh? I wonder who built it.'

Thoughtfully, Ellie stroked the bark of the old beech, her fingers tracing the carved letters: RM L JP.

'Maybe it was RM.' Charlotte was watching her. 'Or JP.'

Ellie shivered. 'Or Indians.' The leaves of the old beech were glinting, like glass did in the sun, giving the hideaway a touch of magic.

Charlotte clicked her tongue impatiently. 'Don't be a dummy. You wouldn't get Indians here. More like Grandfather playing at cowboys. Only he was a bit old for that.'

Ellie giggled. Charlotte held up a hand for silence.

'We won't show this to another soul,' she declared. 'It'll be our secret. Swear, Ellie!'

'I won't tell.' Ellie was indignant.

'On your life.'

'On my life.' She didn't like it when Charlotte got serious. Her thoughts began to wander.

Charlotte frowned. 'You're not concentrating,' she complained. 'Swear you'll have your hair all cut off if you tell!'

Ellie hesitated. Her hair meant more to her than anything – apart from Charlotte of course. She twirled it between slim fingers. It was fine and blonde. Like silk, Mother said, when she brushed it every night. It was Mother's one routine, so Ellie knew how important it must be.

She shrugged. 'I swear,' she repeated obediently. 'Now you swear too!'

'I shall never tell another soul,' Charlotte intoned. 'On the life of my sister Eloise who I love more than I love myself.'

They stared at each other for a long moment, Charlotte's hazel eyes burning into her, as if forcing her to accept this truth. Then she reached out to hug her, long and slow, just like Dad used to hug her all the time. Why had he stopped? She couldn't even remember when he had stopped. Not knowing why, she began to weep into Charlotte's thin shoulder.

'There, there.' Her voice was an adult one. She was the mother Ellie had never really had. 'I'll always look after you, Ellie,' she said. 'I'll always be here.'

'Always?' Ellie clung to her. She could feel Charlotte's heart thumping as if it were her own. She knew her almost as well as she knew herself. Better maybe, because you could rely on her. Charlotte didn't have strange moods that no one could understand, like Ellie did. Like Mother and Dad did. Especially Mother.

Gradually the crying stopped. Charlotte could always make the crying stop. That's why Ellie had learned to run to her first. She would never let her down. Charlotte could always be trusted to make the pain go away.

One day Rolf called them into his study after dinner. He pushed aside the accounts he was working on.

'Have you enjoyed your summer?' he asked them.

Ellie saw him dig deep for the smile. She couldn't look at Charlotte, but her fingers curled into her sister's palm. Neither could miss the note of finality.

'Ye-es,' they said in unison. Warily.

'School starts soon,' he reminded them.

It flooded back into Ellie's mind. Boarding school. An awful tea party on the lawn. Open day. The housemistress beaming at Charlotte with lips too thin and tight to stretch into a proper smile.

'Do I have to go?' Charlotte spoke very quietly.

Rolf frowned. 'You know it's decided,' he said. 'The local school isn't enough for you at your age. You're thirteen. It's time to start considering what you're going to do with your life.'

Charlotte looked helpless. What was happening? She was never helpless. She was strong. So why didn't she stop this?

'Thirty miles isn't so very far away,' Rolf said.

'You can't make her go.' Ellie's voice was only a whisper.

Rolf looked at her. Her green, slanting eyes were flecked with the same kind of dreaming that had made him first fall in love with his wife. She even had Olivia's slightly hesitant smile. A smile that made you want to shield her from pain, damage, knowledge even.

He turned and stared out of the window.

Olivia was wandering across the lawn. The late summer roses she'd been picking were lying across the basket she carried. Her fine blonde hair kept blowing into her face as she walked, and every so often she pushed it back. She was smiling, but lately her smile had become more far away, more distant, as if she were leaving them too.

Rolf sighed. He was only seventeen when he'd met her, and from the start he'd adored her. She made him forget everything that had ever mattered. She was the unattainable, but his longing wasn't because of that. It was something that he'd never been able to grasp. He supposed it was a kind of love.

She would waft by, hardly aware of him, head in a musical world that he'd never comprehend. He was there to remind her of what day it was. What books she needed for school. Small things, but a beginning.

He could hardly believe it when she let him hold her hand. Then she offered a kiss, and even at that first touch he'd ached to give her everything. One day she told him she wanted to marry him. He might never have risked asking.

'Say you'll always look after me, Rolf,' she pleaded. 'You're the only one I can trust.'

Still, after all these years, he wanted to catch her, needed to pin her down. But he had never been able to. He watched her sometimes as she played the piano, her long, slender fingers stroking the keys as if music could give her what nothing else could. She would have been brilliant if she'd ever bothered to practise, and sometimes he told her so. But she brushed it aside, uncaring. So he watched her, and wondered where she was when she was lost in that music. Because she wasn't sitting at the piano in their living-room, that was for sure. She'd drifted so far away – from their life, from him.

It was hard to believe that she'd chosen to spend these years with him, had given him these two children. He was an ordinary man. He'd never been able to live up to her expectations, sweep her off her feet with strong arms and poetry. He never even told her that she was his world, too afraid she'd look at him and laugh. He couldn't bear that. At least living his way he was sure of not being a fool. Even if it meant not delivering adventure.

'Why can't Ellie come too?' Charlotte asked.

'She's too young. And your mother couldn't bear it if you both left at the same time.' Still Rolf stared out of the window.

Outside, Olivia saw him watching. She waved. Rolf turned away, his brown eyes hardening against the pain.

'You can't make her go. You can't!' Ellie's eyes were wet with tears. She buried her face in Charlotte's white T-shirt. She felt so helpless. But Charlotte hardly moved. She remained stiff and unyielding, her brown arms staying by her side, offering no shred of comfort.

'Charlotte—?' Ellie begged.

But she gently pushed her away. Her face was white underneath her dark tan.

'She'll be back in the holidays,' Rolf said. 'Just think what a good time you'll have then.'

They both stared at him.

Ellie turned towards Charlotte. Why didn't she say something? Why didn't she scream and shout?

But it wasn't her way. Her face was as cold and hard as if she had no feelings left. Ellie felt the desolation eating into her.

Then Charlotte turned around, gripped Ellie's wrist so hard that it hurt, and stalked out of the room, dragging her along. Ellie struggled for a moment, wanting to protest further, but Charlotte wasn't giving her the chance. And something told her that this was between the two of them. She couldn't interfere.

They trailed up the stairs.

'If you told him how miserable you are,' Ellie said, when they were in their attic bedroom. 'If you cried for long enough. He'd change his mind then. He would!'

Charlotte laughed without humour. 'It doesn't work for me.'

'Then *I* could—'

She put a finger on Ellie's lips. 'It isn't the way. It wouldn't do any good.'

And Ellie knew that it was useless to say more. She couldn't stop it. Charlotte would go.

They slept together that night, each cuddling into the other's warm body for comfort. But the parting was already haunting Ellie. And a small voice was whispering, making her wonder. Perhaps Charlotte hadn't protested because deep down she really wanted to go. It was the first time that Ellie wasn't sure. The first time she knew her world wasn't safe any longer.

The next day Olivia took Charlotte into town to buy her uniform. There were preparations to make, bags to pack. Everything changed. Ellie mooched around in all their special places, but it meant nothing without Charlotte. The wistful beauty of the wood and cliff had slipped from her grasp. Pencraig was no longer the most wonderful place in the world. She'd rather live anywhere else than be here without Charlotte.

'There'll be the holidays.' Charlotte clung to her for a final hug before she and Olivia boarded the train. 'There'll always be other summers.'

But Ellie didn't want other summers. She wanted the only one she couldn't have.

* * *

Mother was very bubbly when she got back.

'She's in a charming dormitory,' she said. 'And she's got a sweet girl called Jane Parkinson sleeping next to her.'

Ellie hated Jane Parkinson. Whoever she was.

'I was talking to her parents.' Olivia's green eyes took on the dreamy quality they all knew so well. 'He's in banking. They live outside Manchester somewhere. She showed me a photo – sweeping drive in and out. Ah!' She clasped her hands together in appreciation. The delicate gold bracelet she always wore slipped to her elbow. 'She'll love it. I know she will.'

Ellie tried not to listen. It was Mother's rubbish but she didn't want it to be real rubbish.

Olivia started wandering around the room. She was wearing a dress made of chiffon, like the scarves she tied Ellie's hair with sometimes. It billowed out at every small step.

'I've been thinking, Rolf.' She turned to face him. 'It's been bad for the girls being so isolated here. Even in this one summer, Charlotte's grown unused to socialising. She used to be such a dear, sweet thing. And now she's almost become a tomboy.'

Ellie stiffened. More change was in the air.

Rolf Morgan raised one dark eyebrow. 'You said before it was what we all needed. To get away. You wanted to come here to live when the old man died. It was supposed to be a new start for us.'

Mother twisted the diamond and emerald ring on her little finger. 'Of course. But we should still see people.'

Ellie sensed that she was nervous.

'We should have guests. Visitors.' She turned to her daughter. 'You'd like that, wouldn't you, Ellie?' Her poppy-red lips parted slightly.

Ellie knew she was being used. 'Not specially.' She wouldn't make anything easy. She wouldn't forgive them for sending Charlotte away. Not yet.

'Why are you being difficult?' Olivia sighed as she smoothed back her hair. It was wound loosely on top of her head in her usual style, but some fine strands were escaping from the confines of thin, golden hairpins.

Rolf was staring at her. His brown eyes were expressionless. 'What visitors?'

'Hmm?' Olivia turned to face him, distracted.

'Who do you want to invite?'

'Oh, I don't know.' She wandered over to the drinks cabinet, poured some clear liquid into a tumbler.

Ellie watched her. It seemed as if she had to keep moving.

'Denise and a few of the crowd. Anyone, really.'

Dad's eyes became curiously glazed. 'Time you were getting ready for bed, Ellie,' he said.

'I won't have a row!' Olivia spun around, drink in hand. 'I won't have a row about it.' Her green eyes were blazing, and she sounded like a petulant child.

'Ellie?' Dad was going to insist.

Reluctantly Ellie left the room and went noisily up the stairs. Then she tiptoed down again.

It was quiet. She guessed they were kissing. They always kissed when Mother wanted something.

'I thought we'd left all that behind us.' His voice was strained.

'We have.' Ellie imagined her threading her fingers through his hair. Or rubbing his shoulders. She tried to peer through the keyhole but it was blocked.

'It won't be like before,' Olivia said. 'But I need people. I can't be trapped like a caged bird—' Her voice was quickening into hysteria.

'All right. There, there.' He would be holding her in his arms now. Comforting her like Charlotte comforted Ellie.

'I'm scared, Rolf.'

Ellie jumped back. She didn't like that. She didn't want to hear those sorts of confessions.

'Don't worry. I'll always look after you. I'll always be here.'

Those words, the exact words that Charlotte had used. Echoes spun and danced in her head as Ellie raced back up the stairs. She wanted to scream. Throwing herself on the bed, she buried her face in the pillow. The words were still dancing. Laughing at her. She had to make the words go away.

Mother needed people. People meant parties. It would be like before. She started to weep. It wasn't a new beginning at all. Everything was going horribly wrong. It was only the beginning of a nasty kind of end.

2

Crouching in the bivouac, waiting for Charlotte, Ellie heard the sounds of approach at last. It was seven years since that first summer at Pencraig. And an hour since the car had screeched on to the gravel lane outside the house. Ellie had cramp. She moved gingerly. Why had Charlotte taken so long? She must have known where Ellie would be.

But something wasn't right. She leaned forward, her face against the bracken wall, to listen. Two voices? They were faint at first. Then—

'Wait till you see the bay. You won't believe it!'

That was Charlotte. She sounded excited and breathless, as if she'd been hurrying. Perhaps she'd been trying to get rid of him since they arrived. She wouldn't have *wanted* him to come here, would she?

'I'm ready to believe anything, sweetness.' The voice was low, melodic, slightly husky. 'Lead the way.'

Ellie frowned. Ridiculous. Charlotte might be lots of things, but she certainly wasn't sweet. She should snap this person back into the folds of a romantic paperback where he clearly belonged. She eased herself into a squatting position, rubbing at the grassy imprints on her knees. What was Charlotte playing at – bringing him here?

They both laughed. Or at least, he laughed. Charlotte giggled in a stupid way that didn't sound like her at all. What had happened to her? She'd never acted this way before.

In the meantime they were coming closer. If she wasn't careful she'd be trapped. She waited, poised to run, half-knowing the next step.

'There's a hideaway through here.' Charlotte's voice was only a whisper, but she knew how voices carried in the quiet of their wood.

No. Ellie caught her breath. What the hell was she doing? How could she tell some stranger their secret? How could she tell *anyone*? The pain of the cramp assaulted her again and she bit her lip, tasting the blood.

'A hideaway!' He laughed again. 'I didn't realise you were such a baby!'

Ellie didn't like his words, reducing the hideaway to some sort of fantasy of long-lost childhoods. And she hated the way he said them. Caressing. He had no right to speak to Charlotte like that. Especially in their wood. How could Charlotte stand it?

'Let's see this hideaway then.' There was a rustle. Heavy footsteps. Not far off. 'Where is it? Through here?'

'No!'

Ellie knew that Charlotte was embarrassed, recognised the note in her quick denial.

'I'll show you later,' she whispered. 'Ellie might be there.'

Before she could panic, Ellie eased herself free and ran like a rabbit from the bivouac, until she was out of sight behind a nearby tree trunk. Thirty seconds later they appeared.

'Go on!' His arm was slung round Charlotte's hips. It was possessive, yet casual. Ellie closed her eyes.

'Go and look,' he said. 'I'll stay right here. I promise.'

Would she really do it? Ellie opened her eyes to stare at Charlotte, praying for some sign of indecision. She was walking, slowly but surely, towards the bivouac. Ellie was too far away to make out the expression in her dark eyes. The brackenish touch of the leaves grazed her face, just like Charlotte was grazing her heart.

Charlotte seemed larger than life as she got closer, and so wonderfully familiar in her jeans and checked-cheesecloth shirt. As Ellie watched, she pushed her dark hair from her forehead with the back of one hand, and this old gesture of childhood seemed to make their closeness return. Ellie wanted to run to her, hold her, speak to her. It had been a long time. More than a year. There was so much she needed to say.

But something stopped her. Some unwelcome stranger, who was supposed to be just a friend, not a threat. And even as she watched, Charlotte looked back at him in a way that said it all. As if he had become everything to her, and all this had become nothing. Ellie's stomach heaved as she flattened it against the rough bark. She wanted to push. To hurt. Anything would do.

'We said no secrets, remember?' he called, teasing. He was tall, dark and rangy, quite unlike anyone she'd seen before. And he was a threat to everything.

'Don't tell me you've forgotten already? You haven't forgotten the rest of that night though, have you, sweetie?'

Ellie held her breath. What night?

'Don't do it, Charlotte,' she whispered. There was still time to turn back.

But he was following Charlotte, and they were very close.

'Hang on,' Charlotte hissed. 'Wait here. I want to check she's not in there.'

Ellie hated her. It was the first time, and it was almost a relief. She felt the flush of it pour through her, hot and insistent. Their wood. Their hideaway. Betrayal.

You promised! Ellie wanted to shriek. As it started to burst out of her she had to stuff her fingers in her mouth. She tore frantically at the fine, blonde hair that she could now almost sit on, recalling the moment from that other summer. But it was too painful. She had to let it go.

She could hardly watch as Charlotte picked her way through the dense bracken, approached the beech, bent down to peer inside the entrance of the bivouac. She didn't realise that he was right behind her, hadn't heard him ploughing through the delicate bracken path, flattening plants and destroying the path's long-guarded obscurity with a recklessness that made Ellie want to strike out. To hurt him.

'Caught you.' He tackled her, dragging her down on to the grass. Charlotte shrieked with laughter, and twisted round to hit him playfully. He grabbed her wrists. He was on top of her. They both exploded into wild giggles. He bent his dark head towards hers.

That's when Ellie knew that she'd lost her. She dug her fists into her eyes. And then she ran.

'Where've you *been*, Ellie? We've been looking for you all over.' Charlotte had changed into a green dress for dinner. It made her look grown-up and remote.

'Ellie's a wanderer,' Rolf Morgan said. 'Wandering here, there and everywhere. It's no use trying to pin her down.'

Charlotte stared at him in surprise. Jeff cleared his throat.

'I've been around.' Ellie toyed with her food. She glared at Charlotte, unable to resist. 'In all the usual places.'

At least Charlotte had the grace to look ashamed for a

split second. Then she turned to him. 'I wanted you to meet Jeff.' She sounded proud. 'Jeff Dando.'

'Hello, Jeff.' Ellie stabbed at a bean.

'Hello, little sister.'

Ellie looked directly at him for the first time at close quarters, ready to dislike what she saw. There was a certain surprise in the blue eyes, rapidly replaced by challenge. He wasn't the type to be fazed by anything. He'd been around. He was much too wicked for Charlotte. And he wouldn't look away.

'What are you staring at?' she snapped.

'Ellie!' Charlotte smiled an apology at him.

'You made her sound like a child.' Jeff smiled slowly. His mouth was wide and his teeth were very white. 'I was expecting some young kid.'

Hypnotic eyes. He was like a snake. She knew he was laughing at her. He still wouldn't look away. She felt young and uncomfortable.

'You two are very different,' he said. 'For sisters.'

'Eloise is like her mother.' Rolf poured out another glass of wine. 'Just like her mother.' There was an uncomfortable pause.

Jeff Dando filled it. 'And Charlotte's like you,' he supplied.

Ellie glanced up at him quickly, then back to her plate. He was a banisher of silences. Probably all he was good at. Oiling the rusty bits of life. Removing creaks. Keeping everything running smoothly at all costs.

Rolf drank deeply. 'Yes, she's like me, poor child.'

'I'm not a child, Dad,' Charlotte said. 'Not any more.' She turned away. 'How's school, Ellie?' she asked.

Ellie could have slapped her.

* * *

As the evening progressed the tension magnified between Charlotte and Ellie. They all played cards, the fraught atmosphere dragging them into one polite round after another. Only Jeff seemed in control – drinking steadily and winning almost every hand.

But at last they were alone in the attic bedroom the two of them used to share. Ellie had been waiting for this moment, only now she was so strung out that the separateness between them seemed more like a gaping chasm.

'I shouldn't have brought him.' Charlotte sat heavily on the bed.

'Why did you then?' Did this new Charlotte Morgan really require approval?

'Listen—' Charlotte grabbed her by the arm as she passed by. 'I know I should have come before. I know it's been over a year since I last came. And I know it's been hard for you since Mother left—'

'You don't know anything.' Ellie pulled away. 'Do you think I care whether you're around or not? What difference do you think it makes to me?' She should have told her. It just cuts me inside. It's just every lonely day without you, making me bleed. That's all.

'Okay. I should have come back before.' Charlotte's shoulders sagged, and her dark eyes were so sad that Ellie almost forgave her. But there was something she couldn't forget.

'You showed him the bivouac.' Ellie's voice was only a bitter whisper.

Charlotte rubbed at her temples, avoiding the accusing stare. 'Where were you?'

'Close enough.'

'Oh, Ellie.' She got up, placed her hands on Ellie's

shoulders. Looked into her eyes, but not with the old intensity. 'What does it matter if I did show him?'

Ellie shrugged. She looked past Charlotte's left shoulder. She could see Charlotte's back in the mirror. Tall, upright, statuesque. Beautiful. She'd filled out a lot in the last four years. She was twenty now. All grown up. All lost.

'After all, it's only kid's stuff, isn't it?' Charlotte tried to laugh.

'Course it is.' Ellie turned to stare out of the window. The moonlit night beckoned to her with long, mocking fingers, waving in the darkness. Charlotte had spoiled it all.

'For heaven's sake—' Charlotte grabbed her hairbrush from the childish white vanity unit and began brushing with strong, powerful, desperate strokes. She'd had her hair cut into a curtain of a bob that hung just above shoulder level. 'I'd have thought you'd have grown out of *hideaways* by now.'

The frustration inside Ellie burned itself out. Kid's stuff – that's all it was for Charlotte now. It was worthless – now that she had him. What a joke. All that waiting – waiting for letters, phone calls, visits. A shred of sisterly concern.

'You should have told me about him before,' Ellie said.

'Would you have listened?'

'Maybe.'

Charlotte looked straight ahead. Their eyes met in the reflection of the mirror. 'Maybe I should. I'm sorry.' She sighed. 'But it isn't only because of Jeff that I haven't been back.'

'What then?'

'It's not that easy. I have to work during the holidays to

subsidise my grant, don't forget. Where could I find work around this backwater?'

Ellie looked away. Once it had been paradise, now it was a backwater.

'Travelling costs money, and I've never got any spare cash.' She put down the brush at last and splashed water into the wash-basin.

'Dad would send you the money. He's always complaining he never sees you.'

'He hasn't got much left,' Charlotte said.

Ellie stared at her, 'How come you know so much about it?'

'He writes to me. Tells me things. Why do you think you never got sent to boarding school?'

Ellie shrugged. 'Does he tell you he drinks a bottle of whisky almost every day?'

'Ellie!'

'Well, he does.' Why should she be shielded from the truth?

'Since—?'

'Since Mother left. Yes.' Ellie sighed. 'He hardly works, he just sits and stares out of the window for hours. He worships the garden because she spent so long snipping at the blasted roses. It's like living in a bloody morgue.'

'Ellie!'

'Well, it is.' Charlotte should know. It wasn't fair. Ellie felt too alone. Her head felt too heavy. 'You don't know what it's like,' she whispered. All the fight left her. The betrayal sank into another part of her consciousness. All that remained was lethargy. She wanted Charlotte to stroke her brow and say she was coming home. She wanted her to take over.

'I didn't know he was drinking that heavily.' Charlotte began to undress. 'Why didn't you write and tell me?'

'Would you have listened?'

'Touché.'

'I did try.' Ellie's voice was muffled. Some facts had to be told face to face. Some kinds of pain. Others stayed hidden for ever.

'It's probably not as bad as you think.' Charlotte's eyes were misty.

With a pang, Ellie realised that she was hardly listening. That was the problem – that's why she didn't seem to care. Charlotte lived in another world now. His world. And it had swallowed all of her. Ellie was alone. She hung her head and began to sob, slowly, pitifully.

Charlotte's eyes darkened. 'Oh, Ellie,' she said. 'Don't cry.'

She cradled her, but it wasn't like it had ever been before. Before it had been pain shared and now it was only pity. Ellie half-expected her to mutter the same old meaningless words of comfort that she'd used before. That Rolf had used before. That everyone used until they were ground down into nothing.

'Come on. We both know Dad isn't stupid.' Charlotte stroked Ellie's fair hair back from her face.

Ellie laughed harshly. The sound seemed to echo in her head. Charlotte had always faced realities before. It was bad all right. Rolf's desperate bid for daily oblivion was born from betrayal. And everyone had different ways of dealing with betrayal.

Charlotte sighed. 'Mother was everything to him.'

Her romantic vagueness made Ellie want to shake her. The real Charlotte would never have approved. The real sister, the old Charlotte, lurking somewhere underneath this bullshit, was the only one sensible enough to hold this family together. Would she come back, or was she a permanent deserter?

'He thought the world of her.' Charlotte smiled.

'Do you think I don't know that?' Ellie snapped. She pulled away. 'Can't you see how much he hates me because I'm like her? You heard what he said at dinner. I tear him apart every time he looks at me, for Christ's sake!' Her voice was shrill. The tears trammelling her cheeks felt like acid.

'Oh, Ellie.' Charlotte's eyes filled. 'He's always loved you. You're so wrong. You've always been the most important one for both of them.' Her voice rang with conviction, as if she had to transfer her own lifelong belief into Ellie's mind.

'That was before she left.'

Charlotte could be so dense sometimes. It was up to Ellie to cope with it. But she wasn't ready to. She could leave home, but Rolf might fall to pieces completely if she did. And where would she go?

'Come and stay in Manchester for a while,' Charlotte said, displaying all the old powers of telepathy. 'You need a break.' She climbed into bed, swinging her long, brown legs over in the same old abandoned way.

Ellie felt a surge of hope. 'Can I?' she said. 'D'you think he'd let me?'

Charlotte laughed. 'I don't see why not. We'd look after you.'

The hope faded. 'We?'

Charlotte flushed. 'I'm moving out of the hall. To live with Jeff.'

Ellie stared at her. 'But you've almost finished your course.' She'd assumed that by next summer Charlotte's Manchester life would be over. That everything might be as before.

'Oh, I've decided to stay in Manchester after I've finished at the uni.' She spoke as if it was of no importance.

Ellie stared at her. She saw the jagged pieces of her world – that she'd been waiting to fit back together again one day like some old wooden jigsaw – shifting apart, way beyond her reach, way from completion.

'Once I'm working full-time I'll come back more often,' Charlotte said. 'You'll see. It'll all get straightened out.' Flopping backwards, she gazed at the ceiling.

The discussion was over. That was it. Sorted. Ellie shook her head in disbelief. What had happened to Charlotte?

'So, what do you think?' Charlotte spoke as if she'd been going through the motions of conversation up to this point. She looked at Ellie expectantly.

'About what?' Wearily, Ellie climbed into her own bed.

Charlotte sat up. 'Of Jeff, dummy,' she said. She almost sounded like a child again. 'Isn't he the most gorgeous man you've ever seen in your life?'

Ellie frowned. 'He's all right.'

'All right!'

Ellie thought she'd explode.

'He's wonderful.' Charlotte fell backwards once more. She stretched her arms out in front of her. 'I love him so much, Ellie,' she breathed. 'If anything came between us I'd die, I know I would.'

Ellie put out the light. 'Don't be stupid,' she said into the pillow.

'Don't you even want to know what it's like? Being in love?'

Ellie knew she was angry. She wanted to be cross-questioned, but Ellie wasn't going to oblige. The sense of betrayal was still hurting much too much. There was only one thing she had to know.

'Have you—? That is—?' You'd think she could at least be direct with Charlotte.

'Been to bed with him? Of course.'

So blasé. Ellie gripped the pillow more tightly. She could see it all. His eyes undressing her. His mouth pressing on to hers. Charlotte's lithe brown body, stretched out in some sort of virginal submission. Innocent. Unknowing. His rough hands scraping her skin. His body heaving on top of her. The sordid intimacy. His words. 'You haven't forgotten the rest of that night though, have you, sweetie?'

What night? Oh, God.

'He's in property,' Charlotte whispered. 'He buys a place, does it up and sells it for a huge profit. Clever, huh?'

'Sounds like exploitation to me.' This was Ellie's word of the week and using it to describe Jeff's activities gave her a warm sense of justice.

'You don't know a thing about it.' She paused. 'You're just a kid. A silly little kid.'

Ellie crept deeper into the bed but it was never quite deep enough. 'At least I'm not a bimbo.'

'A bimbo!' She laughed but Ellie caught the hurt beneath it. 'You don't even know what the word means.'

'You'd be surprised what I know,' she told the pillow. 'I know he's going to mess you around, for a start.'

'Oh, yeah? How?'

'I can just tell.' She waited for inspiration. 'He doesn't look at you as though he loves you.'

A stroke of genius designed for pain. Ellie had no regrets. She wanted to hurt. She wanted to prepare and polish the knife until it was ready. Ready to be plunged straight into Charlotte's breast. Where it had to belong.

'What do *you* know?' Her voice was weak and strained. 'Of course he loves me.'

'Does he want to marry you?' Another stab in the dark.

Charlotte was silent for so long that Ellie thought she was no longer awake. Then she heard the sobs. She hardened her heart.

'You're just jealous,' Charlotte said at last.

Ellie was silent, pretending to be asleep.

In the darkness Charlotte wept on alone. She wanted to share Jeff with Ellie – she'd always needed to share everything with Ellie. But somehow it wasn't as easy as she'd planned.

She hadn't meant to fall in love with Jeff, but when she met him, when she understood what it felt like to have male arms wrapped round her, for him to want her, then she'd begun to see what it was she had to do. Jeff was a man. The first man she'd ever had, and now the only one she wanted. And she needed to know that he was beside her for ever. Christ, she even wanted to have his children – that was how much he'd somersaulted her life around.

She needed to escape from Pencraig, and he sensed it.

'You've got your own life to lead, sweetie,' he'd told her. 'You can't always take on everyone else's problems.'

It was true. She couldn't allow herself to be sucked into the vortex of responsibilities again. She had to break loose. That's why she'd stayed away so long. It was hard to be separated from Ellie – harder than Ellie would ever know. But it was the only way. Because Ellie was part of it.

But she hadn't intended to show Jeff the bivouac. She'd introduced him to Dad, got them chatting, and after an hour had slipped away, hoping to escape unnoticed into the wood, find Ellie, and prepare her somehow. If she'd just been able to get her alone for a while, she could have got through to her, made her understand.

But Jeff had followed her into the wood, caught up with her by the clearing.

'Not leaving me already, are you, Charlotte?' he'd teased.

And his voice had made her melt – as it always made her melt. So she'd let herself forget what she always should have remembered. And now she'd blown it with Ellie.

The wood, Pencraig, everything, seemed ruined with Jeff here. It was not like she'd thought it would be at all. He didn't belong here. And yet she had to be with him, so she too had to find a way of leaving. She felt manacled to him already. Mesmerised by him. She had to give him everything he wanted. Or was Ellie right? Was she imagining love? Was it already too late? Was it all gone?

'All gone,' she said out loud.

The words of childhood. Scraped knee. A kiss and Elastoplast. 'Better now. All gone.'

Charlotte twisted over. Her face was buried in the pillow. 'Damn you, Ellie!' she muttered. 'You'll find out soon enough. Why can't you even try to understand?'

Ellie didn't reply. But she lay awake for a long, long time.

The next day Ellie kept out of the way when Charlotte and Jeff went back to Manchester. She couldn't bear to see how glad they were to leave. Then she took a bus into Aberystwyth. She marched up the main road, holding Charlotte's image in her head so that she couldn't change her mind.

Hazel eyes, soft and questioning. Long brown limbs winding around an old beech tree.

Ellie found what she was looking for very quickly.

'All of it?' the girl asked. She transferred her gum from one cheek to the other and twirled her scissors.

'All of it.'

'Are you sure?'

'Absolutely sure.'

The girl cocked her head to one side. Ellie stared at her in the mirror. She was wearing too much black eyeliner, and she had masses of streaked, permed hair.

'Only some people say they want it really short, and then when I'm finished, or when they get home— well, they change their minds.' She smirked. 'And we can't stick it back on.'

Ellie shot her a withering glance. 'All off,' she said. 'I want it short. Short and spiky.'

One last glance at her reflection. The sad and pale-faced girl with a sheet of long, blonde hair half-hiding her slanting, green eyes, stared back, and then closed her eyes as the stylist began work. Ellie might be brave enough to make the decision, but she wasn't brave enough to witness it.

And she hardly glanced in the mirror when it was done. A strange, cropped, angry face blinked with brief surprise. Then she paid and got out. What had she done? She found a phone box at the end of the street. There was a wildness in her that brought its own freedom. If you didn't care for the consequences you could do whatever you liked. She was beginning to understand rebellion.

'Dad?' she said when he answered. 'I've met a friend from school. Is it okay if I spend the night at her place?'

She wondered what he'd say if he could see her. Would he even notice? He'd be well into the whisky by now. It was after lunch and he'd had to hold back a bit for appearance's sake while Charlotte and Jeff were around. Ellie guessed he wouldn't even want to know where she was staying. She was right.

All afternoon she looked round the shops. It wasn't Manchester or London, but it was full of students, and it catered to the needs of the young. There were plenty of boutiques to choose from – if only she could avoid the mirrors. Rolf had never been mean with pocket money and she'd saved enough to buy herself a black skirt and vest-top. Skimpy and sexy to suit her new image. She stuffed her jeans in a hold-all, went to the public loo in the park to apply her make-up, and then found the nearest bar. No one questioned her about under-age drinking. But several men chatted her up.

Sex was overrated, Ellie decided, as she rode the bus back home the next day. It might make the world go on spinning, but it was a lot of fuss over nothing very much. Almost a waste – all that effort and emotion for a few silly spurts that smelt horrid and still ran down your legs hours later.

He'd been quite nice, the balding man in the red Escort and he'd certainly bought her a lot of drinks. Ellie wasn't used to drinking. Vodka and tonic she drank because it sounded sophisticated and that's what Mother drank. Bloody awful taste though.

She'd panicked when they left the dark-red plushness of the bar. But it had been easy. Really easy. They'd gone to a seedy hotel. A tiny room, flocked wallpaper, grey blankets and a stained wash-basin. He'd felt obliged to talk when talking hadn't been necessary. Nerves probably. And he'd done all the work too. All she had to do was lie there, not look at her watch and make sure she wasn't sick. She felt sick though. She felt sick from the vodka, and sick from the clammy sweatiness of him pounding away on top of her. She could see the sweat clinging to his thick, black body hair, beads of it threading across the fatty rolls of his shoulders and back.

He wouldn't stop. Groping and heaving, breath coming

fast as if any of it was important. Anyone could see it wasn't. Even him, once he was finished. She could tell from the way he looked at her.

'Your first time?' He was astounded. Embarrassed.

She nodded. Pushed off his bulk and got into a sitting position. 'So what?' She adjusted her clothes, and rubbed angrily at the cropped hair. Nothing to use to hide from the world now.

'So nothing, lovely lady. You'll stay?'

'Don't have a choice,' she told him.

He tried again during the night, but she pretended to be asleep. And in the morning she got up while he was still snoring. Ellie had no regrets. She was relieved to see the last of her virginity, no longer hanging round her neck like tasteless pink plastic beads. She was a part of the rest of the world now. The adult world. Not a stupid kid who knew nothing.

Now she knew what the biggest mystery in the universe was all about. And she'd been right all along. It was nothing to write home about. She laughed to herself. It was perfectly meaningless. Which made it quite appealing in a way.

Perhaps she should do it again. Not with the man in the red Escort but with someone different. She wanted to have more experience than Charlotte. Different experience so there wouldn't be any innocence left to be jeered at. And the same experience. She wanted that. She needed to have a man like Jeff look at her the way Jeff looked at Charlotte. And not to care if she never saw him again. That would give her power.

'Say you love me,' she'd begged just before he came. God knows why. It was the only thing she'd said. 'Say you love me.'

'Love you,' he grunted.

He would have said anything by then. That's how weak men were. How ruled by their own needs.

A one-night stand was all right in its way, but it wasn't enough of a weapon to fight with. It fired blank ammunition. Ellie craved emotion. She wanted to be loved. She wanted to lose herself in it. And then leave.

For six months the craziness stirred in Ellie. It drove her relentlessly on. Sex became her drug. Father drank, Ellie had sex and Charlotte never phoned.

Every so often she wrote scrawled notes instead. Things like, 'I'll be over soon,' 'Take care,' 'Love to you both,' 'Always thinking of you.'

Crap. Utter crap. Ellie noted when the address changed and knew she was living with Jeff. The letters made Ellie sick. Sick with longing, hate and the craziness.

She had no one to turn to so she turned to the boys. It was surprising how many of them there were. Boys who pretended to care briefly, at least until their puny bodies shook with premature orgasms.

Then came embarrassment. An embarrassment that Ellie swiftly learned to cope with. Before they had a chance to look at her like she was a piece of dirt they'd picked up on their shoe. Before they could mumble something about phone numbers, before she could see her humiliation in their eyes, she'd be gone. Best to say nothing. It was the closest she could get to honesty.

Love was about honesty. But sex was dishonest. It was a lie from start to finish. It was about self-gratification, nothing more. Ellie hated it and wanted it. And every time she did it, she wondered what it was like for Charlotte. What it was like with Jeff.

Afterwards she had to be on her own. She would go home, take a scalding shower and burn their touch off her skin. Then she would walk through the wood, find a little lonely peace, and dream the rest away. She would clamber down to the bay and stay there until she was truly alone again. That's when she'd start to get restless.

One night when she returned home Rolf was drunker than usual. Or was he sober? Ellie wasn't sure. The two states had somehow amalgamated into one constant.

'Come here.' His voice was thick and slurred.

'What?' Warily, she obliged.

As she approached, he slapped her across the face. Not hard. He just reached out as if he was going to stroke her hair. And then slapped her. Ellie was so astonished that she didn't cry out. She almost fell from the shock of it, though, regained her balance and then slowly touched her cheek. Stared at him. He'd never hit her before.

'What the hell sort of game do you think you're playing?' he demanded.

'I don't know what—'

'Don't give me that.' He had her by the shoulders. He was shaking her. The unaccustomed touch of his hands stole into her, pressing her down.

Ellie was scared. 'Let go of me,' she shrieked. 'Go back to your bloody whisky bottle!'

He let go. She fell, trembling, at his feet. He lifted one foot, one slippered foot. Ellie and Charlotte had clubbed together to buy him those slippers two years ago. She used to come back regularly then. But it had never been the same. Never the same since that first summer.

Rolf kicked her without force. It didn't hurt. It wasn't meant to hurt. Ellie knew it was merely a gesture.

'Two of them have been here. From over the way. Joy Pringle and Maureen Hazlemere,' he said. Sad. Matter-of-fact. Each word heavy and slow.

'Oh.' Ellie sat up. Martin Hazlemere had always been a

sneak. That's why he'd never been on her list. And as for her old teacher – Joy Pringle pretended concern but she was nothing but an interfering busybody.

'It's not just one or two boys, is it?'

She shook her head.

'I can't believe it.' He sat down on the bench-seat by the telephone. His face was lined with pain, and the marks of defeat were sketched on his tired features, dimming the brown eyes. 'Why, Ellie?'

What could she tell him? Would he want to know her reasons? The craziness flooded through her. 'I just needed to,' she said.

He looked at her as though he hated her.

He'd never looked at Mother like that, not even when Olivia had told him about Greg. Ellie knew this because she'd been hiding on the other side of the patio doors behind the lilac tree. Waiting for the showdown between her parents that she'd been waiting for since the first time she'd seen Olivia and Greg in Dragon Bay, wrapped in each other and the sand. Unaware of the sea licking their toes, the breeze building up from the west, the fifteen-year-old Ellie standing on the cliff-top just outside the ring of the trees. Last summer.

Greg was Denise's brother. He had often come to stay at Pencraig since that first summer. He lounged in the window-seat and stared at Mother as she played. He clapped afterwards. 'Brilliant, my dear,' he said. He told her she was beautiful too, and that she had a charming daughter, a wonderful house and a lucky husband. He gave her roses from the garden, sent her silly notes, and even read poetry to her. He was a true Romantic when Olivia must have believed them all lost to previous centuries, and he was just what Olivia needed. Even Ellie knew that.

It hadn't lasted with Greg, of course. For Mother, romance was never intended to be permanent. And what Greg could give Olivia was insubstantial compared with Rolf's solidity. But he had been substantial enough to pull Mother away from Pencraig last summer, with promises of people and parties. Life, love and laughter.

'We're in love,' Olivia had said to Rolf that day.

Behind the lilac Ellie listened.

'Greg and I are in love.'

Ellie felt sick.

Dad said nothing. Just stared at Olivia as if she were a mirage.

'I'm sorry, Rolf.' She played a few notes on the piano.

Even at a time like this she was only half-aware of him. Ellie clenched her fists until the knuckles were white. How could Mother be so callous? So hard?

'Just like that?' Rolf said at last. His shoulders drooped. Ellie sensed his feelings of failure. Perhaps he'd fought once too often.

Olivia looked up, as if not sure for a moment who he was. 'No,' she said. 'Of course it didn't happen just like that. We both tried to ignore it. Tried to fight it but—'

'I don't want to hear that shit.'

Ellie had never heard Dad say the word shit before. It shocked her more than what Mother was telling him. Mother could never be depended on.

'You're not leaving me? For that— that idiot?'

'I'm sorry, Rolf,' she said again. 'I never wanted it to be like this. But he can give me what I need.'

Somehow Mother always succeeded in shifting the blame. Her affair became Rolf's failure. Ellie knew that it was over between them, and she knew that Pencraig had been their one last chance. She hated their failure. They hadn't even tried.

She slunk off, wanting Charlotte, wanting her to make the pain go away, although something told her that even Charlotte could do nothing about this. Life had overtaken them.

Because there was so much to say, so much that would overflow the page and distort the truth, so much that had to be said face to face, Ellie wrote hardly anything to Charlotte. Just, 'Mother's left him at last. Oh, God, Charlotte, I need you.'

But Charlotte didn't reply. She never replied to that letter. It must have been about the time that she first met Jeff.

Rolf was still looking at Ellie as if he hated her. His hair was almost white. She hadn't even noticed him go grey. He was very thin, stooped and angry.

'Little slut,' he said.

Ellie got up, went to her room and started packing. It would have to be Manchester, there was nowhere else. One thing she knew for sure. She couldn't stay here.

3

'Hi.'

Jeff Dando stared at her, not realising for a minute who she was. This bedraggled, waif-like creature on his doorstep looked nothing like the sullen teenager he'd met last summer. But it was Ellie Morgan all right.

Then he saw the suitcase.

'Oh. Hi.' Jeff didn't need this. He opened the door only a fraction wider.

It was bucketing down so hard outside that he could barely make out the grim lines of the Victorian monstrosity opposite that he'd tried to buy. Its twenty converted bedsits now provided a nice little income for the new owner. This was college and university land, which made it bed-sit land. And if Jeff had owned it he might have been able to afford to move away from it – this bloody eyesore that reminded him of failure every time he opened the front door.

He was avoiding looking at Ellie. He didn't want her here. He had a vital call to make that he had to be alone for, and there were only two fillet steaks in the fridge for tonight's celebratory dinner.

Then he did a double take. 'Christ. What have you done to your hair?' It had been her one redeeming feature. A haze of gold flying over a sea of petulance.

'What does it look like?'

Perhaps she hadn't changed so much after all. She was still the last thing he needed right now.

'I'm getting bloody drenched out here. Where's Charlotte?'

'At work.' He opened the door wider, still half-hoping for a reprieve. But she must have come all the way from Wales, so he couldn't turn her away. Families were a pain. Children should be forced into independence and dumped at an early age like puffins. Like Jeff had been.

'Then I'll wait.' She stomped past, her wet coat brushing against him in the narrow hallway.

'Suit yourself.' So she was angry at not being made welcome. So what? Jeff couldn't care less. 'I'll make some tea,' he said. But he didn't move.

Ellie lowered the suitcase. It squatted in the hallway like an unspoken accusation. Meanwhile her coat dripped onto the thick blue pile of the carpet as she blinked the wetness from her eyelashes.

'But I've got an important call to make first.' Jeff glanced at the Rolex on his wrist. 'I shan't be a tick.'

She shrugged. 'I'll wait in the kitchen. Through here?'

He nodded.

'And I'll make the tea. Give you time to make as many important calls as you want.'

Jeff made a face at her departing wet back. She was difficult, but at least she had a bit of fire about her. He liked to have a few sparks flying, as long as he kept control. He shut the door to the sitting-room behind him, but it was hard to concentrate on the information being fed over the phone, knowing Charlotte's sister was in the kitchen. Property deals required one hundred per cent concentration.

'Melanie? How are you, sweetie? Have you spoken to him yet?'

'Of course I have. I told you I would. A hundred and thirty thousand is the lowest he'll go.'

'Hundred and thirty thou?' His voice gave nothing away.

'It's ever such a big drop, Jeff,' she said. 'He wasn't too happy.'

She had a voice like honey. Sweet and sticky. Cloying on the tongue. All right at the time, but sickened you afterwards. Like yesterday.

'Yeah, I know,' he said. 'I could manage to raise that if—' He made some rapid calculations in his head. His voice became more intimate. 'I don't suppose you could get him any lower? You know, hopeless tone in the voice and all that. Show a bit of leg. You're so good at it, sweetie.' His voice dropped still further. Damn the little sister. If this deal fell through because of her, he'd—

'Is that all I'm good at, love?'

Very bold. She was clearly alone in the office, but Jeff didn't need reminding of yesterday. A deal was a deal.

His laugh caressed the phone. 'You're good at lots of things. So good that I'll need reminding again soon.'

She caught her breath. 'How about dinner tonight? Just the two of us?'

'I can't make it tonight. What a drag.' How could he? He'd promised Charlotte. Tonight was special. And then there was little sister to consider.

Her groan of deep disappointment brought a smile to his lips.

'I need you,' she said. 'Soon.'

'Me too, sweetie. If only I could. But you know what it's like. Business is business and this is a biggie.' She was a future problem – he could feel it in his bones and he was never wrong.

'When *can* I see you then?' she demanded. 'Tomorrow? Wednesday?'

'Wednesday would be perfect.' He paused. 'If I can wait that long before I—'

Ellie walked into the room.

'Yes?' he snapped.

'I can't find the tea.'

It was innocent enough. But those slanty, green eyes of hers could devour a man. Eat him up, chew him to pieces, spit him out.

'In the cupboard over the sink.'

Jeff forced his voice to remain casual. It was a useful skill for when deals fell through unexpectedly, and whenever a threat was in the air. No anger, no panic. But this little witch probably knew all that.

He raised his eyebrows and indicated the phone.

Ellie paused, stared, then spun around and walked out, leaving the door wide open.

'Hold on,' he said into the phone.

He got up, walked over, kicked the door shut. Charlotte would always knock. And Charlotte lived here. This cheeky little bitch wouldn't be staying under his roof for longer than he could help.

'Sorry about that,' he oozed. 'Wednesday it is. And see what you can do about the price, sweetie?'

Ellie was slumped over the breakfast bar when he went into the kitchen ten minutes later. At first he thought she was crying, and he felt an unexpected tug of remorse. She didn't know what was going on, thank Christ. He'd been imagining things. She was only sixteen. Or was it seventeen by now? She must have had a rough time, poor kid, and she was Charlotte's sister. Charlotte was the best thing that had ever happened to Jeff.

'Hey, Ellie,' he began.

But she didn't look up. And as he bent towards her he realised she was sleeping. He smiled. She looked like a child now. Much nicer. A child woman. Vulnerable and sad.

Eloise. The name suited her. She was the sort you wanted to protect – biological male impulse or something. Weird. Just give me a dragon to slay and I'll do it. That sort of thing. It was the look of her. She was small-boned and delicate. Pale and wispy. The kind that just floated away. She was all prickles right now, but he could get past all that – didn't he always? He reached out to stroke the spiky softness of her hair. She was really very pretty.

Charlotte never looked like this. Never vulnerable, even in sleep. And she had a will of iron. Jeff was used to women who could be dominated by a male voice so long as it was loud enough. Charlotte was loyal too, different from the willowy women Jeff was accustomed to – mirror in the bag first priority.

It hadn't been long before he'd realised how much she adored him. It was touching, because it wasn't the thoughtless infatuation of youth. Like everything Charlotte stood for, it was considered and total. Jeff's dream. Absolute commitment. Good brains and a beautiful body. A perfect antithesis. A perfect partner for paradise.

She suited him all right. He needed her composure and practicality. He needed her brand of support behind him so that he could risk everything, even her, for an excitement that was like a drug. It wasn't the money. Principles were involved.

Besides all that, she was a challenge. He couldn't imagine her leaning on him, needing him, shuddering with fear. And he couldn't imagine her tears. The only time he'd seen Charlotte lose herself was not in bed, but at her old home in Wales with her sister. This girl had some hold over Charlotte that he didn't understand and didn't like. She was a threat to their closeness.

He looked down at Ellie and she awoke. Confused and open. Then her green eyes blinked, shuttered, and became ready.

'So what's happened?' He made his voice gentle and his eyes compassionate.

'Charlotte said I could come and stay for a few days whenever I wanted,' she said. 'Your tea's in the pot.'

'That's fine by me.' He let the smile linger, before moving behind her. 'But the pot's cold. How about a glass of wine?'

She twisted in her seat. Her eyes widened. 'It's only three o'clock.'

'Four actually. There's not some sort of curfew, is there?'

She smiled back at him then. One of the bricks crumbled. Her eyes softened. 'No. But Dad—'

'Charlotte told me.' Jeff grabbed a bottle from the fridge and opened it with swift, practised ease. It was the Chablis that was supposed to accompany Charlotte's avocado with prawns and crab-meat.

'It doesn't mean we're budding alcoholics. I happen to feel like it. You?' His eyes held a challenge.

Ellie was up to it. 'Why not?' She accepted the glass. Her fingers were slender, white. On her ring finger was a filigree silver band.

'Do you want to talk? Sometimes it's easier to talk to a stranger.' He sat down. Leaned towards her. Established an intense brand of eye contact.

It was suddenly vital that this strange creature confided in him. It would make things better for him and Charlotte. It might forge them together as lovers, and even give him the extra piece of power that he needed to break through.

'You're hardly a stranger.' Ellie looked at him over the rim of her glass. But she was relaxing. He could feel her relaxing.

'I don't know you. We've never talked. Okay, so I'm a friendly stranger. The kind that you don't have to be frightened of.'

She laughed. 'Maybe.'

'Is it your father?'

'No. It's me. I had to get away. I was going crazy. Everything was going wrong—' She was close to tears.

'Hey, steady on.' He took her hand and patted it like an affectionate uncle might. Strange how small it felt in his. 'It happens to everybody. We all need a break from time to time.'

She looked directly at him. 'I thought I hated you,' she whispered.

He laughed and she pulled her hand from his. But at the same time he felt she'd drawn nearer to him.

'For taking Charlotte away?' Jeff had never consciously thought of this before. But now the truth of the statement seemed indisputable.

She stared at him again. 'You think I'm a stupid kid.'

His arm crept around her. 'Don't put thoughts into my head, you stupid kid,' he teased. 'Maybe I just understand more than you give me credit for.'

'I'm sorry.' She drained her glass.

Jeff took his arm away to give her a refill. Perhaps it was a waste of good Chablis, but what the hell. You always had to go with the moment because it wouldn't come again. And much to his surprise he was enjoying this moment.

'I haven't taken her away,' he said. 'She was already going. Your sister's an ambitious lady. You know that, don't you?'

She nodded. 'That's what makes it worse.'

He smiled. She was really quite sweet. 'Stay as long as you like.' He felt expansive.

Her whole face lit up. She had a strange, eerie kind of beauty that made him uncomfortable. And yet he wanted to see her smile again.

'I'll show you round the place,' he said. His dark-blue eyes were thoughtful as he reached out and took her hand.

Charlotte came in an hour later. She was tall, dark and elegant in a navy suit, and he restrained the urge to try and rip it off. Charlotte had made the transition from university student to cool, efficient businesswoman with an effortless ease that made him want her more than ever.

She blew him a kiss. 'How's it going?'

He grinned lazily, watching her as she breezed into the kitchen. 'Not so bad.'

'You haven't started dinner yet.' Her voice was light and teasing.

'I thought you might have changed your mind.' Jeff grabbed her round the waist, pulled her towards him and kissed her with a passion that somewhere in the middle of the kiss turned into desperation.

Eventually Charlotte emerged for air. Her dark eyes were startled. 'Wow. What was that for?'

'I just felt like it.' Grabbing salad from the fridge, Jeff began chopping ferociously at a radish. He didn't feel cheerful any more. 'Eloise is upstairs,' he told her.

'What?' Her face drained of colour and expression.

'You heard.'

Already she was moving back towards the hall.

'Wait.' He blocked the doorway. 'I don't think she wants to talk right now.'

'*You* don't think—'

Jeff hadn't seen these flecks of anger in her eyes before.

She'd never spoken to him like that either. She looked like a female tiger protecting her young. Was it maternal, then, this thing between her and Eloise?

'Just hang on a minute,' he said.

'Why? What's happened?' She grabbed his arm. 'Is she all right? Is Dad all right?'

'Everyone's fine.' His words were soothing. 'Take it easy.'

There was doubt in Charlotte's nod. She stared at him as if he were an enemy. 'Let me past then.' She pushed through and ran swiftly up the stairs. 'Ellie?' she called.

There was laughter. Muffled, excited voices. And then silence.

Charlotte seemed to be up there for ever. Jeff continued with an air of martyrdom, preparing the meal that was supposed to be a joint effort, clattering pans and slashing at the avocado. Some bloody celebration dinner this was going to be, with little sister stuck in the middle of it.

Eventually Charlotte returned. She'd changed into a scarlet dress that he hated, and was wearing a matching lipstick and dangling gold earrings. He turned away.

'What are we going to do about dinner? Divide it like the loaves and fishes?' She grabbed at plates and cutlery with uncharacteristic jerkiness, avoiding looking at him. 'Ellie will be staying here for a while.' Her voice was low. 'She's had a terrible row with Dad. I don't know what it was about.'

What in hell were they doing up there all that time if she wasn't filling Charlotte in on the details?

'Shall we tell her?' Jeff tossed the salad so violently that tomato and cress were decoratively deposited on the floor.

Charlotte looked blank. 'Tell her?'

'About us. About the wedding.'

A panic flared in her hazel eyes. 'Don't you think she's got enough to cope with at the moment?' she snapped.

Jeff felt his shoulder muscles go rigid. He'd been right. Little sister was a threat. 'She's got to know some time.'

'I know.' Charlotte sighed. 'Okay. We'll tell her tonight. Over dinner.' She laughed nervously. 'We've got to explain the Chablis and the steak somehow.'

'Eloise wouldn't know a Chablis if it got up and stuck its label on her face.'

'How would you know?' Charlotte tightened the belt of the scarlet dress. 'And why are you calling her Eloise? No one else does.'

'It's her name, isn't it? And that's how I know.' He pointed to the empty bottle.

'You've drunk it all?' She looked disbelieving. 'You and Ellie?'

He knew she was hurt. He wanted to hurt her for his feeling of exclusion. But she looked so miserable that he relented. 'I thought she needed it.' He held out his arms. 'I don't want to argue. Not tonight.'

'Not any night.' She came to him, folded herself against his chest. 'Not any night, Jeff. You mean everything to me.'

'I know, sweetie. You're everything to me too.'

Over her shoulder Jeff saw Ellie descend the last few stairs. She hesitated, then came into the kitchen. She had reapplied her make-up and washed her hair. She stared at him but didn't smile.

He couldn't make her out. Why had she come here? He felt sure that she would try and come between him and Charlotte. The only question was – how was he going to stop her?

* * *

At dinner Ellie eyed the avocado warily. Candles too, and a lace tablecloth. Was he loaded, then? She glanced up at Jeff as the first small spoonful went into her mouth. He caught her eye and grinned.

He was very attractive. His dark hair curled around his ears, and occasionally fell into the kind of deep-blue eyes you should be able to swim in. He was dangerous too. She knew it, although she couldn't say why.

Perhaps Charlotte was lucky having a man like him. And yet— There was the phone call. Old habits die hard and Ellie hadn't been able to resist listening outside the door when he came over all secretive and shut himself in the sitting-room. Even a one-sided conversation gave away some clues. So was it lucky Charlotte – or poor Charlotte?

She scrutinised him once more. Magnetism. He had it in large doses. He smiled at her again with an utter confidence that irritated her.

'Did you make the deal?' she asked. Utterly casual.

'What deal?' Charlotte glanced from Ellie to Jeff. 'Has something come up?'

Ellie giggled.

'Behave!' Jeff glared at her. But the corners of his mouth twitched in response.

'He was making some very important calls,' Ellie teased. He deserved to be teased. She'd like to bet that most people didn't dare.

'It's none of your business.' Charlotte's voice was sharp. 'Just remember that.'

'How could I forget?' Ellie slumped in her chair.

Charlotte wanted to exclude her from this adult circle, she knew it. She talked to her like a kid when Jeff was around. Came over all matronly and started clearing plates, polishing her fork and frowning at elbows on the table, as if she was trying to qualify for a housewifery degree. My God, she'd be fulfilling herself with the vacuum cleaner next.

Was it work or was it Jeff Dando who had transformed her into this disapproving soul? Glimpses of the old Charlotte were few and far between, and restricted to the times they were alone. Ellie hated it. It was worse than being at home. At least at Pencraig there was escape and oblivion.

Manchester was a horrid place. The air was thick and grimy. A bleakness sat on the city, squashing it into miserable obscurity. Grand Victorian architecture meant less than nothing to Ellie. In the taxi from the station the Wilmslow Road seemed to go on for ever, and things gradually improved – apart from the weather. But Didsbury was still a suburb pretending to be an interesting village just because it had a picture postcard pub down the road. She should have stayed in Wales. At least the air was clean.

'Who'd want to live in Manchester?' she grumbled.

Jeff leaned back, sipping his wine, watching her. 'Perhaps we won't be here for much longer,' he said.

'Why not?'

Abruptly Charlotte got to her feet and started piling dishes on to a tray. Her face was flushed.

She didn't want Ellie to know about their wedding. Jeff frowned. Now, why would that be? Still, he stared at Ellie, challenging her. She'd thrown down the gauntlet by mentioning his deals, and Jeff was sure that he could rise to the occasion.

'We're getting married in the spring.' He tapped Charlotte lightly on her bottom.

'No!' Ellie sat up straighter.

Her eyes weren't slanty any longer, Jeff noted. They

were wide and surprised. He smiled with secret satisfaction. Gobsmacked was the word that sprang to mind. Served her right.

'Honestly, Charlotte?' she asked. 'Is it true?'

Charlotte nodded, but wouldn't look at her. She disappeared into the kitchen.

'Absolutely true, little sister.' Jeff watched her. 'Surprised?'

Ellie turned away. That was it then. It had gone much further than she'd realised. No hope of getting Charlotte back now. She wouldn't even be Charlotte Morgan for much longer.

After a few minutes of awkward, stunned silence, Charlotte reappeared with the steaks. She'd given herself only a tiny portion.

'I've been scared to ask you—' she began. 'But how's Dad? Is he still drinking—?'

'A bottle a day? Not far off.' Ellie was glad of a change of subject, but this subject was just as bad. It was hard to think of Dad, alone now at Pencraig without feeling guilt. She speared a kidney bean. 'He's in no state to look after himself. He needs help, Charlotte. But—'

'I know. But should it be professional help, like the doctor or something? Or—'

'It has to come from us. But I don't know what to do.'

They stared at each other. Ellie was relieved to see compassion in Charlotte's hazel eyes. So she was concerned at last. She reached out for her hand, squeezing it gently.

'Don't you two ever let each other finish a sentence?' Jeff laughed. He stared pointedly at their clasped hands.

Charlotte took her hand away. 'You were right. This isn't going to go away. He's sick.' She seemed to have forgotten her dinner. The small piece of celebration steak was becoming a corpse on the plate.

'He's still grieving.' Ellie sighed. It was hopeless. Parents were supposed to be your support – your roots and your backbone, all that kind of stuff. They were supposed to be there when you needed help with your problems, not provide new ones for you to worry over.

'But I know I can't go back there. I can't just sit by and watch him destroy himself.' Destruction must be in the air at Pencraig. And yet the opposite was supposed to be true.

'You can't just leave him on his own, either.' Jeff's voice was accusing.

Ellie scrunched some French bread into a ball between her fingers. 'It's not easy living under the same roof as an alcoholic, you know. Especially when he's your father.'

She glared at him. What did he know about it? All he wanted was for her to leave – and pronto. He didn't give a shit about what she'd be going back to. All that kindly advice stuff this afternoon had been nothing but a load of crap. He was a selfish bastard. And he'd screw Charlotte up. She just knew he would.

Charlotte frowned at him. 'Why should Ellie take all the responsibility? I've left it up to her for far too long.'

Ellie smiled and helped herself to more salad. That was more like it – at last Charlotte was taking her side against him.

'Okay, okay.' Jeff reached out to put his hand lightly on Charlotte's knee. He glanced across at Ellie.

Fascinated and repelled, she watched it slide around Charlotte's stockinged lower thigh. Watched the thumb knead the flesh. She even thought she saw goosebumps appear under the thin mesh. Smarmy creep. He sure could turn it on when he wanted to.

Finally she slammed down her knife and fork. 'So what do *you* suggest we do?'

Jeff removed his hand. 'Bring in a professional. Tell whoever has to be told. Find out about the problem. Get him some constructive help instead of sitting here squawking about it. You should try and persuade him to join Alcoholics Anonymous.'

Charlotte put her head to one side. 'Maybe he's right.'

'And maybe that'll make him hate me more than ever.' Ellie didn't want Jeff ever to be right.

'Everyone pays a price.' Jeff's voice was silky-smooth.

Ellie scowled at him. He was making this dinner-table into a battlefield. She hated him – hated what he was doing to Charlotte.

'I'll talk to Dad. I'll go and see him.' Charlotte glanced at her. Ellie averted her eyes.

'He does know you're here?'

She shook her head.

'For heaven's sake!' Charlotte's knife and fork clattered on to the plate. 'He'll be worried sick!'

'He might be sick,' Ellie conceded. 'But he won't be worried. And I wouldn't bother to phone him at this time of night. He'll be well out of it by now.'

'I've got to.' She moved towards the phone, looking to Jeff for support.

'Do you want her to?' he asked Ellie.

'No.' At least Jeff treated her like an adult. At least he appreciated that she was old enough to make her own decisions. She cut into her steak. It was rare. She liked it that way. She looked at him. He was so attractive. His eyes were almost too blue.

'He'll guess where I am,' she told Charlotte. 'Stop fussing. I'll phone him tomorrow.' When would Charlotte stop behaving like a mother-hen? It was driving her crazy.

Charlotte hovered, clearly unsure of her responsibilities. Jeff refilled Ellie's glass. She smiled her thanks. As he handed her the glass their fingers touched. Only for a second. The briefest of touches – but it was still a shock for Ellie.

'Oh, leave it, Charlotte, for Christ's sake.' Jeff smiled back at Ellie.

The corners of those very blue eyes crinkled up into almost nothing when he smiled.

'Tomorrow.' Jeff raised his glass. There was a promise in his eyes.

'Tomorrow,' Ellie echoed.

Charlotte sat down and pushed her plate away.

The letter came the following morning. Charlotte read it with an expression of mild curiosity that soon switched into horror.

'What's up?' Jeff came down in his dressing-gown, unshaven and muffled from sleep.

'Read this.' She thrust it at him. 'It's from Dad.' She felt sick. She couldn't think straight. She couldn't believe any of this was true. But Dad would never have made it up. It was disgusting.

He started reading, blinking blearily at first, then frowned, and raised his dark eyebrows. 'Wow,' he exclaimed softly.

Operating like a machine, Charlotte started making sandwiches. She had overslept after last night's session and now she was late. They'd stayed up till gone two, talking about everything imaginable – except why Ellie had appeared on their doorstep. And now they apparently had the answer to that too.

'How could she do it?' Charlotte muttered. 'How could she?'

'Do what?'

'Behave like a tramp, of course.' Charlotte waved the knife at him. The violence she felt surprised her. 'You've read it. Aren't you shocked?'

He didn't look shocked. Taken aback, yes, but not shocked. And that was Jeff for you. Charlotte knew he'd been around. He'd never made any secret of it. So he'd probably come across far worse than Ellie. Probably *slept* with far worse than Ellie.

Charlotte shivered. She didn't want to think about that now. Jeff loved her. They were getting married. All she wanted was Jeff. His love, and yes, his children. A desire melting inside her. An urge that surely couldn't be merely biological. If she had a child— If she could hold her child in her arms, and be needed. Then surely she'd be secure with him.

But Ellie had been wrong last summer at Pencraig when she'd planted those awful doubts in Charlotte's mind. Ellie. How could she?

'She's only seventeen, Jeff,' Charlotte wailed. 'She's still a kid.'

Jeff snorted. 'Some might say seventeen is quite late to lose your virginity.' He yawned, got up, stood behind her and cupped one hand around each of her breasts.

She pushed them away. 'How the hell can you think about sex at a time like this?'

'Easily. That letter reminded me.' He kissed her shoulder.

'If only I could understand why—' Charlotte spun round, her hazel eyes intent and passionate. She felt that she ought to understand. That the answer was within reach if she could refocus correctly. 'I'm so worried about her.' Her voice was despairing.

'You worry too much. She's not such a kid any more.' He turned away, poured out coffee.

'I can't help it. I was brought up to worry about her. No

one else did.' She was worried sick. Scared too. What was happening to everyone? Dad, and now Ellie. 'What on earth must people be saying about her?'

'Perhaps she doesn't care.'

'She only pretends not to care.' Charlotte was confident. 'I know her.'

She would phone Dad when she got home from work. And talk to Ellie. Oh God. She wasn't looking forward to that. What would she say to her? Could she even bring herself to look at her? 'I have to talk to her,' she muttered.

'Don't forget to talk to me too.' Jeff pulled her back, as she made for the door. 'Don't take the whole world on your shoulders, sweetie. I know they're broad. But they're not that broad.'

She smiled. Rested her head for a moment on the dark forest of his chest hair. His skin was so warm and inviting. When they had their child – and she felt in her heart that it would be soon – they would be properly together at last.

How long could any couple go on making love as often as they did without using contraception and without conceiving?

When they had a child, her skin would be soft and warm and comforting. She would be Charlotte's bright light – her star of hope. And Charlotte would care for her as she had not been cared for. She would teach her with love. Her child wouldn't let her down as Ellie had let her down. Ellie was a weight – pulling her into the darkness of a love and responsibility she couldn't cope with any longer. But Charlotte couldn't cut the strings that tied them.

'Look after Ellie for me,' she said.

All day the words in the letter tore away at Charlotte,

dancing like little devils in her brain. She couldn't concentrate on her work. Couldn't organise her own thoughts, let alone Leonard's day and Leonard's diary, while transcribing Leonard's illegible scrawl into perfect manuscripts of French, Italian and German.

One day there'll be a little machine that does my job, she told herself. PA in big business tourism. Chief interpreter will become little processor. No need for the personal touch.

She arrived home to find Ellie and Jeff playing backgammon. Laughing and drinking wine. Again. 'Busy day?' she enquired.

'Yep. Only got in half an hour ago.' Jeff stretched, loosened his burgundy silk tie, got to his feet and kissed her.

She tried to kiss him back, but it felt wrong. It was hard to respond with Ellie there. Just like last night – even with a bedroom wall between them. She couldn't let herself go. There was a vicious kind of tension in her that wouldn't be smoothed away.

She gazed across at Ellie. She was wearing faded-blue jeans and a white shirt. She looked even younger than last night. So defenceless. Why did Charlotte feel so damned responsible for her? Why did everything about Ellie complicate her life, overloading her with guilt? It seemed to be getting even harder to break free.

'Have you phoned Dad yet?' Charlotte knew she was looking at Ellie with distaste. And she sounded like an old schoolmarm. Her fists were tight balls of anger. Where was it all coming from?

'No.' Ellie swirled red wine around the glass.

She was playing at freedom. Determined to join in grown-up games. Trying to make a point and only showing how childish she was.

'You shouldn't be drinking so much.' The tension was snip-snapping around Charlotte. In her voice, tunnelling through every vein of her body.

'Why? Are you afraid I'll end up like him?'

They eyed each other like two boxers in a ring. Wary, pretending confidence, afraid of failure.

Charlotte sagged first, faintly aware of Jeff's glance of surprise. 'I'm sorry,' she said. 'It's been a hard day.'

Ellie was generous in victory. 'Poor darling. Come and sit down.' She propelled her into a chair. 'A little drink?' She snapped her fingers, green eyes flashing at Jeff. 'Consideration for this lady, please. She's been out earning a crust just to keep you in deals.'

Jeff laughed.

'A cushion, madame?' Ellie fetched one. 'A stool for your poor old feet?' She dragged Charlotte's feet on to a stool, and untied her shoes. 'A hot Radox bath for your aching bones?'

Charlotte giggled. 'You're making me feel about eighty,' she protested. But actually Ellie was making her feel like a girl again.

'Good, good.' Ellie rubbed her hands together. 'Nice to know you're feeling so young.'

'Isn't she a fool?' Charlotte looked into Jeff's eyes as he bent to hand her a glass of wine.

She could drown in those eyes of his. Sometimes she thought she loved him too much. Certainly too much for any room to be left over for Ellie's kind of consuming love. But the times when she longed for him the most, the times when the desire shot through her body like some hot burning liquid, were the times when he was away. When he was away she'd take his shirt into bed with her – the one he'd been wearing that day. She'd hug it, sniff it, then cry into it.

'I'm gonna phone Dad.' Ellie left the room.

'She'll be okay,' Jeff whispered. 'Let her go.'

Charlotte knew what he meant. She stroked his dark hair as if she'd never touched it before. Wondering. 'Kiss me,' she said.

His eyes misted in the way that she loved. The way that told her he was giving in to passion. He bent closer. The dark shadow of his jaw almost touching her. And then his lips were on hers.

Ellie was only two minutes. Jeff and Charlotte broke apart as she burst back into the room, but there had been enough time for them to become close again. Idly, Jeff began playing with her fingers.

'There was no answer.' Ellie looked thoughtful. 'I suppose he's out for the count.'

The worry nagged at Charlotte, but she pushed it away. She didn't want it to begin again. Later. She would worry later.

'I'll make dinner,' Jeff announced. 'Give you two the chance to talk.'

Charlotte nodded reluctantly as she released his hand. She didn't want to talk. She was scared to talk. She wanted to do absolutely nothing.

Ellie sat down at her feet.

'Jeff's told you about the letter?' Charlotte wondered what he'd said. If he'd been embarrassed. Probably not.

Ellie nodded. She looked up at him as he left the room.

'Why, Ellie? Why did you do it?' Charlotte felt so weary.

'That's what Dad asked me.' Ellie buried her head in her knees. Her voice was muffled. 'At first I needed to feel grown up. Like you. And then it took me over. I don't know why. Do you know?'

Charlotte couldn't see her face. How could she know?

She reached out and gently ran her fingers through the clumps of short blonde hair. 'You shouldn't have had it all cut off,' she murmured. Ellie's hair had been so beautiful. It had meant so much to her. Charlotte hands became still. Had she hurt Ellie so much then?

'I didn't know what else to do.' The words sounded as if they were being torn from Ellie.

'Ssh now.' Charlotte put her hands on Ellie's slim shoulders. 'It's over.' But it didn't feel as if it was over. It felt as if it was only just beginning.

Had Ellie's wild promiscuity been only a bid for independence? Charlotte didn't think so. There was too much desperation in it. And what about Charlotte's own need to break free? She hadn't meant to hurt Ellie. Never would she mean to do that. But Ellie had been part of the burden of Pencraig that she'd had to get away from. There was another world outside Pencraig. There was the future of a family of her own.

Under her hands she felt Ellie relax as she sank back against the chair. And Charlotte gradually began to understand, as the hopelessness crept up inside her. No easy solutions. Always a price to pay.

All evening there was no answer from Pencraig. It was the same story at seven the following morning. Charlotte was conscious of more and more twinges of alarm. But there were so many other possibilities. He might have gone away, there might be a fault on the line, anything.

'More likely he's sleeping it off.' Ellie seemed unconcerned. 'He usually is at this time of day, believe me. He wouldn't even hear the phone.' Her green eyes were huge in the paleness of her face as she looked at Charlotte. 'I'll go back, if you're that worried.'

'No. I'll go.' It was time for Charlotte to do her bit – the chance had come a bit earlier than she'd envisaged, that was all.

'Thanks, love.' Ellie glanced at them both and left the room.

Jeff sighed. 'Isn't there someone you could phone to go round there, take a look?'

Charlotte shook her head. No neighbours. No close friends. There was Joy Pringle, Ellie's old teacher. She'd always seemed concerned. But she couldn't involve her. For one thing, although she liked the woman and had felt an odd unexplained bond with her ever since the first time she'd run into her strolling down the lane that led to Pencraig, when it came down to it she hardly knew her. There was no doubt about it. Charlotte was the one who should go.

'I want to see him anyway.' She was checking the train timetable. 'Leonard can't spare me today so I'll go straight after work. 'I'll catch the 5.18.' Charlotte ignored the pinpricks of apprehension. What could possibly have happened to Dad?

'I could drive you.'

Her heart leapt. She didn't want to go alone. But it was Wednesday and he had a dinner engagement. Business. And she could see the unwillingness in his blue eyes. She shook her head. This was something she had to face alone. 'You go on out. Ellie can have an omelette. The train's no problem.'

Jeff shrugged. 'He's probably just not answering the phone,' he said.

'Probably.' She kissed him goodbye. But her smile contained more than a hint of misgiving.

She had to change at both Crewe and Shrewsbury, and it was a quarter to ten by the time the taxi she'd got at

Aberystwyth station dropped Charlotte outside the house. It was pitch-black and she stumbled by the white gate.

Her unease grew stronger. There was one light burning in Pencraig – in the sitting-room. It had been the heart of the household before Olivia left. But according to Ellie it was more like a mausoleum to her memory these days. No one played the piano any more.

'Dad?' She used her own key but shouted loudly to warn him. Her voice wavered in trepidation.

No reply.

'Dad?' She tried to stifle her fear. If only she'd admitted to Jeff that she was scared to come alone. What she wouldn't give for the warmth of his hand. He would have come if she'd only asked.

Charlotte gently opened the sitting-room door. Maybe he was reminiscing, sleeping even. 'Dad?' she whispered. A hundred alarm bells began ringing in her head.

He was sitting in Olivia's favourite chair. The one that no one else had ever used because it was too pretty and delicate and belonged exclusively to Mother. The one that faced the garden.

The curtain was open and the moon illuminated the buddleia tree, quilted with lemon blossom, while the rest of the garden remained in shadow. It was eerie. Charlotte felt her heartbeat quicken into panic.

'Dad?' She crept towards him. There was a whisky bottle – empty – on the small table beside the chair. And another bottle too. Olivia's sleeping pills. She must have thought she wouldn't need them in her new life.

'Dad!' She shook him. Terrified now.

The head lolled horribly. The eyes gaped, the jaw sagged.

Charlotte shrieked. Her hand covered her mouth. Her breath was coming in stuttering gasps. She stared, trying not to see too clearly, knowing how precisely this vision of him would be latched on to her memory.

She knelt down. 'Wake up, Dad. Get up. Wake up. Please?' Her voice rose.

Silence.

'I should have helped you.' The words were a desolate whisper. She took his hand. It sank heavily into her palm like a stone. 'I'm so sorry, Dad,' she said.

After a while Charlotte reached out to close his eyes. She rose stiffly and went to the phone. Control. She must keep control. She phoned the police first.

'My father has taken his own life,' she announced clearly. 'I've just found him.' She gave the address. 'Yes. I'll wait here.' She replaced the receiver. Took a deep breath. Redialled.

From somewhere she registered that Jeff's voice sounded strange. Blurred. And there was something else wrong too, only she couldn't think about that now.

'Charlotte? Is that you? Is everything okay?'

'Ellie, please,' she managed to say. She wanted to laugh. Hysteria was lurking close by.

'What? I can hardly hear you. What's happened? You sound weird. Charlotte?'

Why couldn't he understand? 'Ellie, please,' she said loudly. 'I have to speak to Ellie.'

'Why can't you talk to me? Oh, hell—'

There were noises as the phone was passed over.

'Charlotte?' She sounded frightened.

'Ellie.' All the breath went out of her body. 'He's dead, Ellie.' The sobs came long and rasping, stretching her body as if she was on a rack, beginning in the pit of her stomach and rising into her throat like nausea. 'Tell Jeff to bring you here. Now. Tell him—'

'Dead?'

Would Ellie be able to take this? Charlotte didn't know. 'Get here as soon as you can,' she begged between sobs.

'What are you talking about? How can he be dead?'

She hadn't absorbed it. Simple instructions were best. 'Tell Jeff to bring you now,' she repeated. 'Come to Pencraig.'

'Hold on,' Ellie said. 'I'm coming.'

Charlotte put down the phone, collapsed on to the bench-seat. She had understood. Thank God. The police would be here soon. Ellie and Jeff would be longer. Could he make it in two and a half hours if he drove fast? She must be strong. She rocked herself back and forth. She had to be strong for Ellie.

4

The motorway was like a neon runway streaking through her world of black. Every so often Ellie closed her eyes, and when she opened them again they were wet with unshed tears. Hypnotised by the bright, flashy motorway, the darkness of the bordering countryside that couldn't pretend to be countryside any longer, the approaching headlights howling and sparking through the tears like mad Catherine wheels. Out of control, unpinned from fences. Coming closer and closer. Bearing down on her. All of this scene – even Jeff's humming – seemed totally unreal. Perhaps it wasn't happening. Perhaps she wasn't speeding back to Pencraig at all. Perhaps—

Jeff was driving too fast. Ellie knew he was drunk but she was past caring. How could she care when she couldn't feel?

If she closed her eyes very carefully, and gripped the edge of her seat she could replay it all. Desperately, as if the dialogue must be memorised at all costs. At least it was safer than thinking about the other thing. About death.

Had she half-expected it? There had been so many barely shuttered challenges. Circumstances. It was always down to circumstances in the end.

Much earlier tonight, Jeff had slammed the front door on coming in just as Ellie cracked an egg into a bowl for her omelette.

'What are you up to?' He lounged against the door-frame. Watching her like some sort of big cat. Arrogant bastard.

His way of staring flustered her. She could feel him looking her up and down, and felt ridiculously shy in her tight-fitting black jump-suit. Why had she bothered? To show him what he was missing?

'What does it look like?' Ellie frowned, added a little milk.

He tossed his black leather jacket on to the nearest chair in a territorial gesture. 'Fancy a Chinese?'

From the expression in his blue eyes those words could mean anything. Ellie quickly looked away. 'I thought you were going out for dinner tonight.' She poured oil into a pan. 'Isn't that why you didn't drive Charlotte home?'

'Home?'

'To Pencraig.'

'Oh, that home.' He grinned. It was a grin that made him look about twelve years old. A thoroughly disconcerting grin. 'I changed my mind.'

'Just like that?'

'No, not just like that.' He glanced towards the cooker. 'Your oil's burning.'

'Bugger it!' Ellie tipped the egg mixture into the pan and it spat at her. 'Ouch.'

'Your punishment. Nice girls don't say "bugger it".'

What would he know about nice girls? 'Nice girls don't have to cook omelettes,' she said. 'They get taken out for dinner.'

'I've offered take-away Chinese.' He pretended to be hurt.

'I bet she didn't even ask you to drive her.'

She glanced across at him as he moved with long, lazy strides over to the door. Jeans suited him. He had the longest legs Ellie had ever seen. Not too fat and not too skinny. Long legs and a tight bum.

'No, she didn't ask me. She wouldn't.' He hovered by the door. So he was going out after all.

Ellie was conscious of the dip of disappointment. She bored him. He was probably going out to meet some woman. Poor Charlotte.

But he came over to peer into the pan instead. Pulled a face, then turned to smile at her. 'But naturally I offered to drive her. Being the sort of guy I am—'

'Oh, yeah?' She couldn't help smiling back. His humour was infectious. 'Kind, giving and terribly unselfish?'

'That's me.' Mock amazement on his face. 'How come you realised so quickly?'

'Very funny.' She poked at the omelette with a wooden spoon to reveal a burnt underside. 'Yuck.'

'I suppose you think you know Charlotte pretty well,' he said.

'I do.'

He shook his head despairingly, either at her or the burnt eggs, she wasn't sure which. But there was a teasing glimmer in his blue eyes that appealed to her. You could forgive this man a lot when he turned on the charm. It shone out of his come-to-bed eyes, and oozed from the huskiness of his voice. Such a massive dose of sex appeal in one man alone shouldn't be allowed. Poor Charlotte.

'How can you contemplate eating this shit?' He frowned. 'Can't I tempt you into thinking Chinese?'

'It does sound nice.' Ellie licked her lips.

Jeff moved towards her, about to speak, and then shook his head as if he'd changed his mind. He turned away.

'What about the omelette?' she asked.

'Easy.' In one swift movement he grabbed the handle of

the pan and tipped the contents into the bin. 'What omelette?'

Ellie laughed. 'Are you always this crazy?' Charlotte was lucky. Life must be fun with Jeff. Dangerous but fun.

'I'm usually worse.' He riffled in the drawer for a menu. 'Any preferences?'

Together they pored over the red and white leaflet, his dark head close to her blonde one, but not quite touching. Most of it meant little to Ellie because she'd never tasted Chinese food before. It was beginning to seem as if she'd never lived. Here she was, alone with a man of the world, and she knew nothing. Not even what food to order from the menu of a Chinese take-away.

She should be able to impress him, let him know that she was a force to be reckoned with. But how? Strategies that worked with boys her own age would roll right past Jeff. He made her feel inadequate. He stared at her as if he knew what colour knickers she was wearing. And through her as if he could read her mind. He made her feel such a kid. Only Ellie knew that she wasn't a kid. Childhood was long gone – lost and drowned in the waves of Dragon Bay.

She'd seen all her shelters collapse. She'd been given too much space for contemplation. She'd had responsibilities bequeathed to her that she wasn't ready for. And then Charlotte had nurtured her first seeds of cynicism – bestowed them like a gift, wrapped in her desertion and betrayal. Ellie shivered. No, whatever he might believe, she was far from being a child.

'Definitely prawn balls,' he said.

'Mmm. Definitely.'

'Sweet and sour of course.'

'Of course.'

'Chicken. With chow mein. Do you like chicken, Eloise?'

'Love it.'

'Bombay duck?'

'Duck's my absolute favourite.'

Jeff laughed. 'Apart from the fact that you've obviously never eaten Chinese in your young life, and that Bombay duck is a kind of dried fish, is there anything you don't like?'

She sighed. Might have guessed he'd find her out. 'Not that I know of.'

He was gone for half an hour, returning with burdens of delicious-smelling foil parcels. He got out plates and opened some wine.

She hesitated then. It was as if she'd been catapulted into an adult world that held too many unknowns. But this was what she'd wanted, wasn't it? This freedom.

Then he cleared the coffee table of papers and magazines with one sweep of his hand, poured the wine, and the moment of uncertainty was lost.

The food was so good that for several minutes they didn't speak. Then he grabbed a barbecued spare rib, leaned back, and eyed her speculatively. She began to wonder if the bright red sauce had dribbled down her chin.

'What are you going to do, little Eloise?' he asked. 'Tomorrow or the next day or next month or whenever? What are your plans?'

He was trying to find out when she'd be leaving him and Charlotte alone. She didn't want to think about it. It was a gaping chasm of unknowns. What *could* she do? She wasn't qualified like Charlotte, she had no money, no home. Nothing to hang on to. Nowhere to start.

'I'm not going back to school.' At least she could manage a few negatives. 'And I'm not going back to Pencraig.' She picked up her wine glass.

Jeff was loading more forkfuls on to his plate. 'What are you good at? What do you like doing?'

Ellie shrugged. She was going to say sex, but he probably wouldn't be amused. And anyway, she didn't like sex. There was something it gave her that she needed, but it never satisfied her. It only dug the hole a little deeper and left her more lonely than before.

'There must be something. Come on. Give us a clue.' He sucked in air between certain words, accentuating them, as if ensuring that she realised he was making memorable conversation.

'Music, I suppose. Mother taught me piano and I had private sax lessons.' She laughed bitterly. 'Great, huh? Charlotte went to posh boarding school to get a decent education, and I learned to play the saxophone. A fat lot of good that'll do me.'

'Can you sing?'

'Why? Are you in the music business all of a sudden?' She eyed him with distrust.

'Don't be so prickly. I'm just interested.'

That was hard to believe. Self-interest was the only kind of interest she'd associate with Jeff. Or interest from a healthy fat investment.

'Mother says I can sing like a dream,' she told him, half-laughing.

'Really?' He leaned forward, elbows on his thighs, staring at her in that way he had.

'Really.'

'Tell me about your mother.' Jeff opened another bottle of wine.

She narrowed her green eyes. 'Boy, you really want to know it all, don't you?'

He shrugged. 'Charlotte never talks about her.'

'She wouldn't. She blames her for everything.'

But it was too easy to do that. Too easy to make it that simple. Charlotte had always been charmed by Olivia – everyone could be charmed by Olivia if she put her mind to it. But Charlotte had never liked her. Loved her, yes, she was easy to love, or at least to adore. But she wasn't so easy to like, and Charlotte would never understand her motives. It was different for Ellie.

'Do you ever see her? Charlotte refuses to.'

'Charlotte's too loyal to Dad.' Ellie sighed. 'She thinks Mother betrayed him. So Charlotte cut her out of her life. Just like that.' She made a gesture like someone's throat being cut. Charlotte always seemed so certain about what was right, what she wanted.

Jeff nodded with understanding. 'So what *is* she like, your mother?'

'Beautiful. Remote. Not like a mother at all.'

'And your dad loved her to distraction, I suppose?'

'Yes, he did.' Ellie frowned.

There was a bitterness in Jeff's voice that made her wonder about him. Why was he so interested? Was he thinking about his own parents, perhaps? He was so compact and self-assured that it was easy to forget he had a background of his own. A past that had shaped him, helped to make him what he was. What was he? She didn't have the faintest idea. So far he was a mass of contradictions.

'It was more like an obsession,' she told him. 'Dad had this thing about her. It was a kind of worship.' She shivered. Why was she telling him all this?

'Hmm.' He glanced at her thoughtfully, and sucked in breath. 'It's easy to understand— sexual attraction. Need. Even love, I guess.' He laughed. 'The most overworked word in the English language. But obsession? No, I can't relate to that.'

'It's kind of spooky. You can't reason with it.' Ellie tucked into the chow mein. 'He even mistook me for Mother one time.'

'Did he?' He leaned closer. The pupils in his eyes were tiny darts. There was little genuine compassion to be seen. 'What happened?'

'Oh, he was drunk. Pissed as a fart actually.' She giggled. She'd never told anyone this before, not even Charlotte. 'I came in late with a scarf round my head. It was freezing that night. He was standing at the top of the stairs.'

'And he thought you were Olivia?'

'Sort of. Only he didn't act like he always did with her, so maybe he knew the difference deep down. His eyes didn't come over all spaniel – like they did when he was with her – gooey and sloppy, like he wanted to pant all over her, you know?' Ellie pulled a face.

Jeff grinned and nodded.

'No. His eyes were fiery. And he yelled, "What the hell are you doing here?" Or something like that. Really fierce.' She shuddered.

Jeff put down his fork. Ellie knew she had a captive audience. 'So I pulled off the scarf.' She mimed this action. 'And I said, "It's only me, Dad. It's Ellie."'

'And?'

'He ran down the stairs, lost his balance, almost fell, grabbed me and started rambling— "Why? Tell me why you did it. Why did you leave? You destroyed me, you bitch."' Ellie's voice became louder. Abruptly her shoulders sagged. 'All that kind of stuff. He wouldn't stop.'

'What did you say?'

'I put my arm round him and kept saying, "It's me, Dad, Ellie. Mother isn't here. She's not here." Over and over. And eventually he calmed down.' She'd miss out the tears. Those horrible, scary tears that seemed to be wrenching him apart. And the guilt she'd felt. For not being Mother. For being too like Olivia. For wanting to leave him.

'I took him up to bed and he was sleeping like a baby ten minutes later.' She shook her head as if she could shake the memory out of existence. Then she grabbed a prawn ball. 'These balls are delicious.'

Jeff stared at her. 'You two had a bit of a weird upbringing.'

Ellie smiled. 'We pretended we were the old married couple. We were reflections of Mother and Dad. I was like her, and Charlotte was like him. They were the irresponsible kids.'

'Only it wasn't you who left her.'

She noticed the expression in the dark-blue eyes and wished she hadn't told him all that. 'I suppose we remembered we weren't them in the end,' she said vaguely. The end. It was a long way from the end.

She couldn't make him out. He seemed to have so much sympathy, so much understanding, and yet in the next moment he'd deny it all. But he made her feel special. Everyone likes to feel special. And he was bloody good at it.

How many girls felt special with Jeff? That was an interesting one. Ellie munched thoughtfully on a prawn cracker. Would she ever dare ask him?

'Do you understand why she needed to have affairs?' He moved his plate away.

The words were casual, but Ellie sensed a precariousness. He was so sure of himself. How many affairs had he had since being with Charlotte? Several probably. Most men wouldn't provide much competition for a predator like Jeff. And most women wouldn't resist.

She'd like to bet that he could hold most women in the palm of his hand. In the large, strong, brown-skinned hand that she couldn't take her eyes off. And how he'd enjoy pulling the strings.

For the first time Ellie wondered if she was drinking too much wine. But it was soft and velvety and slid down her throat like some kind of forbidden delight.

'Of course I understand,' she said at last. She spooned the last of the chicken on to her plate. 'She felt trapped by him. Caged up in that house. Isolated. And he didn't want her to have friends.'

'Perhaps he was worried friends might lead to adultery,' Jeff observed.

'Not having friends was even more risky. It would make her desperate. And if she was desperate she wouldn't care about the consequences.' Ellie could imagine the suffocation of it. Poor Olivia, immersed in the sweet, sickly stench of that hangdog kind of love.

'What do you think she got out of her affairs?' He was persistent, she'd give him that.

Ellie cleaned her plate, let out a deep sigh of satisfaction, and put the napkin to her lips. 'Excitement,' she said dreamily. 'Adventure. Escape.'

'Some women read Mills and Boon.'

'Then they're cowards.' She stretched like a cat who's drunk too much cream, and felt the tautness of the lycra jumpsuit pulling at her skin. 'That wouldn't be enough for Mother. It wasn't her fault she couldn't love him in the way he wanted. He expected too much.'

'What about you?' His eyes became misty as he watched her, and his voice was low and husky. 'You're one of the most unusual girls I've ever met. Will you have affairs or read romantic fiction?'

He was laughing at her again. She'd said too much. She should never have opened up her feelings to him. She'd never allowed another human being to get so close before.

Except Charlotte. And this man should be her enemy – in a way.

'I'm not a child,' she whispered.

'I know.' He pushed a strand of blonde hair gently back from her brow, allowing his hand to linger for a moment longer than necessary. 'But do you think the adventure of having an affair is worth it in the end? Worth the pain it can cause?'

Ellie felt nervous. Was she mad?

'No, I don't. Sex is ridiculous. All that squirming around and panting like animals on heat. I don't even like sex.'

He laughed. But the laughter was thick and she knew what was coming.

'Maybe you had the wrong partners.'

She shook her head. 'Don't give me that crap. Men are all the same. They're all pathetic if you want to know the truth. They think it's so bloody crucial.' She sighed. 'Until the end, when they realise it's worthless. If they only knew how ridiculous they look, bouncing away. Sweaty shoulders. Hairy legs. Bums twitching. Dogs look more dignified than men.'

It was the drink talking, she knew that. But it was fun – the thrill of being daring. And he was laughing. Really laughing. His self-confidence wasn't fragile then. She'd known it wouldn't be. Thank God. She could say anything to Jeff, he was unshockable.

'You're precious.' He took a slug of his drink. 'You are really funny. I like you, Eloise.'

She giggled. 'Perhaps I'm just frigid. Everyone else seems to enjoy sex.'

Jeff raised his dark eyebrows. 'You couldn't be further from the truth.'

Ellie shrugged. Originally she'd hoped to find herself in sex. To make sense of it all. But it hadn't worked. Then she'd wanted to lose herself in the sexual act, needed to lose herself in it, because it was the only thing left. But she hadn't been able to do that either. Suddenly she wanted to cry.

'I can't believe you're frigid.' His arm crept, insidious and comforting around her shoulders. His face, male and alien, was very close to hers. The dark shadow of his jaw seemed to brush against her skin. 'I bet you've never even been kissed properly,' he murmured, hot into her ear.

She was surprised by the sharp spasm of pleasure. 'Get off!' But she giggled again.

'I could show you how to kiss,' he said. 'In a brotherly kind of way, of course. Complete the education you say you've missed out on.'

'Of course you could,' she mimicked. The desire shot through her like a rocket. She pulled back, but the agreement was a glimmer in her slanting, green eyes and Jeff wasn't the kind to ask twice.

So he kissed her. Only it didn't stay brotherly for very long. About half a second Ellie would say. If that. And then his fingers found the zip of her jumpsuit.

Jeff was a revelation. For a start he was a great kisser. His kiss wasn't wet or slimy. His kiss was warm, deep and sweaty. There was a jet of heat in his kiss like the rush of heat that would assault you if you broke the skin and burrowed quickly into a delicious, giant baked potato.

It went on. It couldn't stop.

He touched Ellie in all the right places. He didn't leave her behind and he didn't go too slow. Every time she tried to hold back, he did something with his tongue or fingers that made her forget.

Over and over he made her close her eyes and cry out, in almost the same way she'd closed her eyes and cried out to bring boys to rapid orgasm when she was bored. But it wasn't the same way, because now she couldn't help herself. She wasn't in control.

Jeff's body was not an intrusion into hers. That was the chief sensation. For the first time Ellie didn't feel violated – she felt welcoming. She wanted to welcome him inside like a long-lost friend.

He was beautiful. There was nothing to avoid. No adolescent rashes or sweat-streaked blubber. Nothing she didn't want to touch. He fascinated her. She watched him when she could keep her eyes open long enough, drinking in the look of his lean, hard body. The tense muscles rippling under brown skin. His eyes were glazed – he wasn't with her, she knew that. So that was how it was with Jeff. He had to separate himself from the act, from her. He'd learned how to lose himself in it then.

They were on the floor – the carpet burning into her back and her shoulder blades as he pushed further into her. She felt her skin being rubbed red-raw.

His fingers dug into her flesh as he pulled her towards and on top of him, grinding mercilessly on, until she knew she had no power left. She was submerged, lost in him and the passion.

She threw back her head, her lips parted, every sense quivering, and groaned with an abandon that was utterly strange to her.

After her experiences in the sand, on muddy pathways and in the back of cars, Ellie would have chosen comfort with Jeff. But there simply wasn't time. This was consuming. They had to have it all and they had to have it now.

Jeff was a practical lover. He got on with the business. Pushed her into different positions, evaluated their success, probed into her, then tried a different one. And he never once looked her in the eye. He worked on her, tantalising, teasing, teaching.

Once she glanced up and imagined she saw Charlotte's shadow standing by the Georgian fireplace, dark eyes mocking her objections as she watched their bodies making whatever it was that seemed more powerful than love.

Charlotte was naked. As Ellie watched, she ran her fingers along the length of her brown thighs. She threw back her head – abandoned. She massaged her nipples with her fingertips. She knelt and reached out her arms to Ellie.

Ellie's passion came from nowhere. It thundered through her, rush upon wonderful rush of it. She clutched at his shoulders gratefully. So she could have passion. Better than that, she was made for it. It was her first orgasm. The brilliance of it took her by surprise. It was—

'Wow,' she breathed. 'Mmm mmm. Wow.'

She felt him let go, free to go on with what he wanted.

What would Charlotte do now? Ellie looked up, but she'd gone. What did Charlotte do to him now? What would he say to Charlotte?

'Say you love me,' she whispered.

He grunted.

'Tell me you love me,' she repeated. Urgently. 'I want you to love me.' The words took on his rhythm.

'Want me to do it or bloody talk about it?' he gasped.

Seconds later he came. 'Charlotte,' he yelled at the moment of climax.

'Christ Almighty, Jeff—'

'Sorry, sweetness.' He shuddered into her.

'That's worse,' she muttered. 'Don't call me that.'

'You're a strange girl, Eloise.'

'Hold me,' she said. 'Just hold me.'

Please be better than all the rest, she thought. Don't push me away now that it's afterwards. Don't treat me like shit. Be worth more than that. She didn't dare look at him.

Let him be worth something. Let him see some value in all this.

He drew away from her, tracing the bones of her face with his finger. 'What a beautiful girl you are.'

'I've got too many knobbly bits.'

He smiled. It was a smile that made her heart flip. And then the phone rang.

Jeff answered it, rolling his eyes at Ellie before pasting innocence on to his face, as if he knew it would be someone he must lie to.

Please don't let him ever lie to me, she thought. Please, whatever happens, let me be the one he never lies to. I'll accept everything about him. When I want him to lie, one day, don't let him.

'Charlotte? Is that you?' he said. 'Is everything okay?'

Ellie was strangely glad that it was Charlotte. She wanted her to be part of it. She wanted to feel closer to her. Feel that they shared every possible experience. That they were involved in every possible way.

Now, she felt she was on the way to discovering the real Charlotte – the new Charlotte who'd evolved since that first summer when she'd gone to school, then university, then here.

The sexual part of Charlotte was the part that would be a mystery if it wasn't for Jeff. Ellie stretched, relishing the wet and the warm. She smiled, pleased and saturated. Now Charlotte would never be able to leave her again.

'Why can't you talk to me?' he asked.

Ellie yawned. Sleep would be nice.

'Oh, hell—' He thrust the receiver towards her. 'She won't talk to me,' he said. 'She wants you.'

Ellie felt the shaft of satisfaction, before all the combinations jelled. Jeff's face and voice, Charlotte at Pencraig, wanting to speak to her. Something was very wrong.

'Charlotte?'

Charlotte sounded impossibly unlike Charlotte as she spoke, very soft, very low. And it was impossible to take in, because of course Dad was perfectly fine, despite the drinking. How could he die? It was ridiculous. She and Jeff had been making love on the carpet, so how could he die?

She must have made a mistake. Only Charlotte didn't make mistakes. Charlotte needed her.

For a moment Ellie recalled that time when she'd seen Olivia with Greg in Dragon Bay. And the day Olivia left. How she'd cried out for Charlotte. But she hadn't come because of Jeff. Charlotte hadn't heard her. Because of Jeff.

She put down the phone. 'We have to go to Pencraig,' she told him in a surprised kind of voice. 'Charlotte needs us. My father's dead.' Which came first?

And then she heard what she'd said and he grabbed her as she fell. Held her head close to his chest.

She listened to the thumping of his heart, felt the dark hair curling against her skin.

'I'm here, Eloise,' he said. 'Don't worry. I'll look after you. I'm here.'

Soon they would be there.

There was no guilt in Jeff, and she was glad. Guilt was for women, or selfless men like her father. Her father, who cherished expectations, who wouldn't be feeling guilt any more.

'I left. He's dead.' The words rebounded in her head, accompanying the swish of the cars on the motorway. 'I left. He's dead.'

'Not your fault,' Jeff said. He closed his hand over hers.

Guilt. It swamped her. Ellie hadn't realised she'd spoken aloud. 'Not my fault,' she echoed. Obedient to the end.

5

They stood, Charlotte and Ellie Morgan, staring at the flowers outside the Chapel of Rest. That was a joke. Ellie was angry. She resented everything. None of the bodies here were indulging in forty winks. Why not just call it the Chapel of Death and be done with it?

And as they stood in regulation black, close together and yet miles apart, all the faces came to pay their respects. Faces from the village – rooted in the world Ellie had left behind her, and faces she didn't recognise. Faces with frowns, sometimes sad eyes and sometimes even tears. Some of the faces turned out to have arms which they tried to wrap round Ellie, but she resisted. She stood, straight and distanced, with dry eyes and a hating heart. What did they know – any of these faces? It was all a bloody farce.

'Thank you for coming. It was so sweet of you. Thank you for the flowers. You've been very kind.' Charlotte sounded as though she was operating on auto-pilot.

When Ellie and Jeff had arrived at Pencraig on the night of Rolf's death, it had seemed a deep yet simple sadness that could be shared. The sisters collapsed into each other's arms with tears of relief and loss. Together they dealt with the looming practicalities. Together they stood tall against the rest of the world.

Neither uttered a word of recrimination or regret. Neither dared to reminisce or consider the future. Instead they both accepted some sort of superficial pretence that had only ended up pulling them further apart. And now there was merely cold comfort between them. Charlotte's cold hand shook other cold hands. Charlotte's voice said all the correct words and even got the order right. Ellie just stood there.

Faces. Empty faces and black. Black. An interesting colour for different perspectives. A superb backdrop for whatever you chose to place on it. Anything would shine. Ellie smiled to herself. That was the problem when it came down to it. Any star shone brightly in a clear night sky.

'Are you all right, sweetie?' That was Jeff talking to Charlotte. Doing his concerned, manly bit. 'Is there anything I can do?'

Ellie watched him hesitantly put one hand on Charlotte's shoulder. Amazing. Surely a man like Jeff knew all the right moves? It was true that men only saw the simple things clearly. But still—

'I'm fine.' Charlotte shrugged his hand away.

Ellie saw that she didn't want the physical contact. There was something vital missing between these two – something that maybe even held them together. Was that why Jeff had seduced Ellie? If seduction was the way to put it. Ellie had been right all along. Jeff was much too wicked for her sister.

'Where's Mother?' Charlotte hissed. 'Why the hell isn't she out here doing her bit?'

'Perhaps she feels she isn't part of the family any more.' Ellie dug up a perfect piece of turf with the pointed toe of her shoe. Why were crematoria so perfect, with their neat flowers and shorn grass? Would any alternative be in bad taste? She gazed around at the grassy slopes, the discreet planting – nothing too bright and daring. The concrete and the hearses. The wreaths and stiff, upright bearers in their black suits and starched collars.

'Why did she bother to come to his funeral then? What a hypocrite.' Charlotte's hazel eyes were blazing.

The hatred must hurt her. She was dreading a confrontation – Ellie could see it hiding behind her anger. In the brooding, hunted expression on her face.

'You knew she'd come.' Ellie sighed. They'd both known.

And Olivia had certainly made an effective entrance – wafting down the aisle to claim her rightful seat at the front of the chapel. Adultery and divorce conveniently erased from memory. Everyone else was already in place, avoiding the gaze of the coffin. Everyone was waiting. Perhaps people would always wait for Olivia. And she'd always shine. She was like a vision – not quite there, liable to float away at the first insult. And beautifully ethereal in black. The stark contrast against her pale skin and hair only increased her fragility. It made her a victim.

Ellie had begun to wonder if Mother was too caught up with her life and whoever filled it these days, to make the effort. But she'd misjudged her. Olivia would always travel for a stage. And this was the ideal platform for her talents. So with moments to spare, almost as the chaplain drew breath, she created the perfect entrance. Like a bride. Ellie wanted to laugh. Like Rolf's bride of death, in a way.

There he was waiting for her – her dead husband. It was so hard not to stare at the coffin. Hard to imagine Dad's body underneath that expensive and terribly tasteful mahogany. But after a while Ellie let herself be drawn to it, to what was left of Rolf. As the chaplain droned on she heard only Rolf's voice. As the sea of faces around her became indistinguishable, she saw only Rolf's face.

His voice wasn't slurred and weak as it had been near the end, but hopeful, like it once was. Full of love. And his features had returned to the original. His light-brown eyes were bright and alive again, and his lower lip wasn't drooping from drink and self-pity.

Ellie was glad. She wanted to remember him the way he had been when he was invincible – that distant father, hardly ever there for her. When their relationship had existed mainly in her imagination. For he spent little time with her in those early days. His time all Mother's until she began to let go and let him down. It was then that he looked around him to see what else he had apart from Olivia. Then he'd discovered Ellie.

But until that time he'd had his eyes fixed only on Mother. And Ellie hadn't minded. After all, she was only a reflection and he was a fairy-tale.

Faces. Faces and flowers and Charlotte's voice.

'So kind of you. So thoughtful. Yes. We'll all miss him.'

Will you, Charlotte? Even though you hardly ever saw him in the end?

Ellie closed her eyes. She couldn't get away from it. Today the indisputable fact of her own mortality was brushing against her mind like a half-remembered chore that had never made it to the right list. She felt she'd moved up a generation. He had created her – or at least half-created her, along with the whimsical creature she called Mother. And now he was gone. Did that mean Ellie had sprung to adulthood at last? Or did that only happen when you spawned children of your own and moved smoothly into the next gear?

'Oh, my dear. My heart goes out to you.'

For a few moments the face changed from indistinct blur into the face of Miss Pringle, her old teacher. Of needlework, cookery and how to be a door-mat when you grew up. Talking to Charlotte. How did she know Charlotte?

'Thank you.' Their hands clasped as though they shared something important.

Ellie blinked. Joy Pringle was actually crying, for Christ's sake. How dare she? How dare she pretend to have any kind of loss?

Quickly Ellie forced the face back into non-recognition. She couldn't speak to her now. She couldn't speak to any of these faces now.

'Bloody cheek,' she muttered. 'What right have they got to come here at all?' It was loud enough to be heard.

Charlotte turned towards her. Her face, with high cheekbones and proud, dark eyes, was flushed with anger. 'What would you prefer? Dad to be buried in the garden at Pencraig?'

'It'd make more sense.'

'Ellie, for heaven's sake.' Charlotte's angry whisper was close to hysteria. But at least she was letting out some emotion at last. 'Can't you keep your bloody rebellions for a different time and place? I don't want to hear it right now. I can't cope with it. To tell you the truth, I could do with some support for a change.'

'It's a farce.' Why couldn't Charlotte see that? Charlotte had almost become part of the farce.

Ellie knew what she was doing and she couldn't help it. Push, push, push. It was like some little devil inside her that wouldn't stop dancing. She hated it. The hypocrisy. Christ. The fact that he was dead at all.

Jeff, standing behind the two of them, bent his head close to hers. For a second, despite her despair, Ellie was forced to drink in the male scent of him. Forced to remember what had happened between them. It shot through her, the desire, with the force of the orgasm he'd given her.

'Your sister's entitled to some consideration,' he said. 'She's doing all the work around here. Do you think it's easy for her?'

'I know what it's like for her. Rolf was my father too.' Her eyes challenged his. At last he looked away.

'Pack it in then,' he said.

'Oh, go to hell.' Conventions. That was what was wrong with them all. Conventions. The proper way. It meant you weren't allowed to feel any more.

They'd been standing here for only minutes, and yet it felt like hours. Jeff and Charlotte deserved each other. Ellie wandered closer to the flowers. They were in a neat line, separated by only a slightly bigger gap from the next line. The next body. The next death. She walked along to the final wreath. It was a conveyor belt. Very lifelike. Everything in lines – the pews, the mourners, the flowers. Even now the next lot were filing in, a line of black silent dashes.

Ellie clenched her fists and stretched out her arms, allowing one of the roses from an elegantly arranged spray to brush against her skin. Neat and perfect, much more like death than life. These roses had never been close to the soil of a garden or felt a breath of wind. They were nothing like roses should be. They were buds and would probably stay buds until they withered on their dead, erect stalks.

She bent low and sniffed. They didn't even smell of anything. Only artifice. They were scentless, meaningless, nothing roses. Worse than plastic. And more to the point, Dad would have hated them. It would have been better to bring a bunch of windblown white tea roses from the garden.

She reached out again, desperate for something to convey meaning. The rose she touched was damp. Dew perhaps? For a second she brightened. And then she realised it was wet with her tears. Tears for the sad roses or tears for Dad, at last?

Instinctively, like a child, she groped her way back to

Charlotte. As she approached, Charlotte looked up, her hazel eyes also wet with tears, and held out her arms. With a groan, Ellie sank into them. She was shaking.

'I'm sorry I screwed up,' she said. 'I should never have left him on his own. I should have known he'd do something stupid.'

'No.' Charlotte held the blonde, cropped head against her shoulder. Her fingers began to stroke the pain away. 'You couldn't have known,' she whispered. 'I'm not going to let you take the responsibility for this. It was his life. His decision to end it. He might just as easily have done it while you were still living there.'

Ellie shivered.

'It's just as much my fault. More.' Charlotte's voice was still low. 'I ducked out of my responsibilities, didn't I?'

'Let's get out of here,' Ellie muttered. 'It smells of death. I'm stagnating. Bloody drowning in it.'

'Yes. Yes, we will.' Charlotte drew away, her hands still on Ellie's shoulders. 'I've just got to remind people to come back to the house for tea.'

'I don't know why you bothered.' Jeff was watching them, his eyes cold and remote.

Charlotte touched Ellie's wet cheek with a gesture of love. 'They're family and friends. It's the right thing to do.'

'And you must do the right thing, mustn't you, Charlotte?' He began walking towards the cars. 'But I want to get back to Manchester tonight.' He called over his shoulder. 'Business.'

'Business. Bloody business,' Charlotte said softly. 'It's always the way with you.'

Ellie looked at her. 'He's right though,' she said. 'You don't owe this lot anything.' Faces would always drift away.

'I know. But there are practical things we have to do. Talk to Mr Barton for a start.'

Ellie groaned.

'There's the house. All his things— Lots of things—' Charlotte's voice tailed off. Ellie felt her body tense.

She looked up. Olivia was coming down the path towards them. Where had she disappeared to? Trying to chat up the chaplain perhaps? Ellie smiled, her first one of the day. Mother was like a breath of fresh air in this revolting place.

'There you are!' Olivia waved as if she'd seen them an hour ago, instead of having left them all two years ago to go off with another man.

'I wasn't expecting you to come.' Charlotte held herself back, stiff and remote.

'Why not?' Olivia took Ellie's hands in hers. 'Hello, darling. It's wonderful to see you.'

Was it? Was it really? Why did Ellie remain unconvinced?

'Hello, Mother.' She looked better than ever close up. Desertion suited her. 'Are you coming back to Pencraig? We've done tea and stuff.'

Charlotte swung away from them. Ellie could see the anger in the tightness of her shoulders, her rigid back. But when she looked back at them her dark eyes were lost. She seemed like an orphan.

She is our mother, Ellie wanted to say. She was his wife. We've forgiven each other. Can't we reach out to her too?

'Of course I'm coming back to the house.' Olivia sighed dramatically. 'I want to have a nice long chat with both of you.'

'What for?' Charlotte glared at her.

'Charlotte's upset.' Ellie took Olivia's arm. 'Don't take any notice.' She turned to Charlotte. 'We can't let her go without even talking.'

Charlotte shrugged.

'We're all upset. I'm sorry, my darling.' Olivia held out

her arms to her elder daughter, and this time Ellie saw Charlotte's body twitch in response. She was fighting some secret battle.

'Oh, for Christ's sake, Mother.' Instead of succumbing, she turned, stomping towards the car where Jeff was waiting. 'Come if you must.'

'Do you want a lift with us?' Ellie squeezed her arm. Mother was impossible, but she'd chased away all those faces and she lightened Ellie's heart.

Olivia smiled. 'Mr Barton is bringing me. I'll see you back at Pencraig.' She walked gracefully with small steps towards the short, fat, balding solicitor standing by the black Bentley.

Hardly Mother's type. But certainly the power of the moment, Ellie supposed. She watched her, and she watched Mr Barton, Mother's temporary, almost drooling knight in shining armour, as he took her hand to help her into the car. She'd never change.

What was it she had? Ellie shook her head in half-amused despair. Well, whatever it was, she wished she had it, that indefinable something or other that brought out the knight in the most unsuspecting and unlikely men. Had her mother passed it on to Ellie? Or would she always keep it – like her men – exclusively to herself?

Back at the house Jeff loosened the black silk tie, took off his designer-label jacket, and prepared for a few hours of boredom, watching Charlotte and Eloise dish out tea and sympathy. He wanted to be out of here, back in his own territory where at least he felt he knew who Charlotte was again. Here at Pencraig she seemed to become someone quite different and he wasn't sure he even liked her much.

Besides, the world didn't stop with death. There were things he had to do. People to meet, deals to make. Could he risk using the phone? He caught Eloise's eye and beckoned to her.

She came over. 'What's up?'

'Would anyone notice if I made some calls? The phone's still connected, isn't it?'

He wanted to touch her. She looked small and vulnerable, and the sun shafting through the big bay window was sending highlights of gold through her hair. Touching her would make him feel stronger. He hadn't touched her since the day her father died, but he knew he would do it again.

'Would anyone care?' She looked as pissed off as he felt. 'You haven't exactly made a vast contribution so far.'

Jeff grinned. On reflection, she was about as vulnerable as a black widow spider.

'I don't belong here,' he said. Her family. Charlotte's family. Old acquaintances. What did he have to do with any of them?

Her green eyes sparked with anger. 'No. It's this lot that doesn't belong here. Load of bloody vultures. Look at them all. The odd death here and there gives them something to live for. They're practically dribbling with the excitement. They love a bit of suffering with their tea, so long as it's someone else's.'

'You're too young to be cynical.' He smiled at her. With a girl like this one you didn't have to pretend. She had the look of innocence, the sensuality of a siren and a mind that could cut into slices what other people left unsampled.

'I'll cover for you with Charlotte. The phone's in the study.' She pointed.

'You're an angel.'

'Hardly.' She looked him up and down in that considering way she had and smiled slowly.

When would he have her again? Jeff watched her walk away. Strange girl. She hadn't tried to use what had happened between them. She'd never even referred to it. It might never have happened, which was rather off-putting. Apparently immune – after a fuck like that, which didn't happen to anyone very often. Was he losing his touch, or what? Had he been mistaken about her – about that night?

No way. She'd enjoyed it as much as he had. Maybe even more. And eventually she'd let go with a passion that had amazed him. Bloody marvellous in bed, and still only a kid. But as good as any professional already. If he'd met her first, would he and she—? Probably not. She was too young. And part of the attraction was the connection with Charlotte, he knew that.

Jeff blamed himself. He should never have allowed it to happen. He hadn't intended it. He'd meant to walk in, get ready to meet Melanie, go out, do the business, come back and give Eloise a chaste goodnight kiss before they went to their separate beds. That was what you did with the sisters of your women. Anything else was strictly taboo.

But then he'd seen her standing lost and lonely in his kitchen, all big eyes and spiky blonde hair, cracking an egg into a bowl and looking much more sexy and intriguing than a girl of her age had any right to look. And he hadn't been able to do any of those things.

Jeff laughed at himself as he turned away, heading for the study. He had let Melanie go screw herself – hadn't even phoned to tell her he wasn't coming. So he'd risked the entire deal blowing up in his face after all his hard work with the old tart. Ah, what the hell. He'd enjoyed himself. It had all been worth it. Eloise would never risk Charlotte finding out. And he'd get round Melanie eventually, although it would cost him a fortune in red roses.

But he didn't want the deal to blow up in his face. If he

lost it, it would be the second one running to fall through. Worrying, that. Mind you, if he couldn't unload the shop for the right price he might have to wave goodbye to Melanie's deal in any case. And that would be a shame. Because Melanie's deal was a beauty – he'd hate to lose it – a flash detached number in Bowden Vale, swimming-pool, summer-house, the whole caboodle.

His fists clenched, an involuntary action that Jeff wasn't used to. He didn't get wound up, he was always in control. But he had to get that shop off his hands. It had seemed a snip at the time. But the bastards who were interested either ground the price down to nothing, or else turned out to be time-wasting prats who backed out at the first wave of a contract. All talk and didn't have the balls or necessary readies to go any further.

No doubt about it. Things were getting twitchy on the property market. A nice legacy for Charlotte wouldn't go amiss. The men with the money were holding back, waiting. Interest rates were soaring and everyone was getting out quick or drowning. Building and property had been hit by this recession more than he'd estimated. Bad mistake that.

Maybe he should diversify. Get into antiques perhaps – he'd always had a yen for that sort of thing. Reckoned he might be good at it too. It couldn't be that difficult – look at some of the brainless yobs who were doing it these days. Easy money.

None of the shady stuff though, stuff off the back of a lorry or conning little old ladies. None of the crap either. Jewellery perhaps? There was money in that if you knew what you were looking at. He'd find out the business, even buy a few books, get himself a gold-testing kit. No harm in checking it out. He knew a man who had a brother in antiques. Maybe he should fix up a meet.

Respectability was a must. He needed at least the illusion of it to keep Charlotte happy. She was so straight – that was one of the things he liked about her. She'd never mess him around.

The study was empty. Jeff sat down on the desk and began to dial – humming softly to himself. Joy. The telephone was his lifeline. There was absolutely no way he could exist without it.

'Melanie?' His voice was husky. 'God, I've missed you, sweetie. When are you ever going to forgive me? If I don't get to run my hands over your delicious body soon I won't be answerable for the consequences.'

He leaned back and smiled lazily. Stupid bitch.

'You've been avoiding me all afternoon.'

Charlotte was almost afraid to look at her. She knew all about Olivia's powers, and she didn't want to forget what she held against her. She looked cool, elegant and self-assured. But her green eyes showed no traces of affection. Of love, or even regret.

'I've been busy. There's a lot of people I haven't seen for so long—'

'People you hardly know.' Olivia carefully placed one slim white hand on Charlotte's arm.

But Charlotte wasn't deceived. People might think Olivia was delicate as porcelain, but Charlotte knew she was as tough as old wellies. And she hated not being appreciated. Did Mother know how Charlotte was shaking inside? The blame was so mixed up with the longing, that she wasn't even sure which was which any more.

'I still have to talk to them. They were kind to Dad.' Her hazel eyes were challenging.

'And I wasn't?'

'You said it.'

Olivia sighed. 'I want you to talk to me too. I'm your mother. I insist.' The grip on Charlotte's arm strengthened. 'Put away those ridiculous teacups and come outside. At least listen to what I have to say.'

The old spells. The right noises. Mother was good at all that. But she'd only ever wanted a doll to play with. That was what Charlotte should have been. A doll to dress, with hair to brush, who could be forgotten for a few days when Olivia had other things on her mind. More exciting games to play. More beautiful ornaments to cherish. Damn and blast her. There was so much more to motherhood than that. Couldn't she see what she'd done?

'There's nothing to say.' The pain of death and the stings of resentment held Charlotte upright.

'There's plenty to say.' Olivia's hand became a vice-like grip.

It was a struggle between them. Charlotte felt as if the blood was being sucked from her body by that hand. The contours of Olivia's aristocratic face were set with a determination that wouldn't be thwarted. Her eyes were strips of green steel. Charlotte knew that it was hopeless to resist.

'Mrs Morgan.'

Thank God. For a moment Charlotte contemplated escape, as Bert and Maisie Jupp appeared. They'd helped out in the house and garden in the good days. When Pencraig had been a family home.

But one look from Olivia made her stay where she was. Mother would catch up with her sooner or later. She couldn't run for ever. So she watched with interest as Olivia switched into Lady Bountiful mode.

'The roses just aren't the same these days, Bert.' Olivia shook her head mournfully. 'My poor roses.'

'Any time you want a man in the garden, ma'am.' Bert

pumped her free hand up and down in his large sunburned paw.

Olivia smiled weakly. 'I know. You're the man for the job.'

Charlotte stiffened. As if this place had anything to do with Olivia any more. She had forfeited that right when she left.

'That's the way. Just say the word.' Bert grinned. 'Some of them weeds can be right stubborn buggers.'

'You're so right.' With apparent difficulty, Olivia extricated her hand and Charlotte felt a smile twitching at her mouth for the first time in days.

Before she had the chance to hide it, Olivia glanced her way with startled eyes, for a split second looking so much like Ellie that Charlotte was taken aback. Maybe she'd missed something. Maybe they could even have been friends.

'So.' Olivia scrutinised her briefly as she led the way through the patio doors. 'How are you and your young man getting along?'

Charlotte raised dark eyebrows. 'Jeff wouldn't appreciate that. He likes to pretend he's world-weary.'

Olivia laughed – soft and silvery. 'You must introduce us properly.'

Must I? Should I? Charlotte was silent.

'Are you happy?'

'Of course.' Charlotte knew she'd answered too quickly. She wanted Mother to think that she had all she could ever dream of, that Mother hadn't touched her – hadn't caused any pain.

But the truth was, she didn't have everything that she needed, and only part of it was Jeff. The rest was Ellie, and it was wanting a baby, and it was all mixed up with Mother and Dad.

Since Dad's death she and Jeff had lost all connections. Their timetables had become so hopelessly scrambled. She was lost and yet she couldn't reach out for him, she couldn't admit her need. She required a patience in Jeff that he didn't possess. He wouldn't waste time hanging around with a handy shoulder for her to cry on. Not Jeff. If she wasn't ready when he offered it the first time, then he'd be off. Wheeling and dealing. God knows where. She never knew what he was up to – he never told her anything, never gave her any truth or trust to hold on to. No comfortable cushion of togetherness.

He was never there when she needed him. Why had he been home on the night of Dad's death? The question tore at her. If that business meeting had meant so little to him, if it could be cancelled so easily, then why hadn't he insisted on driving her to Pencraig? Did she mean so little?

How could she marry a man so self-centred, so wrapped up in making money, so obsessed with deals? Before long he'd have them tossing a coin to see who'd use the bathroom first.

'Love's never easy,' Olivia said.

She should know.

'And it takes you by surprise.' She looked up at the blue, almost cloudless sky. Her voice changed. 'I never dreamed he'd do such a thing, Charlotte. You have to believe me. Couples often separate. Even in my generation marriage isn't for ever any more, is it?'

'Apparently not.'

'I can still hardly believe it. That Rolf could take his own life.' Olivia shivered.

She had no idea. She'd taken away Dad's self-respect, and she didn't even realise that he couldn't live without it.

'Perhaps you're right to blame me.'

Charlotte absorbed her words as they sat down in the

sun-faded hammock, and began swinging gently, back and forth. She could smell the delicate, drowsy scent of the wisteria growing up the wall behind her. If she reached out she'd be able to touch it.

For a while they were quiet. Charlotte thought of other summers when she and Ellie had sat here. Listening to Mother's playing wafting through the house and out of the windows, listening to the birds and the distant water. And listening to the rows.

'I made a big mistake,' Olivia admitted at last. 'Your father and I should never have got married.'

'Why did you marry him?' Charlotte had always wondered.

Olivia's eyes misted with the memory. She let out a deep sigh. 'It's a long story. One I'm not particularly proud of. I was frightened. Frightened of the alternatives.'

'How d'you mean?' Charlotte stared at her with wide, dark eyes. It scared her how much she wanted to believe in Olivia.

'When I was a girl your grandfather had mistresses,' she told her. 'It was taken for granted. My mother knew before I had any idea. I just wondered why Father was never home.'

'Didn't Grandmother mind?'

Olivia straightened her shoulders. She was staring sightlessly ahead. 'It wasn't important to her at first. It didn't affect her life. We never really discussed it – you didn't in those days, but I always thought she was disappointed that marriage wasn't the ideal she'd expected. And then perhaps grateful.'

'Grateful?'

'If anything, it released her—' Olivia paused. 'From what she would have called the more distasteful side of marriage.'

'You said, at first?'

'It changed. All the easy deception that had become meaningless. You see, he met a woman who was rather different.'

Charlotte was spellbound. She'd never known any of this. Her grandmother had died before she was born, and neither Mother nor Dad was the type for family reminiscences or poring over old photo albums. But was this Mother talking, or was she on stage again?

'Why was she different?' she asked, knowing the answer already.

Olivia's hand trailed across the purple flowers. She was wearing an opal ring on her slender middle finger that shone multi-coloured like a kaleidoscope in the sunlight. Charlotte remembered it from a long time ago. Had that hand ever tucked in the sheets of a baby's cot – of Charlotte's cot? Or had her hands only ever played the piano and tantalised men?

'He fell in love with her.' Olivia's voice was so quiet that Charlotte had to lean towards her to hear. 'And once he fell in love with her, nothing was the same any more.'

'Did he leave?'

'Not at first. But Mother saw the difference in him, and it wasn't long before I realised what was going on. Men aren't good at hiding these things.'

Charlotte thought of Jeff. He was good at hiding everything.

'I was sixteen then. I already knew your father.' Her mouth curved wistfully. 'But I didn't have a lot of time for him, I'm afraid. He was nice, but—'

'Not very exciting?'

'Exactly.' She smiled. 'I suppose I wanted a dashing hero from some romantic fairy-tale. Someone to sweep me off my feet. Maybe I still do.'

'But you changed your mind. Why did you marry him?'

Olivia leaned back and closed her eyes. 'Father left eventually. It was dreadful. Mother was totally destroyed. I could hardly bear to see her, wandering around doing all the same things, clutching on to all her little routines, while inside— Inside, she'd simply given up.'

Charlotte knew this wasn't the end of the story.

'She became ill. It was cancer – it started in the lower spine and spread so fast—' Olivia shuddered. Her face had a wild look about it. 'Before we knew what was happening, her whole body was riddled with it.'

Charlotte touched her mother's lacy black sleeve. Compassion flooded through her. 'What did Grandfather do?'

Olivia's green eyes hardened. 'He came back. Left that woman and came back. Out of pity. But it was never the same.' She began to rock the hammock faster. 'I think Mother hated him for it. For coming back when he hadn't wanted to.' She stared at Charlotte. 'Mother died, and he couldn't take it. He lived alone for the rest of his life.'

'I'm sorry.' Charlotte didn't know what she was apologising for. Or was she just sorry that such things ever had to happen? It was a sad story, and it was part of her own family history. It made Mother seem more human. But what did it have to do with Mother and Dad?

'Grandfather must have felt terrible,' she said.

Olivia laughed without humour. 'Oh, yes, he felt terrible. And I never forgave him. Like you won't forgive me.'

Charlotte felt the full intensity of her stare. But she was silent.

Olivia's shoulders slumped. 'He knew I could never forgive him, even though I knew what it was like—' She thumped the hammock with her fist.

Charlotte flinched. She'd never seen Olivia like this

before. Her self-control seemed to have slipped away as she relived the past that had made her what she was.

'I couldn't forgive him, even though I knew too. How easy it was to keep falling in love.' Olivia rose slowly to her feet. Her face was very pale.

'You see, Charlotte, I couldn't bear the thought of the same thing happening to me. That's why I married your father. A man I could rely on. Who would live with me and love me until death. Including death.' Her voice had a hollow, melodramatic ring to it.

Charlotte felt sick. Had Dad ever suspected all this?

Olivia spread out her hands and gazed at them as if they belonged to someone else. 'Rolf was there,' she said simply. 'He wanted to look after me. He wanted to give me everything.'

'But it wasn't enough for you.' The words escaped before Charlotte could even consider them.

'No.' Olivia gave her one last look before she turned to walk away. 'It wasn't enough for me in the end. And if you want to blame me for that, then that's up to you. I don't expect you to understand.'

Charlotte stayed in the hammock, still rocking, tracing the flower pattern on the fabric with her index finger, thinking about what Olivia had said. Not even knowing how much she blamed her or how much she blamed herself. What did it matter, now that he was gone?

'Mother,' she whispered out loud. Why had Olivia never been a mother? Charlotte could have forgiven her almost anything if she'd only been a mother.

She laid her hands on her stomach. Would she find out soon, what motherhood was all about? The feelings were getting stronger. Already she was a fortnight late, and Charlotte was normally as regular as clockwork.

Jeff didn't know how much she wanted it. She hadn't told

him the truth about this ache. This ache that was stronger than anything she'd ever experienced. She smiled to herself. Anyway, they'd be married soon.

By the time Charlotte returned to the sitting-room her guests were dispersing and Olivia and Ellie were huddled together in conversation with Mr Barton the solicitor. When she saw Charlotte, Ellie drew her aside.

'Can you believe it? We're not even beneficiaries. Dad's left everything to Mother.'

Charlotte stared at her and Ellie began to giggle. 'Besotted to the grave.'

Charlotte grinned. Ellie always helped her get things in proportion. 'Who would have believed it? What about Pencraig?'

'I told you. Everything. Especially Pencraig. He was determined to make her live here. It was his last ditch attempt to make her love the place like he did.' Ellie rolled her eyes and grabbed Charlotte's arm. 'Isn't it awful? Oh, God. It's so awful it's funny.'

Charlotte was conscious of a sense of relief, a glimmer of freedom. She took Ellie by the shoulders and hugged her. 'Who cares? It's only money.'

'Don't you mind at all?' Ellie whispered into her ear.

'It seems so far away these days. Wales, Pencraig, all of it.' For a moment she felt Ellie's body tense. Because the memories were still close for them both. Charlotte smiled ruefully. 'But I wouldn't have minded enough for a wedding dress.'

She looked round. Beside Olivia she saw Jeff smiling and being charming. Which of them would outcharm the other?

'That's the good news,' Ellie said. 'The bad news is that Mother wants to take us all out to dinner and Jeff's agreed.'

Jeff had agreed? Charlotte eyed him curiously – he'd been desperate to go home a few hours ago. She herself would have preferred to think things through and soak today away in a really hot bath. But she supposed Mother was making an effort.

'Okay. Let's do it. Let's give Dad a family send-off after all.'

Olivia chose a restaurant in the village, and they sat around a circular walnut table, divided from the next table by midnight-blue drapes. It was very plush. All four of them were still dressed in funereal black, and it seemed as if none of them knew what they were doing together at all. It had nothing to do with Rolf. So far he hadn't even been mentioned.

Ellie was on some sort of artificial high – as if determined to enjoy herself or die in the attempt, while Olivia was positively sparkling. Charlotte would say she was flirting with Jeff if it hadn't been so absurd. And if Olivia hadn't been her mother. She'd changed again from the woman of this afternoon. Now she was brittle and uncaring. Always playing a bloody different role.

As for Jeff, he was clearly enjoying himself for the first time that day. He kept the conversation running smoothly, and kept the smiles on the faces. He liked it, Charlotte realised miserably. The attention of three women. That was all he needed to be happy.

But it was wrong. All wrong. This was supposed to be for Dad, and yet Dad had got lost like an unmissed bubble in the champagne Mother was buying as if rationing was beginning tomorrow.

Charlotte's lips got thinner and her frown got deeper as the evening wore on. By the time coffee came she'd had enough.

'Anyone would think this was a celebration,' she remarked.

The other three stared at her.

Is it me, she thought. Is it me who's crazy?

'It is a celebration in a way,' Olivia said. 'It's certainly a reunion.'

'Without Dad.'

There was silence. Ellie fiddled with the soft wax on the top of the red candle, Jeff stirred his coffee very slowly, and Olivia folded her napkin and her face at the same time.

'We've done that bit, Charlotte,' she said. 'Life goes on.'

'For some of us life has always gone on.'

Olivia sighed. 'The trouble with you, Charlotte, is that you take life too seriously. You should lighten up a little.'

'Like you do?'

Ellie and Jeff exchanged worried glances. Charlotte saw it and it made her angrier still. They were all against her. It was a conspiracy.

But Olivia didn't respond to the gibe. Instead she turned her back on Charlotte. 'When's the wedding?' she asked Jeff. 'I love weddings. Any excuse to buy a new dress.'

'We want a quiet wedding.' Charlotte was close to tears. 'We're only inviting people we love and trust.'

She didn't look at him, and he said nothing, but Charlotte knew Jeff was furious. She could feel the vibrations of it. But she didn't care.

'Weddings, funerals,' Olivia said at last, in her dreamy voice. 'Sometimes I wonder if there's any difference. The same people singing a different song.'

Ellie looked down at her coffee cup. Jeff stared at Olivia as if she'd said something meaningful. Charlotte looked from one to the other of them with disgust, scraped back her chair, got to her feet and stormed out.

She went straight to the loo. The familiar cramp doubled her up, and the blood appeared like a sadistic reminder.

Here it was then, the dull monthly ache and the terrible sense of loss. The same old story. Only it got worse as time went on. She put her head in her hands, and she wept.

6

'Don't get me wrong.' Charlotte sighed. She tapped her fingernails on the rustic wooden table, impatient with herself rather than anyone else. Why did she feel like a traitor? 'It's not that I don't want her there. I like having her around. I adore Ellie. You know I do. We're as close as anyone could be. We always have been. It's just that—' She looked up at the sky for inspiration. But there was only blue. Nothing but blue.

'Two's company?' Leonard suggested.

'Not even that. Not really.'

So what was it exactly?

Charlotte had imagined that these few days in another location might give her a clue to what had gone wrong. But so far it hadn't worked out like that. She was simply glad to be away.

'How does Jeff feel about it?'

'He treats her like a kid sister. Sort of. Moans about her making the house untidy, and teases her all the time.' But what else? Jeff also loosened up when Ellie was around. Nothing wrong with that.

'He's home more, as if he doesn't want to leave me alone with Ellie. Sometimes he even talks business to her. As if Ellie can understand that stuff.' He never talked business with Charlotte. She laughed, but it sounded unnatural.

'Maybe he likes having someone young and innocent around to show off to,' Leonard suggested.

'Maybe.' But that wasn't it. Ellie had this way of kidding around that made Jeff laugh loudly and throw back his dark head with an abandonment that Charlotte hadn't seen before. Of course Ellie was outrageous. She'd always been able to get away with anything.

'I think Jeff's getting quite fond of her, in a funny sort of way,' she admitted.

'That's good.'

Charlotte smiled. But was it? She should be glad. Didn't she want her two favourite people to like each other?

She finished the colourful salad decorated with nasturtium flowers, and drank the last of her chilled white wine. Heaven. This place was paradise on earth.

'And how does Ellie feel about Jeff these days?' Leonard spoke as if he already knew the answer.

'She likes to pretend that she wouldn't give him the time of day.'

'But—?'

'She looks up to him.' Charlotte had noticed how Ellie brightened when he was around. 'Maybe she's even got a bit of a crush on him.'

She laughed again, but Leonard just looked thoughtful.

'I always wanted to be able to have both of them. So I've got what I wanted, haven't I?' She recrossed her long brown legs in khaki shorts, and rubbed the goose-bumps from her arms. Why did she feel so miserable? Was it just because this other desire was so entrenched – this longing for a child that simply wouldn't go away?

'I don't know what's wrong with me. I'm probably being silly.' She looked with pleading dark eyes at her boss. Leonard would understand.

He leaned back against the wooden seat, swirling the wine around in his glass, gazing into its blackcurranty depths with an expression of regret.

'You may be many things, Charlotte. But you're not silly.' Leonard downed the last of the wine and got to his feet. 'Come on. Time to go.'

She looked up at him, screwing her eyes against the sun, her curtain of dark shoulder-length hair falling away from her face. He was a tall, solid sort of man. It had only taken three days of French sun to bronze him like a native.

Something always happened to Leonard when they went on one of their business trips abroad, and it fascinated Charlotte. He left the starchy side of Leonard in England with his rather dowdy grey English suits and the dowdy, grey English climate. And he became— What? Approachable? A peer rather than a boss? Sexy?

'We'll have to remember this place for next time,' he said.

Next time. Would there be a next time? Why did Charlotte feel as though something she treasured was coming to an end?

Reluctantly she followed him under the bougainvillaea-threaded arbour towards the dusty brown car park and the black Renault. They'd had three blissful days in the south – staying in Tourrettes for a base, where Leonard had a contact, and doing business in Cannes, St Raphael and St Tropez. Leonard was a firm believer in mixing business and pleasure and so it had seemed more like a holiday. But now they were going home. And she wasn't sure that she wanted to.

He seemed to sense her mood. 'It's been wonderful, Charlotte,' he said as he held open the passenger door of the hire car for her. His voice was deeper than usual, and there was a note in it that she chose to ignore.

'It hardly seemed like work at all.' She forced a bright superficiality into her smile that she was using more frequently with Leonard these days. 'I feel rather guilty.'

'Even when you've got no reason to?' He laughed. But there was regret again – there behind the laughter.

'Must be the way I was brought up. Pain and pleasure, you know? Paying for each piece of happiness.'

He stared at her for a long moment before shutting the door.

'It's very flattering.' He got in beside her, fastened his belt, turned the key, checked the mirror, each movement measured and methodical.

'Flattering?' The car began to move and Charlotte gazed out of the window at the countryside that she was beginning to love more and more with every trip to France.

They were heading towards Paris, deep in the Burgundy region now, where fields of sunflowers were stacked side by side like miniature forests, above the banks of vineyards. She knew that every so often they'd pass a tiny village with stone cottages whose roofs folded like cardboard above shuttered windows. With bright pots of flowers perching outside, as if they wanted to tumble on to the roadside.

'Why flattering?' Charlotte repeated.

'Because usually you can't wait to get back to him.'

'Hmm.' She glanced at Leonard. He was dressed casually too, in beige loose-fitting trousers and a short-sleeved shirt. The arms holding the steering wheel were matted with dark hair. He'd put on sunglasses that made him look younger.

'Am I that transparent?' She felt guilty. She didn't want to hurt him. She enjoyed Leonard's company, but it was true that she was usually itching to get back to Jeff and Didsbury.

'Perhaps I just know you better than you think. You can't work with someone, take business trips with them, without getting to know them. This time you've been different. More relaxed.' He took a deep breath. 'Have you enjoyed it, Charlotte?'

'Of course I have.' Carefully now. 'France is such a beautiful country.'

'Why do you think I want to live here?' Lightly, no pressure.

But Charlotte felt the tension in the car. Leonard wanted her to come to France too – he'd already put out feelers. He wanted the entire company to be based here. Maybe that's what this delicious trip had been all about.

'Is it definite? Will I be out of a job soon?' She made her tone bantering, trying to diffuse the tension.

'As far as I'm concerned you'll never be out of a job.' He kept his eyes on the road. He drove not too fast, not too slowly. 'You know I want you to come along. Nothing's certain yet, but if it works out, would you consider it?'

'It's a big step.' Charlotte found herself thinking of Wales and Pencraig. It might belong to Mother now, but it still seemed like home.

'There'd be shares on offer. I'd give you a good deal. Great opportunities. And promotion.' His voice was casual.

'I see.' Shares, opportunities and promotion? What else besides? Charlotte had no illusions about her talent. She was reasonable at her job, a pretty good linguist and an adequate personal assistant. But she was still inexperienced and hardly indispensable. So why was Leonard trying to lure her to France? Was he asking her to consider him?

She thought of Jeff's words before she came on this trip.

'Watch your step, sweetie. That man's got designs on you.'

'Leonard? Don't be ridiculous.' Charlotte found herself choosing her most unflattering clothes to pack in the brown leather case, as if this would deny Leonard's interest.

'It's true. Believe me. He's got a *big* thing going for you.' Jeff licked his lips and grinned as he passed her a sexy black halter-top from the wardrobe. 'Perfect for those balmy, sweaty, evenings.'

She threw it at him. 'Leonard isn't like that.'

'All men are like that. He's got the hots for you, sweetheart. If you watch him closely you'll see it dripping out of those soulful brown eyes of his.'

Jeff laughed. Walked away and laughed as if it meant nothing. Was he so sure of her then?

Charlotte blinked herself back to the present. 'How could I move to France?' she asked out loud. 'What about Jeff?'

There was silence.

'Think about it,' he suggested.

But she didn't want to. Charlotte was fond of Leonard who was generous, kind, loyal and unselfish – all the things that Jeff most certainly was not. But Leonard had to belong in a different compartment. Why create complications? Jeff was the man she was marrying – the man that she loved, the man who could give her a child and answer her needs.

'Maybe Jeff could find work in France.' Leonard was giving away no clues to his feelings.

'Maybe.' It was a lovely dream. If these frequent trips were part of a plan to make her fall in love with France, it was working. And it wasn't just the beauty of the place. France was chic, the French had their lives in perspective, she felt. She liked their temperament and she loved their climate. In England, today would be cool and breezy, whereas here you could feel the warmth of spring almost seeping into your bones. But could Jeff ever be a part of all this?

'It's not that I don't miss him,' she said guiltily. 'I always miss him when I'm away. But it's a good idea to have a break from time to time. Absence makes the heart grow fonder, and all that.'

'Sure.' He nodded.

But Charlotte wasn't even convincing herself. What had happened to the days when she couldn't bear to be apart from him? Now, she felt almost relieved. What had gone wrong? Why did Jeff sometimes seem so far away?

'I suppose all relationships get less frantic as time goes on,' she murmured, half to herself. That was one of the nice things about Leonard. He allowed you to have these personal conversations with yourself. 'No one can keep up the intensity of the first months for ever. Otherwise life would be love and nothing else at all.'

'At least he won't be lonely with Ellie around.' Leonard swung into a sharp left-hand turn.

Charlotte frowned, her thought pattern disturbed. 'He'll hardly see Ellie. He'll probably be out most of the time. Making the most of me being away.'

She didn't want to consider what Jeff did when she was away. He was too attractive – too irresistible to women. She saw them in restaurants and just walking down the streets, giving him furtive glances as they went by.

At first it bothered her and she'd cross-question him constantly. But it was no use. When the rows it caused threatened to destroy them, Charlotte forced herself to become casual about his lifestyle. You couldn't get close to possessing Jeff.

It worked. There were fewer rows and he'd clung to her more since she'd cut some of the ropes that tied them together. But perhaps Charlotte had needed those ropes to love him.

'He'll be fine,' she said. 'But Ellie will be lonely.'

Poor Ellie. Lost and for ever misunderstood. She

experienced a sudden glimmer of understanding. No, it wasn't a case of three being a crowd. It was more a question of balance. It was as if Ellie couldn't be a background person in Charlotte's life. That was the problem. That was what spoiled the closeness between Charlotte and Jeff. Spoiled the closeness between her and Ellie too.

Because Ellie wasn't a background person, not for Charlotte, and not for anyone else. She wasn't made to be one. And so if Charlotte was going to stay with Jeff – and she was, because they were getting married, weren't they? – then Ellie had to go. She was just surprised that she hadn't realised before. Living with Jeff and Ellie was an ideal, and ideals weren't close enough to reality ever to work.

'Sorry, Ellie,' Charlotte whispered.

'I've got an idea for Ellie.' Leonard glanced at her.

'A job?' Charlotte had asked him some time ago, on the off-chance, but nothing had come of it. Ellie and work didn't match. But she couldn't move out without a job, without money. Charlotte's handouts couldn't go on indefinitely.

'It's in the wine bar in St Ann's Square. Sarah's looking for someone.' Leonard wound down his window. 'It's only waitressing and bar work, that's why I didn't mention it before. But there is a bed-sit above the wine bar – next to Sarah's flat. It's not much, but it's cheap. What do you think?'

Charlotte sat up straight, her hazel eyes brightening. 'Perfect. That would be perfect for her. As a start anyway. She refuses to go back to school.'

'She wouldn't be offended? She's obviously a bright girl. She wouldn't think bar work's too menial?'

'Beggars can't be choosers.' Charlotte felt pleased. 'Maybe it'll teach her a lesson. She's got to stand on her own two feet some time.' She sounded like Jeff. With him she was always defensive about Ellie. But with Leonard she could be honest.

Charlotte thought of Rolf's letter about Ellie and the local boys. It still rankled. And there was new resentment, new anger that surprised her. 'She doesn't have a choice. She's brought it on herself. But do you think Sarah would take her on?'

'If I recommended her I'm sure she would.'

Charlotte smiled to herself. Sarah Freeman might close up like a fan when Charlotte was around, but Charlotte knew that she was crazy about Leonard, and would probably do anything he asked. And who could blame her? Leonard was special. Sometimes, when a certain something crept to the back of her brain, Charlotte knew that she could, that she might have—

'Thanks, Leonard.' Her smile was wide and grateful. 'If we could get Ellie settled before the wedding, it would be such a load off my mind.'

Uncharacteristically, Leonard braked too hard, too quickly at some traffic lights, and glanced across at her. 'You're really going through with it then?'

'Of course. You know we are. You're invited. This summer. July or August, we haven't decided yet. It has to be in the summer. At Pencraig.'

'That's terribly traditional of you.'

She didn't like the sarcasm in his voice. It wasn't like Leonard. 'It's not because of tradition,' she said. It was because of Pencraig. How could they hold the wedding anywhere else? As for Mother, Charlotte would have to put up with her, Ellie and Jeff had closed ranks to persuade her of that.

'Divorce rates are increasing all the time,' Leonard remarked. 'Take my advice and stay as you are. Why rock the boat?'

Charlotte laughed. 'Because if you don't rock the boat it never takes you anywhere.'

She used to believe that Leonard's own experiences had soured his ideas about marriage. And God knows he'd had the lot. His only child had died in a tragic, unexplained cot death, and as if that wasn't enough, he'd gone through a messy divorce after discovering his wife's affair. He'd even had a vasectomy, as if he could ensure that he'd never love like that again. But now she wondered if he was simply jealous. How could she continue to work for him if Jeff was right? And why did life have to get so bloody complicated? Charlotte closed her eyes.

'Just because it didn't work for you, that doesn't make marriage a bad institution,' she said.

He grunted. 'It's still an institution.'

Charlotte felt angry with him. 'That's an old line, Leonard, and it wasn't hilarious ten years ago.' She sighed. 'I have to find out for myself.' Quietly. Leonard probably didn't even hear.

It wasn't a long drive from Ringway airport to the Didsbury house, and they shared a taxi – Leonard would go on alone, back to the heart of the city where he worked and lived alone.

Charlotte went in, feeling strangely nervous. The house was a tip. There was no sign of Ellie, and Jeff was working, tapping demoniacally on the typewriter. Charlotte smiled to herself. His dark hair was tousled as if he hadn't brushed it since she'd gone. She crept up behind him, playing one of their old games, whispered 'Hi,' in his ear.

He grinned, and she leaned forward until their faces were touching, cheek to cheek. She slid her right arm round his shoulders and tangled one of his dark curls around her little finger.

'Hi, stranger.' Suddenly he reached back for her hand, grabbed and kissed it. 'Where've you been all my life?' Letting go of her, he spun the black typist's chair so that he was facing her.

'Around.' Smiling at him, she dumped her bag on the floor. It was a long time since they'd played one of these games.

Jeff pulled her on to his lap. 'And how was France?'

'Wonderful.'

He kissed her on the lips, but not with passion. 'Didn't you miss me?'

She laughed. 'Of course.'

'But you had Leonard.'

It wasn't only jealousy. Jeff disliked Leonard, she knew that. 'And you had Ellie,' she said.

His lips came down again on hers. Hard this time. His tongue briefly touched her teeth, her gums, her tongue. She opened her eyes. His deep-blue eyes were already open, unseeing. She knew that he wanted to go to bed.

'Where's Ellie?' she whispered.

'Don't know.' His voice was thick. 'And I don't care.' He pushed her gently to her feet, led her out of the room and practically pulled her up the stairs. 'Come with me, woman,' he said. 'I've got something very interesting to show you.'

Charlotte giggled. France and the sun had made her feel sexy. She wanted him.

Ellie spotted the bag as soon as she came through the door. And then she heard the noises from upstairs. She went into the living-room. Christ! He couldn't wait. She hugged her arms around her breasts. Only a few hours ago he and Ellie had been screwing like they had only minutes to live, and now Jeff couldn't wait to get his dirty paws all over

Charlotte. Perhaps he thought he could make the last few days go away.

She put on a record – loudly so they'd know she was back. With Charlotte away she'd felt almost like a wife – playing house, planning meals, having tea and toast in bed with Jeff. Talking. Making love every spare minute when they weren't eating. She giggled. As if they always had to have something in their mouths.

And then this morning, frantically making the bed, changing sheets, piling the old ones into the machine, collecting crumbs from the carpet. And yet the house still looked messy, like a lovers' meeting-place. Even now the sheets were jiggling away on the line in the breeze outside, just like she and Jeff had been jiggling away. Would it show? Would the stains ever completely disappear?

Would Charlotte know that Jeff had been with another woman? Probably not. Jeff was a master of disguises. And Charlotte wouldn't want to guess. It would have to be spelt out for her, and even then she wouldn't believe it.

But would she notice the difference in Ellie? Would she know that Ellie had been with a man who had taught her to let go at last? Ellie peered in the mirror over the mantelpiece. Her pale face looked the same as usual. But inside she was full of him. Full to bursting. Full to exploding point.

She'd been determined that there wouldn't be a second time. She told herself over and over how it would be if Charlotte ever found out. How, instead of pulling them together, it would tear them apart.

But Jeff wouldn't leave her alone. He teased and cajoled at every opportunity – whenever Charlotte was out of sight, and sometimes even when she wasn't. He stalked Ellie as though she was his prey.

'C'mon, Eloise. You know you want to—' Stroking her bare arms, making her skin tingle. 'It would be *so* good—'

Kissing her neck, hitting all the right spots. A talent for all the best games. 'Don't do this to me, Eloise. I need you—' Finding the small of her back and pressing her towards him. Pinioning her wrists with his other hand. His breath hot on her face. 'Remember last time?'

Until she could stand it no longer. Until she folded against him with a moan of desire, and he took her, in the kitchen, against the cupboards, right where they were standing, five minutes before Charlotte got in from work.

After that it was anywhere and everywhere. Once in the bathroom when Charlotte had gone to the shop round the corner for sugar. Once in Ellie's bed when Charlotte was in the bath. It was insanity. God, it got worse and worse. She couldn't get enough of him.

The night before Charlotte left for France he'd come into her room at 4 a.m. With Charlotte sleeping next door! He'd stroked her legs, her stomach, her breasts, until she was writhing in her dreams.

And then he woke her as he plunged into her. Stifled her half-scream with his mouth. And she'd welcomed him. That was the worst. Welcomed his passion and even the thrill of risk that she saw in his eyes in an unexpected shaft of moonlight.

It scared her. He scared her.

'Do you love me?' she begged, after the rush of her first orgasm had died. 'Say you love me.'

'What's love got to do with it?' He ground on, into her.

'Everything.' But she only wanted love so that she'd feel strong. She didn't want to fall for Jeff, be dependent on him. Desperately, during these passionate encounters and through every day living with him and watching him with Charlotte, she searched for a weakness – something she could twist and trample on. But he was the strongest person she'd ever met.

'Sex is nothing without love,' she told him, tangling slim fingers through his dark curls.

'Balls. You know that isn't true.'

'What is true then?' Her darting green eyes were demanding something, but even Ellie wasn't sure what.

'I want you, Eloise. I want your body. Isn't that enough?' His eyes burned into her.

Enough to turn her into liquid desire, that was for sure. And as for the rest—

What was it about Jeff? Was it the same for Charlotte?

He left her, ragged and saturated only half an hour later. Half an hour. He must have gone back to Charlotte's bed reeking of sex. Reeking of her.

No matter how hard she tried, the guilt wouldn't come through the pleasure. So she rationalised it. If it wasn't her it would be someone else. And at least she left him whole for Charlotte.

She couldn't help smiling. That was the best thing about Jeff – no guilt, no deep conversations, no analysis. He'd run a mile from all that. All she could do was enjoy it while it lasted, and hope to God that Charlotte didn't find out.

It couldn't go on. Ellie knew it mustn't go on, it was a madness. But she couldn't get away until he let her go. He had a power over her. The bastard had unleashed her sexual need.

She tried to read a magazine but her concentration wasn't with it. It was upstairs with them. Was it better for Jeff with Charlotte? It felt incestuous – as if they were her parents or something.

It was no good. Ellie closed the magazine and shut her eyes. She had to escape from this place. Get away from him. Perhaps even lose Charlotte if there was no other way. She didn't belong here. And what would happen when they got married? It couldn't go on.

Charlotte kept giving her money as if she was a charity. Jeff gave her money as if she was a prostitute. It seemed that everyone wanted to keep her. Everyone wanted to stop her from being independent, from leaving.

'We should move house,' Jeff said as they lay still afterwards.

Charlotte sighed. She'd noticed that all conversations about change came after sex. Was it sex that brought them to light or did making plans make Jeff randy? She stared at his lean brown body that was relaxed at last. 'Why should we? I like it here.'

'It's all right, I suppose.' Jeff got up and paced over to the window. He put his elbows on the sill and stared out.

He was restless. Always restless. Charlotte watched him with love in her eyes. It had been good for her this time. The best it had been for ages. But he worried her. Just when she began to think that everything might work out, he had a habit of turning things upside down again.

'Only all right?' She yawned. Travelling always made her sleepy. 'This is a lovely house. You're never satisfied.'

'Yeah, but I don't want to stay here for ever. In a dirty street with lots of big dirty houses.'

'Didsbury's nice. It isn't like living in the city.' She was beginning to feel almost at home here. She didn't want to be uprooted – not yet.

'It's not far enough away from it for me. There's nothing classy about this place. And there's no garden.'

She sighed. 'You don't even like gardening.' How had this conversation happened? Jeff distanced himself so quickly after sex that it was almost obscene.

'That's not the point.' He turned to face her. 'I've got no intention of staying here for ever,' he repeated irritably.

'For ever's a long time. It suits me just fine for now.'

From downstairs, Charlotte heard music and realised that Ellie was home. She sat up guiltily, stretched long brown limbs. 'Want some coffee?'

He spun round. 'Why does she have to have the music so bloody loud?' There was a dense irritation in his blue eyes.

'She wants us to know she's back.' Like a child. Ellie was like a child wanting attention.

'Why should she want us to know she's back?' He glared at Charlotte as if it was her fault.

It was starting already, almost as soon as she'd walked through the door. One rapid sexual interlude, followed by a row. Back to bickering and defensiveness as if she'd never been away.

'Oh, God, Jeff. How should I know? Maybe she's embarrassed. It must be obvious what we're doing up here.' Everything was spoiled, the mood, the moment, the closeness. She pulled on her white towelling robe and grabbed the red flip-flops that had been discarded when Jeff had half-thrown her on to the bed.

Jeff snorted. 'Nothing would embarrass that girl. She just wants to make things as awkward as possible. It's our house, for Christ's sake. What does it matter what we're doing up here?'

'Do you want her to leave?' Charlotte looked in the mirror at her dishevelled appearance. Automatically she took off the robe and began pulling on some jeans instead.

'You see.' Jeff ran his fingers through his dark hair. 'You're getting dressed to go downstairs for coffee. If Eloise wasn't here you could do it naked.'

'I could do it naked anyway if I wanted to.' Charlotte tried to laugh. 'But I wouldn't.'

'Prude. I would.'

She gazed at him, so resplendent in his long-limbed,

dark, muscular nakedness. So unselfconscious. 'You would, even with Ellie around,' she said. 'You'd probably enjoy it.'

She saw his erection rise before he turned away. It fascinated her. Men were all the same. She felt unaccountably depressed. 'Do you want her to leave?' she repeated.

'At least we'd have some privacy.' He came up behind her and rubbed his unshaven jaw lightly across her shoulder. She could feel the heat of his erection against her back.

'I never have you to myself any more,' he said.

She told him about Leonard's idea for Ellie.

'We need some more time together. Now that we're getting married.' Charlotte looked at him doubtfully, wanting reassurance. Why did she keep thinking of Pencraig and the hideaway in the woods? Why did she feel guilty of betrayal?

'I want to move house when we're married.' His hands began lightly to massage her shoulders. She leaned back against him, and his fingers found her collar bone, slid down to her breasts. 'I want to live in some huge detached number with at least four bedrooms. Maybe do it up myself. In the country, with a jungle of a garden and a pond.'

Charlotte laughed. 'You and your dreams.'

'They're not just dreams.' He gripped her shoulders more tightly. 'This is our reality, Charlotte. It's going to happen. It's what I'm working towards.'

'But what about *my* work? Where would I be commuting from every day?' Charlotte shrugged herself out from under his hands. Jeff's dreams always left her feeling like an appendage – somebody's luggage or an extra pair of hands. Useful sometimes, but not indispensable.

He began pulling on his clothes. His blue eyes were hard

and determined. 'I don't want my girl to work,' he said. 'I want you to be a lady of leisure once we're married. You can have coffee mornings and credit cards.'

Charlotte felt a sliver of fear inch into her belly. 'But I've got a job,' she protested, half-laughing. 'I don't want to be a lady of leisure.'

He smiled, but his face darkened. 'I thought Leonard was moving to France.'

'He is.' Charlotte sat on the bed, hunched and miserable. She didn't want this conversation. It was taking her into directions she wasn't ready to face yet. If she didn't have a job to distract her from a dream of motherhood that was becoming a nightmarish fixation, then what would she have left?

'But France is a beautiful country,' she said. 'Maybe we should think about moving there ourselves.'

'No.' He glared at her. 'I warned you about him, didn't I? Didn't I tell you he had the hots for you?'

She hung her dark head. 'It was only an idea. It's got nothing to do with Leonard.'

He laughed harshly. At times he seemed like a stranger to her. 'It's not part of the plan. We're staying in England, job or no job.'

'But there are other jobs, Jeff.' She felt angry, upset, confused. 'I like working. I'm not the stay-at-home type.' Unless she had a child. A child. The words echoed in her head. She mustn't think about it. It was dangerous to think about it. She put her hands to her temple.

He sat down next to her. She couldn't look at him, but the heat emanating from his dark body seemed to be threatening her. She shivered.

'But not when we have kids.' His voice was low, persuasive. 'You won't want to work when we have kids, will you, Charlotte?'

Something stuttered into life inside her. 'Who says we're ever going to have any? Nothing's happened so far. Why should it be taking so long? We're always having sex. Maybe there's something wrong. Maybe we should have tests, see a doctor, make a chart—' She began to sob. Heavy sobs that were coming from some part of her she'd been trying to deny even existed.

'Hey, hey— Charlotte. What are you getting so het up about?' He held her chin with one hand, stroking the dark hair away from her face with the other. 'I didn't know it was so important for you, sweetness.'

'It isn't. It is— Oh, Jeff. It's been months. Can't we do something?' The desperation, strung up inside, now poured out of her.

'Relax, sweetie.' He pulled her head closer, into the warmth of his shoulder. 'Just relax. You're worrying too much about this. You leave the worrying to me.'

His voice was soft. He calmed her. If only she was more sure of him, he'd be everything she'd ever wanted in a man. And he'd give her a child.

'Children can wait,' he said. 'We've got plenty of time. All the time in the world. Weddings come before children, didn't your parents ever tell you that?' His fingers were massaging her head, moving down to the back of her neck.

She made a muffled noise of assent into his shoulder. He was right. He was always right.

'We'll wait a bit. After a few months, if nothing's happened then we'll go to a doctor, okay? I promise.'

'Okay.'

Gently he drew away to dry her eyes with a tissue. 'You just take it easy. I'll make the coffee,' he said.

A few minutes later Charlotte heard him arguing with Ellie. She should go downstairs, but she couldn't find the energy. She was drained dry.

The intensity of her longing was beginning to scare her. The almost unbearable ache of each monthly disappointment. With the appearance of the dark-red stain each and every month her desire had slowly grown into such a need. An obsession. She wanted a child so much. It was hurting some deep primeval part of her.

She found herself staring at babies in prams, smiling and then turning away from the tears while something tugged at her inside. Transforming her from a reasonable individual into an emotional mass of pure desperation.

None of it made sense. She'd seen enough of Olivia's brand of motherhood to be put off for ever. And she herself had been more like a mother to Ellie in the old days. But some good or bad fairy of ancient biological impulses had tapped her on the head one night, and made everything else seem insignificant next to creation. She laughed. Creation. The most perfect deed, the most vital role for a woman to play.

'I want a baby,' she'd told Jeff at last, on the night he asked her to marry him. 'I want us to have a baby.'

She'd expected resistance. Men like Jeff didn't want to be tied down by children. It didn't suit their image.

But a wide grin of delight had transformed his features as he rubbed his hands together with barely concealed excitement. 'Yes! A baby. I'd like that. We'll get married, have a baby, do everything right. What's the use of having everything you want, if there's no one to pass it on to?'

Jeff wanted a child for a taste of immortality – for the line to go on. It was just a small part of his dream – to belong. And Charlotte would give him that. She must give him that.

But above all, the child would be for herself. Without it life would be worthless. It would be a charade with no heart.

7

Someone was writing a cheque.

'What's the date?' he asked.

'August 21st.' Ellie's voice was low. August 21st. It was a date stitched into her mind. The exact anniversary of the day when that first summer was as good as over. Nine years ago. The day Rolf had called them into his study at Pencraig and reminded them that Charlotte had to prepare for school. The day that had been the beginning of the end.

She could still feel the utter desolation. A child's desolation that she'd never feel these days. She was almost prepared for things to fall apart now.

Today was also the day before Jeff and Charlotte's wedding. Tomorrow they would all be back there again. Back in Wales. Back home at Pencraig. Tomorrow her sister and her lover would be married.

What changes would there be? Would that little piece of paper bring instant fidelity? No chance. Ellie laughed, and the man with the cheque book glanced up, surprised. Would Charlotte drift so far away that Ellie wouldn't even be able to catch faint glimpses of her any more? God knows, it was hard enough now. Or would everything stay the same, apart from the certificate in Jeff's desk drawer and a small bundle of photographs?

Ellie took a sip of her tonic water and looked around her. It was before seven, and the place was empty, apart from people eating early to catch a film or a play, she supposed.

Being close to the Royal Exchange, they were at their busiest pre-show and for late night suppers. This was the kind of place that mixed Bohemian atmosphere with class, and it worked. People of all kinds flocked to Pasha's.

And what was she doing here? Who would have ever imagined her working here as a barmaid, still trying to make sense of what was happening to her. With Jeff. With Charlotte. Charlotte. Ellie closed her eyes for a few seconds. She'd seen her this afternoon. She'd phoned, her voice hurried and breathless.

'Ellie? I must see you. Are you working?'

'No— no.' Reluctance. She was never totally at ease with Charlotte any more. Always slightly afraid and wondering – if she knew, or was about to find out. If a look, a word might betray her.

'Can you come over?'

'Aren't you supposed to be going home this afternoon?' Ellie hedged. Home. Pencraig was still home to both of them. Olivia was more like the visitor.

'There's plenty of time.' A pause. 'Please, Ellie?'

She could hear her desperation. Surely Charlotte wouldn't have a change of heart? 'I'm on my way,' she said.

She took a bus, watching all the familiar sights along the Wilmslow Road pass her by as they'd passed her by so many times before, and when she got to the Didsbury house Charlotte the bride opened the door. She was wearing floor-length white taffeta, with her veil and head-dress slung over one shoulder.

'Wow. Are you having a rehearsal?' Ellie stared at her. 'I hope you haven't let Jeff see you. It's bad luck, you know.' Her way of finding out if he was around. She didn't want him to be around – it made her uncomfortable.

'He's out. Look at all this crap.' Charlotte threw the veil on to the kitchen table. 'I look ridiculous.'

'You look beautiful.' And it was true. Charlotte had scraped her hair back from her face, and with her height, classical profile, high cheekbones and flushed face she looked almost regal. Her hazel eyes were proud and defiant – just like the eyes that had challenged the nine-year-old Ellie in that first summer at Pencraig.

'Unzip me.' Charlotte turned round, arms folded.

Falteringly, with tears in her eyes, Ellie groped for the zipper. It could have been so different between them. So many 'if onlys' tucked into the folds of this voluminous white dress.

'I feel as if I'm deceiving everybody. Pretending to be some pure white virgin, when Jeff and I have been living together for ages.' Charlotte climbed out of the starchy dress, glaring at it as though it was an animate object – with reservations of its own. She let it fall to the ground and began pulling on a black track suit.

'You're not deceiving anyone. It's just tradition. That's the point.' Ellie turned to hide her tears.

'The point is that I'm waltzing up the aisle in white, with enough flowers to fill an old people's home, because that's what Mother wants. That's the point.' Her voice rose.

'Jeff wants it too.' Ellie stared at her. But what did Charlotte want? And why the hell couldn't she even ask her?

'Only because it's the done thing. Sometimes I wonder if that's the only reason we're getting married at all.' She grabbed Ellie's hand and led her into the living-room.

They sat on the couch.

'Do you like Jeff?' Charlotte asked. 'Tell me honestly.' Her dark eyes were pleading.

Honestly. Their bodies were almost touching. 'Charlotte—' she began. But the words wouldn't come. She wanted to tell her there and then, for Christ's sake. But how could she? How could she hurt Charlotte, whom she loved more than anything? How could she take that risk?

'Of course I do,' she said. The moment was gone. There was more she could have said. He's too wicked for you, Charlotte. Much too wicked. Don't do it, Charlotte.

Ellie felt her sister look deep into her eyes and wondered if she could possibly tell what she was thinking. Once she would have been able to. Not now. Now they were miles apart.

Still perilously close to tears, she glanced at her watch to hide her emotions. 'I've got to go. My shift starts in half an hour. Sarah will be pacing the floor.'

Charlotte nodded. 'Tomorrow, then,' she said. There was a disappointment in her eyes. An air of so much being left unsaid.

'Tomorrow.'

Ellie came back to the present, and to a young couple at the bar waiting to be served. He was jingling coins importantly in his pockets, and she was fiddling nonchalantly with her hair. Love's young dream. Both drinking bacardis. Longing to be seen in all the right places.

'Thanks, love,' he said as she gave him the change. 'Have one yourself?' He looked her up and down so fleetingly that Ellie hardly caught it. But she was used to covert leering. The glimmer behind the turd-brown of his eyes said he was proposing a fuck as clearly as if he'd spoken.

'Cheers.' She took the small change and sauntered back to the corner where she had a bar stool and the best view of the door. And she didn't give the boy even the small satisfaction of a smile.

It hadn't taken Ellie long to learn the ropes. This job

didn't pay much and a girl had to live. So you took tips, but kept your dignity. You accepted them as your right rather than smirking with gratitude. No amount of tips would buy Ellie. She'd either give herself totally out of choice or hold back on even a smile.

She was just a part of the pub scene – the presentable barmaid who you could pretend would be yours for a gin and tonic if you weren't already taken. And if she wasn't working. And if you had the guts. And if they sold condoms in the loo. Nothing wrong with fantasies.

There were always a few men at the bar, swanking and drooling over a pint of ale and Ellie's legs in black stockings. Men who were stupid and shallow enough to believe she could be so easily impressed. Men who were stuck in the male menopause between the ages of eighteen and sixty (after that they sometimes became a bit more sensible, thank God). Determined to engage her in conversations crammed with double meanings, but would probably run a mile if she were actually to invite them upstairs.

'How's tricks?' Tom was ordering drinks for his first table. Pasha's not only provided bar snacks but also had a reasonable restaurant pandering to the current trend for Mexican food. He consulted his waiter's red notebook. 'Two halves of lager and lime for the ladies—'

Ellie fetched glasses. 'It's going to be a busy night.' She replaced a pin in the blonde hair loosely piled on her head. It had regained at least some of its former glory. 'Harold's not around, is he?' That was the down side of the job. Coping with Harold's hands, Harold's inanities and just Harold – part of the money behind Sarah's management – was nothing short of a nightmare.

'Not yet. But Sarah's behaving a bit strangely, I can tell you that, Miss Morgan.' He leaned forward, adopting a bad

Russian accent. 'She's drinking vodka and doing the books upstairs.'

'So what?'

He laughed. 'She's got through half a bottle already, that's what. So take an old hand's advice to a new girl and watch yourself.'

Ellie raised her eyebrows. 'Thanks for the warning. What's eating her? Money? Men?'

'She should be so lucky.' Tom shrugged. 'Who knows? Don't ask me, I only work here.' He glanced at his notebook again. 'And two shots of whisky for the boys.'

The door swung open as Ellie stood by the optics.

Tom glanced round. 'Get a load of that.'

Ellie grinned. It was Jeff with three other guys. The sight of him made her stomach lurch with an unexpected and absurd somersault. 'That's my future brother-in-law,' she said with a forced laugh. 'So hands off. And don't let Peter catch you admiring other men.'

'He'd agree with me.' With a melodramatic sigh Tom grabbed the tray of drinks. 'Might have known he'd be on the other side.'

Jeff strode lazily up to the bar. As always he looked dark and immaculate in a maroon silk shirt, charcoal grey trousers and a wide leather belt. He grinned at her.

'Eloise. Sweet thing. Let me introduce a few of the lads.'

Why did men become lads in the pub? Did it happen as they walked through the door, or did alcohol strip off years and common sense?

His blue eyes were slightly glazed. He'd been drinking, but as always, remained in control. It would be nice to see him fall over for a change. At least then she could pick him up.

In one movement he took her hand and leaned forward to kiss her, with an absolute self-confidence that drew and repelled her simultaneously. He had that rough, unshaven look that was so sexy on men like Jeff.

'Stag night, I presume? What can I get you?'

She sounded cool, but her heart was thumping madly and she was shaking. He always had this effect on her. It was looking at his hands that did it. Looking at his hands and remembering what they'd done to her the last time she'd seen them.

'Whatever you want to give me,' he said. 'This is a night to remember. The last night before the shackles tie me down.'

Ellie smiled. 'I can't see any shackles doing that.' But already she was thinking. Planning, wondering. Where would he want to spend the night? Surely not here? Not tonight, the night before his wedding. He'd never come here before. But he was here now, wasn't he?

'Your latest?' Jeff nodded with scathing disinterest in Tom's direction.

'Hardly.' Ellie pulled on the pumps.

Jeff shrugged and glanced around. 'Nice place. Classy decor.'

Ellie followed the direction of his gaze. It was mostly black. Black and chrome – which wasn't as cold as it sounded. With clever lighting the effect was interesting. Art deco lamps and stained glass warmed the wine bar and created focal points. But right now Ellie only had one focal point. And from the way he was staring at her, Jeff felt the same.

'How are you getting on here, Eloise? Right in the cultural hot-bed of the city?' He chuckled. His gaze lingered on her breasts, until she wondered if her thin black blouse was see-through. And then it slid downwards to encompass her short black skirt, sheer black stockings and high heels.

Was he making small talk? Didn't he know that she'd be his if he just grabbed her like some neanderthal and heaved her up the stairs?

'I'm getting on just fine.' It suited Ellie, although she knew it wouldn't be for ever. She enjoyed watching people, and being a little disdainful. It was even fun, flirting, getting the assholes going, watching the world getting drunker and then having coffee and nightcaps with Tom and Peter afterwards. Discussing the personal attributes of every customer. It was an awfully long way from Wales and Pencraig.

'The two of you certainly look friendly enough,' Jeff said.

'We are. But we don't share a bed.' Ellie loved his jealousy. 'No one told us that it was compulsory for friends to sleep together,' she concluded innocently.

One of Jeff's companions laughed. Ellie looked at him. He was small, fair and wimpy – Jeff's opposite, as if his prime purpose in the world was to set off Jeff's appearance to perfection.

'Very funny.' Jeff shot her one of his sardonic, appreciative looks as he led the others to a table near the bar. He sat on the far side, practically ignoring the men he'd come with. Staring, making Ellie feel uncomfortable.

Jeff didn't have proper friends. The people he spent time with were acquaintances who might be able to do him a favour in the future, or had done him a favour in the past, thus becoming a link in Jeff's chain.

'More drinks, please, you gorgeous creature.'

Ellie wondered if Jeff had heard Tom. He stood at the bar with his hair slicked back, in his tight black trousers and fancy shirt. Surely Jeff must realise?

Eyeing up men was just a joke for Tom. On the third finger of his left hand was a gold band, identical to the one Peter wore. And in his left ear-lobe was a silver love knot. Tom and Peter were more married to each other than anyone else Ellie knew – despite not having the certificate to prove it.

It was a shame that gays were unavailable. They had fewer hang-ups, were more fun, and they weren't threatening. So what if they lacked the scruffy machismo of some men? That was something most women could live without.

She gazed at Jeff. But he was macho without trying to be. And that was the best kind. The only kind. He was long, lean, beautiful and dangerous.

As she watched, he grinned at her and raised his glass. 'To me and Charlotte. To the wedding of the year!'

Bastard. His teeth were big and white. He was a shark. Ellie wanted him. She was crumbling to pieces, wanting him.

'Good God. Look what the cat dragged in.'

Ellie turned. Sarah Freeman was standing behind her, one hand on generous hip, a glass of vodka in the other. She was attractive in a buxom, red-headed kind of way, but drinking didn't suit her. She was looking at Jeff.

'Do you know him?' Ellie grabbed a bottle of pale ale from the shelf.

'Know him?' Sarah's voice was slurred. 'I sure do, my dear. And I avoid him at all costs. He's a blood-sucking leech. An evil son of a bitch.'

'You don't like him then?' Ellie joked. Although they'd had a wary relationship at first, and Ellie had sensed that Sarah was prepared to dislike her, they'd gradually become firm friends over the last four months.

'Like him?' Sarah laughed with a harshness Ellie hadn't

heard from her before. 'You've got to be joking. What is your sister doing with that man? Leonard knows about it. He's tried to tell her—'

To her annoyance, Ellie missed the next few sentences. They were busy, customers were clamouring to be served, and God knows where Peter had got to.

'It's no skin off my nose, I can tell you. Why should I help her, of all people?'

'What's Leonard got to do with it?' Ellie poured out five sherries. Sherry. Yuck.

'I could tell you some stories—' Sarah downed another glass of vodka in one.

'What stories?' Ellie wanted to scream with frustration.

Half-listening, she doled out change, beer, shorts, cokes, more change. The beermats were soaking. There was no one to wash up more glasses and they were running out fast. The narrow bar was three deep in people waiting to be served. This was so unlike Sarah. Normally she would muck in and take charge. The efficient running of her wine bar, to transform it into a successful business, was supposed to be the most important thing in Sarah's life.

Peter returned from changing a barrel, and Ellie continued serving. She kept catching glimpses of Jeff's dark head through the tables, and beyond the customers milling at the bar, and then she'd panic in case he'd left without her noticing. Jeff would never make an effort to say goodbye.

At ten thirty balding, flabby Harold turned up, with his wet and watery eyes and hands that would dive-bomb into a grope at the slightest opportunity. Ellie would have liked to slap that disgusting leer from his creepy face. But she couldn't. Sarah had warned her that the first slap would be her last.

'Find another way to deal with him,' she'd said. 'Laugh it off.'

Ellie was surprised. It was sexual harassment and Sarah was the last person she'd expect to put up with that kind of crap from men. Did Harold have some hold over her?

Sarah smiled grimly. 'One day, Ellie. You can come with me and we'll both tell him to go to hell.'

In the meantime Harold and Sarah had disappeared, and the crowd around the bar was thinning when Jeff came for more drinks. His blue eyes were pure, unshuttered invitation, and when Ellie gave him his change, he grabbed her hand, leaning forward to whisper in her ear. It shot through her, the warmth, the excitement.

'Later?' was all he said. It was enough. Enough to make the tops of her thighs wet.

By half past eleven he was almost the only customer left. Sarah was nowhere to be found, while Tom and Peter's curious glances were beginning to irritate her. 'I'll lock up,' she told them.

Less than fifteen minutes later she shot the bolts and turned the key. She turned to face him, her back against the door. 'Are you coming up for coffee?'

Silently he watched her, his eyes travelling the length of her body.

She moved from the door, passed his table, very close, almost brushing against him.

'If that's what you prescribe, little sister.' He got up and followed her, out of the bar, up the stairs.

'It's certainly what you need.'

'What I need—' His hands reached out, travelling swiftly up her legs and under her short black skirt as she moved in front of him.

She paused, thinking she'd heard a cry.

'You're so sexy,' he said. 'I want you so much it hurts.'

Ellie could hardly make it up the last steps. 'You smooth

talker, you.' But her voice was husky, and she felt such a tightness in her throat that she could barely breathe.

At the top she turned to face him. He touched her cheek with his fingertips, pulled the pins out of her hair one by one as if engaging in a sexual ritual. Then, as her blonde hair tumbled free, he took her left nipple between his thumb and index finger, massaging, playing with it between the fingertips. It hardened, erect under the skimpy black blouse.

'I want you,' he repeated. 'God, I want you, Eloise.'

'Even when you're marrying my sister tomorrow?' Her breasts ached. The nipple became harder still.

'Especially when I'm marrying your sister tomorrow.'

The knocking woke her. Then a faint shout. 'Ellie!' Louder now. 'Ellieee.' Irritation. Anger.

What was going on? What the hell time was it?

Ellie scrambled from the tangled sheets, half-falling out of bed, glanced blearily at the illuminated dials of the clock. Three in the morning. Who the hell would come here at three in the morning? She didn't have time to consider.

'Ellie!'

Recognising Sarah's voice, remembering the cry she'd heard last night, Ellie grabbed the outsize stripey shirt she used as a robe, pulled it on, and unlocked the front door of the bed-sit. Sarah was standing there, with Olivia beside her. 'What on earth—'

Sarah was angry. Her small blue eyes looked piggy in the brash light of the hallway – as if she'd been crying, and her face was pale and drawn.

'Your mother's decided to pay you a visit.' She glared at Olivia. 'On impulse.'

Olivia took off her neat, navy hat and gloves, and opened her bag. She found lipstick and a mirror, which she consulted briefly before speaking to Ellie. 'Hello, darling.' She offered a cheek.

Ellie and Sarah stared at her. She didn't seem quite real.

'You're supposed to be at Pencraig. What on earth are you doing here?' Ellie was still half-asleep. But even through this unreal chain of events, she remembered only too well who was sleeping in her bed. Somehow she had to stall. But Olivia wasn't having any of that.

'I'll tell you in a minute. I need to sit down.' Olivia began to edge past.

Ellie grabbed at her arm to stop her. 'I'm really sorry Sarah,' she called. But already the pink-robed figure was halfway down the landing.

Olivia turned to watch the retreat. She sniffed delicately. 'I don't know if I altogether approve of you living here.'

'I probably won't be for much longer.' Hastily, Ellie pulled the green velvet curtain that shrouded the bed from the rest of the large bed-sitting room, further across. How could she hope to hide Jeff for more than a few minutes? He was bound to wake up – if he hadn't already.

'What are you doing here?' she hissed again.

'Why are you whispering? Oh—' Olivia paused. A gleam of disapproval appeared in her cold, green eyes, then she smiled. 'You've got someone here, haven't you?'

Ellie grabbed the chance. 'Yes I have. Look, Mother, this is really embarrassing. You can't come in. I'm sorry.'

Olivia dismissed this with a wave of her slender, bejewelled hand. 'I'm already in.' She sat gingerly on the edge of the tatty armchair and Ellie noticed how white she was. She looked like her own ghost.

'I've got nowhere else to go. Are you going to throw me out on the streets?'

'Don't be silly.' Ellie filled the kettle. It was three in the morning. She couldn't believe this was happening. What *was* she going to do with her? What was she going to do with Jeff?

'Why aren't you with Charlotte?' she asked. A sudden thought occurred to her. 'Charlotte's not in Manchester, is she?' She was conscious of a spiky kind of panic performing a war-dance in the pit of her stomach.

'I don't know where she is. She never turned up. I came to find her.' Olivia leaned back in the chair and closed her eyes. She was wearing a dusty-blue eyeshadow and eye-liner. She'd had time to put on her make-up then.

'Why should she be here?' Ellie wanted to scream at her. The panic returned in waves, hurting her.

'Where else could she be? I've been phoning the Didsbury house all evening and no one's there. Not even Jeff.'

Ellie looked down at her bare feet. Oh God.

'She's supposed to be getting married tomorrow.' Olivia's eyes snapped open and her voice rose into hysteria.

'Calm down, Mother.' If only she wouldn't make such a racket. Jeff was a heavy sleeper. But how could she get them out of here? Mother's car? Suggest driving to Didsbury?

'How did you get here?'

'By taxi of course.'

'Taxi!' Ellie sat down like a stone on the chair beside her. 'Christ Almighty, Mother. That must have cost a fortune.' She didn't know whether to laugh or cry. Mother had no idea of reality. She was on another planet – a planet dictated by her whims. And Ellie was completely sunk.

'What does money matter? I needed to see you.' Olivia sighed. 'I would have phoned, if you'd ever bothered to give me the number.'

Ellie hadn't seen her in this mood before. Could she

really be worried about Charlotte? She'd never seemed to care before. Was she right to be worried? Ellie hugged her arms to her chest. She was wide awake now.

'If anything had happened to Charlotte, we would have heard.' She felt sure that Charlotte had gone to Pencraig. The answers would be there, not here in Manchester. She stared at a stain on the red carpet. What should she have said to Charlotte this afternoon? What had Charlotte been looking for? Ellie should have known, or at least tried to find out.

'Do you think we should phone the police?'

'No.' Ellie poured boiling water into the teapot. 'Damn, I've forgotten the bags—' She dropped them in. Charlotte needed space, not search parties.

'You don't think she's changed her mind do you? She wouldn't do that to me, would she?'

Olivia's face was still white with panic, and Ellie realised that this was the root of her fear. Olivia had invited everybody who meant anything to her – regardless of whether or not they knew Charlotte. Any excuse for a party. Any excuse to fill Pencraig with people and noise. So that was it. Prospective humiliation was in the air.

Had Charlotte changed her mind? The thought had occurred to Ellie earlier today. It was the kind of thing she herself might do, or Olivia. But no, not Charlotte. Charlotte wouldn't let people down. 'No. I don't think she's changed her mind.'

'Changed her mind about what?' The green curtain was swept aside, and Jeff stood there, looking at Ellie with a bleary question in his eyes. He was stark naked. He didn't acknowledge Olivia's presence or his own nudity. He just stood there. Tall, rangy, and completely naked.

It was a horrific moment. Ellie closed her eyes and opened them again to find that despite her swift prayer, he was still standing there and he was still naked. She looked him up and down, discovering to her surprise that a smile was twitching at her lips. She sneaked a sidelong glance at Olivia. Olivia's mouth was wide open.

'Changed her mind about getting married,' Ellie supplied. 'Do you want some tea?' It was always safer to be doing something.

Jeff nodded.

'And who could blame her?' Olivia looked from one to the other of them in utter disbelief. Her green eyes were glittering with fury. 'You two?'

For the first time Jeff glanced at her, still without a trace of self-consciousness. And why not? He had a beautiful body, dark, muscular and lean like an animal, with none of the visible drooping hang-ups of the human race. And he loved shocking people.

'She must be devastated.' Olivia's chest was heaving. 'How could you? What sort of a man are you?'

'The normal red-blooded kind.' The naked and unrepentant Jeff gazed right back at her.

Ellie wanted to giggle. There was no way Mother could cope with this. Poor Mother. Torn between her hopeless romantic dream, her inability to accept that her younger daughter was no longer an innocent child, and her own experience of the power of sexual need. Sex overtook most loyalties, it seemed.

Jeff grabbed his shirt and trousers from the crumpled heap by the bed. 'Charlotte doesn't know. And she's not going to find out.' He zipped his trousers with a flourish.

'Well, I certainly wouldn't tell the poor child. You can be sure of that.' Olivia looked down at her white ringed hands as if she was embarrassed to look at him now that he was fully clothed.

'Where do you reckon she's gone?' he asked Ellie.

'A thinking place.'

He smiled slowly. 'And where would that be?'

'Pencraig. In the wood.' There was nowhere else. Ellie stared into her cup. 'In the bivouac she showed you. Our hideaway.'

His eyes were burning into her. Dense, and very, very blue. Slowly she looked up, and their eyes met for a long moment before he swung round to face Olivia. 'Did you look there?'

'Don't be ridiculous.' She had recovered some of her poise, but the shock of what she'd witnessed was still on her face, an echo of it in her eyes. 'I'm hardly going to start wandering around in the woods in the middle of the night.'

'But Charlotte would.' Ellie put her hand on his arm. 'Let's drive there. We'd be leaving in five hours anyway. I'll go and find Charlotte. Then I'll take her back to the house and come and let you know she's okay.'

'How can you be so sure that's where she is?' Olivia's face was slowly regaining some colour.

'I just know,' Ellie told her. And she did.

'You don't think she's changed her mind then?' Momentarily Jeff looked like a young boy, and again Ellie envied Charlotte for having so much of him.

She shook her head. 'She loves you,' she said.

Before they got in the car to go back to Wales, Olivia pulled her aside. 'It's very wicked of you, darling. But I think I can understand it.'

There was a smile on her red lips, and Ellie knew that she didn't understand – why it had happened, or what there was between the three of them. She felt almost disgusted by her mother – by the easy acceptance of what should have been sordid.

In that moment Ellie knew that childhood was over. She

and Olivia would never have the same relationship again. There was no going back now.

Charlotte had put her bag down in the shadows by the garden gate and she'd walked, following the path up to the ring of trees and into the wood. She wasn't frightened – she and Ellie had often sneaked off for forbidden night-time adventures in the wood, for midnight feasts in their hideaway.

And sometimes they'd climbed down to the bay to swim. Negotiated the rocks hand in hand in silence. Undressed, left their clothes behind on the pebbles and run naked and free into the cool water. What a feeling it had been when the water level crept up their thighs, and the first waves splashed on to their bare backs. She'd never forget.

And she would have liked to do it now. But those days were long gone. And it wouldn't be the same alone.

Charlotte sat down on the tree stump next to the old beech. She used to hold Ellie's hand when they were in the wood, because Ellie always got scared. It hadn't only been a difference in age. She had wanted to care for Ellie – even then perhaps the ache to be needed had found its place in Ellie.

So she'd never minded that Ellie was scared by the rustles of tiny scampering animals and the occasional eerie screech of night birds. And scared by the shadows. She almost wanted her to be.

Charlotte was never scared of shadows. She could always see beyond them – knew which hand holding a sword was really a branch of the horse-chestnut tree, and which grisly mask was the rose-hip bush. She knew it all so well – everything in the wood. That helped. Ellie had always let her imagination take over.

She stretched out her long legs. Charlotte loved the

particular quiet of the night. The stillness. All the night noises only emphasised the peace that she'd always been able to find here. A peace that she needed now more than ever. Now that the doubts were tumbling in her head. Now that she was taking the biggest stride away that she'd ever taken in her life.

It had always been special – returning to Pencraig – and not just because it held the roots of their happiest childhood summer. It was special because it had been special to the generations before her. And because there was a magic that she believed could always soothe her. Always show her the right way to go.

She had missed the wood when she'd stayed away from Pencraig for too long in those later years. But whenever she did come, she always visited the wood alone, when everyone else was sleeping. That first time she'd brought Jeff here, he'd wanted to meet her when the house was asleep, to come to the wood and make love.

It had been a temptation – she'd shown him their hideaway, hadn't she? And deeply regretted it afterwards. But she hadn't agreed. She hadn't wanted Jeff to have the soul of the wood. The soul of the wood that she liked to think still belonged to her and Ellie. It had been passed down to them. It was the kind of thing that couldn't be put in a bank or written on a piece of solicitor's paper. It meant much more than that.

Wherever she went, when she was at Pencraig this place was her refuge. A retreat from the world when she needed to think.

Some of the trees had been damaged by a storm since her last visit. Charlotte stroked the bark of the horse-chestnut. Nothing could destroy the horse-chestnut. She walked through the ring to the edge of the cliff, to the rough grass and stony path cut into the cliffs that led down to the bay.

It was a windy night and the sea was rough. Great dark waves reared and bucked on to the black rocks. There was little moonlight – there were too many low clouds. Charlotte hugged her arms close to her chest, and drank it in. The drama seemed to seep into her senses.

After a while she wandered back to the hideaway. She couldn't go to the house. The house held Olivia, small talk and careful conversations. And besides, she wasn't ready.

Was she ready to be a married woman? Was Charlotte Morgan ready to become Mrs Dando?

She bent down and crawled inside the bivouac. Would a married woman want a hideaway? She had always assumed that Jeff was what she wanted. Since the day she'd met him and almost drowned in those blue eyes. But was he? Was he really? Or was it only a child she wanted? Was this ache only for a child who would need her, like Ellie once had?

She shivered, the truth clasping icy fingers around her heart. She loved Jeff – of course she did. She'd never love another man the way she loved Jeff. He made her laugh, he was intelligent and good company. He was wonderful in bed and he was going to make money. But did he need her? Would he ever want her to hold his hand in the darkness? Would he ever – like Ellie – need her to fight away shadows?

And what of the child? The child who wouldn't come. Who hid from her desperate embrace although Charlotte needed her like she needed the air she breathed? The child hadn't yet come – and yet she was as real to Charlotte as if she were already flesh and blood, lying here beside her.

If she closed her eyes, she could even smell her. The baby scent, mingling with the damp, rotting smell of leaves and wood that was already in her nostrils. She could almost taste it.

This baby was worth waiting for. But how long could she

bear to wait? And was she right about Jeff? Was he the right man to give her what she needed? Were Jeff, his baby and Ellie destined to be for ever mingling inside her head? Making her half-crazy with longing and sadness?

She groaned, a low sound stifled by the earth beneath her. Charlotte didn't mind about the dirt. It was a warm evening now that she was out of the wind. She must stay here. Just for a few moments to think it through, she told herself. It might, after all, be her last chance.

The next thing she knew, someone was kneeling beside her and there was thin sunlight filtering through the branches of the bivouac.

'I knew it,' a voice said. Someone chuckled.

She stretched and cautiously opened one eye.

'Charlotte?' Ellie whispered. 'Are you all right?' She was hunched in the entrance, her eyes concerned.

Charlotte felt as if she'd had the best night's sleep for a long time. 'Wonderful,' she said. 'I feel wonderful.'

Ellie lay down beside her and hugged her. 'Crazy, crazy person,' she murmured in her ear. Her fair head stayed close to Charlotte's dark one. When they drew apart at last, they smiled. Charlotte squeezed her hand and together they crawled out.

'You might feel wonderful, but you look terrible.' Ellie brushed some dirt out of Charlotte's matted hair. 'You'd better come back to the house and have a bath. You're supposed to be getting married today.'

8

Jeff made the call from the car phone in his black Volvo, twenty minutes after leaving the estate agent's office on Deansgate, to coincide with Bob Butler's lunch hour. Bob was a man of regular habits, as well as a man who played it strictly by the book, so timing was crucial.

When she answered he could tell that she'd been waiting.

'Are you all alone yet, you sweet thing you?' he purred.

She giggled. 'Bob's at lunch and Reggie's out viewing. So, yes. I'm holding the fort.'

'I wish you were holding me.'

'Jeff Dando, honestly!'

But she liked it. He knew that she liked it. Polly was just another sucker for the right sexy innuendo and the wildest of compliments. She was at that age. Too old to be brave, careless and single, too young to have stopped caring. Another girl in her late twenties who was too plain to be choosy and who'd been married for five years – about right for Jeff's purpose. She was bored.

He'd seen it the first day he'd walked into Butler's Estate Agent's office, and he'd noted it for later. Boredom – such a useful state of mind. Now Polly's time had come. The deal was there for the taking. He had laid the foundations. She was ripe for the picking.

'Now me, I prefer straight talking.' Jeff stared at a long-legged brunette crossing the busy road in front of him. As always, Manchester was buzzing. He was in Piccadilly – the modern heart of the city some called it – a great square of hotels and shops, with a central oasis of lawns and flower beds, all looked over by the towering Piccadilly Plaza. 'If everyone said what they thought, we'd all be better off. Less confused for a start.'

'What *do* you think, Jeff?'

She sounded very coy. He wondered what she was doing during this conversation. Pictured her freckled face with greenish-blue eyes and shy smile, framed by light, straggly brown hair. God, things would be different if they ever brought in those phone viewer things. He'd have to work bloody hard to keep the right expression on his face.

'I think we should get together, sweetie. And not in your office either.'

He heard the faint intake of breath.

'That old house you mentioned, in Alderley Edge. The one you were typing the details for. It's empty isn't it?' His tone was absolute innocence.

'It might be,' she hedged.

She was making it so easy for him. 'When my mother said "it might be" in that tone of voice she always meant yes. Have you got anything in common with my mother, Polly?'

'I might have.' She laughed.

'So how do you fancy a picnic? Smoked salmon, a bottle of decent Chardonnay, just you and me? I've always liked the scenery in that neck of the woods. Especially at night time.' She lived out towards Wilmslow – he'd checked. It wouldn't be far for her to go. But he had plans for her to go a lot further.

'I'm a married woman, don't forget.'

Oh, he hadn't. No chance. They were the safest. And the most willing – the rush of excitement behind her words was unmistakable.

'And I'm a married man,' he said. 'But it doesn't stop me

wanting you.' The games you had to play. He tapped his fingers on the steering wheel. Maybe he'd get some driving gloves. Black leather.

Jeff didn't mind the chase – often it was the best part, but sometimes women pissed him right off. They wanted so much reassurance. It wasn't enough, apparently, to show you fancied them. You had to fill in the spaces with a hundred other details, most of them phoney, before you could even get them into bed.

A black taxi pulled into the rank behind him. Jeff checked his mirror but the driver didn't seem to care that the Volvo was taking up a taxi space. He just pulled out a copy of the *Manchester Evening News* and started reading.

'Jeff, really!' Her accent was harsh but appealing. 'You're terrible, you are, honest.'

'It's the effect you have on me,' he murmured. When would women realise that they were asking to be lied to? Most men only wanted stimulation, success and a hot meal every night.

'You're interested in buying Alderley Towers, aren't you, Jeff?' Her voice hardened unexpectedly, and he blinked with surprise. Maybe he hadn't been subtle enough.

He made a split-second decision not to lie. 'Yes, I am interested. It might be just what I'm looking for. I want to see it as soon as possible. With you.'

'How did you find out about it?' She sounded wary now.

'Oh, you know how it is, sweetie. Word gets round.' Jeff had heard about the house on the dealers' grapevine – more necessary for a result than a deposit tucked in your jacket pocket.

'No one's supposed to go round there yet.' Polly lowered her voice. 'Until it's cleared with Bob. But the owner's dropping the key off with me this afternoon, about four.'

'Perfect.' He was glad she couldn't see his smile.

'And he needs an early sale. My guess is that he's strapped for cash. He'll be open to offers all right.'

'Really,' Jeff drawled. That's what he'd heard too. 'And when he comes in, you of course will take down all his particulars. You'll be terribly nice to him. An absolute angel. And then being the clever girl that you are, you'll tell me, so I can contact him direct.'

'Bob will go loopy.'

'Bob will never know.' He had her now. In the palm of his hand.

She paused. 'What do I get out of it?'

Jeff smiled to himself. She was brighter than he'd thought. Less desperate too. 'What do you want?'

'I've heard about you, Jeff,' she said. 'You've got quite a reputation.'

He groaned. He hadn't figured on that. 'Is it time to move to a different town?'

'Oh, it's not that bad.' She stifled another giggle. 'But I've got a friend who works in Mason's.'

Melanie worked in Mason's. Damn her to hell. 'Who just happens to know Melanie?'

'Apparently she never stops talking about you.'

Jeff pulled a face. 'Hell hath no fury—' He'd always known Melanie was going to be trouble.

'But don't worry. No one takes any notice of her. She's such an old tart.'

He raised his eyebrows. Women. They never ceased to amaze him. 'Far be it for me to disagree.' Jeff quickly ran through his mental file of the female faces in Mason's. 'What's your friend's name?'

She giggled again. 'I don't dare tell you.' Her voice changed. 'And I don't want to be dumped when you've had enough of me. I want an agreement. A hundred pounds on the table for the information I give you.'

'If I buy,' he said.

'If you buy.'

'Done.' He wondered if that would be classed as prostitution. 'Are we still on for that picnic?'

'Of course. That's included in the price.'

Jeff laughed. He liked her style. 'Wonderful. Tonight?'

'It'll have to be. We've got to move fast. Seven o'clock? You know the address? It's a bit off the beaten track.'

That's why he wanted it. It was close enough to Manchester for commuting, and yet Alderley Edge was more than just an illusion of the countryside. It was the real thing. It had character and it had style. Wonderful views – on a clear day you could see as far as Wales – and more than a touch of class. 'I'll find it,' he promised. As if he hadn't driven past the place three times already. What did she think had drawn him to Butler's Estate Agent's in the first place?

Jeff was thoughtful as he put down the car phone and turned the ignition key. He pulled out into the line of traffic. He didn't fancy Polly much. She was a mousy individual, too skinny for his taste, and a tad common as well as having a laugh like a witch. But she'd be very useful. He knew it. She was a practical girl. Maybe it was time to branch out a little. Maybe sex wasn't enough – it could lead into a maze of complications, like it had with Melanie. But a girl like Polly— If Polly was into profit and not just being taken to bed, then she'd work even harder. A good investment. Just as long as she didn't get too greedy.

Charlotte was home. Her dark hair was tied back in a ponytail. She was wearing white jeans and was cleaning her red high-heeled shoes.

'You're home early.' He kissed her neck. 'Got the sack?'

'Very funny. I'm getting ready. We should be leaving soon.'

'Leaving?' For a moment his mind was blank. Then he looked at the shoes and remembered. Olivia's birthday. They were invited to Pencraig for the weekend. For dinner tonight and a party on Saturday. He groaned.

Charlotte stopped polishing to stare at him. 'You hadn't forgotten?'

'Yeah. I had.' He filled the kettle, wondering how to handle it. 'The thing is, Charlotte—'

'No, Jeff.' She got to her feet. Her hands were on her hips. She was ready. More than ready. He could see that. She was spoiling for a fight.

It was eleven months since they'd promised to love each other for better or worse, and in that time they'd hardly stopped rowing for long enough to do it.

'You're not going to tell me you've arranged something else,' she warned him. 'Because if you have, then you can un-arrange it right now. This is important to me.'

'Sweetie, I can't help it if things come up.'

Her body became tense and rigid. 'Don't they always? Anything you want gets priority. Everything I care about gets swept under the carpet and conveniently forgotten.'

Jeff sighed. Here we go again. Children. Hospital tests. They were back to all that stuff, and God, he was sick of it. It was a nice idea but Christ— What was her hurry?

He flung his jacket on the chair, grabbed two mugs. 'Tea?'

'Damn the tea.' She was upset. Her face was drawn and angry.

'Come on, sweetie, don't be like that. I didn't arrange this.'

'But you could cancel it.'

'No way.' There was no contest in his mind. Polly and Alderley Towers were both more important than Olivia

Morgan and her daughter's tantrums. He wouldn't contemplate cancelling, not for anyone.

'I can't reschedule this, sweetness,' he repeated. 'It's business. And it has to be sorted tonight.'

'Damn your bloody business.' She sank into a chair. 'I hate it. Business always comes first for you. Before me, before our life together.' The anger had left her voice. Now it was only bleak and empty. That hurt him much more.

'Charlotte—?' he began.

'I'm sick of it.' She leaned heavily on to the table, her shoulders bowed in defeat. 'Sick to death of it.'

Jeff went up behind her, and began gently to massage her shoulders. 'It's for us, sweetie,' he murmured. He had to make her see. 'Everything I'm doing is for us. I'm trying to make enough money for us to have our dream. You know, the cottage in the country, the jungly garden—'

'That's your dream, Jeff. Not mine.' She pulled away.

'I thought you wanted it too.' What was the matter with her? Why was she making everything so difficult?

'You never asked me what I wanted. You promised to drive us to Wales tonight. Ellie's even taken the night off. You've let both of us down.'

'She won't mind.'

'That's not the point.' Her voice was rising again. 'If you really want to know what I want, then I'll tell you. What I really want is for you to keep one of your lousy promises.'

'Oh, for God's sake—' He was irritated. How could she be such a hypocrite? She'd never made any secret of her feelings about her mother. So why the hell was it so important not to miss her birthday? 'What do you want to go there for anyway? You can't stand Olivia.' And God knows he didn't want them all together. He had enough to do when they were apart.

'It's not that.' She sighed. 'I just want to go back to Pencraig. With Ellie. It means a lot to me, Jeff.'

'I know, I know. I'm sorry.' God, she was really turning the screws now. He didn't know what had got into Charlotte lately. He used to be able to rely on her support. But now, coming home meant one bloody battle after another.

'I'll take you first thing in the morning. I promise.'

'Tomorrow is too late, Jeff.'

There was a hardness in the hazel eyes that scared him because he'd never seen it there before. But he couldn't back down now. How could he, when this deal was so important? And it wasn't just this deal. Who knew what else Polly might have in the pipeline?

'I'll make it up to you, sweetie.'

'I don't want you to.' Her voice was cruel. 'I don't want your cheap schoolboy grins and expensive bottles of wine. I don't want flowers. I don't want your hole-and-corner deals that never give us any time for ourselves, and I don't want—' She broke off. She was shaking.

He slumped in the chair next to her, a feeling of lifelessness taking him over, as if the blood was draining from his body. 'Me. You don't want me, is that it?' He hardly recognised the sense of uselessness that he felt. He wasn't accustomed to it, and he couldn't imagine what to do about it. But it brought back, all too vividly, childhood memories that he couldn't stomach.

'Don't you want me any more, Charlotte?' His voice was bleak and hopeless. It would be a release to cry, but he couldn't. He wouldn't lose control. All his tears had been shed at the age of nine when his mother had pissed off to live in Spain with a bloody waiter she'd met on holiday, and then a year later his father had left him in care because his new stepmother had kids of her own and didn't fancy any more. He'd never cried since then. And he wasn't going to start now.

Charlotte knelt down next to him. She smelt sweet and musky. 'You know I want you,' she whispered. 'I love you. But we may as well not be married, for the amount we see each other. The real time we have together.'

He untied the red ribbon to release her hair. It was so thick and dark that he wanted to bury his face in it. 'I love you too, Charlotte. You know I do.' He didn't want her to get this close. Part of him wanted to shove her away. Quick, before he got hurt himself.

'You never tell me anything about all these deals of yours,' she said. 'I never know what's going on. You fob me off with silly excuses. You patronise me. You let me down. Constantly. You're always letting me down, for Christ's sake.'

She was close to tears. She still cared enough to cry. So he was all right then. Everything was fine. Charlotte was still his. The relief overwhelmed him.

'Is that all?' he murmured.

The half-smile was barely visible. But it was there. 'I've had enough of it, Jeff,' she repeated. 'I deserve more.' Slowly, she rose to her feet.

'I know you do.' He got up to make the tea, an air of penitence on his face. 'It's not that I'm trying to keep things from you, sweetie. It's just that I'm used to operating on my own.'

She didn't seem convinced. He'd have to tell her.

He turned. Ran his fingers through his dark hair. 'A house called Alderley Towers has come on to the market. It's between Wilmslow and Alderley Edge. Heavy duty, big, and almost derelict. It needs a lot of work doing to it, but it could be a real bargain.' His voice rose with excitement. He couldn't help it. He grinned and grabbed her hands. 'There's a massive garden. Two acres of it. And wonderful views. It's got so much potential, Charlotte! We could keep an acre and still apply for a building plot. Even two.'

His voice levelled out at the lack of enthusiasm in her blank eyes. Her hands seemed lifeless too. He let them go. What was wrong with her?

'So far I've only driven past. But I've heard the owner wants an early sale. And I've been given the chance to look round it tonight. I'll be the first person to see it.' He spoke slowly, waiting for the words to sink in. Didn't she realise what a chance this was? Why wasn't she jumping for joy?

Charlotte slumped into a chair.

'So you see why I can't drive you anywhere tonight,' he appealed.

She was silent.

'Shall I come and look at it with you?' she asked at last in a weary voice.

Jeff hesitated. Bloody hell, he hadn't thought of that. 'I think it's best for me to see it on my own first, sweetness,' he said. 'Without distractions, you know?'

She was silent.

'But if it looks right for us, then just you wait. I'll be dragging you along there before you know it.'

'I see.' It didn't look as if she did. It looked as though she was seeing something quite different.

'It'll take almost all we have.' Jeff was thinking aloud. 'But we've got the dough from the shop, and this could be a gold mine.' He reached out to trace a line along her cheekbone with his thumb. It was still wet with her tears. 'This could set us up for life, sweetie.' Where was her vision?

'Would that mean no more wheeling and dealing, Jeff?'

'Christ, Charlotte.' He took his hand away. What was the bloody point? He got up and paced over to the sink, stared at the tiny square of patio out the back. It was a long way from being a jungly garden. Didsbury was all right in its way – probably enough for some people. But not for Jeff. It reminded him too forcibly that the dream was still some distance away. And Charlotte's attitude wasn't bloody helping.

He slammed his fist on the stainless steel drainer, which rattled ominously. 'What do you want from me? I'm doing my best. I'm working my balls off for us.' He thought of all the girls he knew who would happily become fools for love. The thought fuelled his sense of injustice. Who did she think she was?

'You know the work I do. Okay, so it means doing odd hours. And when something like this comes up, I have to change our plans. But it's what I do for a living. It's who I am. If you wanted something different you should have married a different man.'

'Maybe I should.' She turned from him.

'Charlotte—' His hands fell to his sides.

She moved to the door. 'I'm going to phone Mother and Ellie.' Her voice was deadpan. 'Can we leave by nine in the morning or will another deal materialise before then?'

He shook his head. 'Tomorrow, I'm all yours.'

But she didn't respond. Instead she looked at him for a few moments, turned and slowly trailed up the stairs.

Once she was out of sight Jeff concentrated on the things that mattered – what was ahead. Charlotte would come round – she always did. He got on with some paperwork, ordered the food by phone, and eventually went upstairs.

She was lying on the bed, curled into a foetal position, and she wouldn't look at him. He bent to kiss her petulant lips. She looked so sexy when she was sulking, that he was tempted not to stop. To keep going until he kissed away this black mood of hers.

As he looked at her, the thought of Eloise rose unbidden

into his mind. And yet they never looked alike, even when they were sleeping. He'd rarely seen Eloise asleep since that first day she'd turned up here and fallen asleep in the kitchen. It would be about the only time she'd be defenceless. When those slanting green eyes were closed. When her long, light lashes skimmed the soft, pale skin of her cheeks. And her lips were slightly parted.

Jeff didn't want to lose her. But neither did he want to lose Charlotte. He was making plans. There were two options, and he wasn't sure which way to go. But for now it was imperative to get Charlotte away from here, since Didsbury had become a battleground. And the battleground was preventing him from operating both effectively and smoothly. He needed some space here alone, where Charlotte wasn't nagging him about hospitals and babies and deals. Space to operate, and, yes, time for Eloise.

And if Charlotte was tucked away somewhere safe— His lip curled. Away from that drooling, pathetic boss of hers, for a start, not to mention away from Eloise. Then she would be dependent. Ready for him at weekends, waiting to make babies. And if all went well she could come back to Alderley when it was finished. His dream house. His family.

As for Eloise. She was dangerous, but she intrigued him – she always held something back, something that he sensed would never belong to him. But he had to try for it. She wasn't the same as all the others. She saw him in a way that no one else did, understood him as no one else did – perhaps because they were alike.

Yes, they were alike. And she was part of Charlotte. They were unique. Two halves of a whole. Together they could satisfy him like nothing he'd ever known.

He stared once more at Charlotte, almost seeing them both – the two sisters – lying there on the bed. He blinked rapidly. He didn't have time for this. No time for reflection, and certainly no time for sex. Besides, he had to conserve his energies for later. It would be the first time with Polly. There were first impressions to be made.

'Bye, sweetie.' He touched her flushed cheek, but still Charlotte wouldn't look at him. She'd been crying again – he saw it, although he pretended not to. It was there, stamped into her eyes.

He got off the bed. In his mind he was gone already. He'd make it up to her later. No worries.

At six o'clock he picked up the provisions, bought the wine and drove to Alderley, humming softly to himself. Charlotte would be back to normal after a couple of days at Pencraig. That place always cheered her up. It boded well for the future. Everything would be fine.

Jeff couldn't help feeling bubbly. On a high. A bit of business always cheered him up. And he hoped Polly would be doing much more to him than that.

If Ellie frowned and concentrated hard on the lemon and cream hollyhocks just outside the patio doors, the sound of Mother's playing could easily transport her back into childhood summers.

Then Jeff and Charlotte coming into view from behind the buddleia spoiled the fantasy. Especially because they were arguing – again. What was wrong with them all? Everyone had changed in the past year.

She turned to stare through the open window at her mother. Olivia had that far away look in her eyes again. Her fair hair was neatly coiled on top of her head, a few fugitive strands stroking her slim, white neck. There were pearls at her throat, on her fingers and in her ears. She was pale and transported – as she usually was when playing. But she was wilting like a flower from lack of nourishment.

She didn't belong here. It had been different at the party last night when some city slimeball – probably destined to be her next lover – was pouring gin down her throat and dancing with her all night. But now, her lights had dimmed again. It didn't suit her living at Pencraig. She was still beautiful, but there was no life in her. Nothing that grabbed you as her beauty always had in the past. And there was a new bitterness about her that frightened Ellie.

Jeff was different too. On the surface nothing had changed. He was still running from one deal to the next, before running to Ellie, who still opened her arms for him against every instinct and every better judgement she possessed. But the running was frantic, as if the finishing flag itself was racing away from him all the time.

How long could it go on? Sometimes she didn't see him for weeks, and then he'd appear in the wine bar as if she'd seen him only yesterday. Once upstairs they fell on each other in desperation, often barely making it into her room before they began. Devouring, soaking up the other's passion, storing it away for the lean times.

Ellie sighed. She picked a few daisies and began making a chain. The lawn at Pencraig was always covered with them. How often had she and Charlotte made daisy chains in that first summer? Queen of the May. Daisy crowns circling one dark head, one fair. Daisy bracelets and daisy belts.

She'd tried to break free of Jeff. She really had. After Christmas, when traditional family celebrations had left her tasting only sour flavours, she'd told him it was over.

'We have to break it off for Charlotte's sake,' she said. 'What if she found out? It just isn't worth it.'

'If that's what you want, Eloise.'

His voice was smooth. No protestations of love, no attempt to make her change her mind. Nothing. Hardly a glimmer of regret in those sexy blue eyes. That's how much she meant to him.

During January and February Ellie went to bed with a string of other men, to put a lid on it, so to speak. Or to flush Jeff out of her sexual system.

But each man left her colder than before. She even tried to manage alone. But she needed it – not sex, not someone to love her, but the right body in her bed. Even if it was only sometimes. And instead of easing the guilt, not having Jeff had left her feeling more distanced from Charlotte than ever. As if he could stand between them even then.

So when she went to dinner with them at the beginning of March she wore a low-cut, tight-fitting black dress that emphasised every slim curve, and glanced at him just once, in a way she knew he'd recognise.

'I've missed you,' she said softly. Charlotte was in the kitchen making coffee.

'Me too,' he said. Then he kissed her and put his hand up her dress until she was afraid she'd come, right there at the dinner-table.

She told Charlotte that she had to get home, Jeff offered her a lift, and they made love in a pub car park two hundred yards down the road. If they'd driven any further they would have crashed the car.

'It's no good,' she moaned. 'I can't stay away from you.'

'Then don't try, Eloise.' His voice was husky. 'Please don't try.'

But Ellie was miserable. She was miserable and she knew that Charlotte was miserable too, although she didn't know why. Something, somewhere along the line had gone wrong. Having Jeff hadn't brought Ellie and Charlotte together at all. It had only brought betrayal. And a tight knot to her stomach, just thinking about it. It made her sick. She had to push it away, fast, before she was scarred for life or something.

Olivia made the announcement at lunchtime. One minute Ellie was eating toast and paté, and the next her world was falling apart.

'I've come to a decision,' Olivia said. She rearranged her knife and fork on her plate and pushed it away. 'I'm leaving Pencraig.'

'What?' Ellie spoke, but they all stopped eating to stare at Olivia. Except Jeff. He merely raised his dark eyebrows.

'I'm selling the house. I want to live in London. It doesn't feel right, living here.'

Ellie thought of the slimeball. There always had to be a man behind Olivia's decisions. 'But you can't.' She looked to Charlotte for support. 'It's our family home.'

Olivia's green eyes were impatient. 'Houses get sold. It belongs to me. I can do what I like with it. No one keeps a house for ever. This isn't some kind of ancestral mansion, Ellie.'

'But Dad loved this house.' God, she was so insensitive. 'He never meant for you to sell it when you got bored. He meant it to be for all of us.'

Olivia glared at her. 'It isn't a question of boredom, Ellie. And what your father wanted is neither here nor there. He left it to me to do as I like with. And I'd like to sell it.' She folded her napkin.

She was right. Absolutely right. Rolf in his foolishness had signed away what he'd always promised would be theirs for ever. And if his aim had been to make his wife fall in love with Wales, then he'd failed miserably.

Ellie felt shaken to the roots. It wasn't just a house.

Somehow she'd imagined she would come back to live here one day. That her children – if she had any – would play here.

'To be honest,' Olivia confided, turning to Jeff, putting her slender hand on his arm, 'this place is a millstone round my neck. I can't possibly begin to get over Rolf's death while I'm living here.'

Ellie waited for the explosion from Charlotte. She wouldn't let Mother get away with that statement, surely? But Charlotte was silent, and her dark, morose eyes were giving no clues. What on earth was wrong with her?

So, Ellie was fighting this battle alone. 'Don't be ridiculous, Mother. You and Dad got divorced.'

'You're too young to understand, my dear.' Her hand was still on Jeff's arm. Her eyes challenged Ellie.

Ellie stared at her, stared at the slim white hand that seemed a symbol of possession. Was she threatening them? Since the night she'd discovered them together, Olivia was always playing games with Jeff. Teasing. Smiling secret smiles. Pushing him, seeing how far he was prepared to go, telling him she knew his rules.

Ellie didn't like it one bit. She had told Mother that it was only a one-night stand, but did she believe her? And could Ellie possibly trust her? If Olivia told Charlotte, it would be the end of everything.

Maybe this was another one of her games. 'You're not really going to sell Pencraig, are you, Mother?'

'Of course I am.' Olivia removed her hand. 'How else could I afford to live in London?' Her eyes were wistful.

'You could rent it out. You don't have to actually sell it.' To a stranger. So it's lost for ever.

'Don't be silly, Ellie. Who would want to rent this place? Besides, the rent would hardly keep me in clothes. I want to buy myself a nice little flat in Kensington.'

Ellie felt the tears welling in her eyes. 'Jeff—?'

Charlotte looked up swiftly.

But Jeff's deep-blue eyes had become the pound and pence signs of a cashier's till. And he didn't even seem surprised.

Rather fastidiously, Olivia chose an apple from the crystal fruit bowl. 'There is one way it could be kept in the family. You could buy it, couldn't you, Jeff?' She bit into the apple.

Ellie felt that the crunch of it had bitten into her heart.

'You could live here, couldn't you?' she persisted. 'You and Charlotte?'

Ellie frowned. What was Olivia up to now?

'Don't be daft, Mother,' she said. 'How could they possibly live here? They both work in Manchester.'

Olivia smiled. 'But Leonard's going to France, which puts Charlotte out of a job. And besides, Jeff and Charlotte are looking for a country retreat, aren't you, darlings?'

'Are you?' Ellie willed Charlotte to look at her.

'Maybe one day.' Charlotte pierced a cocktail sausage, keeping her eyes low. 'But not yet.'

'Jeff told me it was the sooner the better,' Olivia said sweetly.

'Then Jeff was wrong.' Charlotte glared at him.

Ellie looked around the circular table at the faces she was supposed to know so well. What was going on? Anyone would think that Jeff and Olivia had discussed this before. But when could they have done that? She glanced at him again. His mind was working overtime. Jesus, no!

'It would stretch us,' he said quietly. 'But it would be perfect. A perfect place for us.'

The anger bubbled in Ellie's head like a volcano. Her brain was the boiling lava that might spill over any second and ruin Olivia's immaculate white linen table-cloth.

It must never be perfect for Jeff and Charlotte without her. Never. Not here. Not anywhere. But especially not here.

'I don't see how you can even consider it.' Charlotte sounded vague and irritated. 'Especially when you're so set on that place you looked at last night.'

Ellie glanced at Jeff and raised her eyebrows. Last night?

'And whatever he may do in the future, don't forget that I am still working for Leonard. He's been considering France for so long that when it comes down to it he might never go.'

'You're the one holding him back.' Jeff's voice was smooth and slippery as satin.

'What?'

Ellie groaned.

'He won't go while you're around.' Jeff buttered some bread. 'You know he won't. He wouldn't dream of leaving you without a job. He wouldn't dream of leaving you anywhere.'

'What rubbish!' But Charlotte's face was flushed.

Ellie stared at Jeff. He was so clever. He knew just how to play her. He knew all the pressure points, and he operated them with precision. It was as if he'd programmed her innermost feelings, emotionally charted and calculated how best to use them against her. But he hadn't. It was all instinctive with Jeff. Either that or he was the most manipulative bastard she'd ever met.

'It's true.' Jeff's tone changed. 'All the time you carry on working for him he sees you every day, thinks there might be hope. France is what he wants, but he can't do it. Because it would mean leaving you. He'll waste his whole life waiting for you.'

Everyone was silent, absorbing this information.

'It could be just what we need,' Jeff whispered.

Suddenly Ellie knew that Charlotte would give in.

No. She couldn't bear it. Not Charlotte and Jeff – here, without her. She gripped the edge of the table.

Charlotte's eyes grew vague, as if she could move in any unpredictable direction.

Ellie held her breath.

'I know it could happen for us here.' Jeff's voice was silky-soft. He was speaking as if the two of them were alone in the room.

Ellie closed her eyes.

'If you gave up work for a while— Relaxed, stopped worrying. It might just happen.'

What the hell was he talking about? What might happen? Ellie frowned.

'It would be a perfect place for us—'

'No—' Ellie wanted to scream. She had to stop his voice – his hypnotic voice, drilling into her head, drilling into Charlotte. Yes, this was a perfect place. But it was her perfect place – hers and Charlotte's place. Not Jeff's.

Everyone turned to stare at her. Ellie felt angry and utterly alone. She wanted to lift the table and up-end it complete with cloth, best dinner service, food and crystal. To see it smash to pieces. She wanted to stamp her feet and get what she wanted. She wanted—

She stood up, and rushed from the room.

That night he came to her as she'd known he would. She was sitting hunched on the rocker, knees up to her chest staring out of the window of the attic room she'd shared with Charlotte.

'I suppose she agreed?' Ellie didn't want even to look at him.

Jeff sat on the bed. He nodded. 'It won't change a thing, you know. I want you to come here as often as you like.

Weekends, holidays, any time.' He reached out to run his fingers lightly up the inside of her thighs.

She put her feet down on the floor, began rocking. 'Big deal.'

'I want you to think of Pencraig as your home too,' he said. 'You know that.'

'It is my home.' She glared at him.

'We'll probably see even more of each other than before. After all, I'll be working in Manchester a lot of the time. And Charlotte will be here.' He smiled.

Out of his way. Out of their way. Out of the way, while Jeff got on with life. He had no idea. 'Stupid bastard,' she muttered.

'What?'

She got to her feet, leaned on the window-sill. 'For someone who makes a living out of being in the right place at the right time and gauging the right reactions, you can be pretty dumb.'

She glanced at him over her shoulder. He looked like a boy. Like a boy who knew everything. Who was innocent but held the secret of sexuality in his little finger. She turned back to the window. For a moment she thought she saw a shadowy figure entering the wood.

'How d'you mean?' He moved in closer behind her and rubbed his palms across her breasts.

She groaned, pulled away. 'That's not always the answer, Jeff.' Often enough though, often enough.

'Well, what do you mean?'

She turned to face him. 'I don't care about seeing you more often. I'd rather be free of you. Don't you see?' She clenched her fists. 'But I don't want Charlotte to be so far away.'

He laughed. 'C'mon now, Eloise. You can do better than that.' His eyes shone wickedly in the semi-darkness. 'You don't want to lose Pencraig to me and Charlotte. That's it, isn't it?'

She looked away.

'I know you and Charlotte are both nutty about this place,' he said. 'All those wonderful memories of your mother screwing around and your father drinking himself into oblivion. Who could blame you?'

She lifted her head. 'You're right. I'd rather it went to a stranger. I don't want you and Charlotte living here. While I'm— while I'm—'

'Miles away?' He tilted her chin and kissed her. Just a small tantalising promise of a kiss.

'You wouldn't understand.'

'We need this, Eloise. Me and Charlotte. *You* probably wouldn't understand that.' His mouth was nuzzling into her neck.

'God, I want you,' he muttered.

His hands were under her thin nightie. She shuddered. All her proud intentions melted into liquid desire when she felt the touch of those hands. He bent down, towards her belly, and she pulled his dark head closer, until the rough stubble of his jaw was grazing her skin. She moaned, so softly that it could have been a prayer.

'You smell so good.' His voice was thick with longing. 'My Eloise. I've been watching you and wanting you all day.'

Her fingers tangled through his hair. 'Bastard,' she murmured. 'I want you too.'

Her lips parted as his tongue explored her warm and eager flesh. All of her straining for him, wanting him so much that she could hardly breathe. He must know how much she wanted him.

But for how long? Things were changing so fast, and she was scared. How long could it possibly go on this way?

9

In Pasha's wine bar Ellie was glad of the overhead fan that kept her cool. This summer so far had been sultry, as if a distant storm was brewing. She was faint with the airlessness that seemed to hang like a cloud over Manchester as it had never hung over Wales or Pencraig, with its sea breezes and gentle waves. This would be Charlotte's first summer there since the sale had gone through. And Ellie could still hardly bear to think of it.

She had just started her mid-session break when Sarah called her over.

'Ellie. I want you to meet Melanie.'

'Hi.' Ellie barely glanced at her. Nice-looking in a tarty kind of way. Too much make-up.

'Hi.' Melanie smiled back. A nice smile.

'Ellie Morgan. Jeff Dando's sister-in-law,' Sarah declared.

'Oh, yeah?' Melanie's expression changed.

'So?' Ellie looked from one to the other of them, half-surprised that Sarah hadn't enlarged further on the relationship between Ellie and Jeff. It was common knowledge in the wine bar that, since Charlotte had been living back at Pencraig, Jeff had been spending most of his time with Ellie. She wasn't even sure how they'd drifted into it. Circumstances, not enough will-power, too much sex. It wasn't even because of Charlotte any more. No. Jeff had a much greater power over her now. He had made her fall hopelessly in love with him. Hopelessly under his spell. He was tearing Ellie and Charlotte apart – she knew it.

'He's a rat.' Melanie's words were slightly slurred, dipping into the Mancunian accent. 'He didn't half leave me in the lurch. I hope your sister knows how to take care of herself.'

Ellie got to her feet. She didn't want to hear this.

'Ellie! She's got something to say that you ought to hear.' Sarah was following her through the crowded tables of the wine bar, out of the double-doors, up the stairs towards the bed-sit. 'Why won't you listen to me? Why won't you listen to her?'

'I'm not interested.'

'Ellie, I'm trying to help you, for God's sake. You're making a fool of yourself.'

'And you're not?' Ellie turned to face her. 'Everybody knows about you and Harold. For Christ's sake, Sarah. That man is revolting. How could you?'

'At least I'm not screwing my own brother-in-law.' But Sarah's kind, full face was flushed. She sank on to the top stair. 'Harold may not be God's gift to the female population, but he's not cruel.' She looked up, her eyes like cold steel. 'And he gives me what I need.'

'Which is?'

'Money.' Sarah looked beyond Ellie, her eyes tinged with regret. 'If it wasn't for Harold, this place would have folded a long time ago. Believe me.'

'I thought it was strictly a business arrangement.' Ellie's voice was sardonic, but her heart went out to Sarah. So she'd been right all along. This wine bar was the most important thing in Sarah's life. She'd even prostitute herself for it. So much more important than love.

'It was. At first.' Sarah's voice was low, barely a whisper. 'But things got worse. The bank was going to foreclose. I panicked. I couldn't see a solution. I tried to talk to Leonard, but his mind was on other things.' Her voice was bitter. 'On your darling sister for one.'

Ellie sat down next to her on the stairs. 'So what did you do?'

Sarah was crying now, huge tears coursing down her cheeks. 'Harold made me an offer. He said there was an easy way out. I knew what he meant. I drank a lot of vodka. An awful lot of vodka, Ellie. And I took it.'

Ellie put an arm tentatively around her shoulders. 'It was the night before Charlotte's wedding, wasn't it?' She spoke as if to herself. 'The night when you were doing the books. You got drunk. And Mother turned up at three in the morning.' The cry. She remembered the cry. Jeff's hands chasing her up the stairs. Passion and terror. Charlotte in the bivouac.

Sarah nodded. 'I kept thinking, if I kept going over the figures, I might not need to— It was supposed to be just the once.'

'I know the feeling. It was supposed to be just once with Jeff.' Just the once. That was a laugh.

Sarah grabbed her wrist. 'But don't you see? That's why you've got to stop this now, before it's too late. Before it destroys your life.'

'Maybe it already is too late.'

'Not for you.' Sarah spoke with urgency.

Ellie stared at her. 'What do you mean? Why is it too late for you? Leonard doesn't know about Harold, does he?' She'd known that Sarah held a long-term torch for Leonard even before Charlotte had told her. But Sarah and Leonard had remained just good friends.

Sarah nodded. 'He turned up one day. I wasn't expecting him. He just walked right in. He always does – or used to.'

Ellie sighed. 'Maybe he'd understand, if you explained—'

'Would Charlotte understand?'

'Of course not. But that's different.' Ellie didn't want to think about it.

'It always is.' Sarah's voice was weary. She took a deep breath, then grabbed Ellie and shook her by the shoulders with a sudden energy. 'But Jeff's not what you think. He's rotten. Just listen to what Melanie has to say. You owe it to yourself. Please?'

Ellie sighed. Why was it so important to Sarah? Did she hate Jeff that much? Didn't she know that Ellie had no illusions about Jeff Dando – that his dubious morality was all part of his attraction?

'Five minutes. Only five minutes, Sarah.'

'That's all she needs.' Sarah got to her feet and reluctantly Ellie followed her back to the table.

Melanie was still knocking back the gin and tonics. Sarah nudged her. 'Tell her, then.'

'He said he loved me.' Melanie frowned. 'He got me to find out about loads of properties that were coming on to the market, to give him the names and addresses of the owners, that kind of stuff.'

Ellie raised her eyebrows and pulled a face at Sarah. It didn't surprise her. It only surprised her that anyone could be so gullible.

'He even tried to get me to sleep with one of them. He thought that would persuade him to lower the asking price.'

'You could have said no.' Ellie wanted to escape, but Sarah, standing there with angry eyes and arms folded, forced her to stay put.

'She trusted him,' Sarah told her. 'She was renting a flat, but she was chucked out illegally when the owner wanted to sell to Jeff. Who wants a sitting tenant?'

'Not Jeff.' Melanie sniffed. 'He said we'd buy a place together, he got me to sign something. I don't know what. I believed everything he said. I loved him. If Sarah hadn't taken me in until I found a new place, I don't know what I would have done.' She was crying now, tears smudging the mascara and eyeshadow around the baby-blue eyes.

'He's a male whore.' Sarah's voice was dangerously low. 'Now do you understand? He'd sleep with anyone for the right price. What's your price Ellie?'

'What's yours?'

Sarah turned away, an expression of disgust in her eyes. 'Some people just won't be told.'

Ellie felt the anger flush through her. With Sarah for trying to run her life when hers could do with more than a quick vacuuming over. With this girl for her stupid gullibility and vacuous blue eyes. With Jeff for being such a bloody fool. And with herself for being part of it. For not being enough for him and for being unable to give him up.

'At least he's going down the financial drain.' Melanie's expression was one of grim satisfaction. 'Him and his latest.'

'His latest?' Ellie stared. She felt an old fear slicing through her.

'Some silly cow from Butler's Estate Agent's. They've been running a right little racket, but he won't be interested in her any more, now that she's got the sack.' Melanie took a long swig of her drink.

Ellie decided that she hated her.

'And I hear he's up to the eyeballs with the bank because he didn't get rid of my flat at the right time. He always was a greedy sod. As if that wasn't enough, he's got his hands full with that dump in Alderley Edge, because he got ripped off in some Welsh deal. Alderley bloody Towers. I ask you.

Talk about delusions of grandeur.' She laughed. 'I've heard he can't even afford to pay the builders.'

'You seem to have heard quite a lot.' Ellie got to her feet. She turned to Sarah. 'Satisfied?'

Sarah shrugged. 'You had to know sooner or later.'

But Ellie didn't believe half of it. This silly cow was bitter because she'd been dumped. Jeff was preoccupied, yes, but men like him didn't fail. Not ultimately. They'd always find a way out. There was an invincibility about Jeff. Whatever the problems, he'd pull through, laughing all the way to the bank.

'She doesn't believe you,' Sarah said. 'You're wasting your breath. He's got her eating out of his hand.'

'What? I thought you said he was married to her sister—' Melanie glanced at Ellie, and for a moment there was an expression of pity on her face.

Ellie felt the tightness in her chest. The doubts curdled in her stomach. She'd always known what he was. So was she making the wrong decision? Did she have it all as neatly compartmentalised as she'd believed?

The door opened and instinctively she looked up. It was Jeff. He was dressed in a black leather jacket and close-fitting jeans that hugged his long legs. His hair, dark and untidy, curled around his neck. There was a distant half-smile on his lean face as he paused to wave at her. Then the smile faded and he stopped in his tracks. He'd spotted Melanie, sitting with her back to the door. Without further hesitation, he turned around and walked straight out again, back into St Ann's Square.

Ellie just stared at the door swinging behind him. It was true then.

'Are you going after him?' Sarah put a hand on her arm as if to stop her. 'Don't, Ellie. He's not worth it.'

Ellie couldn't look at her. 'I've got work to do.' She

walked to the bar, began stacking glasses like some well-oiled machine. But inside there was a confusion and a terror. Things were getting out of her control.

When she'd finished, she stared, mesmerised, at the glasses. Rows and rows of shining tumblers, racks of wine glasses, gleaming optics. She leaned back against the counter, her back aching, and closed her eyes.

'Are you okay?' It was Sarah. 'I'm sorry, Ellie.' She put her arm around Ellie's waist.

Ellie was afraid she was going to crumple and cry on Sarah's shoulder. She didn't want to do that. Not now. 'I need some time off. Just a couple of days.'

She needed to go home. She needed to go to Pencraig. She needed to see Charlotte and she needed to think. She had things to tell Charlotte that wouldn't wait any longer.

'Sure.' Sarah smiled kindly. 'You take as much time as you need.'

Charlotte wrapped the red beach towel closer around her, not because she was cold, but to draw herself inwards. Tightly curled and safe, like a foetus. She wanted to be a tiny red speck in this bay. Isolated and imprisoned by it.

Around her the shingle lay undisturbed by the tide, slowly drawing in to give the stones their twice daily wash-over. And Charlotte was watching its steady progress, astounded at the way one hour flowed into another and then disappeared. Like the water, like the clouds, like these summer days.

She curled her toes around some smaller pebbles, enjoying the dry chalkiness next to her skin. This was all so different from her city life. She was a different person here.

Although Charlotte had been at Pencraig only since last October, her Manchester life was gone and might as well never have existed. The stacked, grimy landscape had become as unreal as a distant picture on some distant wall. It had no relevance to what Charlotte had now.

And what did she have now?

All the time in the world to think. To live, rather than arbitrate on what would slip past and what could be caught, grabbed and momentarily experienced, before it was time to go on. It had always been like that in the city. The rushing and buzzing like forests of flies. Going on to the next thing, quick before it's too late. For ever moving, never stopping. Clockwatching. No time to think.

Now, entire days disappeared with Charlotte hardly noticing. They simply drifted away, and all concept of time went with them. When Jeff rang he brought only a faint disturbance to her days. He changed their natural patterns. Charlotte was forced to accept that it was 'after dinner' or 'before lunch' or 'so late you should be asleep'. He introduced reluctant routines into her world that didn't belong here. Charlotte didn't want to have routines from her before-life. She wanted to forget them. She wanted to let go, ease herself out of all tension.

The sun disappeared behind a cloud, and she decided to swim. Her sunburned brown body in bright-yellow bikini felt parched and dried from the heat and the haze. She walked easily down the shingle to the water's edge as she'd done since childhood, waiting for a few seconds while the tiny waves curled prettily around her toes. Letting out a small cry, as if she was trying to communicate with the hazy sun, the world or the water in Dragon Bay, she strode in, gasping, loving the contrast of cool water on hot skin. She let out a shudder of pleasure, waded deeper, and bent into her first breast stroke of the day.

After a while Charlotte slipped over to float on her back, arching her long neck, squinting her eyes as the midday sun reappeared. If she were to die, she'd choose to drown.

There was no violence in that. It would be natural to stop breathing. So, so easy. Sinking lower and lower, drifting through the weeds of the sea, hair flowing and fanning behind floating, weightless limbs. There was a kind of beauty in it.

With a start she realised she'd gone under – as if living out the fantasy of death. She struggled, trod water, then turned back on to her belly and swam again, hard, out to her favourite rock.

Devil's Rock, she called it, because of the two limpeted appendages that jutted out like scabby, twisted horns. Charlotte climbed up, lying flat between the horns, her tanned limbs gleaming wet. She rested, relaxing every muscle, meditating on the dizzle-dazzle pictures dancing behind her closed eyelids as the sun burned down on her. Toasting the flat belly that she'd rather wasn't flat any more.

Charlotte sighed. She'd give anything for it to be swollen. Anything for morning sickness, cramps, heartburn – the lot. And, like Jeff had once said, this would be a paradise to be pregnant in.

But there was no baby. There would be no baby – Jeff was hardly here, and according to the doctor she'd seen yesterday, she herself possessed a 'reluctant reproductive system'. Still worse, he'd laughed when he said it.

'Early days, Mrs Dando,' he told her. 'Early days.'

'It's two years since we got married.' She could tell him the months, weeks and days, but then he'd think she was really crazy.

'That's not so long. It's a delicate business, is conception.' He prattled on about periods, temperature charts, and low sperm counts.

She knew all that already.

'I can refer you to a gynaecologist at the hospital. They'll give you all the guff.' He glanced at his black-faced digital watch.

Was his queue of patients building up into unmanageable proportions?

'But I wouldn't worry.'

No. Why should you? It isn't your affair. It isn't your failure, your heartache. 'No. I shouldn't worry.' She looked down. She'd been fiddling with her wedding ring and the gold band had cut into her skin. There was no blood. It didn't even hurt.

'Worry doesn't help, eh?' Another rapid digital check-up.

Charlotte shook her head. 'No. Worry doesn't help.'

'They'll want to see Mr Dando as well, when you go up to the hospital,' he said. 'After all, it takes two to tango, wouldn't you say?'

Charlotte scraped her chair back. 'Perhaps I'll leave it a while.' She couldn't bear to look at him. At his pasty face and bloodshot, pale-blue eyes. She should have gone to Dr Hill at the village surgery. He would have been more understanding. But he was also too close to home.

The doctor nodded. 'Up to you, Mrs Dando. We often find that Nature knows best.'

Charlotte left, quickly, before she became hysterical. She must talk to Jeff again, she must make him come with her. She needed to know the reasons, needed to move on to the next stage – whatever it might be. For her own sanity, she had to move on.

Fertility obsessed her day and night, and because Jeff was home so rarely she saved it for him until it dominated their conversations. Sometimes she couldn't even wait until after the first cup of tea. And it dominated sex.

She lay with her body rigid while he pounded into her. At first he hardly noticed. Then he changed.

'Relax, sweetie, just relax,' he began to say.

He'd start much more slowly, stroking her and easing her into it until she wanted to scream. She began to want it over.

'Give me a break, Charlotte.' His blue eyes held a question that she couldn't answer. Even Jeff couldn't help her now.

The time had to be right, conditions must be favourable. Like a channel swim. Take it easy. A slow, sure rhythm that she tried to lose herself in. But her body stayed rigid and her mind thought babies.

No wonder sex had become strained between them. They weren't doing it for themselves any more – they were doing it by order of Charlotte's temperature chart. To be fertile or not to be fertile. Tough luck if they'd rather read a book or take a cold shower. They had to do it instead. And enforced sex was unpleasant. Sometimes Jeff couldn't get it up, and Charlotte had to coax him, feeding some sort of prostitution into her fingertips.

'Christ, Charlotte,' he said. 'What are you doing to me?'

Each stared into the other's eyes, afraid of what they might see, trying not to read what they saw – not wanting to know.

She sat up – too quickly, and gazed out to sea. It was hard, knowing that she was responsible for sending spontaneity scuttling out of the door. But how could she help it? What else could she do?

'Save it,' she'd whisper. 'It's the wrong time.'

Then she'd watch him wilt.

Save the sperm. But who the hell would save her?

Jeff stayed away. She couldn't blame him. He didn't understand her desperation, and his incomprehension tore them apart. Slowly. Fibre by fibre, strand by strand. While Charlotte waited, and prayed, and dreamed of holding that tiny someone, of feeling the beating of a tiny heart, of holding an infant to her breast.

Sometimes it wasn't just a fantasy. Sometimes it was a real dream. Just like before, only becoming more and more vivid. She dreamed of a baby girl, living and breathing. So real that sometimes she awoke to her cry. The silence in the house brought absolute despair.

Was she losing her mind?

'It's not the end of the world if we can't have kids,' Jeff said. He said that often.

She was silent. It might as well be.

'Why do you want them so much anyway?'

'I just do.' He had wanted them too, but his need had been of a very different nature, soon forgotten.

'Kids tie you down. Your life's not your own any more once you have kids.'

Maybe she didn't want her life to be her own. A baby is life. Primeval urges. Man is the hunter, woman gives birth. But this woman was doing bugger all. If she was left alone, would her spirit eventually break?

Charlotte climbed down, slid into the cool water and swam back to the bay, back to the red towel. She wrapped it around herself once more. Her dark hair, wet and salty, hung like strands of seaweed brushing against her smooth brown shoulders. She stayed hunched within the towel, head bowed.

She was no longer her own woman. She was dependent. Now that she wasn't working, everything came from Jeff. Had he planned it that way? Had he tried to deceive her?

She felt deceived. She thought back to that conversation, when Jeff had persuaded her that they should come to Wales. That they should buy Pencraig from Mother – buy the inheritance she'd never had, and leave Manchester. She thought of Ellie and remembered how hurt she'd been.

And yet at the time it had seemed imperative to stop Pencraig going to a stranger. She knew Mother. And Mother wanted to sell. She'd had more than enough.

Poor Ellie. She hadn't understood. And who could blame her? She wasn't to know that Charlotte wanted a child more than she wanted anything else in the world. And that Jeff had promised she would have one here at Pencraig. Charlotte couldn't share any of that with Ellie. It seemed like a betrayal somehow.

And at least this way she could come and visit whenever she wanted. Only she didn't. They were even further apart. Ellie was independent now. Since going to Manchester, she'd forged her own life with her own friends. She hadn't needed Charlotte for a long while. How many times, in those Didsbury days, had Charlotte phoned her when Jeff was out, wanting to get together. Only to find she was busy, evasive. Every time. Ellie might have followed her to Manchester, but she'd lost her just as quickly. They only belonged together when they were here.

Perhaps one day they would be as close as they used to be. Perhaps.

She sighed. They were all so far away from her now. It had seemed the right thing to do – keeping Pencraig, giving Jeff his perfect dream, leaving her job so that Leonard would be free to move to France, maybe find a woman who could love him as he deserved to be loved.

And something had to change – she was going crazy in Manchester. Mindless and aching. Row after row, each one followed desperately by bed. Tears and pretences of solutions.

Only nothing had changed, not really. Leonard hadn't gone to France. He was still working from Manchester, and he even phoned her sometimes, his voice worried and distant. She wanted to invite him over, but how could she, now that Jeff had transferred him from a friend into a potential lover? If he came here she might go to bed with him. And that would be a mistake. That wouldn't save her. Leonard might be able to give her compassion and tenderness, but he'd never be able to give her a child.

And Jeff was never here, so he wouldn't give her a child either. He wouldn't even try out his dream.

She closed her eyes again. Felt the salty wetness on her cheeks. Here at Pencraig she felt tranquillised. Perhaps there was too much time. Too much time, too much space, too much solitude. She didn't miss Jeff like she missed Ellie. The thought made her sit up straighter with surprise. Perhaps it was just that Ellie would always be a part of this place. Ellie belonged here. It felt wrong without her.

Charlotte was alone, and barren as the stretches of sand between the rocks, exposed to the harshness of the sun when the tide was low. If she stared for long enough at the waves she could almost see her sanity slipping. Teetering on the edge of Devil's Rock. Would it go? Falling, screaming. Slowly submerged.

Hunger made Charlotte wander back towards the house. She walked slowly through the wood, stopping by the hideaway, thinking for a moment of those two girls and how they'd changed. Charlotte had always been the leader, but her strength had been sapped by circumstance. Now Ellie was the independent one, with a life and friends of her own.

How many friends did Charlotte have? Who missed her?

The path emerged from the wood, and because Charlotte had been thinking about Ellie, and because her mind wasn't tied too closely to reality these days, she took no notice of the slightly battered, burgundy-coloured Mini parked outside Pencraig. It was only when she saw Ellie herself flopped on the daisy-dotted grass outside the front door, that she did a double take. Followed by a rush of pure pleasure that almost made her forget the ache inside.

'Ellie!' She hurried up the path.

'Charlotte?' Ellie rubbed at her eyes as though she'd been asleep. She glanced down at her wristwatch. 'God, you've been ages. It was too hot to come looking for you, so I just flopped.'

Charlotte held out her arms and Ellie sprang up to run into them. Her skin smelt sweet, of grass cuttings.

'It's so good to see you.' And it was. Charlotte drew them apart so she could look at her properly. She was like a dream come true. All the trappings of city life that stood between them when they were in Manchester simply crumbled into dust at Pencraig. 'Why didn't you let me know you were coming?' She would have got herself together for Ellie, bought shopping, even tidied the house.

'It was a mad impulse.'

'One of your better ones.' Charlotte played with the ends of the fine blonde hair that hung past Ellie's shoulders now. Her face was fuller, more healthy. But the soft, green eyes had a troubled expression. There was something bothering her. Or she wouldn't be here. Charlotte blinked, the thought souring their reunion.

'And I wanted to surprise you.' Ellie was wearing a big straw sunhat. She took it off to fan her face. 'God, I'm sweltering to death out here. Let's go inside.'

'Okay.' Charlotte lifted the azalea's clay pot and scrabbled in the dirt for the key.

'I never dreamed you'd still keep it there.' For a moment her eyes glazed and she grabbed Charlotte's arm as if she was about to fall.

'Ellie?' Charlotte led her inside. 'Nothing's wrong is it?'

'It's just the heat.' Ellie spoke quickly, her gaze shifting away from her.

'I'll make some coffee.' Charlotte felt jumpy and ill at ease. Was it so long since she'd been sociable? This was Ellie sitting on the poppy and bluebell couch. This was the two of them, together at Pencraig.

'Juice for me.' Ellie got up to follow her into the kitchen, apparently unaware of the tension, although she was acting pretty strangely herself. 'It seems funny, me visiting you here. As if it should still be the other way round.' She paused. Glanced at her. 'Is everything all right?'

'Why?' Charlotte heard her own question rattle around the primrose walls of the kitchen.

Ellie frowned. 'Because you look tired. Worried. Thinner.' She surveyed Charlotte critically, reaching to brush the salt, that had dried in the sun, from the dark hair. She looked down at her equally dusty feet clad in red flip-flops. 'Are you eating properly?' Grabbing a cracker, she bit into it hungrily.

Charlotte laughed. 'You sound like someone's nanny.'

'Or someone's mother.' Ellie grinned. 'But not our mother.'

'Definitely not our mother.' Charlotte began to relax. It would be all right. She just needed time to adjust to company – even Ellie's company.

'Just so long as you're looking after yourself.' Ellie's green eyes narrowed. Charlotte could tell she wasn't convinced – she always had been able to see more than Charlotte wanted her to.

She wanted to tell her. She could feel the ache in her, this tight bud of pain, needing to burst into the open. If she was ever going to be released from it, she'd have to let it out – this desire, snapping into a longing that seemed to obliterate the rest of her life. But she felt ashamed of wanting a child that much. It wasn't natural, was it?

So she laughed, a weak kind of explosion that wouldn't fool anyone. 'You're imagining things.'

Ellie stared at her, her eyes unfathomable. She swung away. 'Why isn't Jeff ever here? He was the one who couldn't wait to get his hands on this place.'

She sounded so bitter. Had she minded that much? 'I always thought he wanted it for me.' Charlotte sighed. But what did she think now?

Ellie snorted. 'Who are you kidding? When didn't Jeff think of himself first and everyone else second?'

'I thought you liked him.' She never had thought that, not really. She'd assumed that they tolerated each other. Only sometimes Ellie seemed to know him better than Charlotte did herself. And she could always make him laugh.

Ellie shrugged. 'Was he right? Is this what you want, Charlotte? Never seeing him from one week to the next?'

'He's still busy with Alderley Towers. Even Jeff can't be in two places at once.' Charlotte hated the name of that house. Why was she bothering to defend him? Why didn't she just tell Ellie how miserable it all was? Being here alone.

Ellie clicked her tongue impatiently as though she didn't like the name of it either. 'Yes, I know. But that's not the point.'

'Then what is the point?' Charlotte led the way back into the sitting-room. And why had she come? There must be a reason.

Once more, Ellie settled herself on the couch. 'The point is that you're unhappy.'

So she had noticed after all. 'Maybe he wants to avoid me and my hang-ups.'

'You don't have hang-ups.' Ellie reached for her hand.

'Maybe not once upon a time.' Charlotte looked down at

the slim fingers entwined with her own, at the filigree ring that she'd given her. 'But now—'

'Everything's different now.' Smiling sadly, Ellie reached to brush some dried salt from Charlotte's cheek. 'You're sea-stained.'

There was a pause. If only Ellie could be here with her. Then perhaps even the worst kind of deprivation could be borne.

'Do you miss this place?' Her voice was soft.

Ellie looked out through the open window into the garden, and Charlotte followed the direction of her gaze. The hollyhocks were in full flower, lemon and cream in front of the buddleia.

'I'd like to frame it,' Ellie whispered. 'Sometimes, when I'm in the bed-sit, I imagine it all. Sometimes I can even smell this garden.'

Charlotte nodded, understanding perfectly.

'It's another world.' Ellie's voice grew dreamy. 'When I'm here I feel I could never leave. And when I'm away it pulls at me, and I have to push it out of my head to be able to do anything else at all.'

'I know what you mean.' Charlotte's voice was a whisper. She drew her chair closer. 'It's trying to make me put down roots.' She laughed uncertainly.

Ellie glanced at her, the worried frown returning. 'You don't have to stay here.'

'It seems like I do.' How could she begin to explain? But maybe she didn't have to with Ellie.

'I dream of coming back here to live one day.' Ellie smiled a secret smile. 'Maybe sooner than you think.'

'Can't be soon enough for me.' Their eyes met. How could she have ever thought she could live here without Ellie? It was no wonder she was going crazy.

Ellie looked away first. 'What about Jeff?'

Charlotte shrugged. 'He was always talking about country retreats and jungly gardens. A place where he could breathe.' But what did he talk about now?

Ellie raised sceptical eyebrows. 'Isn't that what Alderley Towers is earmarked for?'

'He wouldn't even stay there. He only liked the idea, not the reality. He was just dreaming. City bred, city dreaming.'

'We were city bred.'

'But we escaped.'

Ellie smiled. 'You're right. Jeff needs people too much. He really would go crazy here.'

'He does.' Charlotte stretched out long brown legs. Thought of his blue, restless eyes, his feet itching to be gone. 'He arrives on Saturday, and by Sunday afternoon he can't wait to leave. He probably only comes here for sex.'

That wasn't true. The opposite was true. She was trying to be light-hearted, expecting Ellie to laugh. But she didn't.

'Don't you mind?' Ellie's voice was low.

'Sometimes. Maybe things will be different one day.' That wasn't true either. Why was she bothering to pretend with Ellie?

It seemed useless, and yet a small part of Charlotte still had to believe that if Jeff made an effort, if they were together more, if he began to understand, then they could still be a partnership in every sense of the word. There was still so much connecting them. If they had a child, the rest might fall into place so easily.

'Perhaps you're right.' Ellie looked at her. 'But you don't look happy. You've got bags under your eyes, and you've started biting your nails again.'

Charlotte laughed. 'Stop it. Let's talk about you for a change.' She was beginning to relax at last. The breeze was blowing the old fragrances of the garden through the open window, and she reached out for Ellie's slender white hand. 'You're looking good. What's been going on? Have you found a new man or something?' No. She didn't want it to be that. A new man might stop Ellie from coming to Pencraig.

'No—' Ellie hesitated.

'What then?' Charlotte was casual, and for the first time in ages she was smiling.

'I'm pregnant,' Ellie said.

Charlotte stared at her. There was an awful, creaking silence in the room.

The first thing that Charlotte was aware of was the odd sensation of the word being played around in her head. Pregnant, pregnant, pregnant— the echo went on, as if the word meant something quite different. Soft and distant it was, and then so loud that Charlotte wanted to put her hands over her ears to stop it. Only that would be no use, because it came from inside. And things on the inside couldn't be muffled so easily. Then the pain came.

'Well, say something!' Ellie sounded nervous.

Charlotte was unable to grasp it. 'What did you say?'

'I said I'm pregnant.' She sounded exasperated now. 'With child. Expectant mother. Bun in the oven. Up the spout or whatever it is.'

'There's no need to be like that.' The fury arched through her entire body. The resentment. Against Ellie who had always got everything she ever wanted. 'Why do you have to be so bloody flippant? That's your trouble, Ellie, if you really want to know. You never take anything seriously.'

Ellie stared at her for a long moment, then shrugged and transferred her gaze to the hollyhocks.

Charlotte grabbed her arm. 'How can you be pregnant?

It's ridiculous. What are you talking about? Is this your idea of a joke?'

Ellie pulled away. 'No. You're hurting me, Charlotte.' She rubbed at the red fingertip-bruises on her skin.

Charlotte took a deep breath. Somewhere there was control. She just had to find it. Think mundane, that was the trick. 'Have some coffee.'

Ellie stared at her again. Her slanting green eyes were confused and hurt. 'I don't want any coffee.' She spoke slowly. 'It makes me feel sick. Because I'm pregnant.'

'I wish you'd stop saying that.' Charlotte took a few paces towards the door. 'I'll make myself some.' Stop looking at her. Leave the room. Just for a few minutes.

But she stayed where she was as if rooted to the spot, tense and unmoving. 'How can you be pregnant?'

How could she? How could it happen just like that for Ellie? When Charlotte wanted a baby so much that every barren month tore her insides to shreds. As if that was where all the blood was coming from. How could it have happened to Ellie? She managed a few more paces, but couldn't make it to the door. 'How did it happen?'

'Do you want me to tell you the facts of life, Charlotte?' Ellie's voice seemed unbearably sardonic and cruel.

'Shut up!'

Ellie looked away.

She was lying, feet up, on the bluebell and poppy couch, almost draped across it in a pose of relaxed fulfilment. Blooming, flowering, fulfilled and pregnant. Oh God. It was unbearable. Charlotte hated her. She dug her fists into her eyes to stop herself slapping Ellie's bright face. Ellie was alive. Next to her, Charlotte felt old and wasted, like an ageing grandmother with breasts sagging down to her stomach, whose reproductive organs had shrivelled and died. Like Charlotte's might as well have done.

She backed out of the room, then seconds later re-appeared. 'Whose is it? Who's the father?' It was hard to keep her voice steady.

Ellie pulled herself upright. 'That's not important.'

'Not important!' She was close to exploding point. Ellie was unbelievable. What was wrong with the girl? How could she take a gift like this one and pretend that it meant nothing?

'How can you say that?' Her voice rose. 'There's a man wandering around, God knows where, who just happens to be the father of this child— And you say it's not important who he is. Isn't it important for him, that he's the father of your child? Your child, Ellie. Your child—' Charlotte stopped abruptly. She felt dizzy.

Still Ellie stayed on the couch, silently watching her. Her face was paler than ever, her eyes wider.

Charlotte put a hand to her head. 'Or maybe it was an immaculate conception? Is that how it happened, Ellie? My God!' She gripped the back of the armchair by the door. Otherwise she'd fall. 'You have to go one better, don't you? You're so selfish. Always, always so bloody selfish. Have you spared a thought for the child? Won't it matter to the— to the—' She faltered. That word was hard. 'To the baby. That its mother doesn't have the least idea who fucked her into conception?' She was shaking and panting uncontrollably.

In one swift movement, Ellie rose to her feet. 'It's all right, darling.' She took Charlotte's arm and guided her back to her chair. 'It's all right. Don't worry. Calm down.' She knelt at her feet. 'What is it? Tell me what's wrong with you.' There was a passionate urgency in her voice.

But Charlotte couldn't answer her.

'It's okay now. It's okay, my darling.' Ellie reached for

her hand but Charlotte snatched it away. She couldn't even bear to touch her.

Ellie got up, immediately distant once more, her green eyes lost and unfathomable. 'I'll make you that coffee you wanted.'

She came back with a steaming cup five minutes later. Warily she placed it on the coffee table next to Charlotte and then sat down again on the couch opposite.

'You don't know who the father is, do you?' Charlotte felt numb. It was beyond her comprehension. She couldn't understand promiscuity – it was hard enough to give yourself to one person. And to get pregnant! Not know whose genes were mingling with your own.

'Yes, I know.' Ellie looked down at her orange juice.

'Who is it then? Why won't you tell me?' Charlotte's voice was rising again. The cup was rattling in the saucer.

'He's attached. Married.'

'Married! Jesus, Ellie. How could you let yourself get involved with a married man? What the hell are you playing at?' She might have guessed – judging by Ellie's past record. 'Does he know? Have you told him?'

Ellie shook her head.

'Has he got children of his own?'

'Does it matter?'

Charlotte slammed down the cup and saucer on the coffee table. 'Of course it matters. How can you think it doesn't matter? How can you be so— so blasé about this?'

Ellie shrugged. 'I didn't mean it to happen. But it did. Screaming about it won't make it go away. I don't know what's got into you, and you're obviously not going to tell me. But if I'd ever dreamt you'd react like this I'd never have come here. This would have been the last place I'd have come. You can be sure of that.' She sniffed. 'Why did

I imagine I should tell you first? What an idiot. Why should you understand?'

Charlotte gazed at her, almost sightlessly, suddenly aware of the vulnerability behind the façade. Funny, she'd always known that about Ellie and yet she'd forgotten about it today. Her brave face, her ways of coping with fear. Ellie wasn't blasé or arrogant. She was worried. She was scared too.

'What are you going to do?' she asked in a softer voice.

'I haven't made up my mind. I came here because I needed to think things through.'

Charlotte shivered. A sudden thought struck her. 'You're not thinking of getting rid of this baby are you, Ellie?' In a moment she was on her knees, next to the couch, as if this could prevent Ellie from considering the option.

'I don't know yet.' Absent-mindedly, Ellie began to stroke Charlotte's thick, dark hair. 'I'm sorry, love,' she said. 'I shouldn't have sprung it on you like that. You're right. It was a bloody stupid thing to let happen.'

Charlotte grabbed her hand. 'Don't, Ellie.' Her voice was thick with urgency. 'This baby is alive. A living being. You can't murder it.'

Ellie shuddered. 'I didn't realise you felt like that about abortion.'

'I don't. I didn't.' How could she tell her now? How could she tell her that the idea of abortion was like a death to her too. Ellie held the decision in the palm of her hand. She could go either way, knowing Ellie, depending on how the mood took her. And yet if she kept it— Charlotte couldn't think of Ellie with a baby. She was still a child herself.

'Promise me,' she said. 'Promise me you won't do anything rash until we've talked this through. Promise me you won't do anything without telling me.' Promises, promises.

For a moment Charlotte was transported back into that other summer. 'Promise me—'

'Okay.' Ellie got up and wandered to the window.

'Should I tell Jeff?'

'No!'

Charlotte blinked hard, not realising she'd spoken aloud. But she couldn't blame Ellie for wanting to keep it quiet. Times had changed but even Ellie wasn't as liberated as she liked to pretend.

'It's a big responsibility.' Frantically Charlotte sifted options through her head. If Ellie didn't want the baby— if Ellie couldn't cope with the baby— Maybe? It might be the answer. After all, the baby would be almost family. Ellie was such a dreamer. How could she take on motherhood? It would be too much for her. How could she cope as a single parent with no income and no home?

The pain was diminishing. The baby was a gift. A part of Charlotte too. A lifeline. There was no father. Ellie was right – the father didn't matter. They could manage without him. Because Ellie had Charlotte to look after her and the baby. Charlotte felt reasoned and capable again. They were a family already.

She looked fondly at her sister. Charlotte wanted to take care of everybody now. She needed to do that. It would help her. And it would be all right. There was no need to worry. No need at all.

10

The following day heralded more blistering heat – three days of temperatures like these, and it was an English heatwave. By mid-afternoon Jeff was sweating in the white long-sleeved shirt he'd worn to the meeting with the bank manager that morning. The heat was on all right. He waited for Charlotte to answer the phone.

'Come on, woman.' The ringing tone continued. Where the hell was she? Jeff pulled off his tie. Still no answer. It was the seventh time he'd tried today. He tapped his gold-plated pen impatiently on Sylvie and Reg Stoddart's dining-table.

Above the table were two narrow shelves filled with tacky mementoes of Sylvie and Reg's holidays in Clacton, Torquay and St Ives. And under the table and round the room the patterned carpet waged war with the equally abrasive pattern of the curtains and wallpaper. 'Scrambled eggs and fireworks,' Jeff murmured.

'Come on, Charlotte. Answer the bloody phone.' She was getting so vague these days that sometimes Jeff wondered if he'd screwed up by uprooting her and taking her back to Pencraig. It had seemed the perfect solution when Olivia mentioned it, too good a chance to miss. Not exactly the right time – he knew that, but when opportunities fell into your lap you didn't always check your watch.

Jeff had never wanted a career woman, although he often believed that he did. What he wanted was someone to take care of him while he got on with the business. Someone to be there at all the right times. He'd never wanted a door-mat though – he admired independent women. Just so long as they knew when to give in. And he didn't want women docile in bed. In bed he definitely preferred his women wild.

But he should have waited. It was no good like this – the control was slipping through his fingers. He should have waited until things were sorted in Manchester, so he could spend a bit more time at Pencraig himself. He needed to keep a closer eye on things. Right now there was so much craving his attention, clawing at him for time, that Charlotte and Wales were well out of the frame. And the way she was acting wasn't any inducement for him to spend time with her. This baby thing was getting well out of hand.

But at the time it hadn't been that simple. There was Olivia itching for London and itching to do the deal. Women had no patience when it came to deals – they decided on a direction to take and wanted to arrive there yesterday.

He wanted his woman – the right woman, Charlotte, to be waiting for him. But as it was, she wasn't waiting for him, docile or otherwise, because she wasn't answering the bloody phone. Again.

As Jeff sighed and began to shift the receiver from his ear, she answered.

'Hello?' She was out of breath.

'Charlotte? Where've you been?' Jeff spoke more sharply than he'd intended. He wasn't after a long-distance row.

'I was in the garden. It's such a beautiful afternoon.'

As if he hadn't noticed. The heatwave had hit the entire British Isles. 'I've been trying to get you all day.' He couldn't keep the peevishness out of his voice. Peevishness was supposed to belong exclusively to women.

'You can't expect me to hang around by the phone waiting for you to call.' She paused. 'Or is that what you do expect, Jeff?'

He could hear it in her voice – the old snap, snap, snap that got him going. All the time he tried to make her meek and mild, docile as a lamb, producing beef Stroganoff one minute, and a see-through black body stocking the next, Jeff knew that he wouldn't still be with her if it wasn't for the snap, snap, snap. It hadn't been there for a while and he realised with a shock that he was relieved to hear it now. Without it, she'd seemed to be drifting away from him.

'I can't help worrying about you, sweetie,' he soothed. 'You know me – I get on edge. You're such a long way away.'

'And whose fault is that?' She was quick as a flash.

'I miss you, Charlotte.' His voice was only a whisper. It was true. Sometimes. But was it often enough?

'It wasn't *me* who decided to live here.' Her voice was brisk. She didn't want to hear protestations of love, he could tell. And could he blame her?

'I know that. But I thought I'd be there with you. I didn't expect to be so tied up in Manchester.'

'It was your dream. Remember?' Was there a wistfulness in that soft velvet voice of hers? Or did he just want there to be?

'But you love living there. You always said it was paradise.'

'Even paradise gets jaded without anyone here to share it.'

He caught his breath. Was the old Charlotte coming back to him at last? 'I know, love. I'm sorry.'

'Jeff? When will you be home?'

He hadn't heard that excitement in her voice for a long

time. He licked his dry lips, wanting her. 'Things are still on the sticky side. I'll have to stay a bit longer to keep everyone on their toes. But I'll be there soon. I promise.'

'Still so indispensable?'

''Fraid so.' He crossed long legs and leaned back in the fragile cane chair. 'Jesus, it's such a bore. I'd much rather be there now, with you.' He made rapid calculations. How soon could he make it? He had to see Eloise first, find out about Melanie and her big mouth. And then he had to wait for the builders to finish the job. Bloody load of skivers. 'Maybe next weekend?'

'Hmm. Can't you make it any sooner?'

Something had happened. Charlotte's moods didn't change so quickly for no reason. But what the hell could it be? What could happen to Charlotte in a place like Pencraig? There was nothing there.

Sylvie knocked lightly and entered the room, with a whisky bottle, a jug of water and a glass on a tray. Jeff put his hand over the receiver. 'Thanks, sweetie. I'm almost finished here.'

She flashed him a smile as she left the room. Open invitation. Sylvie was a tart, but any woman who fancied Jeff couldn't be all bad.

Reg was off out tonight, and Jeff knew that Sylvie would be open to offers. She'd have to be pretty persuasive though, because Jeff wasn't intending to abuse their hospitality. With the Didsbury house full of lodgers, he didn't have too many choices when Eloise was unavailable. He'd certainly been reluctant to test the water there for the last two days. And although Reg wasn't a mate, he and Jeff went way back. Reg was more useful as an ally than an enemy. And Sylvie Stoddart wasn't worth the risk.

The trouble with women like Sylvie, who needed to persuade themselves that they'd still got what it takes at forty-five, was that they wanted their husbands to know it too. That's when the trouble always started.

'I hate to think of you all alone, sweetness,' Jeff murmured into the phone. He loved it really. All alone and waiting for him. Delicious thought. It had been a long time.

'I'm not.'

'How d'you mean?'

'Ellie's here.'

Jeff sat bolt upright in the chair. 'Eloise?' Jesus, no. Not at Pencraig with Charlotte.

'Yep. She just turned up out of the blue.'

'Oh yeah?' Sure she did. Out of the blue. Just like Melanie had been sitting in the wine bar. Talking to Eloise. Out of the blue. He couldn't trust Melanie to keep her mouth shut. But could he trust Eloise? That question had been plaguing him since the night before last.

The answer wasn't long in coming. Not the way he could trust Charlotte. Because Eloise was still an unknown quantity for Jeff. He hadn't yet discovered what really made her tick.

How had she taken it? Had she gone crazy or told Melanie to go to hell? He didn't know. Or had she come over all holier than thou, about to blow the whistle with Charlotte? Jeff tasted panic.

'You're right in a way.' Charlotte's voice was mysterious. 'There was a reason for her coming. Something she wanted to tell me.'

'What?' His palms were sweating and the telephone receiver was becoming wet and slippery.

'I can't tell you what.'

Because she didn't know yet? Because Eloise was playing one of her little games?

'I wouldn't believe everything you hear.' He laughed. 'We all know that Eloise has got one hell of a vivid imagination.'

'Do we?'

He recognised the defensive note in her voice that materialised whenever Eloise was mentioned. It made him sick. In a way it would be satisfying for her to find out. To see her face when she discovered that her darling sister wasn't as sweet as a summer's day. That little Ellie had been fucking her husband since before they were married. Since the day their father died. She wouldn't be so bloody defensive then.

'She exaggerates,' he said. He was handling this badly. He knew it. Not so long ago he'd been able to talk his way out of anything. The challenge of doing so had been a pleasure in itself. But lately Jeff had seen the grinning face of failure peering over his shoulder in the mirror while he was shaving. Waiting for a turn with the razor. Since he'd bought Alderley Towers. Since he'd bought Pencraig. He'd overstretched himself badly. He'd made a mistake. And it had changed his vision of himself as much as it had scared him. Self-confidence, apparently, was a tenuous thing.

'She's always had it in for me,' he grumbled. 'Maybe she'd hate anyone who took you out of her clutches.'

'Don't be stupid.' Charlotte sounded surprised. 'Who said it's anything about you?'

'But if it's not about me—' He got no further.

'Listen, Jeff. I have to run. I'll call you later – okay?' She put the phone down before he had a chance to reply.

Jeff held on to the receiver for a while, staring into an empty space peopled only by the figures on Sylvie's wall-paper. He had to think fast and act even quicker. He was helpless while he was so far away. There was nothing else for it. He must get to Pencraig tonight. He had to get to Eloise before she told Charlotte everything.

'Damn,' he swore softly. Damn Melanie for doing this to him. And damn Eloise too.

He told Sylvie where he was going, ignored the unveiled regret on her face, picked up his car keys and a few things, and was out of the door within fifteen minutes.

He drove quickly and confidently down the motorway. He should never have bought the bloody place. He'd hoped to pick it up for a song, but Olivia had driven a hard bargain. Mean old cow – somehow she'd got the better of him. God alone knew how, although the night before his wedding had been mentioned.

'Charlotte would leave you if she ever found out.' Her green eyes, so like Eloise's eyes, were half-hidden by the brim of her black straw hat.

'I don't intend that she ever will.'

Olivia shrugged. 'It may not be up to you.'

'Is that a threat?' Jeff stood tall, towering over her – the only way he could feel strong enough to deal with this woman.

'Don't be ridiculous.' She laughed. And he felt ridiculous.

Jeff had been forced to take on a massive mortgage, because of his financial commitment to Alderley Towers, and because he had no hope of shifting the Didsbury house until the market improved. And he had to accept a loan from Olivia. There were no other avenues.

'No interest. As long as you behave yourself.' She put her slim hand on his arm.

What the hell was that supposed to mean?

'I'll have to give you something.' No way was Jeff going to owe this woman a bean. He couldn't afford to. She'd destroy him first.

She brushed this aside. 'We'll come to an arrangement later. But don't forget that I still have an interest in Pencraig.'

He looked into the green eyes. That's exactly what was worrying him.

'And don't tell the girls.' There was a certain breathiness in Olivia's voice. A few fine tendrils of fair hair escaped from the confines of the black straw hat. 'It'll be our little secret.'

Silly bitch. Too much money to play with, and not enough sense. 'You must want something out of it.' Jeff looked her up and down, from the perfectly made-up face, past the elegant black dress into which her slim body was moulded, and down the length of her slender legs in their sheer black stockings. She was still in very good shape. He had to admit that.

'Nothing. Yet—' She smiled slowly. 'But you're a man of the world. Perhaps you could give me some advice— on my investments.'

'My pleasure.' His voice was sardonic, and he lounged, hands in the pockets of his jeans as she pulled some papers from her bag. But his expression slowly changed and his frown deepened as he heard what she had to say.

'You've got that much to invest?'

She laughed – a tinkling kind of laugh. 'Oh, there's lots more. Believe me, Jeff. Lots more.'

'I bet.'

But it was one hell of a shock, discovering just how much she'd walked away with, and that she didn't mind him knowing – virtually flaunted it in his face. Bloody shame as well, because Jeff could have done with some of it. What would Charlotte and Ellie say if they knew? Charlotte always said that her father had drunk the last of his money.

But if that was the case – then where was all this dosh coming from?

Olivia had come to Manchester twice since that day, to discuss her 'stocks and shares'. Although Jeff was never sure if she was worried about her money or checking up on him. Ensuring that the night with her younger daughter had only been a one-night stand, not the beginning of some sort of ménage à trois or long-lasting affair.

Or did she come with something much more basic in mind? Jeff smiled. He wouldn't put it past her. She was high-class material, but also the kind of flirt who needed a damn good seeing to. He chuckled softly. The idea of sex always cheered him up. But not with Olivia. Now there he really would draw the line.

Jeff put his foot down harder on the accelerator. He had to get to Pencraig. And the sooner the better.

In the garden at Pencraig Ellie was suffocating – from the weather which was sultry once more, and from Charlotte who was much the same. She followed Ellie around with only one topic of conversation. The baby. The baby had rapidly grown in importance. Grown and multiplied and taken over. At least taken over Charlotte.

She criticised everything from Ellie's diet to whether she might strain herself swimming. Christ, she was driving her crazy. Ellie was beginning to feel as she'd felt as a child – with no say, no mind of her own. Not even a body of her own now. Only a will – for ever frustrated.

Yesterday it had been pleasant to laze around being waited on, fantasizing about a remote kind of motherhood that was free from practical restraints. It was easy for Ellie to slip into this kind of mood with Charlotte, because it had always been a bit like that with Charlotte – no tension, no strings. Just Charlotte taking the lead. A mother figure, almost.

But it had gone on for too long. This wasn't what she'd come here for. She'd come to talk things through. She needed advice and comfort. Not all this mothering shit.

'Want some milk?' Charlotte poked her head round the door. She smiled. 'Jeff phoned earlier, by the way. He wanted to know why you're here.'

'No milk, thanks.' Ellie smiled back, imagining what Jeff must be thinking. The uncertainty would do him good. It was about time he wasn't so sure of her.

'Don't sit in the sun for too long. You'll get a headache.'

A frown replaced the smile. 'I like it.' Ellie pushed back her huge sunhat and spread out her arms to the sun. She was feeling contrary – like a child herself.

'Have some milk then,' Charlotte coaxed.

'I hate milk. You know I hate milk. I've always hated it.' Even the thought of it made Ellie feel sick. I'll have some juice instead.'

'You shouldn't have too much acid in the stomach. Milk's better for you.'

'I bloody hate milk,' Ellie snapped. Charlotte was being unbelievably irritating. But she'd never got mad with her before.

'All right, all right.' She came over to plump up cushions on the hammock as if Ellie was an invalid. 'Don't get yourself into a state. It's bad for the baby.'

Ellie glared at her again. The baby. Damn the wretched baby. What had happened to Ellie when that egg got fertilised inside her? How had she become a mere incubator? Much more of this from Charlotte and she'd begin to hate the baby.

She stroked her stomach. Of course she wouldn't, not really. She'd been surprised at some of the good feelings that pregnancy had given her – along with the inevitable morning sickness. Ellie had never wanted a baby. Noisy, messy things. There were enough cretins in the world already, she felt, without adding to the population.

But this baby would be special. If she kept it. It was a dark thought. But adoption might be a way out. Gooey biological sensations wouldn't get up in the middle of the night when the baby was crying. When it came down to the nitty gritty, she was a single girl who'd hardly begun to live her own life. Did she want to be saddled with nappies and tantrums?

Charlotte brought out the juice. 'We should think about names.' Her hazel eyes were dense and dreaming.

'That's a bit premature, isn't it?' But it was a pleasant thought, quite remote from those uncomfortable practicalities. And it was one she'd had already. 'Alex. I thought I'd call the baby Alex.'

'Girl or boy?'

'Either.'

'Well, which do you want?' Charlotte leaned closer.

Ellie smiled. 'A boy who's so good at pretending that he never loses face—' She laughed. 'Or a girl who's judged by it.'

'Cynic.' Charlotte took hold of Ellie's hand and began playing with her fingers.

'A girl.' Ellie looked at her. A girl to replace the girl that Ellie once was. Not any more though.

'When does the doctor say it's due?'

Ellie looked away. 'I haven't actually seen a doctor yet.'

'Ellie!' She seemed horrified. 'You are sure about this?'

'Unless missed periods and two positive home pregnancy kits can mean something else.' Ellie laughed humourlessly.

Charlotte smiled. 'That's good.'

'It is?' Ellie shook her head with bewilderment. What had got into her? She'd reacted like a spitfire when she first heard the news, and now anyone would believe this was a pregnancy planned in heaven. Was Charlotte going crazy, here alone at Pencraig? It was beginning to seem that way.

'Of course it's good!' Charlotte grasped her arm. 'This is a living being, Ellie. A part of you. This baby is a gift.' Her nails bit into Ellie's flesh.

She pulled away. 'Don't talk like that. I don't want to hear that shit. I haven't even decided what I'm going to do, for Christ's sake.'

'Do?' Charlotte paled. A spear of pain shot through her dark eyes. 'Please don't say you're going to—'

'I think it's too late for that.' Ellie sighed. 'I'm over four months gone already.'

'Thank God.'

Ellie turned from her in disgust. Olivia would have been more in tune with her needs than Charlotte had proved to be. And who'd have thought she'd ever say that?

'You'll have to see a doctor.' Charlotte ran fingers through her dark hair. 'A good doctor who'll look after you through to the birth. Give you the proper ante-natal care. Then there's the National Childbirth Trust. They do classes – I could come with you. Doctor Hill is a lamb and—'

'Charlotte!' Ellie stared at her. 'I won't be going to Doctor Hill. I won't be having the baby here. I'll be in Manchester.'

Ellie surprised herself with these words. It was true that she'd half-thought of coming back here, although she'd also wondered how on earth she was going to live. Wasn't Pencraig still home? Wouldn't it always be? But Charlotte had made that impossible. Now Ellie just needed to get away.

Besides, how could she stomach the looks from the

people in the village, who would all turn round and say I told you so. The gossip from the interfering Miss Pringle and all the rest, the thought of Doctor Hill who'd given Ellie her first contraceptive pill and lecture on sexual behaviour! It was horrible to contemplate. Far better the clinical approach of a big city hospital where you could be a nobody. That was safer every time.

'Oh.' Charlotte looked deflated. 'I wanted to help you through it all. I thought you'd want to be here.' She looked at Ellie as if she'd suddenly become a bewildering stranger. 'I assumed you'd come back here to live—' The expression in her hazel eyes was pure desolation.

'Why do you want me to?' Ellie felt the need for bluntness.

'So I can give you moral support.'

'But why?' The moral support she was getting from her right now had slipped into the minus stakes.

'Because you're my sister of course.' Charlotte looked away. 'I care about you.' Her voice was husky.

'Don't give me that.' Ellie knelt in front of her. 'Tell me what this is all about. Tell me what's wrong with you. I know you care about me, but there's more to it than that. You're acting so crazy. You seem like you're in another world. I'm knocking on the door, but you just won't let me in.'

She took hold of both Charlotte's hands, lifting them in rhythm with her words. But she still wouldn't look at her.

'What's wrong?' Ellie let go of her limp hands and they fell back into Charlotte's lap. 'You're not thinking of what's best for me, are you? You're only thinking about this baby.'

When she spoke these words, Charlotte raised her head, and as she caught sight of the pain in her dark eyes, it all fell into place for Ellie. Of course. It explained everything.

'Why didn't you tell me, for Christ's sake?' It was only a whisper.

Charlotte looked as if she was going to cry. 'We've been trying for ages. It's been a nightmare. I couldn't tell anyone.' Her voice was an emotionless monotone, and her shoulders drooped in defeat.

'You poor darling.' Ellie took her in her arms. Why hadn't Jeff told her? Jesus, how could he have let this happen to Charlotte, without telling her? How could he leave her here alone in this state of mind? It was almost as bad as murder.

Charlotte drew back. There were tears on her cheeks, but her eyes were eager and brighter. 'This might be our chance, Ellie.'

'How d'you mean?' A sense of foreboding settled on Ellie's mind.

'I'd have to talk to Jeff of course—' The words tumbled out of her. 'But don't you see? This could be the answer to everyone's problems.'

As her meaning gradually penetrated, Ellie's world sprang into nightmare. Charlotte wanted her baby. That's why she was being so motherly. She wanted her baby. For her and Jeff. So much for caring. Charlotte didn't give a shit about what Ellie was going through. She was too submerged in her own problems.

Ellie twisted away. 'Thanks for consulting me about my baby's future.' Her voice was brittle and cold.

'I thought it was too soon.' Charlotte took Ellie's face in her hands like a lover might. 'Don't be angry. We could work it out, you and me. You know we could always work anything out if we tried.' Her voice tailed off as she looked into Ellie's eyes. 'It just seemed like such a good idea.'

'For you perhaps.' This baby obsession must have taken

over Charlotte's senses. She didn't even realise what she was proposing. That Jeff should adopt his natural child. But of course, Charlotte wasn't to know that. And she wasn't to know that Jeff mustn't be told – not yet.

'Don't tell Jeff.' Ellie's voice was strained with urgency. 'Promise me you won't tell him. Please?'

She had to tell him herself. She'd been scared he might jump to all the wrong conclusions. And she'd needed to tell Charlotte first, although now she was beginning to wonder why. But now she must tell Jeff. Because Charlotte was right. The father did matter. He was part of the whole picture. The whole cluttered, chaotic picture. Ellie hung her head. Her fault. She should never have allowed it to go on for so long. Allowed passion to drown what little common sense she retained when Jeff's body was near her own.

Charlotte nodded. 'I promise.' She tugged at Ellie's sleeve. 'I do love you, Ellie. You know how much I care about you. It's just that – can't you understand? I want a baby more than anything.'

Something protective stirred inside Ellie. She moved away from Charlotte as if she were hostile, a threat.

'I'm sorry,' she said stiffly. 'I had no idea.' It would happen at Pencraig— Jeff's words came back to her. He had used Charlotte's longing to get her here. The bastard.

No way. There was no way in the world that Jeff and Charlotte would ever get this baby. The idea was obscene.

'But will you think about it?'

There was such an air of urgency about her, that even now, as she shrank from her, Ellie was unable to deny Charlotte absolutely. She seemed just too desperate and sad. Jeff would have to break it to her. About time he did some of the bloody work. He'd had it too easy all along.

She looked at Charlotte, trying to imagine what it must

be like to want a baby that much. And considering the irony of what had happened to her – forgetting contraception for a few precious days, and conceiving from the very same man.

'I'll think about it.' Ellie hated the lie. Damn bloody Jeff. He'd built a wall between Ellie and Charlotte that was just about insurmountable now.

She looked at her watch. 'But I've got to be getting back to Manchester. Back to work.' Back to Jeff. She had to see Jeff, tell him what had happened. Tell him that it was over.

Charlotte was wringing her hands. Her eyes had a wildness about them. 'You will come back?'

Ellie sighed. 'I'll phone you.'

If only Jeff had told her how much Charlotte wanted a baby. If only she'd been more careful. If only—

'My life's a bloody mess.' Ellie got slowly to her feet, and went inside to get her things.

Jeff arrived at Pencraig a short time later, to find Charlotte pacing the kitchen with a broom in her hand. There was a vapidity in her eyes, as she turned to face him, that repelled him.

'Where's Eloise?'

'Gone.' Charlotte started sweeping. 'The house is a mess. It needs cleaning.'

Jeff grabbed her arm. 'Gone? Gone where?'

Charlotte looked down at the hand. 'And I've missed you too, husband mine,' she whispered.

She looked up at him with ringed, red-raw eyes. It shocked him. She shocked him. What had happened to her since he'd spoken to her on the phone? Had Eloise told her – about Melanie? About him and Eloise? She must have.

Taking a deep breath, he released her arm and drew her gently towards him, half-expecting her to struggle, claw at him.

'Sorry, sweetness.'

She didn't resist him, but she was trembling like a frightened animal. All the self-containment, Charlotte's control that he'd often wanted to dent, was lost. Never before had she allowed him to get this close. And never had he felt so far away. It scared him. The snap, snap, snap was all gone.

'What's happened? What's she been saying?'

Charlotte looked as if she'd lost her world. So she cared about him more than he'd ever suspected. Eloise had told her, and Charlotte had sent her away. As he tangled his fingers through her thick dark hair, Jeff began planning his defence.

But Charlotte was silent, only burrowing into his shoulder for some deeper comfort. Then she cried for the first time since he'd known her, in his arms. He held her, patting her back, stroking her hair, making the right noises but still planning his defence.

'Don't cry.' He forced her a few inches away so that he could see her eyes. 'What's happened?' Rule one – find out how much you've got to deny. Only defend the absolute minimum.

She shook her head fiercely like a dog coming out of water. 'I can't tell you. I promised Ellie.'

The anger came from nowhere, burying his sympathy. So Eloise still came first. After everything she'd done. 'Then I can't help you, can I?' His voice was cold. He turned, ignoring her pleading dark eyes. He would only be her hero if she trusted him. There was no room for secrets here.

'When did she go?'

'You must have passed her on the road.' She moved with

some kind of automatic control now, away from him, to pick up a duster from the table. She resumed her robotic cleaning.

'Did you tell her to leave?'

'Of course not. I'd never want Ellie to go.'

No, of course she bloody wouldn't. Jeff clenched his fist and smashed it down on the table. 'Where's she gone?'

'Back to Manchester.'

He frowned. What the hell was Eloise playing at? He stared out of the window at the blackness outside. He had to see her, he was becoming half-crazy himself with the need to see her. 'I'll have to go back,' he said to himself.

'But you've only just got here.' Charlotte stared at him. 'Why did you bother to come? You said you were too busy.'

'I am.' He took her by the shoulders. Her shoulders felt bony. She was getting skinny. It was a long time since Jeff had seen Charlotte naked. 'I'm worried about you, Charlotte.'

Her eyes were blank.

'But if you won't tell me what's wrong—'

She hung her head. With a sigh of frustration Jeff roughly forced her chin upwards and kissed her hard on the lips. It was violent rather than passionate. When he broke away she stared at him, her hazel eyes still expressionless, as she carefully touched her bruised lip with the tip of her tongue.

'Tell me, Charlotte! What's she been saying?'

'She doesn't want me to tell you. And I've let her down enough already.'

'At least I know where your loyalties lie.' Jeff slumped into the nearest chair. 'Some wives tell their husbands everything.'

'Not this wife.' Charlotte leaned against the door-frame. She looked slightly mad, her dark hair dishevelled, her lip swollen and her eyes glazed.

Jeff stared at her. This wasn't the woman he'd married. 'You need to get away from here.'

'I need—' She took a few uncertain steps towards him. 'I need—'

For one insane moment Jeff imagined she was going to try and suffocate him with the duster that was still in her hand. It was bizarre. She looked like something out of *Psycho*.

'What? What do you need?'

She came closer. Closer still. Sank to her knees, and buried her face in his thighs. 'I need a baby, Jeff,' she whispered. 'Oh, God, I need a baby so much.' She was weeping into the duster.

Jesus, not this again. He couldn't stand it. Not now.

'Come with me to the hospital,' she pleaded. She began pounding his legs with her clenched fists. 'I've got all these leaflets for you to read, there's so much we have to talk about. But you're never here. I need you to come with me.'

He turned away from her in disgust. The same old record. She was pathetic. He hated that. It turned his stomach.

'Not now, Charlotte. It isn't the right time.'

To his surprise, she nodded and rose to her feet. 'You're right. We should wait for her to get herself sorted out, think things through, come to her senses. She'll realise it's the obvious answer to everything. And then, who can tell? Brothers and sisters are terribly important, Jeff. I know that. There shouldn't be only one.'

He frowned. Brothers? Sisters? What the hell was she on about? 'Are you talking about Eloise?'

'Of course.' Charlotte reached out for the phone. She dusted it tenderly before glancing up at the piece of paper pinned next to the calendar. She smiled slowly. 'Why don't you stay here tonight? It's far too late to drive back now.

You can't possibly, you'll be exhausted. Go first thing in the morning.'

Jeff wavered. He didn't relish the idea of the drive, he needed to rest and eat. And God knows, sex with Charlotte in this mood would be a new experience. Would she bring the duster to bed? Then he followed the direction of her gaze. The temperature chart. The passion-killer. He shook his head. 'No. Not tonight.'

'Jeff!' She flung the duster across the room. Tears filled her eyes once more.

Something inside him snapped. 'I can't bloody do it to order. With you underneath me, stroking my back, trying to make me come so that you can start playing baby machines. What do you think I am?' He paused. His breathing was thick and heavy. She was driving him into some kind of insanity, and he wasn't going to go there. Not for her. Not for anyone. 'It shouldn't be like that, Charlotte.'

'No. It shouldn't be like that at all.' She stared at him.

Jeff grabbed his jacket. 'I've got to go. I'm sorry, Charlotte. But you're not making any sense. And I can't help you if you won't even tell me what's wrong.'

'Hell of a way to come for a loveless kiss and a row,' she murmured.

Jeff hesitated in the doorway, torn, watching her. What should he do? Of course he should stay with her, hold her, make love to her, tell her that everything was all right, and only leave when she believed him. Maybe he would have done that if she'd only told him what Eloise had said.

But there were more important fish to fry. There was Eloise – he had to get to her, and quick. Wandering around with Melanie's stories in her head, there was no knowing how much damage she could do. And she might throw some light on what was happening to his wife.

'Charlotte—' He was still unsure.

She waved her hand. It was like a dismissal. 'I'm fine. Go.'

It was the absolution he needed. 'I'll be back in a couple of days. Sooner if I can. For a proper stay this time. I promise we'll talk things through. All of it.' He blew her a kiss. 'Take care, sweetie.'

Once he had the time, he was confident he'd sort it out. There was nothing wrong with Charlotte that couldn't be fixed, once he gave her his undivided attention. Outside the door he paused.

'It'll be too late then,' he heard her say.

Bloody temperature chart. Jeff strode to the car. Women and their hormones had a way of buggering things up.

11

Jeff didn't make it in time for Pasha's wine bar, and he didn't fancy getting the stroppy cow who managed the place down at midnight to let him in. So instead he returned to Reg and Sylvie's where he could be sure of his welcome.

Sylvie looked suitably pleased to see him. Reg had gone on to a poker club and would apparently be some time, so Jeff allowed himself to be lured upstairs by a black négligé and a glimpse of a black, lacy stocking-top. It wasn't in the game plan, but Charlotte's behaviour had left him with a frustration and guilt that could be quenched quite nicely by Sylvie's ample breasts. And black stockings had often been Jeff's undoing.

But in the morning he felt worse than ever as he went looking for Eloise, venting some of his anger on the heavy oak outer door of the wine bar.

'What the hell do you want?' Sarah Freeman's angry face appeared, as she poked her head round the door.

He raised dark eyebrows. What was her problem – apart from the obvious? 'I want to see Eloise.' He paused. 'And I want to see her now.'

'Is that right?' Sarah opened the door a few more inches and looked him up and down. Her eyes were bleary. She looked about as bad as Jeff felt.

He sighed. He was in no mood for bantering conversation. 'Yes, that's right.' He glanced at his watch, looked once more at Sarah, and softened slightly. 'Look,

I know it's a pretty indecent hour but—'

'When you've been up half the night, yes, it is rather.' Sarah's hostile eyes sparked into challenge. She looked as though she enjoyed this sort of thing.

'That's hardly my fault.' His voice was crisp.

'Since I've been talking to Ellie till three in the morning, that's a matter of opinion.' Still, she made no move either to let him in or call Eloise down.

Jeff frowned. 'What about?'

'None of your business,' she snapped. 'When she wants to tell you, she'll do it herself.'

If you give her the chance, he thought.

'But I'm warning you—' Sarah stepped closer. She smelled of sleep and a lazy kind of sex appeal.

'Yes?' He smiled. Lesser women than this one had crumpled for his smile.

Sarah hesitated, but a film of resistance came down like a blind over her angry eyes. 'If you kick her while she's down—'

'Yes? What'll you do?' He couldn't resist teasing her. She looked so indignant and serious, standing on the doorstep in her fluffy, pink mules and quilted dressing-gown. He allowed his gaze to rove over her bedtime garb, as insolently as possible.

A hot flush stained Sarah's cheeks. 'I'll bloody finish you, Jeff Dando.' She was breathing heavily, her ample chest rising and falling under the quilted fabric. 'Just see if I don't.'

He laughed. 'Stop it, you're scaring me.'

And then as he saw the fear touch her eyes, he moved closer, the tension sharpening the air between them. He reached out his hand to brush her untidy red hair away from her face.

'You're a wild one,' he whispered. He'd like to bet she

was wild in bed too. Wild and also wasted. Who did she have snoring upstairs in her bed? Eloise had let slip that she had a fancy man who paid all the bills, and that she had a thing going for the stupid bastard Charlotte used to work for. So Sarah Freeman was just another screwed-up lady with a screwed-up life.

Panic flared in her face. She took a step backwards. 'Ellie has lots of friends,' she muttered.

'Then she's a lucky girl.' Abruptly he tired of the game, her words reminding him of his purpose. 'I've got no intention of doing anything to her. Now tell her I'm here, there's a good girl.'

Sarah glowered back at him. 'I'm not your good girl, and she's not here.'

'Not here?' His blue eyes darkened with anger. 'Then why the hell didn't you say so?'

'You didn't—'

'Well, where is she then?' He didn't give her the chance to finish. Where the hell had she gone to at this time in the morning?

'I don't know.' She looked away. 'I heard her go out fifteen minutes ago.' As she spoke, she drew the door towards her.

Frustrated, Jeff put his foot in the way, to stop her shutting it. 'I'll be back.'

She stared at him, putting her weight behind the door.

He realised that she hated him. Oh, what the hell? He twisted around and strode off away from the cobbled square with its exclusive jewellers and high-class boutiques. Damn Eloise. She was so bloody elusive. You could never catch her when you wanted her the most.

He got into the Volvo and drove towards Alderley Edge, calming slightly as he left the city behind. This was more like it. Alderley Edge was a narrow ridge of pink sandstone still scarred by the old mine workings, and planted with Scots pine trees that stood like sentinels on the landscape. But it was more than that. It gave Jeff the sensation that he was on top of the world – looking across Yorkshire, the Lakes and Wales. And he liked that. It was another kind of power.

He pressed harder on the accelerator. And Alderley had even more than that— He glanced out of the window at the field roses in hedgerows and scattered gorse, heather and birch trees. More than a pretty landscape. A classy landscape for the classy houses dotted along the route. Halls and mansions some of them. And best of all, a hint of magic. The wizard of Alderley Edge lived on as far as Jeff was concerned. This place was a piece of history – an old water mill in the heart of the Cheshire countryside. This was Jeff's future.

But his mood changed once more when he reached Alderley Towers, to discover that the builders' truck was noticeable by its absence from the drive. He parked the car. Builders were a different breed. You had to watch them every second, time their tea-breaks and pay them on the nail. That was the hard part. Jeff didn't know where the next wage-packet was coming from. And the plasterer was booked for next week.

He opened the inner wrought-iron gates that led to the house, walked up the broken, weed-fringed slabs of paving stones that made up the path, and stopped dead in his tracks. She was sitting outside the front door, in the porch, between two cracked pots of faded geraniums and in front of a worn-out honeysuckle. She looked as much of a waif and stray as she'd looked when he opened the door of the Didsbury house to her, three years before.

'Well. This is a surprise.' He kept the sarcasm in his

voice. 'How long have you been here?' But he realised that he was glad to see her. Whatever the situation, whatever her mood, Eloise brought a welcome unpredictability to any day.

He held out a hand and pulled her to her feet. She was so light – there was nothing substantial about her at all.

She groaned. 'Too long. I didn't know where you were, I just hoped you'd get here before rigor mortis set in.' She brushed the leaves from the long Indian skirt she was wearing. 'Anyway, I'm getting used to waiting outside people's front doors.'

He wanted to kiss her. But he wouldn't. He had a few choice things to say to her first. 'That's because you don't tell people you're coming. And you never use the phone. You just breeze in and out, taking everyone for granted.' He was angry with her, but had to keep a tight rein on it. Anger wasn't the way to deal with Eloise.

'Unlike you, I suppose.' She shot him a humourless glance from under the fair lashes.

Jeff sighed. No one would ever be able to control her. 'That's different,' he said.

'I thought it might be.' She stepped away from the porch, glancing in all directions. 'You may as well show me around, now that I'm here.'

'I didn't see the car.' He surveyed her curiously. 'Where did you park it?'

'Round the corner.' She grinned. 'I wanted to surprise you.'

'You did that all right.'

She leaned towards him, and he smelled her perfume – musky as opium. Sexy as the night-time blues. 'Where have all the workers got to?'

'A good question. I've got to chase them up.' He glanced at his watch. 'Oh, what the hell— Outside first then.' He took her elbow, steering her rapidly along the path. He needed guided tours like a hole in the head. But he did need to talk to her. 'The front garden.'

'Charming.' She twisted neatly away from him. 'You don't seem very pleased to see me. Are you busy?'

'Am I ever too busy for you?' His voice was dry as he watched her. Somehow, work and mundane practicalities like making money drifted into the background when Eloise was standing in front of him.

She smiled. 'Often enough.'

They made their way through a small rose garden. Jeff walked quickly, eager to get to the house, where he could talk to her without distraction. But she was drifting, apparently engrossed in every shrub and flower. She was the most frustrating girl he'd ever known. He could never pin her down.

He took her hand. 'We have to talk.'

'Later.' She put a finger on her lips. 'Let me look around first.'

What choice did he have? Shaking his dark head in irritation, Jeff led the way round the side of the house. The back was laid out mostly in lawn with narrow ornamental borders, and a small orchard at the far end.

'The back garden.' He folded his arms. She was beautiful, and she was playing games.

'Very nice. Half an acre?'

'And the rest.' Jeff's impatience got the better of him. He grabbed her and pulled her towards the wooden bench that perched under the late-flowering cherry tree. Its rose-shaded petals littered the lawn.

'Lovely!' They sat down. Ellie bent to pick up some of the pale pink blooms, then let them flutter from her fingers. 'Smell these.' She took more, crushed them in her palm and offered it to Jeff.

He grasped her wrist. 'What the hell are you playing at, Eloise?'

With her free hand, she shielded her eyes from the sun. 'I never know whether or not to trust a person who doesn't like flowers. It's a bit like animals. How d'you mean, playing?' She gazed pointedly at his hand. He released her and she stared, as if mesmerised, at the red marks his fingers had made. 'You don't know your own strength,' she murmured.

Jeff got up from the bench and thrust his hands in his pockets. What the hell was he going to do with her? She was impossible. He turned to face her.

'What did Melanie tell you? And how much of it have you told Charlotte?'

'Ah, Melanie—' Ellie got up too and began wandering towards the fruit trees. She half-turned. 'That lady's got it in for you. I'd watch her if I were you.'

'I know that.' He followed her, exasperated. You couldn't keep her in one place for even a few seconds. 'She's jealous. She wanted me to sleep with her and I wasn't interested. Some women get like that, they can't take rejection.'

'Oh yeah?' Ellie laughed. 'And there I was thinking that you didn't have to pretend with me.'

She moved closer, and reaching out to him, allowed her fingers to dance briefly across his chest. 'Do you think I'm a complete idiot?'

'No, Eloise. I don't.'

She grabbed a branch and brought it down between them. They watched each other through the leaves.

'You've got blackfly, darling,' she said.

Jeff leaned against the flimsy trunk which tilted with his weight. She was hopeless. He didn't know what to do with her. She broke too many rules. 'You didn't believe her, did you? I didn't think you were the gullible kind.'

'I'm not, Jeff.' She stroked the bark, and her hand brushed casually against his arm.

She was taunting him. Against his will he felt himself getting a hard-on. Christ, he wanted her.

'Did you believe her, Eloise?' He smiled, daring her, joining in the game.

'Some of it. Most of it.' She moved away and hugged her arms across her chest. 'I suppose I did. She's a friend of Sarah's. No reason for her to lie. I expect it was all true.' She let her arms fall to her sides. 'So. You're even more of a bastard than I thought. What does it matter?'

He was surprised. And pleased.

She turned towards him again, spread her hands in front of her as if she wanted to grab the day. 'What does it matter?' she repeated. 'When we're in a beautiful garden, there's no one in sight, and yet you haven't even kissed me.' She laughed and twirled around. Her skirt flared, black, pink and white paisley, away from her legs.

'God, you drive me mad.' His voice was thick. He came after her, not too fast. Slowly, slowly.

Catching one of her slender arms, he pulled her towards him, rubbed his thumb along the line of her cheekbone, watched the passion touch the slant of her eyes. 'You're a witch.'

She smiled. Lazy, like a cat. 'Ever made love in the open air?' she whispered. 'With the sun beating down on your back?'

He hesitated for only a split second. It was too long.

Her eyes changed. 'Oh, but of course you have.' Ellie frowned. 'For a minute I forgot who I was talking to.'

'Don't be silly, sweetheart,' he murmured. Damn her. She never missed a thing.

But the spell was broken. She was struggling, and he let her go. Still, at least they walked on together.

'If you don't care about what Melanie was telling you, why did you go running to Charlotte? What did you tell her?'

Ellie's eyes hardened, but she smiled. 'I thought you might be worried about that. You don't know me very well, do you, Jeff?'

He shrugged. 'Apparently not. I'm always cynical about the motives of women.' Who could tell what went on behind those pretty faces? He was good at it, but he wasn't that good.

She stopped walking. 'I'm not "women", don't you even know that yet?'

Sometimes she seemed such a child. And sometimes she knew everything. 'Yes, but—'

'How could you imagine that I'd hurt Charlotte because of what one of your stupid little sluts might say to me?' She brushed a strand of blonde hair out of her eyes.

So she hadn't let him down. The relief swamped over him. He should have remembered that Eloise was different. 'Then why did you go there?'

'Why shouldn't I? She is my sister.' She stared at him as if she was reading his mind. 'Surely you didn't imagine I'd tell her about *us*?' Her voice was a whisper.

'Of course I didn't.' He looked away.

'You did!' Her eyes widened. 'You did, you stupid bastard!'

'What if I did?' He raised his voice to match hers. 'You are hurting her, aren't you? What are you doing with me if you're not hurting her?'

She folded – so abruptly that it took him by surprise. 'I'm not hurting her as much as you are.' She was close to tears. 'I thought we had something valuable. Something worth all that betrayal. But I was wrong. It's you—' She choked on a sob. 'You're the one who's cheapened everything.'

He was silent, unwilling to consider the truth of that.

'What's the point of going to bed with every bimbo that comes along?' Ellie's eyes seemed huge in her pale face. 'Was it really just to get information?' Her voice was incredulous. She grabbed his hands. 'That's hard to swallow. Does a deal really mean that much to you?'

'Of course not.' Jeff knew he sounded unconvincing. Eloise was hard to lie to. Sometimes she seemed to know so much about him that she seemed part of him almost.

'It does, doesn't it?' Ellie dropped his hands as if they'd burned her. 'A deal means everything.'

He was reminded of Charlotte. In some ways they were alike after all. But he could afford to be more truthful with Eloise.

'Okay, Eloise. It's true. I slept with Melanie. She was asking for it. But it didn't mean anything to me. You must know that. And it was before I met you.' Only six inches between them, but it felt like a long distance – a lifetime.

She laughed harshly. 'Don't give me that crap. I know you've been seeing someone else – from some other bloody estate agent's.'

He was taken aback. How the hell did she know that? Then he remembered Polly's friend who worked with Melanie. Damn and blast her. 'That was nothing—' he began.

'It never is.' She smiled. 'Only if it's a deal. A deal means everything. Everything second to the deal. Loyalty, love, honesty—'

'For Christ's sake.' He swung away. 'What's the matter with everyone? So, I slept with a couple of pretty girls who gave me the come on. So bloody what? I'm not a saint.'

They stared at each other. Both were breathing heavily, locked in battle.

'Poor Charlotte.' Ellie sat down on the lawn and began to pick daisies.

'What Charlotte doesn't know won't hurt her.' If she was trying to make him feel guilty, it wouldn't wash with Jeff.

'But it will hurt her. It'll hurt you both, even if she never finds out – don't you realise?' Ellie sighed as she eased her thumbnail into a daisy stalk. 'God, men can be so stupid.' She looked up at him. 'Apart from anything else, they're cheap and meaningless affairs that you've ducked into out of greed. That would hurt her.' She threaded the next daisy through. 'Like I said, you've cheapened everything.'

'And us?' He sat down next to her and pushed her hair back from her face. He lifted it and let it fall. It was like a pale gold curtain. He realised that, more than anything, he didn't want to lose her.

'Ours wasn't a cheap affair.' If Ellie had needed confirmation, she would have seen it in his eyes.

'Don't make it the past.' His voice was husky. Sometimes he even thought that he loved her.

She dropped the daisy chain. 'It has to be. What if Charlotte found out? I couldn't bear it. I couldn't.'

Jeff took her in his arms and held her. She still felt like a child. Slender and weightless. Vulnerable and needing him. He held her more tightly.

She began to sob.

'She won't find out. We won't let her.' Jeff stroked her fine blonde hair, his hand cradling her head.

But the sobbing went on. It was more than that, he realised. He thought back to Charlotte's words. There was something else.

'Why did you go to see her? Why, Eloise?'

When he held her like this, close and cushioned, it was easier for Ellie to imagine that they were living in their own small world. Just a pregnant woman and her man. Bliss.

'I can hear the birds,' she whispered. 'It's a perfect place for them here.'

'They don't just live at Pencraig.' His voice was mocking. 'Now, don't you think it's time to let me know what's going on?'

Ellie felt the pressure spoiling the moment. She couldn't put it off.

'I'm pregnant,' she said.

She watched him. It had to be the most dramatic news a woman could ever give. What face would Jeff find to put on? Horror or delight?

He let go of her, abruptly, as if she'd contracted leprosy instead of pregnancy. Not a good start. Ellie sat, utterly alone, watching him in this naked moment. It was her only chance of discovering his true feelings.

His hands slumped to his sides, his fists clenched then unclenched again. He breathed deeply as if searching for control. His eyes were puzzled, and there was a vulnerability to his mouth that was new. He rubbed his hand across it, it resumed the old lines, and at last he turned to her. She knew what he would say.

'Are you sure?'

She smiled because she was right, and nodded. How many women had ever replied: 'No, I'm not sure, but it's a hell of an interesting idea, don't you think?'

Jeff frowned. 'You seem to be taking this very lightly.'

Pompous bastard. How could he say that? He'd known for less than a minute. She'd had the half-knowledge drifting into certainty for three months, resting inside her, developing and changing along with the foetus. Horror and shock had gone a long time ago, although they sometimes returned at night.

'Do you want me to cry some more?' Her voice was cool. 'Is that what you'd like to see?'

He shook his head. 'No, of course not. Only—' He glanced at her.

Already he was looking at her in a different way. She could see it. She wasn't Ellie any more. Just like Charlotte – only for different reasons – she had changed. For Jeff she was now a woman pregnant with his child, no longer his Eloise. A complication. It made her sad, and bitter.

'I'm past tears.' She got to her feet. 'I finished with all that last month. This month I've started laughing at the bloody predictable way that people respond to my happy news.'

She could tell that the flippancy stung.

'What do you want me to do, Eloise?' he drawled. 'Dance for joy?'

'You would if I was Charlotte.' She hadn't wanted to say that. It had burst out from nowhere, this hurt resentment that he wasn't pleased, that no one was pleased, or if they were, they had ulterior motives. But why should they be pleased? Everything was wrong, wasn't it? She wasn't in the correct social position.

Charlotte wanted the baby, Sarah had been horrified. And Jeff would leave her. If she didn't leave him first.

At least Sarah had come through for her, saying she could stay on in the bed-sit, work different shifts cash in hand and draw social. That she'd always lend her a hand. Sarah had done more than she knew – with practical help that was worth a dozen pairs of wringing hands.

'But you're not Charlotte.'

She flinched at his cruelty. 'Mistress, but not the mother of your child, is that it?' she taunted.

'Something like that.' His expression was inscrutable.

'I see.' And she did. How she wished that she could hate him.

'How do you know it's mine?' His voice was rough and he was looking at her as though she were a stranger.

'You bastard.' The second question she'd been waiting for. But that didn't mean it hurt any the less.

She took a deep breath. 'Don't you think I'd rather it was someone else's?' She wouldn't cry. No, damn him to hell. She would not cry. 'Don't flatter yourself. Do you think I want my own sister's husband to be the father of my child? For Christ's sake, Jeff—'

'Sorry.' He got up and grabbed her by the shoulders once more. There was something about him that seemed new to her – some hint of a past pain perhaps?

'It wasn't intentional,' she said. 'It was an accident – you must know that.'

'I'm sorry.' His voice was gentle. 'I didn't mean it.'

She stared at him. 'You bloody did.'

'Jesus—' Jeff buried his head on her shoulder, and together, almost as one, they sank down on to the grass.

For a moment Ellie hesitated, unused to him confessing need. Ready to deny him. Then, instinctively, she took his head on to her lap and stroked the thick, dark hair. Gingerly at first, and then with such passion flowing out of her fingers that it seemed incredible he didn't feel it. Perhaps he did feel it. The current between them was so strong that he ought to.

'It was just a shock.' His voice was muffled. 'We've been trying for so long. For a kid, you know. God knows why she wants one so much. Charlotte's been getting pretty desperate. Jesus, Eloise, I don't know what's got into her. So I couldn't believe that you—'

'I know. She told me.' Ellie held him closer. 'But you should have told me before.'

He lifted his head. His eyes were wet. She couldn't believe what she was seeing. Jeff Dando in tears. Wasn't that impossible? She felt so moved that she could hardly speak. Her throat constricted with a kind of bitter-sweet pain.

'I assumed she'd told you ages ago. I thought you two told each other just about everything.' He groaned. 'I didn't want to even bloody think about it, to tell you the truth. It's taken her over, to say the least.'

'So I discovered.' She frowned, picturing Charlotte's sad and desperate hazel eyes. 'You shouldn't leave her alone so much. It's bad for her.'

'If I could leave you alone, then I might not leave her alone quite so much.' A trace of a smile lifted the corners of his mouth.

'Then leave me alone.' Her tone was a passionate one. 'She's your wife. So look after her, for Christ's sake.'

He stiffened. 'Is it any of your concern?'

How could he even ask that? 'Everything about Charlotte is my concern.'

'And me? Am I your concern?' His blue eyes met hers.

He was jealous. She smiled. 'And you. You're my concern too.' She wound her fingers around the dark curls.

'Why didn't you tell me first?' He reached out and ran his hand lightly, possessively, under her skirt and between her thighs.

'I've always gone to Charlotte first.' He'd never understand. She didn't even want him to.

'She must have gone stark raving mad.' Jeff looked thoughtful.

'She did at first.' Ellie gazed at him. 'Then she wanted the baby. For the two of you.'

'Jesus Christ.' He sat up. 'No wonder she was in such a state. And you said no.'

She turned on him. 'Yes of course I bloody said no. I wouldn't give my baby to you and Charlotte.'

'It's my baby too.'

'What?' She couldn't tell what was going on behind those intense eyes of his any more. And she couldn't believe what she was hearing. First Charlotte, now Jeff. Taking over. She put her hands over her stomach.

'It's my baby too,' he repeated.

'Do you want Charlotte to know that?' she whispered.

A momentary fear glimmered in his eyes.

'Just remember that this is my baby.' Her voice was soft. 'No one is going to take this baby anywhere. Always remember that, Jeff. I mean it.'

He looked away, into the distance. 'What are you going to do? How will you manage?'

'What's that got to do with you?' It was almost funny. First of all men denied parenthood, rejected the responsibility. Then they wanted to control all the decisions. Absolutely bloody typical.

He took hold of her wrists. 'I want to have a say. I want to help you.' He hesitated. 'You've definitely decided that you're going to—'

'Keep it?' Her voice was harsh. 'It's too late for abortion, if that's what you mean.'

'Come on, Eloise. There are other options.' He pulled her to her feet, leading her towards the house, holding her hand, stroking the base of her thumb, rhythmically, hypnotically. 'We don't have to decide now,' he said. 'But we should talk to the right people. I'd come with you. We should take everything into account, think what's best for the baby. I can't be a father to my sister-in-law's child.'

Ellie felt herself lulled by his words. She shook her head. 'Stop it!'

He was silent.

'I'm keeping it, Jeff. I don't need you to be my baby's father.' It was finalised in her mind. There was no going back now.

'Come and have some tea,' he said.

'Only if you promise to stop badgering me. I'm a pregnant woman. You should be looking after me, not harassing me.'

He smiled. 'Then promise me you'll let me help financially at least.'

She looked deep into his eyes. 'No promises,' she said. 'No claims.'

He put his arm around her slim shoulders. 'Whatever you say.'

As they sat drinking their tea a quarter of an hour later, on the bench under the flowering cherry tree, there was a new peace between them. And oddly, Ellie felt that they were closer – that after all the baby would be a bond between them rather than an instrument of separation. But it might be the closeness of friends, not lovers.

Jeff took her hand. 'You're a very unusual girl, Eloise,' he said.

'I know.' She smiled.

'And I'm sorry for hassling you.'

She shrugged. 'I can cope.'

'I want you to know that I'll be here for you— whenever you need me to be. That this is important for me. That I feel good about it.' He smiled. 'I mean it.'

'I know you do.' Could she have expected any more? She

put down the cup. It was so warm and peaceful, everything in her body was warm and peaceful and full to the brim. She leaned against his shoulder, closed her eyes.

'So have you ever made love in the open air, with the sun beating down on your back?' he whispered in her ear.

His lips were so close. His warm breath was caressing her, inviting her, and all she wanted to do was press him closer. The slight stubble on his jaw was almost touching her neck, and she wanted it to rub across her soft skin. She felt herself melting against him, into him. She turned her face towards his. 'Not yet,' she said. 'But there's always a first time.'

The last time, she promised herself. This would be the very last time.

Part II

12

''Appy birfday to me!' There was a loud cheer. It sounded as if Alex had put her whole world into that cheer.

Ellie stopped at the traffic lights by the Hare and Hounds, her signal that she was out of the city and heading home. To Pencraig. She automatically relaxed in her seat and let out a sigh of relief.

'Someone else is supposed to sing it to you, Alex.'

'Who?'

'All the people at the party.' Ellie let out the clutch, drove on, and wondered for the hundredth time just how many people Charlotte had invited. Going to Pencraig for her daughter's fifth birthday had been Charlotte's idea. And not one of her better ones.

Ellie had planned a small celebration back at the flat.

'I was quite looking forward to giving out party bags and balloons for the first time,' she complained to Charlotte.

'Don't be mean. There'll be plenty more times for you.' Charlotte's hazel eyes pleaded with her. Don't deny me this, they were saying.

It was late, late summer, during one of Ellie's rare weekends at Pencraig. Since Ellie's pregnancy she and Charlotte had drifted a long distance apart. It seemed that all of a sudden, there was just too much separating them. The baby that Charlotte couldn't have. And of course the fact that Jeff was Alex's father, the best kept secret in the world.

'I want to organise a family party.' Charlotte's eyes

dimmed with that far away look that Ellie dreaded. The guilt-hook, she called it.

'A big party for grown-ups and children. With lots of food and dancing. Something special for Alex.' She stroked her niece's dark curls. 'Because it's a special birthday, number five, isn't it Alex?'

The child nodded, and grinned the grin that melted most people's hearts the second they saw it. Making Ellie want to laugh and cry at the same time. It was awe-inspiring just how much a child could twist your heart.

'And Alex Morgan is a special little girl.' Charlotte bent down to hug her. Then she looked up. 'Please, Ellie?'

'Oh, all right. If that's what Alex wants.' How could she refuse Charlotte this, when she was clearly itching to start writing invitations and start stacking the house with presents? How could she refuse, when a small share in Alex was all that Charlotte had? Charlotte adored her, but Ellie still sometimes spotted those tell-tale shadows of pain around her eyes as she watched Alex playing, smiling, laughing.

Poor Charlotte. Motherhood had taught Ellie compassion, and she knew Charlotte deserved a child more than anyone. Certainly more than Ellie did. But not Alex. She could never have given up Alex and then stood by to watch.

Maybe if that was all— But it wasn't. Ellie's eyes were drawn instinctively to Jeff. It was hard not to look at him. He was mowing the lawn – which was unusual in itself – dressed only in cut-off denims and worn leather sandals. He moved with lazy strides, stopping every now and then to sweep his dark hair out of his eyes.

She knew that body so intimately, and yet still she couldn't resist staring at the strong, well-proportioned shoulders, the long, brown back, the chest muscles rippling slightly with the unaccustomed effort, the dark, crisp chest hair— She turned her head.

Guilt would always make her give Charlotte what she wanted.

'But don't go too mad,' she warned. 'Just a few friends. Okay?'

Charlotte grinned. 'Leave it to me. Don't worry about a thing.'

Ellie watched her. She was still far from well. It had been a sticky time during her own pregnancy, worrying about Charlotte on tranquillisers, perilously close to a nervous breakdown. And being unable to help. A hugely pregnant Ellie wouldn't have done much for a woman who felt destroyed, because she couldn't conceive.

But the breakdown hadn't come. Somehow Charlotte had found the strength to pull through, and Ellie guessed that part of that strength at least had come from the peace of Pencraig. And maybe some of it had come from the work she now did at the village school, helping Joy Pringle with the children. Not much of it had come from Jeff. He was still hardly ever here.

He strolled towards them. The sweat was resting in tiny beads on his forehead. Ellie had never seen him work so hard before. Apart from making love, Jeff was the one who organised everyone else's activities. He was carrying a baseball cap, which he pulled on. It hid the blueness of his eyes but made him look sexier than ever.

'We're going to throw a party for Alex,' Charlotte told him.

He grabbed Alex, lifting her high in the air, spinning her until she was screaming for mercy and shrieking with childish laughter.

Ellie looked away. She liked seeing them together,

but it scared her. With every day that passed, Alex was turning more and more into a carbon copy of her father. It was incredible that Charlotte hadn't noticed. But there was always the chance that she'd notice one day.

'Make sure she keeps it low-key,' she told Jeff.

'How can I stop her?' He laughed. 'You know what Charlotte's like. Any excuse for a party.'

That was absolutely untrue and they all knew it. Apart from Charlotte's work at the school she was practically a hermit. But they all laughed.

'We'll have to ask Mother.' Ellie and Charlotte exchanged a look of apprehension.

Ellie had come to resent Olivia almost as much as Charlotte did, since she'd become a mother herself. Her own motherhood seemed to accentuate the fact that Olivia's kind of caring was nothing more than superficial dusting. It didn't go down any deeper. But still both of them acknowledged the blood tie – Ellie more than Charlotte. Olivia was her child's grandmother. So Christmas cards, little notes, and invitations to birthday parties were unavoidable.

Charlotte grabbed a pen and paper from her bag.

'And Sarah.' Ellie smiled at her daughter. 'Alex adores Sarah.'

'Does she?' Charlotte frowned and nibbled the pen. 'How will she get here? It's a bit of a trek for a children's party.'

'Leonard will bring her. You don't mind him coming, do you?'

Charlotte put her head on one side. 'I suppose not.'

Was she still holding a secret torch for the man who'd loved her for so long, or was she just frightened of encountering people from her past?

'They're the people she loves.' Ellie stroked her daughter's hair. 'It is supposed to be her party.' She wasn't going to give in over this one. Sarah meant a lot to her. And she'd helped Ellie more than she could ever repay, over the last five years.

'You're right.' Jeff tilted Alex's small chin, and looked into the reflection of his own blue eyes. 'It's her party. She can have whoever she wants.'

On the motorway Ellie put her foot down. She hadn't seen Jeff or Charlotte for two months, and Olivia for almost a year. It was a farce having a family party. Sometimes she wondered if she even had a family any more.

'Will Uncle Jeff be there?' Alex's voice broke into her thoughts. He was her favourite. Ironic, that. There was a natural bond between the two of them, and when Alex was around Jeff gave her the kind of undivided attention that he'd never give to his women.

'Yep. He'll be there.' Presumably. What would she feel when she saw him? Love? Lust? Just a barely perceptible fluttering? Or would she feel nothing, now that she felt so much for someone else? Would she finally be able to look Charlotte in the eye without experiencing guilt? Or was this the kind of guilt that went on for ever?

Pencraig had been transformed. One room was crammed with children from Charlotte's school, playing 'Dead Fishes', another with people Ellie hardly knew. Olivia was swanning round in an elegant, jade-green suit and matching, wide-brimmed hat, as if she still owned the place. Jeff was in the kitchen presiding over two huge woks balanced on the Aga. And Charlotte was playing with the children, her face flushed with excitement.

Ellie soon got lost in a sea of anonymous thank-yous.

'Never again,' she told Sarah. 'Never again will I let Charlotte talk me into this. There are people here I've never seen in my life. Where did she get them all from?'

Sarah was unsympathetic. 'You should be grateful. Imagine this fiasco at the wine bar.'

'There wouldn't be this fiasco at the wine bar.' Ellie downed the contents of her glass of champagne and tossed back her blonde hair. 'I would have limited myself to sausages on sticks. And I'd only invite people I like talking to.'

'No family allowed then?' Sarah laughed.

Ellie glanced at her. Sarah was more relaxed these days, since Leonard had finally given in to the inevitable and asked her to marry him. Ellie had waited for month after month since Harold had disappeared from the scene. She noticed Leonard's visits getting more and more frequent. She saw Sarah veering between misery and joy like some teenage adolescent. And she realised that Leonard was lonely.

'You know Sarah's crazy about you,' she said to him one day. 'She's just terrified of what you might think of her – because of Harold.'

Leonard's brow darkened. 'I never understood what she saw in that man.'

Ellie hesitated. Should she tell him – that Harold had been a means to an end? That Sarah had been forced into sleeping with him, in order to keep the wine bar? She looked into his kind, dark eyes. No. Leonard was straight as a die. He might not understand. That part was up to Sarah.

'She'd never let you down,' Ellie whispered. Charlotte had told her about the consequences of Leonard's unhappy marriage.

He glanced at her swiftly, seemed about to say something – about Charlotte perhaps? – and then he changed his mind.

'Don't wait too long, Leonard.' She hoped he'd understand what she was trying to tell him. Perhaps she'd said too much. But the two of them were made for each other. Charlotte would never be Leonard's – not now. Ellie knew that.

And a month later it was as if they'd never been apart. Ellie was rewarded by a brightness on Sarah's face that she'd never seen before, and a knowledge that Sarah was happy at last.

Ellie came back to the present, to catch Leonard's smile. 'There's nothing like a family get-together to bring hostility to the surface,' he said. 'And talking about hostility, how's Jeff these days?'

Ellie and Sarah giggled. They were standing in the hallway, catching glimpses of Jeff through the open door of the kitchen. He was stir-frying mountains of Chinese food, stopping every few seconds for liquid refreshment in the form of red wine, and talking to anyone who came close enough. He was probably the only man who could take two wooden spatulas and a tea-towel hooked into his belt, and give them distinct sex-appeal.

Ellie hadn't even spoken to him yet. She was scared to.

'As gorgeous as ever,' Sarah drawled with sarcasm.

'You'd better watch it. I'm not marrying anyone who fancies Jeff Dando,' Leonard teased.

They all laughed, but Ellie knew they were thinking of Jeff and his tangled relationships. With her. With Charlotte. Ellie prayed that Leonard had got over Charlotte. She glanced at Sarah. She deserved the right kind of love. Someone to put the past away for her and allow her to build some self-belief again.

'Your mother's very pally with him,' Sarah observed.

It was true. Olivia had wandered over, and was leaning over the Aga, pointing at the food, and smiling that vague smile of hers, her hand resting lightly on Jeff's shoulder.

Ellie watched Alex run through a group of people clustered by the doorway, past Olivia and up to Jeff. He automatically shielded her from the hot stove.

'Hi, sweet-pie.' He took the small hand in his, bent his dark head close to hers. 'Let's go and find the birthday cake.'

Ellie glanced towards her mother.

Olivia too, was watching the man and child, smiling, as she dried her hands on a nearby towel. Then she tensed, stared, and drew back as if a sudden understanding had surfaced. She continued to rub the towel over her hands, over and over, faster and faster. Still she stared at Jeff and Alex. Then she caught Ellie's eye. She looked back to Alex.

'Oh, Christ.' Ellie drew back out of sight. She'd been so worried about Charlotte noticing the family resemblance that she hadn't thought of Olivia.

Leonard, taking in the situation immediately, was in the kitchen in five strides, grabbing the towel from Olivia, putting his arm round her shoulders, talking to her in a low whisper.

'My God, no. She can't be.' Ellie could hear her mother's voice through the general hubbub of conversation. Numbly, she sat on the bench by the telephone. The people by the doorway were staring into the kitchen.

'Do you think she's guessed?' Sarah was by her shoulder. 'Surely she wouldn't *dream* that you and Jeff—'

Ellie paled. 'She caught us once. In the bed-sit. That awful night before their wedding when she came to

Manchester. You remember?' She glanced at Sarah's face. Of course she did. It was the same night that Sarah first took Harold into her bed. My God, that was a night to remember.

Ellie got to her feet. Jeff walked back into the kitchen. The voices got louder. Someone shut the door.

'Jesus Christ.' Ellie backed off.

'What on earth did she say? When she saw him?' The expression in Sarah's clear blue eyes was one of incredulity.

'I told her it was just a one-night stand. I think she believed me.' She pointed to her daughter, coming their way. 'But look at Alex. How could anyone not know? She's the spitting image—'

'Of who?' Charlotte came up behind them.

'Of her father, of course.' Thinking fast, Ellie took Charlotte's arm, steering her into the other room where Dead Fishes had become Musical Chairs. They sat down.

'She's got your character though.' Charlotte's voice had that dreamy quality that it often had these days. 'She reminds me of you as a kid.'

'She reminds me of you.' Ellie squeezed her hand. Alex had that same earnest independence that she'd always associated with Charlotte.

Charlotte smiled. 'Thanks for letting me do this. I know you didn't relish the idea. And don't worry, I'll never forget that she's your daughter.'

She seemed about to say more, when the sound of raised voices distracted her. She glanced up. 'What's all the racket?' Getting to her feet, she walked towards the kitchen. 'What's going on? Jeff? Mother? Leonard?' Her tone of astonishment increased with each name uttered.

Jeff and Olivia were standing glaring at each other with Leonard between them like a referee. Olivia was in deadly earnest, but the corners of Jeff's mouth were twitching as if he was half-enjoying her distress.

In the background Ellie groaned and hung on to Sarah's arm.

Charlotte's hazel eyes narrowed. She ran her fingers through her dark hair as she turned on Jeff. 'You promised. Smooth as clockwork, you said.' Her lips crumpled. She looked as if she might cry.

Leonard took a step towards her. Even from this distance Ellie could see the compassion on his face, and she felt Sarah's body tense.

'Don't worry, Charlotte,' he said. 'It's nothing for you to worry about.'

As if reacting instinctively to the concern in his voice, Charlotte moved like a sleepwalker towards him. And Leonard looked for all the world as if he was about to take her in his arms.

'Charlotte?' The voice was Jeff's.

Confused, she turned to him. He pulled her away, into the far corner of the room, talking in low, urgent whispers. Leonard watched them for a moment, and then walked slowly back towards Ellie and Sarah.

'Has he really got over her, Ellie?' Sarah whispered. 'Have I pushed him into this?'

Ellie squeezed her arm. 'It's you he wants to marry, love.' She'd seen Leonard's eyes shutter momentarily when Charlotte greeted them this afternoon. But she didn't know for sure.

'I hope you're right.' Sarah smiled at him warily as he approached.

'Thanks, Leonard. Do you think Mother will be able to keep quiet?' Ellie dreaded the answer to this.

'Who knows? She's pretty upset. You'll have to talk to her yourself.' Ellie thought she glimpsed disapproval in his eyes.

She groaned. 'I need another drink.'

'I'll get it.' Leonard took their glasses back into the kitchen, as if he wanted to check up on what was happening.

Ellie drew Sarah to one side. 'Stop fretting. You two are perfect together. I've got you down in my little black book as the couple least likely to.'

'Least likely to?'

'Least likely to get divorced.'

They laughed.

'I'm glad we're partners,' Sarah said. 'It was the best day's work I ever did, getting you to come in with me.'

Jeff's early legacy for Alex. He had provided the money for Ellie to buy into the wine bar. Ellie didn't know where it had come from, but it had made a lot of difference to her life, that was for sure.

'Not quite.' Ellie grinned. 'The best day's work you ever did was getting rid of creepy old Harold. How did it go? One, two, three—'

'Fuck off Harold,' they whispered in unison, exploding into giggles. He'd had it coming for a long time. Thinking he owned both the wine bar and Sarah's body. That night, the night they'd gained financial independence, had been a night to remember too.

'Your mother knows about Alex.' Jeff was washing up and Ellie was sweeping the kitchen floor. Most of the guests had gone home but Ellie and Alex were staying the night.

'I know she does. I saw the penny drop. D'you think she'll tell Charlotte?' Ellie restrained the urge to leave the room. She didn't want to be alone with him, but she needed to hear about Olivia.

'Not if I've got anything to do with it.' Jeff stretched and yawned. 'She'll cool down.'

'Is that why she left so suddenly?' Ellie had steeled herself for a heavy lecture from Olivia at the very least, but Mother had taken off straight after the incident in the kitchen. And Ellie wasn't sorry to see her go.

Wiping his wet hands on a tea-towel, Jeff came closer. 'Probably. Do you care?'

Ellie felt the hairs on the back of her neck stiffen. 'Not really. She's hardly your average loving grandmother. It's just that—'

He moved closer still. 'Just that, like Charlotte, you're always half-expecting her to change?'

'Maybe.' She twisted away from the proximity of him. Jeff had that predatory look that she recognised only too well. And she didn't totally trust herself. When she looked into those blue eyes, when he was this close, his body almost touching hers, she wasn't sure she could resist.

'Something's different.' He spoke softly. 'You're different.' He pushed her fair hair from her face, traced the line of her lips with his thumb.

'Bed-time stories don't take very long when you're five,' Ellie reminded him. She wanted to close her eyes and sink. But where would she be sinking to?

He grasped her arm. 'Why haven't you returned any of my calls?'

'I've been busy.' Why couldn't she just say it? Shout it. No more. Why couldn't she commit herself to that decision?

'Hmm.' He wandered out of the room. 'You're not a very good liar, Eloise. And you know perfectly well that Charlotte will probably read about ten stories,' he said.

That night Ellie sat huddled on the window-seat, wondering what was happening in a certain flat above a certain wine bar in St Ann's Square. Then she saw a tall, slim, familiar figure slip out of the front door and walk in the direction of the wood. On a wild impulse she pulled a towelling robe around her and ran lightly downstairs. But by the time she reached the garden the figure had disappeared.

'Charlotte?' She looked around, into as many shadows as she dared, pulled the robe closer, and made her way into the wood. It was cold and scary. Even her own footsteps, the soft rustle of leaves, and the cracking of an occasional twig, made her jump. But she couldn't turn back. Gingerly, feeling her way past unfamiliar trees and bushes, she approached the bivouac.

'Ellie?'

She jumped. 'Jesus Christ. You could have given me a heart attack.'

Charlotte moved out of the shadows and touched her arm. 'What are you doing here?'

'I was following you.' Ellie felt stupid. Supposing Charlotte had some sort of assignation? They weren't kids any more, they weren't here for a midnight feast. 'What are *you* doing here?' she countered.

'I'm going down to the bay.' Charlotte smiled, her face eerie in the shadowy moonlight. 'Want to come?'

Ellie nodded. She wasn't about to go back to the house alone.

Charlotte took her hand, moving sure-footed, as if in a trance. 'I often come here. It relaxes me.'

Ellie stumbled. How come Charlotte could see so well in the dark? 'Doesn't Jeff think it's a bit weird?' She didn't know why she was whispering. Anything else seemed like sacrilege.

'He's fast asleep.'

So he hadn't intended to come to her room tonight.

She'd half-hoped and half-dreaded. But it was for the best, considering. Ellie sighed, with what may have been relief.

They reached the straggling outskirts of the wood, stepped into the clearing, and Charlotte stood still, hugging herself tightly, staring up at the moon like someone possessed.

'You have to let it wash over you, Ellie.' Charlotte closed her eyes. 'You're resisting. You have to relax. Just feel it. There's nothing to be afraid of. It's just a little bit of peace.'

Ellie stared at her.

Opening her eyes again, Charlotte came closer, reached out a hand and stroked Ellie's hair back from her face, smoothed gentle fingertips over her temple, touched the corners of her slanting, green eyes. She took Ellie's arm. 'Come on.'

Ellie felt like a child again. The darkness and the crashing of the waves against the rocks lent excitement to the adventure. They climbed down to the bay, Ellie's robe catching on jagged rocks and stones continually, until at last she tore it off with a shriek of despair, flinging it down on to the beach below. She didn't feel cold any more.

When they reached the bottom, panting and laughing like a couple of kids, Charlotte slipped off the long white shirt she was wearing, and together, hand in hand, they ran into the sea.

Ellie screamed. But once she'd recovered from the first shock of the cold water on her bare skin she couldn't believe how wonderful it was, floating in the cool, rippling, night-washed water. She closed her eyes, feeling the peace Charlotte had described flowing through her, restoring her. And then she opened them, to stare at the light canopies of cloud and pin-pricked stars dotted against the country-black of the night. Every so often the moon appeared briefly from behind a cloud, then drew back under cover.

'It's beautiful.' Ellie had forgotten this sense of awe. She heard the gentle slapping of Charlotte's arms in the water, somewhere behind her.

In the city this couldn't happen. It was lost to her. When she was out at night – which was rare in itself because of Alex and Pasha's – she was more concerned with crossing busy roads before she could be mowed down by a couple of glaring headlights in Piccadilly. Or with shouting for a taxi, finding a decent restaurant in Market Street, or even gazing into the framed promises of another shoppers' paradise. When there were too many shadowy corners she only worried about being mugged or raped.

But this. This was what freedom was all about.

After the swim they dried themselves with Charlotte's shirt and Ellie's discarded robe, before running, shaking with cold and excitement, back to the wood. They ran all the way to the hideout, shuffling into the entrance, giggling, and fighting over who should go in first. To Ellie's amazement Charlotte had left biscuits and cheese in a blue and white tin, red wine, two glasses, and even spare clothes piled in the corner. On the ground, to edge on to, was a tartan blanket and two big towels.

'Expecting company, were you?' Ellie wrapped one of these around her.

'Well, you never know.'

They huddled close together for warmth, their wet hair dripping on to bare shoulders, both lying flat on their stomachs, Ellie's golden skin touching Charlotte's dark-brown body. With some difficulty, Charlotte poured the wine.

'Something's happened, hasn't it?' she asked. 'You're different.'

Ellie took the glass she offered. It must be more obvious than she'd thought. Charlotte sounded like an echo of Jeff. For a moment she was filled with regret. Of Jeff and what he'd done to her, and to Charlotte. What would have happened, if there'd never been a Jeff?

'Come on. Tell.' Charlotte sounded like a child again. 'Tell me all about it.'

'I've met someone. Someone who's special – I think.'

'You know,' Charlotte corrected. 'You always know.' She twisted on to her back. There was a strange expression in her hazel eyes. 'Tell me about him.'

Ellie remembered the time when Charlotte had first wanted to talk about Jeff. She wouldn't listen. But that was then, a long time ago. And this was now. Everything was different now.

Ellie closed her eyes. 'He turned up from nowhere. Out of the blue. He just walked into the wine bar and hasn't left since.'

She must have been in the middle of her second set when he came in, because by the time the last song was finished and she went over to the bar he was already there, draped over a bar-stool.

Ellie felt the attraction the moment she saw him, and the rapid surge of sexuality took her by surprise. He had eyes like washed-out denim – very cool and sexy, and hair exactly the same shade as her own.

'A haunting number, that last one,' he said, as if he'd known her for years. 'Who wrote it?'

Ellie's heart flipped. The only time it had ever flipped

before was for Jeff, and discovering that it could flip for someone else was such a relief that she could have hugged him, right there and then. 'I wrote it.'

'Great lyrics. You're quite a poet.' He was looking at her with unconcealed admiration. But was it because his heart had somersaulted too, or did he just appreciate her song-writing talents? Much to her confusion, Ellie wasn't sure which she'd prefer it to be.

'I don't know about that. My mother would call it an over-active imagination.'

He stood up, all six feet and quite a few inches of him, and reached into his jeans pocket, pulling out some change. 'Then your mother is a heathen. Want a beer?'

She nodded, although she never drank beer. She'd like to see him call Olivia a heathen to her face.

Patrick was as casual and rough around the edges as Jeff was smooth. He presented himself exactly as he really was – and if you didn't like it, then it wouldn't bother him. But most people did like him.

As Sarah said later, he was such a nice guy. There was no malice or greed in him. His philosophy was to live and let live, and Ellie knew right from the beginning that she could trust him. Patrick would never judge. But would he ever care?

That first night they went for a curry on Deansgate, after Pasha's had closed. As she sat facing Patrick, Ellie knew she wanted to go to bed with him. And she wanted it to be tonight. She was so nervous that her palms were clammy and her thighs kept sticking together. She didn't think she'd ever wanted a man so much.

'How did you get into singing?' he asked her, as they drank coffee out of tiny cups.

His hands seemed too huge for those tiny handles. She couldn't stop staring at his hands.

'I was working behind the bar, and living in the bed-sit upstairs, and—' She paused, not wanting to be the one doing the talking. 'It's a corny story.'

'All the best stories are.' He grinned.

She melted. 'Sarah – you met her – decided she wanted some live music at the wine bar, so she hired a local band.'

'Don't tell me.' He lit a cigarette.

Ellie had to drag her eyes away.

'The lead singer got a sore throat? And you stepped into her place, conveniently knowing all the songs, of course.'

'Something like that.' She signalled for more coffee. '*He* got a job abroad, they were desperate, I got talking to the lead guitarist,' (she didn't add that he wanted to go to bed with her) 'and when they discovered I could sing in tune, we did a lot of rehearsing until I knew their set. I thought it would be fun.'

'And the rest, as they say, is history.' He gulped another cupful. 'But you've come a long haul since then. Writing your own songs is quite an achievement.'

She glowed from the casual praise. Song-writing had, like Patrick, come from nowhere – she'd never even considered it until those long hours alone with the baby, rocking her to sleep with songs that strained to rhyme so hard, she'd been forced to make up her own. And since then she'd had no shortage of time alone to think, write and dream.

Since Olivia had left Pencraig, music had left Ellie – she'd let it go. She knew she had a good voice, and she still remembered that conversation with Jeff which had begun with him asking what she was good at, and ended with sex. But it was song-writing that gave her the fulfilment she needed. It wasn't just something to do in the lonely hours of the night. It was an escape for her trapped emotions. Her relationships with Jeff and Charlotte had screwed her up more than she cared to admit. She needed some sort of release.

Since she'd been writing songs, Ellie had felt more of a real person and less of a cardboard cut-out, as if it had been there all along, waiting for her to discover that she needed it. But she wouldn't tell Patrick all of this – at least not yet.

'Are you still a barmaid as well?' He had one of those semi-Australian, semi-American twangs that always held a question.

'Not exactly.' Ellie fiddled with her coffee cup. Why didn't she want to tell him this? Shouldn't she be proud? 'As a matter of fact I'm a partner now.'

'A partner.' His eyebrows rose. 'You mean like in partner of a business, share of the profits kind of thing.'

She nodded.

'First time I ever heard of a barmaid becoming a partner.' He pulled a face.

'What's wrong with that?'

Patrick shrugged. 'Nothing. Each to his own. I never had you down for a capitalist, that's all.' He glanced at her. 'Don't get heavy. It's not important. I'm just not into ties.'

Ellie felt angry with him. She was getting the impression that everything, with the exception of Patrick's freedom, would constitute a tie.

'It doesn't have to be a tie,' she said.

'Ah.' He leaned forward. 'But you couldn't just chuck it in and go. Could you?'

'Go where?' Ellie was conscious of a strange excitement digging her in the ribs.

'Anywhere. That's the whole point. To go as the desire

sweeps over you.' He laughed. Leaned back, still watching her.

It was appealing. A temptation. If it had just been the question of the wine bar and if someone like this man was ever to ask her— But it wasn't only a question of the wine bar, was it? And why would he ask her anyway? He was the type who travelled alone.

She frowned. 'No, I guess I couldn't.' She looked up into those blue-denim eyes. Would she like to stroke them or just drown in them? They were eyeing her quizzically.

'But there is more to life than just getting up and going whenever the urge takes you.'

'I can't think of anything right now,' he said.

She laughed with him at first. But then she sobered. If she was going to sleep with him – if he was going to mean anything at all before he disappeared – this get up and go stuff was all very well but it was making her feel very insecure – then she had to tell him.

'I've got other commitments,' she said. 'So I couldn't get up and go anywhere.'

His eyes clouded. 'Commitments,' he echoed. 'Now why is that such a depressing word? A man?'

'A child.' She looked over his left shoulder.

'Cool.'

She stared at him. He hadn't leapt out of his seat, backed away, made the sign of the cross, or even frowned. He looked interested.

'I like kids. Boy or girl?'

Again, Ellie could have hugged him.

She told him about Alex. 'I've never been married though,' she added.

He took hold of her hand that was lying on the table between them, and began absent-mindedly playing with her fingers. Jeff had done that once. Charlotte too, but this time thousands of currents of the most delectable sexual electricity shot right through her.

'Who cares? As long as he's not still on the scene.' He had a lovely smile.

'No, he's not. It was a long time ago.' She didn't like deceiving Patrick, but about this one thing she could never be honest. Because of Charlotte.

He smiled. 'A child shouldn't stop you doing what you really want to do, Ellie,' he said. 'What do you want to do?'

'I want to go to bed. With you.' You didn't play games with someone like Patrick. She held her breath.

He grinned. 'Let's go for it.'

They got up.

'Your place or mine?' Ellie's voice was weak. For such a long time Jeff had been the only man in her life. And for such a long time he'd only bothered to call once a week or less. It was hard to imagine another man's body pressing against her own.

He slung an arm over her shoulders, not possessively, just a friendly gesture. 'It'll have to be your place,' he said. 'I haven't got one.'

In bed Patrick was inexhaustible and amazing. She loved his thin, tawny body, his humour and his total dedication to her pleasure. She even thought she might love him, but that wasn't the kind of thing you said to someone like Patrick. Not now, perhaps not ever. You told him that you were having a great time and hoped he wasn't about to run out of the door. Out of your life.

'No strings, Ellie,' he said in the morning. 'But I have to tell you, you are one lovely lady.'

'No strings,' she agreed. But she could see them. They were like a cat's cradle. Closing in on her, closing in on him. He was living in a dream world. Wasn't he?

Within a week Patrick had moved into the bed-sit that

Ellie used to occupy before she and Alex had taken over Sarah's old two-bedroomed flat. And he was spending most of his time with Ellie. He had very little luggage. T-shirts, a spare pair of faded denim jeans that matched his eyes, and a couple of jumpers. He wasn't into belongings, he said, and she knew that he meant people as well as things. But he did have a lot of paints. Two boxes full, to be precise. And he had talent.

Within a month he'd persuaded a city gallery to do an exhibition of his canvases as part of a much bigger show, and he was working like crazy to get enough stuff finished. He was also advertising for portraits in the local paper. 'It's a drag, but it's a rent-payer,' he said. And on Saturday afternoons he could be found doing pavement drawings along Cannon Street. Outside the shop fronts advertising jeans and check shirts, away from the glossy sophistication of the department stores.

He laughed when she questioned him about this. 'Of course I don't need to.' He frowned. Gently touched her cheek. 'But it's important to me. I don't want to lose sight of my roots. Where it all began for me, you know?'

'Is that where it began, Patrick? With pavement drawings?' She was beginning to understand that there was more to Patrick than she'd first seen. And she liked that.

'It's where the life is.' His voice was low. 'Where the people are. Where art begins and ends for most of them.'

She smiled. For the first time in ages she felt happy. Patrick got on well with Alex, Sarah, and everyone else who mattered, and he made no demands.

Part of Ellie had always yearned for conformity, because she'd never had it. With Patrick she felt for the first time a part of a regular couple. She liked going out with him, being seen with him, having his arm around her. Part of a unit, loved, a whole person.

But at the same time she longed for some of his philosophy to rub off on her. She wanted things not to matter. She'd like the world to be pleasantly hazy and stress-free, as it was when they sat in the evenings listening to music, working, and smoking marijuana – an activity that Patrick introduced her to, displaying astonishment that she'd never tried it before.

'It draws repressed creativity to the surface,' he said.

But it pushed Ellie's into the background. She couldn't write a word when she was stoned. While Patrick went bananas with his brush and paints she just giggled and went to sleep.

Patrick had done all the things that had passed Ellie by, because of the sudden and giant leap she'd taken from sheltered childhood into adult life. He had travelled abroad – picked potatoes in Jersey and grapes in Provence. He'd worked as a waiter in Spanish bars and even joined a band of Dutch stunt drivers touring Europe and calling themselves Helldrivers.

Patrick had achieved freedom from every boring routine. It was alluring to Ellie, but she searched for pitfalls. There had to be pitfalls – there always were.

'He sounds—' Charlotte hesitated. 'A dream. Why didn't you bring him to the party?'

'He was busy. And it's not really his kind of thing.' Ellie couldn't tell her the other reasons. Jeff, for one.

'I'm glad you've found a man to care about.' They linked arms as they wandered back to the house.

'It's early days,' Ellie murmured.

'But at least it proves it's possible.'

Ellie glanced at her with surprise. 'What about you? You and Jeff have been together for ages.' She realised how rarely they discussed him. He'd been one of the most important parts of both their lives, and yet he was hardly mentioned between them. Ellie paused. 'Nothing's happened between you two, has it?'

Charlotte laughed bitterly. 'Nothing much does these days. This is real.' She waved into the darkness. 'Everything else seems a bit superficial somehow.'

'Even Jeff?'

Charlotte stopped walking. 'I don't know if I still love him.' The admission hung between them. 'And the world he lives in means nothing to me now.' Her dismissal seemed to include him.

Did he know how far Charlotte had travelled away from him? Was it only convention keeping them together after all – the same convention that made Ellie yearn for coupledom? She was conscious of the irony. Now that she didn't need Jeff, Charlotte was moving away from him too.

Charlotte wasn't weak, but Ellie knew that she was trying to escape. Back to nature, out of the rat-race, trying to find her sense of self, she supposed. Charlotte wasn't the old Charlotte – perhaps she was gone for good. And she was still experiencing a deep pain that made her beyond Ellie's help. But still Ellie felt envious of her. Just as she'd once felt envious of her for being a wife – especially Jeff's wife.

When they reached the house they clung together.

'I love you.' Charlotte's voice was soft. Tenderly, she touched Ellie's cheek with her fingertips.

'I love you too.' Ellie didn't want the moment to end. When they were together like this all she wanted was to stay close to her for ever. No more choices. No more pain.

Back in bed she stared out at the night that was so different on the other side of a window, and thought about Patrick. She missed him – the feel of his warm body next to hers – but would she ever be able to tell him that? He wouldn't want her intensity and she couldn't love without it. She realised that he was scared. Too scared to accept emotional freedom, too scared to have freedom of speech, of expression. He was as hopelessly tied as she was.

She smiled and closed her eyes. Had she found a man she could love without pain, with balanced desire and not a power struggle in sight? As she'd told Charlotte, it was early days. But when it came down to it she still found it hard to accept – that loving a man wasn't impossible, without a heavy price to pay.

13

The phone fell out of Ellie's hand, and a wide grin spread slowly across her face. 'Stay' had won the competition! Her very own song had won Manchester's annual contest for local song-writers. She allowed the victory to sink into her senses. She'd only entered because Patrick had pushed her into it. And now 'Stay' would be released as a single. A single!

'Patrick!' she yelled. 'You'll never believe what's happened—'

Alex was in the living-room doing puzzles. But there was no Patrick.

It was only a month since Ellie had split from the band, which was travelling further into glam rock and away from the kind of music she preferred. She loved the blues; her husky voice suited the music. And the music suited her songs. Sad, soulful songs like 'Stay'.

Ellie started humming it. Then sang softly: 'Tell me I'm not a passing spirit— Tell me you want to see my face— In the bleakest lights— Opened in the morning— Scared in the night. Tell me you're gonna stay—' She tailed off into silence.

She'd written it for Patrick of course. He'd been with them for a year now – a year, six weeks and two days to be exact – and she still wasn't sure that he'd stay.

But now Ellie felt a new surge of confidence. They had so many good times, Alex adored him, he was becoming known as an emerging artist – he didn't even have to paint portraits any more. He couldn't throw all that away.

He wasn't in the kitchen. And he wasn't in the bedroom. He wasn't even in the room she'd turned into a studio for him. Damn. She wanted to share her news.

He had to stay. Patrick couldn't leave her when she was so close to finding the sort of contentment that had eluded her for so long.

He must have gone out – rarely did he tell Ellie where he was going. It was infuriating. But it was part of Patrick. She'd never change him.

Could she phone Charlotte? It was still instinctive to tell Charlotte first. She wanted to. She even reached out for the phone and began to dial. But in the end she couldn't. Patrick should be the first to know. And Patrick always seemed to resent her ties with Charlotte.

Charlotte. It was hard to think of her without some pain. Ellie still went to Pencraig for occasional weekends of peace. But they were getting further and further apart. Because of other commitments. Because of Patrick. And Jeff. But the longing never went away. It was as if Charlotte and Pencraig existed in some sort of limbo. Just waiting.

Ellie had never taken Patrick to Wales. He'd met Charlotte on one of her rare visits to Manchester, but they hadn't clicked. And Ellie hadn't expected them to. Pencraig had become a place for the closeness of the two sisters to reassert itself. Ellie told herself that she and Patrick didn't need whatever it was that the place had to offer, and even that she wasn't ready to share her life in Wales with him yet. She told herself that the most special place in her life belonged to their future. But she wasn't sure if any excuse was real. Pencraig did seem to belong to her future – but did that future include Patrick?

He came in the door half an hour later, a pack of cigarettes in his hand, and the absorbed look on his face that told her he was involved in a painting. He glanced at Ellie vaguely as if he wasn't sure who she was or what she was doing there. She knew it was nothing personal, but it still hurt sometimes.

Normally she wouldn't interrupt this mood but—

'Patrick!' she said. The suppressed excitement spilled over. 'You'll never guess what—!'

That night he bought champagne to celebrate, and they made love in the sitting-room as they'd done in their first weeks together. His tongue travelled slowly from her slim neck down to her small, perfectly formed breasts. She gasped as he took the nipple into his mouth. She pressed his fair head closer, as though she could mould him to her.

'Patrick. Patrick, I love you.'

There, she'd said it again. It was always exploding out of her. And it was always followed by a short silence of hope.

'You're beautiful, Ellie. God, you're beautiful.' His groan was muffled into her breast. It was nice. But they weren't quite the words she longed for.

He had never told her that he loved her. She pushed the thought away. Perhaps the words weren't in him. Perhaps Patrick couldn't give love.

'C'mon, baby.' He eased into her.

His blue-denim eyes were vague, transported, as if he was lost to the passion. His hands, lips, tongue, worked as if they were apart from it all. It was all so easy for Patrick. He was good at pretending to love.

She relaxed. But what did it matter? He might not say it, but that didn't mean he didn't feel it. He had to. You couldn't live with someone for a year and not care. Who needed words?

Ellie clutched at his shoulders, felt him shudder into her. He loved Alex too. They were a family at last. Confirmation would come in time. She must just be patient.

Ellie was dreaming even before she fell asleep. She had this dream of selling her shares in the wine bar – it had always been Sarah's, not hers. And of buying a small house with a little garden. A place for herself and Patrick to work and make love in. A place for Alex to grow up in. It was a nice thought, one that Ellie often hugged to herself on bad days. She'd feel safe if she and Patrick had that. It would work between them if they had that.

The dream was sending her to sleep. Towards a song called 'Stay', and tomorrow. Tomorrow was Alex's sixth birthday, and they were going to the zoo. A family outing – their first.

By morning everything had changed. The Teasmade wasn't working, Ellie had a headache, and Patrick got grumpy when Alex came in and bounced on their bed.

'It is her birthday.' Ellie was irritated. She wanted all Alex's birthdays to be special.

'It can't be. It's the middle of the night.' Patrick wasn't like Ellie. He was never eager for days to begin.

Ignoring him, Ellie began a rendition of 'Happy birthday to you'.

Patrick groaned. 'What are you trying to do to me?'

She ignored him. Sometimes things were so much easier without a man around.

'Stupid, bloody traditionalist song,' he muttered into the pillow.

Ellie wanted to ask what was wrong with tradition, but she didn't. She couldn't rock the boat with Patrick in it because she was never confident that he wouldn't jump out. So she tried not to mind. But the resentment was there. Small things. Easy to give. That's all she asked. It wasn't a lot.

She took a shower to wash the resentment away. For breakfast she'd make scrambled eggs on bagels and then they'd go out.

But he came into the bedroom while she was still drying herself, stuffing toast into his mouth.

'I'm going to work for a while, honey. Just for a few hours. Okay?'

Ellie stared at him. He really couldn't have forgotten. 'But we're going out.'

'How d'you mean?'

'We're going out.' She heard her voice. It was brittle and harsh, and wanted to get very angry. 'I asked you weeks ago, and reminded you yesterday.'

Patrick's expression was a blank, infuriating mask of ignorance. He stood there in his paint-stained overalls, tapping his fingers impatiently on the dressing-table. He wanted to be out of here, she could tell. God, he made her mad.

'Where are we supposed to be going?' His voice betrayed no emotion.

Perhaps he didn't have any emotion. Perhaps she was wasting her breath, her time, her life.

'To the zoo. Alex's birthday outing. Remember?' An old song danced in her brain: 'Daddy's taking us to the zoo tomorrow—'. No daddy. Patrick didn't even remember his promise. Ellie wanted to shake him. What right did he have to be so caught up in his own little world? How could he live with her and ignore *her* world? She was fed up with for ever coming a poor second in his life.

His brow creased. 'I forgot. Sorry.' He didn't sound it.

'It doesn't matter.' It was Alex's birthday. She was supposed to be happy. She wasn't going to allow today to go wrong. She wasn't going to mind.

He ran his fingers through his unbrushed blond hair. 'But I still have work to do, Ellie,' he said.

'Patrick! You promised—'

She stared at him. Jesus. He looked so bloody casual that she wanted to lash out at him, scream, do something absolutely outrageous that he'd never forget.

'I didn't promise.' He shrugged and looked over her shoulder. 'Anyway, what's the big deal? You know work comes first. I've never pretended it didn't.'

'Don't I bloody know it.' She was blazing. Patrick hated rows, and she was determined to have one.

She took a deep breath. 'Why do you always let me down, Patrick?' Her voice was dangerously calm. 'Just when I think we're getting somewhere— Just when I think there's some bloody point to this relationship. You screw it up.'

'Oh, c'mon, Ellie.' Patrick's eyes were confused. Did he really not understand? 'It's no big—'

'If you say that to me again I'll scream. Because nothing's a big deal to you, Patrick, is it?' She looked him up and down with scorn in her green eyes. 'Nothing except your painting. That's safe enough.'

'What's this all about?' He came just one step closer.

'It's about nothing.' Her shoulders sagged. 'That's what we mean to you, isn't it, Patrick? Absolutely bugger all.'

'We never said it was going to get heavy.' He took a step backwards, towards the door. 'I never wanted to put down roots.'

Ellie laughed humourlessly. Roots? Who was he kidding? Even after a year he had little more luggage than he'd moved in with. Every time Ellie bought him a new shirt or waistcoat because he had so little, he hesitated before accepting. Baggage, more baggage to weigh me down, his eyes seemed to say. And that's what his eyes were saying now.

She sighed heavily, and sat down on the bed. What point was there to all this? She was fighting a losing battle and Patrick wasn't fighting at all.

'Alex will be heartbroken,' she said.

He frowned. And was that a hint of guilt in the blue eyes at last? 'Don't lay emotional blackmail on me, Ellie. You can take her to the zoo on your own, can't you?'

'That's not the point.' Didn't he understand anything? 'She wants us to go together.'

His eyes clouded. 'I told you. I have to work.'

'She loves you.' Ellie began to sob. 'You're like a father to her, although Christ knows why. It's her birthday. Jesus! Can't you forget work for one bloody day?' The towel fell from her slim shoulders. She felt naked and defenceless. But better. She had to tell him these things – too much frustration had wormed itself into her. She had to be rid of it.

He stared at her. 'What the hell is all this about? What's the matter with you?'

'Oh, it's no big deal.' She smiled. 'It's just that I realised something.' Her eyes were like slits of green steel.

'What?' He shifted uncomfortably.

'That your idea of freedom stinks. And that I'm getting sick to bloody death of protecting you from the real world.'

'What are you on about? I don't get you.'

But she caught the first flicker of anger in his eyes, and it urged her on.

She got to her feet. Faced him. 'You're a selfish bastard, Patrick.'

He flinched.

She grabbed clothes at random, pulling them on. Old jeans and a T-shirt. Her hair, still wet from the shower, whipped from side to side.

But Patrick stood his ground.

'I'm not her father, Ellie,' he said at last. The anger, what little she had seen, was all gone. 'She's not my kid.'

'I know that.' Viciously she towelled her hair, still crying with frustration. Even this row was a bloody one-way row. Like their relationship. She couldn't even make him shout at her. 'But you're the closest thing to a father she's got.'

He didn't come to her. She needed comforting arms to hold her. A voice to tell her she was loved. But there was nothing.

'I never wanted to be anyone's father.' Patrick seemed to be talking to himself. The worry creased his face once more. 'I don't want to be. I can't.'

'I just wanted us to be a family.' Ellie sank to her knees. She buried her face in the bedcovers. Never, never had she pleaded with a man like this. Never had she felt so angry. And so helpless. If he didn't come to her now—

'I'm not a part of your family.' Patrick had his hand on the door. He was opening it.

He was so far away from her. She couldn't believe that last night they'd held each other as if each was the other's destiny. Or had she only imagined that? He was going. There was nothing to lose.

'I wanted to marry you, Patrick,' she whispered. Loud enough for him to hear. 'I love you.'

He hesitated. She felt him hesitate. She held her breath.

But when she looked up from the bedcovers the room

was empty. An utter hopelessness swept over her. She'd lost him. Never had him really. He wasn't there to be had. She'd been kidding herself all along.

Then the anger resurfaced with fresh intensity. An anger of humiliation. Somehow Ellie staggered to her feet. Followed him into the kitchen.

He was standing at the sink, washing brushes.

'For Christ's sake—' she muttered. How could he think about painting at a time like this?

'Nothing's changed, Ellie.' He turned to face her, pushing her damp blonde hair back from red-rimmed green eyes.

'Everything's changed.' She stared at him. 'We've been living together for more than a year. How can things not have changed?'

Patrick turned away. 'Marriage was never on the agenda.'

'Will it ever be?' Her voice was bleak.

He wouldn't look at her. 'We're happy as we are, aren't we? What d'you want to get married for?'

'What about love?' she whispered. 'Is love on the agenda?'

The blue-denim eyes shifted back to the brushes. 'Not now, Ellie.'

'Then get out.' There was a stark confidence in her voice. This had to be finalised somehow. She couldn't go on like this. She couldn't just pretend it hadn't happened. She couldn't pretend it didn't matter. 'Get out of my life. I don't want you here.'

'Ellie—' he began. But she saw the relief in his eyes. Relief followed by fear. And it tore her in two. He didn't want scenes. And he was too scared to commit himself to something he couldn't control. He'd rather go. That's what was so heartbreaking. He'd rather go.

Patrick walked out of the door. Easy for him. He'd pack

a few things, collect his work and do it. Just walk out of the door.

Ellie made the scrambled eggs for Alex. She had to keep herself together. It was Alex's birthday, for Christ's sake. But she was numb. And she knew that when she allowed herself to start feeling again, she'd be crying for quite a while. She'd be lonely too. Ellie picked up the phone to call Charlotte.

Half an hour later Jeff put down the receiver. He'd do what Charlotte asked, but she didn't know the half of it.

He drove to the wine bar, parked, rang the bell and waited. After a few minutes Eloise came to the door. Her face was red and her eyes swollen, but it only made her look more vulnerable. He could stare at her face all day.

'Jeff!' Her eyes widened with surprise.

She'd been hurt. Jeff gripped his keys until they cut into his fingers threatening to break the skin, but he forced a light smile. How could that lazy, hippy bastard have so much power over a woman like Eloise?

'I've brought a birthday present for my favourite girl.' He pointed to the huge, silver-wrapped package propped against the wall outside. He'd been wondering how to get it to her for weeks – he certainly hadn't relished the idea of calling on them for afternoon tea and polite conversation.

Ellie laughed, and her sad face brightened. He could still do that at least. 'She'll be thrilled. Can you get it up the stairs?'

'No problem.'

He let her go first so he could watch her. Her fair hair was longer. She wore no make-up. And she'd put on some weight, but not much. It suited her – there was a faint voluptuousness about her now. Even in those old jeans.

'How have you been?' It seemed strange asking her that. He'd taken her for granted all those years, assumed she'd always be available. Allowed himself to be distracted – scared off, even. Paid off too. And yet why should she always be available? Eloise was one gorgeous girl – woman really since she'd had Alex. And she had brains. More than that, she had much more than that.

'I'm okay.' She ran lightly ahead. 'We were going to the zoo.'

'Were?' Best to make out he didn't know. Callous hippy bastard, disappointing his daughter like that.

But Ellie laughed. 'Don't pretend you don't know all about it.'

He'd forgotten how easily she could see through him. And yet Eloise had loved him despite that. If it had been love. What did she feel now?

'How did you guess?' he stalled.

At the top of the stairs, she turned. 'Jeff, I haven't seen you for months. Not since Leonard and Sarah's wedding, for Christ's sake. And I was in a right state when I phoned Charlotte. It's a bit of a coincidence you turning up less than an hour later, don't you think? I'm surprised she's not on her way here too.'

He smiled. 'Maybe she is.'

Ellie stood with her hand on the closed door of the flat. 'Are you supposed to be comforting me or what?'

One glance from the slanting, green eyes was enough for the wicked humour he saw there to turn him on. 'Whatever you need, Eloise.'

Despite himself, Jeff remembered that wedding. Not that he wanted to. That had been bloody difficult, seeing Eloise hanging on to the hippy's arm. She was in a gorgeous sea-green dress that perfectly matched her eyes. A sea-green dress with a plunging neckline and a jagged hem.

With blonde hair piled on her head and a gold chain at her throat. She looked like a beautiful mermaid from some lost sea. And she'd hardly glanced his way.

'That's Ellie's new man.' Charlotte nudged him. Pointed at the hippy, dressed from Oxfam. 'He's living with her now.'

So he'd been right. He'd known there was someone. She was out of bounds. Jeff clenched his fists.

'I suppose it's nice for Alex to have a father figure around.' Charlotte sighed. 'Although I wouldn't have chosen him.'

Jeff snorted with laughter. 'He wouldn't be capable of it. Looks a bit of a wimp, if you ask me.'

Charlotte wrinkled her nose. 'Well, Ellie's nuts about him, I can tell you that.'

Failure and rejection were nasty little words. Jeff wasn't used to them and he wasn't going to bloody well start admitting to them now. But he'd missed Eloise. Not the sex, although he missed that too – what man wouldn't, because Eloise was wild. But the rest of it. Women— He'd be better off without them. Eloise had tied him in knots emotionally, and Olivia had tied him up financially. As for Charlotte— Sometimes he wished he never had to see another Morgan woman again.

Except this one.

Ellie opened the door and Alex looked up.

'Uncle Jeff!' Her face became a portrait of animated excitement.

The spasm of joy that streaked across his heart took Jeff by surprise. He put her present down, caught Alex in his arms, held her close and felt the tears come to his eyes. He loved this child.

But he'd never know what it was like to be called Daddy. That hurt – never being able to tell her, knowing that she was so much a part of him. Because he felt a bond with Alex that scared him – they were so alike it seemed he could look into her soul. She was a mirror image for him to worship.

And he felt a responsibility for her welfare that Eloise wouldn't allow. That she'd give without question to that hippy bastard.

'Hiya, sweetiepops. Are you having a good birthday?'

'Not bad.' The small face was very serious. 'We're going to the zoo.' She looked up at Ellie. 'We are still going, aren't we, Mummy?'

'Yes, of course we are. I was just getting ready.' Ellie flicked back her unbrushed hair and put her hands to her face. The sadness returned, touching the green eyes.

He wanted to hold out his arms to her too, take mother and daughter to a place of safety where no hippy bastard could ever hurt them or touch them again.

'I'll take you,' he said. 'I've got nothing else to do.' That wasn't true, but Alex was special. She was family.

'Oh, no. I don't think that's a good idea.' Ellie wrung her hands together in a gesture that was familiar to him.

'Mummy!' Alex's voice was plaintive. 'Why not?'

Jeff pulled the child on to his lap. 'Yeah, why not?' He grinned. He knew perfectly well why not. But he wanted Eloise to suffer a little. Her punishment for absconding from his bed into a hippy's.

Ellie looked helpless. Her eyes pleaded with his. 'We can go on our own. There's no reason why you should come.'

'I want him to.' Alex nestled into his shoulder. 'Please, Mummy?'

Ellie shook her head. 'It's impossible.'

'You're family,' Jeff said quietly. 'I'd like to take you.'

As if he'd said the magic words, she hesitated. 'If you're sure—'

'Absolutely sure.'

'But no funny business. Okay?' The expression in her eyes made the meaning clear.

He laughed. 'Guaranteed. No funny business.'

'Promise?'

He held up a hand. 'I promise.'

She nodded. 'Okay then, I'll go and get ready.'

As Alex planted a kiss on his cheek, Ellie turned to look back at them, regret in her eyes.

'Go on then.' He waved her away. 'Your daughter is going to open her present.' My daughter, he wanted to say. Or even better, our daughter.

'What is it?' Alex stared wide-eyed.

'That's for me not to tell and you to find out.'

She took a deep breath and began ripping off the paper.

It was a gleaming red and white bike with metallic stabilisers and a Minnie Mouse bell. Alex gasped.

'There's nowhere to ride it around here.' Ellie came back into the room. It's too expensive, her expression told him. But nice. 'You shouldn't have—'

'Rubbish. She can take it to the park. Are you ready?'

She nodded.

He grabbed Alex's hand. 'Then let's go.'

If Ellie had ever wanted to spend a day feeling part of a complete family, then this was the perfect one. And it was better than she'd dreamed it could be.

It was the simple things that were special. Like lounging on a bench eating hot dogs while Alex attacked the playground with exactly the intended spirit of adventure. Munching apples, sharing packets of crisps, licking the salt from cold lips.

It was laughing hysterically at Jeff's chimpanzee impression, watching Alex's huge blue eyes drink in his stories.

It was watching Jeff climb up the helter-skelter with Alex, both of them whizzing down the long red tunnel. Knowing he cared for her safety. Knowing he loved her. Applauding her antics on the climbing frame and exchanging those little parental glances of concern, appreciation, delight.

It was deciding which was their favourite animal and all agreeing it was the sun-bear, one last cup of tea, and then 'I spy' on the way home.

'Oh, Jeff. I'm really glad you came.' Alex had gone to bed at last and the two of them were alone in the small kitchen. Ellie felt exhausted, but exhilarated beyond description. 'It was such a wonderful day. I can't tell you how much—' She stopped at the expression on his face.

'It was a wonderful day for me too. The best day I can remember.' His voice had a husky, caressing quality that seemed to soothe her tangled emotions.

She laughed, although he sounded so serious. They'd been laughing all day, but suddenly, without Alex, the mood of the laughter had changed. There was a tension in the air between them.

He came towards her. She shrank back against the kitchen cupboard.

'No funny business, remember?' she whispered.

'God, I've missed you.' He was only inches away. His blue eyes – the eyes she could never forget – were stamping their peculiar power into hers. All she could think of was how different his face was from Patrick's.

Patrick's was a boyish face. A dreamy face. But Patrick wouldn't say that he loved her. Patrick had let her down.

Jeff's face— Oh, Christ, it was nothing like a dream. It was so close, dark and brooding. His jaw was covered in the shadow of stubble. His eyes burned under thick, black brows. A man's face. Never any doubt about that.

Her breathing came faster. The old excitement began to drill through her veins. Hardly even forgotten. Some ancient tribal drumbeat thundered inside her. Heavy, low, dangerously rhythmic. How Ellie had missed that excitement – the thrill Jeff gave to her that no one else ever could.

'I've missed you too.' She couldn't deny it.

Unlike Patrick, Jeff wanted all of her. Patrick didn't want everything, so he got nothing worthwhile.

She threw back her head. She and Jeff were different. They could be one body, one mind. Jeff could understand her, and he was a part of Charlotte too.

His hand caressed her neck. His lips were almost touching hers. He was waiting, holding back, teasing her, ensuring that she couldn't say no. That she wouldn't be able to deny him. He knew her so well.

'I love you, Eloise,' he said.

The words sank into her senses. Again she thought of Patrick. The words he wouldn't say. And the way he'd left her when she'd needed him the most.

But Patrick was fading from her mind. This was where she belonged – with the father of her child. She reached out her hand to twine the dark curls around her fingers. 'We shouldn't.' A hot, moist whisper in his ear. 'What about Charlotte?'

But they both knew that none of it mattered – compared with this. At precisely the same moment, their mouths, arms, and then their bodies and legs cleaved, each around the other, as if their passion could devour them, suck the other into themselves.

Ellie folded against him, he took her, they tore off only the clothes that were necessary, and made a frantic tortured kind of love on the tiles of the kitchen floor.

Some time later Jeff carried her into the bedroom and they

made love again, slower this time, staring into each other's faces. And when Ellie tried to think of Patrick she found that his face had disappeared.

'Hold me,' she whispered. 'Just hold me.'

In the early hours of the morning they turned to each other for the last time, almost too exhausted to move, but so aroused that they had to have one another again, desperately, as if it were an ending.

An hour later Ellie awoke, thought of Patrick and wept. But Jeff slept on.

In the morning Ellie pushed him out of bed, her first thought for Alex. She staggered to the shower. When she emerged, she could hear Jeff and Alex in the kitchen. The smell of frying bacon wafted tantalisingly through. She sat on the bed. They seemed like a regular family.

And then she remembered Charlotte, and she wanted to cry again. Instead, she pulled on jeans and an Aran jumper, went into the kitchen with a wide smile already on her face and stopped dead in astonishment. Jeff and Alex were eating bacon sandwiches. And Patrick was sitting next to them.

Ellie couldn't move – she just stared from one to the other. Patrick seemed calm enough – everybody seemed calm – but how could they be?

'Jesus, Eloise.' At last Jeff broke the awful silence. 'Cat got your tongue?' His face was dangerously angry. He stared at her. 'I've put the sleeping bag back in the cupboard,' he said.

'What?' She felt like a mindless zombie. 'Oh, right.' She nodded. So Patrick hadn't realised. Jeff had fabricated some story. She didn't know whether or not she cared.

But she did know that she was angry too. This morning was so close to last night that she still belonged absolutely to Jeff. She wanted to kiss him, perhaps even make love again. Something deep in the pit of her stomach was reaching out for him as if it knew he was her man. What right did Patrick have to turn up like this? He'd left at the worst possible time yesterday, and come back at the worst possible time this morning.

'Did you forget something?' Her voice was cold. So much had changed between them. She sounded as if she was talking to the man who read the gas meter.

'Ellie, I've got to talk to you—' Patrick's eyes were weary, as if he'd been up all night. He looked even scruffier than usual. But there was something different about him too.

Jeff scraped back his chair. 'I'll be going.' He kissed Alex, but didn't look at Ellie.

'I'll see you out.' Ellie followed him out of the door and down the stairs, in silence.

'Will you take him back?' Jeff turned, as they reached the bottom.

He was freezing her out. His eyes were well below zero.

'I don't know.' She hugged herself. Looked down. 'Will you go on living with Charlotte?'

'That's different. We're married. And she is your sister.'

That was cruel. She waited for the pain to ebb away. 'Don't give me that. You can't expect me not to have a life of my own.' She grabbed his arm. 'You can't expect me to hang around waiting for you all my life. For your weekly visit. It would never be like it was yesterday. We'd never be a proper family. We're kidding ourselves.' It hadn't felt like that yesterday. It had seemed very real. Part of her wanted him to deny the truth of her words.

'She's my daughter.'

This wasn't the man she'd been with yesterday. And loved all of last night.

'My daughter,' she said. 'And don't you forget it.' Her eyes glittered. No one could stake a claim on Alex. She'd kill them first.

'You weren't saying that last night.' He stood facing her, his face expressionless.

'Last night was different. It doesn't give you any rights over Alex.'

'You can say that again.' He swung away from her. 'See you around sometime.'

She watched him go. He didn't look back. Jeff would never do that. Even if it weren't for Patrick, they'd never be happy. Charlotte would always keep them apart and they'd only be together with Charlotte between them. It was a mess. It would always be a mess while Jeff was in her life. There was no other way. She and Jeff might be sexually compatible, she felt the warmth between her legs – she couldn't deny that. But what else was there? If it weren't for Alex binding them together, then even yesterday would never have happened.

Ellie trailed back up the stairs. As she went into the kitchen Patrick held out his arms. He had no idea. And yes, he looked very different from yesterday. But then yesterday seemed like years ago. Even winning the competition seemed like years ago. Another life.

She walked into Patrick's arms. But they felt alien after Jeff's. And they were demanding something of her that she couldn't give. That couldn't be right – Patrick never made demands. He was talking, but for a few minutes she didn't hear what he was saying.

'I've been really dumb. I want to be with you and Alex,' he said. 'I should have gone with you. I shouldn't let work take me over like that—'

She shook her head. This was all wrong. 'It doesn't matter. We've got no claims on you. You were right –

you're a free agent – you've always said that. I've always known that.'

'No.' He drew back. 'That's what I'm trying to tell you. I'm not a free agent any more.'

'Huh?'

He released her completely. 'I liked to think I was,' he said. 'It seemed to be the only thing that mattered. Once. But these last months—' He grabbed her hands. 'I've been happy with you, Ellie. I don't want to lose you and I can't walk away from you like— like I've walked away from everyone else.'

She stared at him.

He hung his head. 'Last night I was thinking about it. I couldn't stop thinking about it. I let you down yesterday. You were right – I've been a right selfish bastard. Taking everything and giving bugger all back. I can see now I've been scared, Ellie. Just plain shit scared to let myself admit to feeling anything. Scared of being messed around, I guess.'

'What are you saying, Patrick?' Why hadn't he said this yesterday? Why hadn't he come back and said this before—? When it wasn't too late.

'I love you, Ellie,' he said softly. He looked into her eyes. She couldn't doubt the sincerity she saw there. 'I love you. I want to stay with you. And we'll get married if that's what you want.'

'Oh, Patrick.' She knew how much it had cost him. She held him, stroked his blond hair as if he was a child. But she didn't feel what she'd expected to feel. Her heart wasn't jumping for joy. There was only an emptiness. A void. Where was the future for her and Patrick?

'I love you too, Patrick,' she said dully. 'I'm glad you're going to stay.'

14

'You're a bitch.'

Jeff Dando spoke calmly. He was lounging on the burgundy-leather Chesterfield in Olivia's Chiswick open-plan two up, two down.

She was seated at the mahogany desk, busily writing with her gold-nibbed pen – exuding expensive perfume and a patronising smile.

'Vulgarity won't help the situation.' She glanced up, her eyes as icy as a winter's day.

Jesus, she was such a cold bitch as well. How could he ever have thought that Eloise took after her mother?

'Maybe not, but it might make me feel better.' Jeff stretched. 'And you know it's true.'

He enjoyed taunting her, seeing how much she'd let him get away with. And he needed to make himself feel better after last week with Eloise, when that hippy bastard walked in to disturb his breakfast with his daughter. Up till then, that had been one of the most precious moments of his life.

Alex had been overjoyed to see Patrick. He saw it on her face and it knocked him for six. Kids – they broke your heart all right.

What a day they'd had. Jeff sighed. So good, that he'd been on the brink of making the biggest decision of his life. About to suggest to Ellie that they got together. Officially. It would be go for broke – this bitch would ruin him financially. And Charlotte would never forgive them – even if there was bugger all between them any more.

But just think what he'd get in return. His daughter, and a woman who understood him and turned him on more than any other woman ever had before. And ever would again.

'What's the matter with you today?' Olivia frowned, a faint pucker in the perfect, pale foundation she wore. 'Is it Charlotte?'

'No more than usual.' Jeff laughed without humour. He was wasting his life with Charlotte. Wasting days when they hardly spoke. And nights of thankless, gutless, mechanical sex.

Why did he bother? Life would have made sense with Eloise and Alex. But it wasn't to be. When the hippy bastard turned up like a bad smell, Eloise had made it crystal clear where her loyalties would always lie. And maybe she was right. Maybe it would never have worked between them. Olivia had done her best to make sure of that.

Jeff got up and wandered over to the window. Looked out on a drab street full of terraced houses that had become yuppie houses, with yuppie cars parked outside. At the end of the street was Chiswick High Road – crammed with wine bars and restaurants for them to mingle in. He stared into the rain. Oh yes. Olivia had made sure that he couldn't give Eloise the attention she asked for. Olivia had taken care of everything.

He remembered the look on her face when she'd realised that Alex was his child. The wild fury. Spitting venom, she'd been. The only time he'd seen her lose control. At Alex's party.

Angry green eyes looking him up and down with disgust. 'You're filth,' she said. 'You belong in the gutter. And that's exactly where I'm going to put you.'

Somehow he'd stayed casual. 'Can I help it if you've got

two beautiful daughters that I can't resist?' Flattery was the best option open to him. Perhaps the only option.

But she laughed in his face. 'That won't wash with me. You're wasting your breath.' Her eyes narrowed. 'How many times was it? With Ellie. How often?'

'Pretty often.' He kept his eyes fixed on hers. Countless times. What difference did it make?

'Never again.' She snapped her bag open. Got out her cheque book. 'How much do you want?'

'What?' Jeff was flabbergasted. Would she actually buy him off?

'How much do you want to stay away from both of them? Ellie and Alex. For good.'

He shook his head in disbelief. 'I don't understand you.' Why the hell would she want to do that? Since when had she cared about her family's welfare? And she certainly didn't care for him.

'You don't have to understand anything.' She was calm now. The topic of money always seemed to calm her. 'Just tell me your price. I presume that you have a price?'

For a moment Jeff was tempted to tell her to stuff it. It would be a good feeling. To see her face change. But how could he? He was up to his eyes. Already he owed her more than he could possibly pay back. And if he could persuade her to shell out enough, it might get her off his back for ever.

'Thirty thousand.' He stared her out. She'd never agree. Thirty thousand for a woman and his child. Jesus, what a callous bastard he was. He'd sunk to the bottom now. Olivia had only given him the first push to send him on his way.

She raised perfectly plucked eyebrows, but didn't stop writing. 'There's no going back on this, Jeff.' She signed the cheque with a flourish, tore it off and flapped it in his face.

'This is the one and only payment. Otherwise I'll tell Charlotte everything.' She paused. 'And I'll break you. You know that, don't you?'

He nodded. She had more balls than he'd ever given her credit for. She was a bitch. First-class material. No doubt of that.

Jeff turned from the window with its white Venetian blinds that were even colder than Olivia was, and ran his fingers through the dark hair that seemed to be getting thinner by the minute. What did it matter now? He had no claim on Alex. He never would have. Eloise had made sure he realised that. He would never experience fatherhood, never know that needing kind of love that only a dependent child can give. He'd sold it. If it had ever been his to sell.

Charlotte had never needed him, even Eloise hadn't needed him. Who did need him? Certainly not this woman who was such an insidious part of it all.

Olivia pushed the half-spectacles she now wore for close work from her elegant nose. Everything about her whispered elegance. From the delicately highlighted hair coiled around her head to the faintest touch of blusher on thinning cheeks. To the pearls around her neck.

'You don't treat Charlotte very well,' she observed. 'All she wants is a family, and yet you don't make any effort to oblige. You're far too fond of your other pursuits.' The last two words were uttered as if Olivia had wrapped a tissue round them before she could bear to say them.

'Other pursuits?' He mimicked her tone. 'You mean building a successful property business?'

'I wish you would.' Olivia glanced at him over the rim of her glasses.

Jeff could see no hint of humour there. She really was a miserable bitch.

'You've never learned the value of hard work. You expect everything to be handed to you on a plate.' Her voice dripped scorn.

What was she trying to do to him? Educate him or emasculate him? Or was it just power she wanted?

Jeff stared at her. There was a self-containment about Olivia that he wanted to smash. And she certainly craved something. Otherwise why go to all this trouble? Why enmesh herself so totally in his affairs? He couldn't bloody move without her blowing a whistle.

He sat down again on the Chesterfield, and shut his eyes so he didn't have to look at her. Whatever she craved, it wasn't sex – and that was what women usually wanted from him. They disguised it. It became romance, affection or flattery, because women weren't supposed to search for sex. They were supposed to be seduced. Realising this was one of the secrets of Jeff's successful score-card. But in the end it always came down to sex.

He opened his eyes to see Olivia still frowning at him.

'What are you dreaming about?' Her voice was almost tender.

Jeff smiled. He didn't believe in the possibility of her tenderness. She just wanted to see inside his head. 'Wouldn't you like to know?' he jeered.

'Not particularly.' She turned away. 'It would probably be a waste of my time.' She seemed to find it so easy to make him feel as if he were back in short trousers.

'It might be a brilliant money-making scheme.'

'Based on your past record, I doubt it.' She began sorting through the remaining papers on her desk as though she had so many more important things to do with her time.

Jeff knew how much she enjoyed pointing out to him that he hadn't got very far in life after all.

'You're very good at criticising my lifestyle,' he grumbled. 'But I work like a bloody slave. There's a high stress level in what I do. It might look like going out and having a good time. But what you call "other pursuits" is known in the business as nurturing contacts and developing leads.'

She sighed, and put down her pen and glasses. 'I'm not one of your silly bimbos, Jeff. Give me credit for some brains, for heaven's sake.'

Was she including her daughters in that sweeping description of his women? Knowing Olivia, she probably was.

'You're good at balancing books,' he said. 'But you haven't got the faintest idea of what's going on in the real world out there. What the recession is doing to the property market for a start. Not a clue. Everything's changing.'

He helped himself to more biscuits from the porcelain plate on the coffee table. Women and business went together like Stilton and lemonade, in Jeff's opinion.

'Don't be so silly.' Olivia could humiliate with one small lash of the tongue. It wasn't what she said, it was the way that she said it.

She got up, and he watched her graceful figure stoop to switch on one of her Tiffany lamps, then walk to the window to lower the blind. She had a classic kind of beauty that hadn't aged. And she had the sort of coolness in her eyes and voice that made you want to find out what could set her on fire. If anything.

She came to the Chesterfield, sitting carefully on the arm, smiling at him in that remote way that she had. 'You haven't proved yourself so far.'

She was cold all right. Everything about her was cold. From her pale face and white hands, to the bitter eyes. She was soured. And sexless. She was probably frigid. There was probably nothing that would set her on fire. She'd created an unfounded reputation out of her need for attention and romance.

He shrugged.

'I want you to collect some rent for me,' she said. 'From Fielding House. My usual man's gone down with flu.'

'Do what?' He stared at her. Was that all he was now – a glorified rent collector?

'You don't mind – do you?' She smiled.

He recognised the grim determination in that thin-lipped smile. Whether he minded or not wasn't an issue. He'd be doing it, God damn her.

Jeff got to his feet and paced over to the other side of the room. Bloody white walls and smoky glass tables. A chrome-framed mirror on the wall so that she could be sure to see herself often. Not a picture in sight. Hard, cold surfaces, not a trace of warmth to be found. Christ. The place was as soulless as the inside of a freezer. It suited Olivia with her bitter, green eyes and sour-milk smile. And it suited what was between them. Business partnership – it was more like a slow kind of death.

He sighed. It hadn't always been like this. Until six months ago Jeff believed that Olivia secretly fancied him. From their very first meeting, on the day of her husband's funeral, he'd been the object of those veiled glances of hers. And it had kept him master of the situation, however much she tried to demean him. However much she inveigled herself into his affairs.

He'd ask her opinion – partly to flatter but also because Jeff never underestimated second opinions – but he remained the decision-maker. No question. Whoever might hold the purse-strings, Jeff was in control.

But six months ago all that changed. It had been a bad time—

Sex for Jeff had been getting particularly meaningless. New women – mere refurbished versions of what had gone before – came and went so quickly that he could almost blink and miss them. That's how little any of them meant to him. They were symbolic necessities for his self-esteem, like having electric windows and power steering in the car, or wearing a designer suit.

Jeff was worrying about Charlotte, and missing Eloise. Thinking, and getting drunk, and wondering where he'd gone wrong. Something he never used to do. It had been raining all day. He felt like death.

And then Olivia turned up out of the blue. A bit like a gift you wouldn't have put on your Christmas list and yet found you had room for in your bottom drawer. Just happening to be there – remote, still attractive, and even looking a little like Eloise if he had another rum and coke and squinted at her.

'You're a good-looking woman, Olivia.' Granted, it wasn't much of a chat-up line. Certainly not up to his usual standard, but he was pissed and he'd assumed she'd want it.

She turned to stare at him in surprise. Her cherry-red lips parted ever so slightly. He saw the tip of a protruding pink tongue. And he grabbed her. An inexpert and drunken pass – more of a lunge.

Olivia dodged the lunge with the expertise of experience.

She'd said it then too. 'Don't be so silly, Jeff.' Making him feel about ten years old. 'What on earth are you doing? You're my daughter's husband.'

'Don't I know it.' Jeff groaned and put his dark head in his hands. He couldn't look at her. He was Charlotte's husband. And marriage to Charlotte seemed unbreakable.

Representing a stamp of authenticity – almost confirming Jeff's very identity. And Olivia saw that.

'I know you've got problems.' She came up to him, sitting on the arm of the chair. Like she'd done just now. As if she wanted to tantalise him with the fragrance of her womanhood.

'And I'd like to help you, I really would.'

He looked at her doubtfully. It seemed unlikely.

'But *that* sort of thing is out of the question.' She took his arm. Smiled the sort of smile that Jeff would have taken as a direct invitation from anyone else.

'Let's just forget it ever happened,' she whispered.

But every time he saw her – every time she spoke to him with that certain smile in her eyes, he remembered. And he knew she did too.

One lunge had altered the entire balance of their relationship. And it had made Olivia just that little more tempting. Now, he rather wanted her – only to see what it was like, of course.

One lunge had led to his control being whittled away. And now he'd sunk this low.

Her perfume brought him back to the present and reality. She was staring at him, a quizzical expression on her face.

The anger rose inside him. 'I haven't got the time to go bloody rent-collecting,' he snapped. 'Maybe you should try it yourself for a change. Get a taste of how the real world lives. Or are you frightened to get your hands dirty?'

'Very amusing.'

Olivia glanced down at her delicate hands. She knew he'd do it. He always did eventually – he just liked putting up a fight. And he didn't realise that all these little things, all these demeaning tasks that she created especially for him – followed by a generous tip of course – were more links in the chain. The chain that she was forging between them.

At times it was touch and go. But she didn't doubt her power to pull it off. She'd never failed yet. And it had made her a rich woman.

She allowed her gaze to linger on Jeff's lean, hungry body. It made her glad to see him here, in her house. And she allowed the insults, because that was all part of the game. It was all a means to an end.

There had been many men for Olivia since she'd first married Rolf. Men who loved to give her presents. Presents that began with perfume and trinkets, and progressed to expensive jewellery. Diamonds, rubies, gold and pearls, Olivia had them all. In return, if they were lucky, and if it suited Olivia, they got her. Part of her, anyway. She was still a bit of a dreamer back in those days. Not even conscious of the power she held.

Later, after she left Rolf, she realised that she needed financial independence beyond the generous allowance he gave her. She needed it for the kind of lifestyle that she longed for.

She had a sizeable legacy from her father, so she set about finding herself an adviser or two. It didn't take long to learn all she needed to know. And then she was ready to use it – to acquire more, and to acquire power. She didn't dream any more. If you had money and power you had freedom. The freedom to choose. And the freedom to pursue beauty – when you saw the years sucking it out of you and passing it on to others.

Jeff sighed again. He paced from one side of the room to the other, but nothing changed. It was all white walls and a meaningless sort of taste. He felt like a caged animal in this woman's world. It was a prison. And she had him banged to rights. He felt defeat tapping him on the shoulder.

'Okay, I'll do it. Give me the books then.'

She got up, went to the desk, and handed them over with a smile. Touched his fingers for slightly longer than necessary. But you'd hardly notice. Then she sat down again as if he was dismissed.

It was all a question of class. Olivia didn't have to try. She was class – and he admired her for it. Charlotte and Eloise had shrugged it off because they didn't need it. It didn't belong with their generation. It had become redundant but, like dyed hair, the roots of it would always show.

Olivia looked down on him. He could see it in her manner, and in her eyes. Sensing his working-class background with those high-class antennae of hers. Knowing that, at heart, he was a rough one. Knowing he'd clawed his way up, shut away every part of his past behind locked doors. Learned to speak the right words in the right way.

He'd learned it well. But Olivia seemed to know he hadn't been born with it. That was the difference. She looked at him as though he didn't belong. As though he'd married Charlotte to belong. It was all a little too close to the truth for comfort.

Jeff brushed the unwelcome thought away. He stood there with her rent-book in his hand. 'If I bought that flat—' he began.

It was cheap. It could easily be done up. There was money to be made, he could feel it in his bones. And he only needed one good hit – one deal that was outside her scope, and he could be on his own again.

'If *we* bought that flat,' Olivia corrected smoothly. 'It's my money you're trying to spend.'

'You really are a bitch,' he repeated.

How had Olivia Morgan become so involved in his

financial affairs? It was a partnership a million miles from the easy-going one he'd had with Polly. She'd relied on Jeff to make the right moves, and she'd provided plenty of uncomplicated extramarital sex along the way. But when Polly lost her job she had nothing left to offer him.

Olivia was much more devious. This had begun the day she'd offered to sell him Pencraig. From the day she'd told him that the blasted place could solve his problems. She seemed to know what he wanted and she seemed to be offering it to him on a plate. Why? Had she planned so far ahead?

He might have survived, if circumstances hadn't been against him. The property market taking a dive, Alderley Towers requiring three times the amount of money spending on it than he'd estimated. That building firm going bust when it did. If he'd sold the Didsbury house instead of letting lodgers turn it into a doss-hole, then maybe he'd have survived. If he hadn't given Eloise the money that had ended up costing him his business freedom. A whole world of if onlys.

They'd crippled him. He was still making payments to Olivia, the interest was mounting, Olivia's thirty thousand had got lost in the pile of debts, and the bank was threatening to foreclose, when like an angel of death she rose from the storm to take his affairs in hand. To become the partner with all the say. The one holding the purse tightly shut.

Jeff thrust the rent-book into his back pocket, and sat down again, sinking lower into the leather of the Chesterfield. God, he loved that smell. He had to face it. Olivia was breaking him. He'd lost control. He wasn't his own man any longer. He'd been bought. This might be his last chance.

'I don't want to buy that flat.' Olivia's voice held cold finality.

'May I ask why not?' He mimicked the tone. Snooty bitch.

'It isn't a very nice area for a start.' She got a street map out of the drawer, and traced a line of acceptability with her index finger.

'You haven't even seen the place.' Jeff glared at her.

'I've seen the details. That's enough.'

Women. She'd be telling him next that the house was painted the wrong colour. 'What difference does the area make, if we get it cheap enough?'

She wrinkled her delicate nose. 'It's not sound business sense. And it isn't just a question of price.'

'Everything's a question of price.' He found himself wanting to shock her. He could make a killing on that flat if she'd only give him half a chance. But he didn't want her to know all the details. Some things he wanted to keep up his sleeve.

Olivia shook her head. 'In this financial climate the only way to do business is to do business with those that have money. You must know that.'

Patronising bitch. Maybe she had a point, but Jeff would never back down. This was his project, his baby. He'd researched it, done all the wheeling and dealing. But he had to move now. And he couldn't move without her backing. He was strung up. Who the hell did she think she was?

'You know it will be hard to sell. And it needs far too much spending on it.' Olivia folded the map, her decision made.

Jesus. Anyone would think the woman was totally skint. 'We can get a bodge job done for next to nothing.'

She winced. 'That isn't the way I operate, and you know it. Face up to it, Jeff – there's simply not sufficient profit in it.' Her voice was sharp. There'd be no persuading her.

The anger rattled around in his head. Failure was looming. It was standing right behind him, waiting to get in, waiting for the right time. He could almost smell it.

'I didn't know you were such an expert.' He sprawled on the Chesterfield, dirty boots and all. 'Did you sneak off to a business school for very mature students?'

Her eyes flickered, and her colour heightened. Jeff smiled. He hadn't completely lost his touch then. He could still reach a raw nerve or two.

Slowly her colour returned to its original pallor. 'I think I've proved that, out of the two of us, I'm a little more capable of managing money.'

'Beginner's luck,' he jeered. 'Where would you be without me? Who does all your dirty work? Who's got all the contacts?'

'Naturally I wouldn't associate with those sorts of people.' Taking a mirror from her bag, Olivia reapplied her lipstick.

She wouldn't be beaten so easily. Jeff was glad – it made the battle more interesting.

She glanced at him over the rim of the mirror. 'That's why I decided to take you on. Not because I ever considered you a financial genius.'

'You're a bitch,' he repeated.

'And you're displaying a limited vocabulary, Jeff.' She pressed her lips together. Dabbed delicately with the corner of a tissue. 'You should work on it. And perhaps I should warn you not to go too far. There is a limit to my patience, and what I'll endure for my daughter's sake.'

He laughed. Failure was so close now – reflected even in her eyes, that he had to make a choice. It was make or break. Crumple into a kind of security or break free and face the consequences.

Call her bluff. Jeff had always enjoyed a gamble. It had

come to the point where it was no contest really. He couldn't stomach failure – being dictated to by a woman. He'd be nothing then.

'For your daughter's sake? Since when have you ever cared about Charlotte? Or Eloise?' His blue eyes mocked unmercifully. This was war. 'Why did you have children, Olivia? They've often wondered.'

For a moment she sagged in the chair, looking beyond him, somewhere over his shoulder.

'It might have been an answer.' Her voice was soft. 'It might have made it easier to bear.' She shook her head, glanced at him sharply as if she'd suddenly remembered who she was talking to. 'Rolf wanted children. I agreed with him.'

'And changed your mind once they were born and started making demands?' He was practically lying on the Chesterfield now, still staring at her. Quite enjoying himself. He had her where he wanted her. At last. And this was just the beginning.

She flinched. 'You know nothing about it. Good parents foster independence.'

He snorted with laughter. 'That's convenient for you.'

Women— They had no idea. Staking the life of an unborn child on biological impulses that no one could ever hope to understand. Expecting everyone to fall in with their plans. Assuming that it was all their world. Their decision. Their child. And then— and then—

He thought back with bitterness. How could she have done it? His mother. All he had left of her was a faded black and white photograph, so blurred that it was hard to make the features out properly. But he had a vivid enough picture in his mind.

Of the kiss when she dropped him at the school gate. Soft, full lips.

'Goodbye, my darling.'

He turned his face from her dark beauty, so that the kiss barely touched his cheek. What would his mates say?

'Take care.'

For just one moment he looked into those fathomless blue eyes and thought he saw a tear. 'Bye, then.' He raced off.

How could he have known what she was planning? How could he stop her when she hadn't even bothered to say the right kind of goodbye?

Over the years she wrote him letters. He made his mind blank when she tried to explain. He didn't want to know about unhappy marriages, feelings of imprisonment, and a new love she'd found, that cried out to her more loudly than anything had before. More loudly than the needs of her own son. So much for biological impulses. There was nothing to understand, was there? Some rejections had to remain unacknowledged. They hurt too bloody much.

'It's none of your business.' Olivia was eyeing him strangely. 'You don't know anything about it.'

'I know you hardly see them. I know you go to Manchester and hardly ever see your daughter. Or your grandchild. That's bloody weird if you ask me.'

'No one is asking you.' Olivia tore the glasses from her face and half-stood, gripping the edge of the desk. 'You're hardly in a position to talk about loyalty. Or family responsibilities. Don't pretend to be something you're not.'

Jeff stared at her. Suddenly he knew what she was. She was just a scared middle-aged woman who didn't want to accept that her daughters had become the younger generation. That the world belonged to them, not to the likes of Olivia. The birth of her grandchild had slotted her into the older generation, and she just couldn't take it.

A new hope and a new power surged through him. Getting to his feet, he sauntered towards her. He put his hands on the desk directly facing her.

'If this partnership is going to survive, then you'd better understand how it's going to be from now on.' He took the rent-book from his back pocket and threw it on the desk-top in front of her. 'I play the tunes, Olivia. There isn't going to be any other way.'

She seemed to wither under his scrutiny as he leaned closer towards her. He'd got her now. He knew he had her beaten.

'You're mistaken, Jeff.' Her voice was soft, but her eyes remained unflinching. 'You can't browbeat me.' She stood upright and he straightened too, towering over her.

'Is that right, Olivia?' There was a threat in every line of his face, every crease of his mouth and eyes.

'I hope you're not threatening me physically.' Olivia looked up at him, all innocence. 'As a woman, I hardly present you with much of a challenge.'

'Don't be stupid.' He turned away. Jesus, how did she twist things so easily?

Olivia glided past him, through the white archway that divided the rooms, towards the door. She was smiling. 'Now that, you can't accuse me of. The last thing you can call me is stupid.'

Jeff stared at her. His mind groped for another weapon to use against her. But his mind was empty.

'You don't have any choice. It's no use pretending that you do.' She opened the door. 'It's pointless putting up any more of a fight. You're beaten. From now on you have to do as I say. That's the way it has to be.'

He blinked furiously. What had happened to the script?

'Otherwise I'll withdraw all my financial interest in your affairs, and pay that long overdue call on my elder daughter. I'm sure she'll be interested to hear all the news. About the other affairs in your life. Particularly your exploits with her sister.' Olivia's white fingers were still curled around the door-knob.

He stared at her hand – at the huge diamond solitaire and the opal that seemed to glitter mockingly in the light. Then his gaze moved up to her face. There was a self-satisfied expression on her elegant features that Jeff wanted to wipe off, with a very hard slap.

'And I'm sure she'll be happy to get to know your daughter better – when she knows how closely related she is.'

The blood rushed to his head. It throbbed in his temple, and made him clench his fists into tight balls of fury. He wanted to kill her. He wanted to take her by the throat and squeeze. Squeeze until there was no life left in her. No breath left to say these things.

'You leave Alex out of this.'

'With pleasure,' she snapped. 'Who wants a kid that's the product of a sordid little fling like that.' The distaste on her face made him a little crazy.

'It wasn't a fling.'

'I don't want to hear it.' She put her hands over her ears.

'I loved Eloise.' He lingered over each syllable. 'Perhaps I still do. And Charlotte too.'

Walking slowly over to where she stood, he pulled her hands from her ears, and held them while she struggled.

'Did you hate the idea of it so much, Olivia?' He thrust his face into hers. Close. Until he could see the cracks under that perfect foundation.

'No!' she shrieked.

Her eyes met his. They locked in conflict. They were still. Then at last her eyes closed in defeat.

'Yes,' she whispered. 'It's obscene.'

'But all right if there's no love?' His grip tightened. 'Is that it?'

The pain crossed her features. She clutched at his shoulders. There was only one weapon left. Jeff bent his head and closed his mouth fiercely on hers. Hurting and demanding. He felt her mouth soften under his. His tongue penetrated into the moistness and then darted back. He knew that she wanted him. He drew away so suddenly that her mouth remained open and she almost fell against him. He wiped his mouth with the back of his hand. Stared at her in disgust.

'It was never a fling,' he repeated. 'We were in bed together last week. And it was bloody wonderful. We did it all night long.'

Her eyes widened in horror. 'Shut up!' It was a desperate scream. Her control was gone. Jeff smiled. That's what he wanted to see.

'Get away from me.' Wildly, ineffectually, her arms flailed as she tried to push him off.

He laughed.

'I'll tell Charlotte. You just watch me, you manipulative bastard.' Hatred and humiliation burned in her eyes.

'You wouldn't dare.'

'Are you willing to take that risk?'

Jeff squirmed. The bitch didn't give up easily, he'd say that for her. But he'd gone so far, there was no turning back now. He had to call her bluff. 'Even if you did, Charlotte would get over it.'

'Oh, yes.' She nodded. He could see her fighting to regain her control. 'Charlotte would survive. But she'd leave you. And don't think Ellie would ever have you – she and Charlotte are much too close for that.' She moved a few paces closer. 'If it came to the crunch,' she whispered, 'which do you think either of them would choose? You – or each other?'

Jeff was silent. He knew the answer only too well.

She smiled again – the same evil smile.

Was she bluffing? Would she really do that to her own flesh and blood?

'Do it then, you bitch.' God, she wasn't a woman at all. She wasn't even human. 'Do it then. But remember that you lose everything too. If I go down, I'll make sure I pull you down with me. All the way.'

She wavered. He saw her wavering and inside he was jubilant. He'd won.

'You've said more than enough.' She wouldn't look at him.

'Oh, no. Not nearly enough,' he murmured. Roughly, he tilted her chin and stared into the cold eyes. 'But one word to Charlotte and we're finished. You can take all your bloody money. I'll start from the bottom again. I don't bloody care – at least I won't have to see your worn-out ugly face again.' Opening the door, Jeff walked out with just one quick glance behind him. And he had the satisfaction of seeing that face twist with pain before she slammed the door shut.

He'd won – he knew it. He'd phone her tomorrow, apologise and tell her he was buying the flat. He'd talk her round. Women could always be ground down eventually. It had been a struggle there for a while. But the truth was that women weren't aggressive enough for the kill. They weren't made for it – it was as simple as that.

The important thing – the thing he had to hold on to – was that Jeff had faced up to failure and sent it packing, tail between its legs. So he could hold his head high again. Maybe he was invincible after all.

15

It was a June morning some months later. Olivia awoke at six o'clock and eased herself gently from under the bed-covers to avoid waking him.

Some people might find her morning routine unnecessary. Tiptoeing around the house, getting washed and flawlessly made-up, before the rest of the world experienced its first yawn. But Olivia realised that it was vital. She knew better than anyone the importance of creating the right impressions. And she also knew how cruel the morning light could be to a woman – especially to one no longer in the first flush of youth.

Jeff looked peaceful, his dark tousled head not seeming out of place on the white laciness of her pillow, because Olivia had always imagined it there. Right from the start. The entire bedroom had been furnished with him in mind.

She sighed. And now that he was here, she felt a little more contented at least. His lithe, lean body was even more desirable than she'd ever imagined. All her hard work had been worthwhile, to have this man in her bed, in her territory, under her control. It could only get better.

By the time the final stroke of the eyebrow pencil had been made she saw that it was after seven. Olivia was ready for the world, but he still hadn't woken, so she sat on the edge of the bed and kissed one dark eyebrow. He frowned in his sleep.

She glanced at her watch once more. She had to make an early start, so she'd leave a note. Besides, it was better for him to wake alone on this first morning. She considered carefully.

No endearments to make him feel trapped. Keep it casual. 'Good morning,' she wrote. 'I've taken your advice and gone to visit Charlotte. You were right of course. I should see her more often.' She sucked the pen thoughtfully. 'Don't worry – I won't tell her where you are!' That was about the required tone, the right hint of humour.

But she wasn't going because of anything Jeff had said. Olivia was going to Pencraig to fulfil her promise to herself. She would see Charlotte, but she wouldn't go to Manchester. Ellie had always been her favourite child – despite everything – but these days she hardly saw her. She couldn't bear to see the brat. Ellie's brat reminded Olivia of her own age almost as much as she reminded her of that night in Ellie's bed-sit.

My God. She caught her breath. Olivia had never forgotten the contours of his hard, brown, naked body and the open challenge in his blue eyes. The fact that he didn't care. She'd wanted him since that day. She'd simply been unable to resist that challenge. And what a coup it would be. To claim the man that neither of her daughters could keep. The final triumph.

Jeff stirred in the bed, and Olivia reached out to run light fingertips along the warmth of his arm. He'd been worth waiting for.

Thank God he was out of Ellie's clutches now. It had given Olivia quite a start to realise that it was serious between them. And that Jeff hadn't been bought off as easily as she'd imagined. The real threat had always been Ellie. Because of Alex. And because of what Ellie was. Olivia straightened. Her daughter in every way. Ellie had handled Jeff badly. But he wasn't easy. Even Olivia had handled him badly in the beginning. And she had years of experience.

Olivia glanced away from the dreaming face on her pillow. She wasn't looking forward to this visit. It wouldn't be easy. It wasn't true that she felt nothing for Ellie and Charlotte. On the contrary. But it was true that she'd never wanted them.

She walked over to the bedroom window with its white, frilly Austrian blind. And she found herself thinking of Rolf. Of the day, that dreadful day, she'd discovered she was pregnant with Charlotte. The day she'd told him.

'But that's wonderful, darling! Absolutely wonderful.' Belatedly, he seemed to notice the expression on her face. 'Isn't it? Aren't you pleased, my darling?'

No she wasn't. She dreaded it. She groaned. 'It's not the right time. There are so many things coming up.' Parties, parties, and more parties. 'You realise I'll miss the whole summer! I'll probably spend the entire time being sick and buying maternity dresses.' She knew that she was whining. But she'd married Rolf because she could depend on him to stand by her. Not to have his babies.

He hadn't understood. Rolf had never understood her. And even Olivia couldn't bring herself to tell him that no time would have been the right time.

None of her predictions came true. Olivia made a charming picture at all those summer parties, drinking tonic water, and swanning around in floaty chiffons while other women went swimming and messed up their hair.

It was a time for leaning on all the most delectable men, and one thing that Olivia was good at was leaning. The funny thing was that none of the men she leaned on ever suspected that she could support herself just fine, let alone all of them as well. But that was men for you – always lost to a pretty face and flattery.

Even the first days after Charlotte's birth had a certain appeal – lying in bed with fluffed-up pillows, and the best cleavage she'd ever had. Everyone waiting on her. Cuddling a small, sweet bundle who made few demands and presented no threats.

But things changed. The bundle grew, and wanted attention. Men who had once brought flowers, now brought teddy bears for the baby. And no one noticed when she'd had her hair done.

Olivia was losing the spotlight. Not only that, but the new light she was bathed in was the awful non-persona of motherhood. And she didn't want that, damn it. It meant nothing. It wasn't unique. Thousands of women were mothers, but none was Olivia Morgan.

She fought the baby tooth and nail to become centre-stage once more, held the position with dignity for three years, and then to her horror discovered that she was pregnant again.

Oh, God. Olivia put her head in her hands, even forgetting about her make-up. It was a terrible memory.

'I can't have it,' she shrieked at Rolf. 'I won't have it.'

His kind, calm face. 'I understand, my darling. I know it's painful for you. I'm sorry.'

No, no, that wasn't it. She could stand the pain, but she couldn't stand the disruption to her life. What would Clem say? He'd only given her a present of some shares in his company last week. And the week before that an emerald necklace.

'It matches your eyes,' he'd said.

She'd smiled, knowing how much he wanted her.

'I'm not having it,' she told Rolf.

No answering response in his brown eyes. He just had that look – as if this latest tantrum was only one of her whims – to be indulged or ignored. But never denied.

That afternoon, when he went out, she took the hottest bath she could stand. She sat down in it, with a bottle of gin, and started drinking. The temperature was so high that soon her skin was red-raw. It made her head swim with dizziness.

'Get out of me,' she hissed to her unborn child.

She drank and she drank, lying back, as the steam and heat engulfed her body and her mind. Then at last, when she could bear it no longer, she got to her feet, giggled and almost fell. Traced 'Clem' in a heart in the bathroom mirror.

'What the hell are you doing?' Rolf stood in the doorway.

She giggled again. He was a steam-person, he was lost in the fog.

'Get out of here.' Strong hands gripped her wrists, her arms. She was pulled unceremoniously out of the water. 'How could you?' He threw her bathrobe over her. Picked up the empty bottle of gin. 'What have you done?' His voice was barely a whisper.

His hands, his strong, brown arms, his dark face, danced before her like some evil vision. She screamed.

'Help me, Rolf!'

And he, who'd never denied her anything, who would have given her the world, just stood and stared. With something in his eyes that could have been hatred if she hadn't known him so well.

'Help me.' She sank to her knees. If he didn't help her now, she'd die. She had to know he would always be there.

He scooped her from the floor, carried her into the bedroom, dried her shivering body, and covered her with clean white sheets.

She grabbed his hand. 'Tell me you forgive me.'

He hesitated.

She felt a weight pressing down on her head. She knew that the baby was still alive inside her. Tears coursed down her cheeks. She held his hand so hard that her fingernails bit into the flesh. 'Rolf?'

'I forgive you,' he said. 'Rest now.'

They never spoke of it again.

Ellie was born six months later. A beauty.

'She's the image of you.' Rolf was proud. 'The absolute image. Let's call her Eloise.'

Olivia shrugged. Her green eyes narrowed. No one was the image of Olivia Morgan.

You never escape from jealousy. Olivia came back to the bed, stared at Jeff's sleeping form. Once it was there inside you, it only grew. And she'd always be jealous of Charlotte and Ellie. How could she help it when they had taken so much from her, when they had everything in front of them. And they had each other. Boys would have been better. Girls would never let you forget.

She picked up the pen. 'Help yourself to anything you want,' she wrote. 'There's money in the drawer of the bedside cabinet, and a house-key if you want it.' That was a tricky one. To give and yet take away.

Olivia had taken everything from Jeff Dando. Employed every weapon in her possession to break him. Money and timing – they were both so crucial.

Olivia had won, because Jeff hadn't recognised when the real battle started. It had been tempting last year, when Jeff made his drunken pass at her. Oh, God. If he'd only known how she was melting inside. But that was the real difference between men and women. Women were strong enough to resist those vital temptations. They had to be.

She smiled. Last night had been the right time. She'd waited for him to come to her—

'You know why I'm here.' His blue eyes were aggressive and hostile.

'Because you need money? Because you've got yourself into a mess again? Dug another financial grave?' Yes of course she knew. The estate agent had phoned her as she'd asked him to do. Olivia had made it her business to know every move that Jeff tried to make, before it even occurred to him.

'It could have worked if you'd backed me.' Jeff knew that he had finally failed. She could see that he knew it. It was in the slight droop of the broad shoulders, the lack of arrogance in his eyes.

She was his last hope, and he must also know that she'd show no mercy this time. It had been make or break. And God, he'd come close to breaking her.

'It wasn't the right place for us.' Victory was sweet. She tasted it on her tongue. 'You shouldn't have tried to fight me.'

'I had no choice.' He sat down. He wouldn't look at her. He seemed like a child.

'It doesn't have to be like this, Jeff.' Standing in front of him, she bent and took his face in her hands, cradling, and feeling the roughness of his jaw. 'It could be so much nicer,' she whispered.

His eyes met hers. A faint understanding dawned. 'What do you want from me?'

'I want you to sign one small piece of paper.' She laughed. 'And then I want you.'

He was still puzzled. She took his hands and guided them under her dress.

He groaned, buried his face in her thighs. She knew that she'd won at last.

She reached for the paper and a pen, and watched him sign it all away without even reading the small print. Not that it mattered.

'I'll look after you, darling.' She led him up the stairs. 'You don't have to worry about a thing any more. As long as you give me what I want.'

His blue eyes were glazed and expressionless as he followed her. But she didn't care. He belonged to her now. There would be no going back. She'd give him everything that he thought he needed, and keep the rest to hug to herself.

'Back in a few days. Have a good time,' she wrote, signing her name with a flourish. Bestowing the good time so that he could never use it against her.

She blew him a kiss. And then she left the house. She had to think of Charlotte now.

Olivia parked the sleek white sports car close to the painted white gate that brought back a few too many memories for comfort, slid her smooth legs away from the cool leather interior, adjusted her cream linen dress and walked towards the garden of Pencraig.

She saw Charlotte at once, sitting in the shade of the buddleia, staring at her in that disconcerting way she had. She was a strange girl. Olivia had always thought so, but these days she seemed quite mad. It was this place, it had a way of making everyone half-crazy.

'It's been so long, darling.' Olivia kissed her on both cheeks. She was such hard work. Despite all Olivia's efforts, she'd acquired no social graces whatever.

'Since Alex's birthday party.' Charlotte eyed her warily. She looked tired. Her hazel eyes were huge in her thin face, and her hair was lank – needing a good wash and condition, no doubt.

'Yes.' Olivia sat down, admiring her cream strappy sandals as she did so, smoothed her dress once more, and opened her bag to check her make-up in the mirror. 'I'm sorry I had to rush off that day. I had to get back to London.' She made her voice brisk. The last thing she intended to do right now was give Charlotte explanations of her behaviour. And she certainly didn't want to recall that awful day.

Charlotte shrugged.

Olivia knew that it meant less than nothing to her. When had she lost this daughter? Had it been when she first handed the small bundle to a nanny? Or had it been later – when she didn't bother to watch her growing up? Perhaps it had been when she left Rolf— She thought of Rolf's funeral. No, she'd still had a part of Charlotte then. When they sat together, mother and daughter, in the hammock, and she told Charlotte about her father. She could still have regained her trust on that day.

There had been a certain far away look in Charlotte's eyes – Olivia could picture it as clearly as she could picture the wisteria growing alongside. And Olivia wanted to reach out to that part of her daughter. It shocked her. The moment lingered in the air between them, and then, even as Olivia hesitated, it was gone. They snapped back to their realities – Charlotte back to resentment, Olivia to jealousy. And her daughter was lost to her once more.

'What on earth do you find to do here all day?' Olivia looked around them. It was a beautiful summer retreat. But it had no life.

'Most days I work with Joy Pringle at the village school.'

Charlotte got to her feet and wandered around to the other side of the buddleia. She was wearing a loose white smock and cotton shorts, and her brown feet were bare.

'Joy Pringle—' The name struck some chord of memory. Olivia considered briefly, then gave up. Some old acquaintance of Rolf's, no doubt. He'd been obsessed with this place since those holidays he had here as a child. But as far as she was concerned the place was full of heathens. How could anyone have a social life here?

She shook her head at Charlotte. The girl was a mess. No wonder Jeff wanted other women. The desire shot through her as she thought of him. It surprised her. She'd never wanted a man the way she'd wanted Jeff Dando.

She gazed at Charlotte. 'You could always go to college and do a teacher's training course.'

Charlotte shook her dark head. 'I have to stay here.' She stretched her arms, as if to embrace the garden, and the wood beyond. 'I belong here.'

'I never did.' Olivia got up too, and they wandered towards the house. 'I loathed it.' It had been like a prison for Olivia. She turned to face Charlotte. 'How can you live here alone? It must be unbearable.'

Charlotte's eyes misted. 'There's plenty to do. I look after the garden and the house. I go to the woods and swim in the bay. There's a bit of everything here.'

'But no people.' Olivia reached out her hand to caress the cool grey and white stone of the house. They were by the front door.

'Pencraig,' she whispered. 'It was supposed to be a new start for your father and me.' But it wasn't. It hadn't been a beginning for her and Rolf. Nothing could have given them that.

Charlotte turned away. 'I don't want people.'

'Not even Jeff?' Olivia's voice was soft. She loved saying

his name; the sound of it made her feel tender. And she needed to find out how close they still were.

Charlotte didn't seem to notice. 'It's not important. I like being alone. I've got the sea and the cliff and the woods—'

'Hmm. But you can't have them over for dinner.' Olivia's voice was brittle. It was hard to believe that this was any daughter of hers.

Charlotte laughed – the sound was hollow and unreal. 'I'll make some tea.' She led the way inside.

Olivia's cool eyes scanned the untidy rooms, clothes and books flung everywhere, crumbs on the carpet, hardly a thing in the fridge. She frowned and clicked her tongue. 'How much time does Jeff spend here?' She had an ulterior motive for asking, that was true. But really, did Charlotte expect a man to come and see a wife who couldn't provide much more than bread and milk?

Charlotte shrugged. 'Not much.' Her eyes became broody. 'He doesn't belong here like I do.'

Olivia couldn't resist a secret smile. With her, that's where he belonged.

They took the tea outside.

'How's Ellie?' Olivia sipped daintily at the tea in the porcelain cup with the yellow roses on. It was funny how quickly she ran out of conversation with Charlotte. With Ellie it had always been different. But not now. Not now that she had Jeff's brat.

'All right.' Charlotte's voice was flat. As if she didn't care. As if she wanted Olivia to be gone.

Olivia fidgeted in her chair. She felt uncomfortable in this place. She always had and she probably always would. What Charlotte and Ellie saw in it she'd never know. Charlotte and Ellie. They'd always liked the same things, hadn't they? Same places, same men. They'd always had a closeness she envied so much that it had twisted into some kind of evil spirit inside her. Making her incapable of such a closeness herself. Damn them to hell.

'You'd like Ellie to live here with you, wouldn't you?' Olivia's eyes narrowed.

'Ellie's always belonged here too.' Charlotte looked up at the sky. 'She was here last weekend—' She smiled, her face transformed.

Olivia glared at her. All it took was a mention of her precious sister. 'What about that young man of hers?' She tried to keep her voice casual.

'Patrick?' Charlotte sipped her tea. 'Oh, he didn't come.'

'Just the two of you, then. How sweet.' Olivia's voice was a low sneer.

Charlotte blinked at her. 'What are you talking about?'

'You don't think she'll stay with him,' Olivia guessed. 'You'd rather she was here. With you.'

'I didn't say that.' Charlotte was beginning to look flustered. She wiped her brow.

The day was getting more hot and sultry by the second. As if a storm was waiting on the other side of the cliff. Getting closer. Ready to pounce. Olivia stared at Charlotte. How could she be her daughter? She was a stranger. A stranger who had edged into Olivia's life, remained on the periphery and then— What would happen now?

The love for Ellie was burning in Charlotte's gentle hazel eyes. Olivia recognised it, and she felt the jealousy rise in a red dragon of blood and hatred. 'You think you know her so well, don't you?' Dangerously quietly.

'I do.' Charlotte looked away.

Olivia had the power to destroy them. It was there. Ready and waiting. One small sentence would unleash it. She thought of Jeff. No going back now.

'Then you know that Ellie's been sleeping with Jeff?'

That was it. Done. Olivia sat back on the bench, recrossed her legs and waited.

'No.' Charlotte stared at her mother. Slowly, very slowly, a kind of blackness settled over her heart. She closed her eyes. No. It was impossible.

'You didn't know.'

She could feel her mother's smile. It was twisting the knife inside her.

'It's not true.' Of course it couldn't be true. They'd disliked each other from the start. They'd never been close. Of course it was impossible. She laughed. 'How can it be true—? You don't understand— Ellie would never— She could never— They couldn't. I would have known.' Talk, talk, talk. Words – they were the secret. Never get to the end of a sentence. If she never got to the end of a sentence, then Olivia couldn't say any more. 'It's not true.'

'It is, my dear. It's been going on for years. I caught them myself. The night before your wedding. In Ellie's bed-sit.'

Charlotte buried her head in her hands. She thought of that night. Ellie finding her in the bivouac where she'd fallen asleep. The closeness. The warm feeling that this was where she belonged.

'It's over now,' Olivia said. 'He wouldn't have her now.'

Was that why Ellie now wanted to come home?

The numbness broke into a thousand jigsaw-puzzle pieces, buzzing in Charlotte's brain, looking for something to slot into. She stared at the cup with the yellow roses as if she could hypnotise the subject from her mind. But through the yellow porcelain petals the other thing, the unmentionable, was jostling all of her senses.

She got up and ran. Down the lawn, through the white gate, along the path towards the wood.

'Charlotte!'

She thought she heard her mother's stilettoed footsteps following, and she ran faster. Into the wood, past the clearing, down the second path, through the bracken to the bivouac. She sank to her knees.

Now that she was alone Charlotte couldn't deny it any longer. The recognition of truth was eating a hole in her heart. 'Oh, Ellie,' she whispered. 'Is it really true?'

She looked up. Ellie's face filled her mind. The image changed into the beech tree and a fragmented childhood memory. RM L JP cut into bark.

Nausea was winding around her stomach. Still on her knees, she moved round to the entrance and crawled in, with a sense of sad security, as if she was returning to the womb. Pieces of the jigsaw stopped buzzing and began slotting into place with a horrible finality. Clicking and crunching in her mind. Ellie's attitude to Jeff, Jeff's attitude to Ellie. Times when Jeff had been away, when Ellie had been incommunicative. Looks, odd words. Thoughts that had drifted into Charlotte's mind and then drifted unconnected out again, now connected. It was true then.

She stayed in the bivouac for two long, nightmarish hours. It seemed that she would never be able to cope with this thing. She accepted the knowledge. But anything else was impossible. All she knew was that of the three of them, it was Olivia she hated the most. How could she ever have been her mother? How could she ever have suffered for Charlotte? Cried out with pain when her child was born?

'Was there any love? Was there ever any love?' she said softly to herself. It seemed impossible.

And Ellie. How could Ellie have done this thing?

When Charlotte got back to Pencraig, Olivia and the white sports car were gone. But the air of destruction she'd brought with her remained, festering into a black numbness that crept close to Charlotte's heart.

She went inside, not knowing what she was doing. She collected a few things in a small bag as if she was going on a journey. But she didn't know where she was going. She glanced in the mirror at her dry eyes and left the house, walking. But she didn't know where.

She only knew that she was in danger. Moving stopped her from thinking. And at the moment she couldn't think. That would come. She couldn't think about this betrayal. Not yet.

16

At the station the sense of other-worldliness that usually assaulted Charlotte when she returned to the city after months entrenched at Pencraig was muted. She hardly registered the core of vital lifelessness, so estranged from the natural world she'd made her own. The bustle and noise – even at this time of night, the whistles and screams of Manchester's Piccadilly station, were only a dark blur to her. Part of the general coating, like city grime. She seemed incapable of seeing anything other than this blur.

She'd been pulled here – shocked to discover she had her cheque book in her bag and could therefore pay for her rail ticket from Wales – just as she'd had enough cash to get her to town on the bus. But she knew she must have put them there herself. Part of her at least was preparing for confrontation.

The rest of her was tranquillised. Holding her bag close to her tall, narrow frame, eyes fixed on the path ahead, she moved like a woman with a single purpose. Whatever was controlling her had deposited her on the platform, installed her in a railway carriage, and even given her a nap consisting of about three stations on the way. It was weird.

She was swept along with late commuters heading for home – busy, unknowing people. Never seeing who was in front of them, not hearing their voices, not caring for any other blob of humanity. And Charlotte too felt nothing.

Perhaps she should have stayed at home for a while longer. Taken the time to think things through. But she needed to be moving, and she needed to see Ellie face to face. Only then could Charlotte decide what her next step could possibly be.

She walked out, and took a deep, automatic breath of the evening air before recalling that it was Manchester air – smoky and damp. Then she made her way towards St Ann's Square – along Piccadilly Road and then Market Street, every shop window a blur, every detail of the familiar Gothic landscape meaningless.

What could she possibly say to her? What was there to say? Did the details even matter – when it had happened, how it had happened, and why? Charlotte stared around her. Yes. Every detail mattered. She had to know everything because for so long she'd known nothing. The full picture was what she'd come for – irrespective of how much it hurt.

There were so many cars in this city. So many cars and so many people. Manchester belonged to the old days. The Italian restaurant with the blue and white tablecloths where she and Leonard often had lunch, the small library theatre where she'd dragged Jeff to more than one fringe production. And then Pasha's – the wine bar where Ellie still worked, although they had a manager now.

She stood outside the door, on the cobbles, looking up towards the flat. It hadn't taken long to get here. Her journey seemed to be over before it had properly begun.

The wine bar's night life was in full swing as Charlotte groped her way through the swing-doors. How could Ellie live here with all this racket going on? How could she stand it – the constant smoke, pollution, traffic and noise? It was a million miles from Pencraig.

A gang of young men with slicked-back hair and arrogant

eyes pushed past her as she was deposited inside. She grabbed a nearby pillar and held on until they'd gone. Just for a moment, to steady herself. But her disorientation was getting stronger. Why had she come here?

A group of people in the corner began to stare, and Charlotte was suddenly aware of her smock top and shorts – hardly typical of wine bar attire. The last thing she wanted right now was to be stared at. But further in there were far too many people for her to be noticed. Stacked three deep at the bar, crammed around tables, packed into every available space. Unknown, unfamiliar faces behind pints of beer and parrot-coloured cocktails.

Oh, God. Quickly she side-stepped into the inner hallway, rang the bell on the door marked 'Private'.

'Please hurry,' she whispered. Even confronting Ellie couldn't be worse than this nightmare.

Minutes passed. Supposing she was out? Charlotte felt dizzy. She'd never make it out of this hell-hole again. She had bitten all the fingernails of her left hand down to the quick when she heard footsteps on the stairs. Thank God.

Patrick opened the door. She stared at him. She'd forgotten about Patrick. Tall, skinny, blond and scruffy. He looked like an overgrown schoolboy. The first thing that came into her head was – did he know? Did he approve of free love? Was he laughing at her right now?

'Oh, hi.' His voice was infuriatingly casual, and he was frowning as if to place her, but he certainly wasn't laughing.

'Hello, Patrick. Is Ellie around?' She watched his brain attaching a name to a face and a role to a name as he realised who she was.

'Not right now.' He smiled vaguely, but Charlotte couldn't help glaring at him. Up till this afternoon she'd been jealous of Patrick. And now she was angry. After all, he hadn't been enough for Ellie.

But what about before? What about the night before she and Jeff were married? Charlotte remembered her doubts. Her reasons for marrying Jeff. So complex and so mixed up with having a child and her love for Ellie. But as it turned out Charlotte hadn't even been enough for Jeff, had she? And she still didn't have the child.

'She's not back yet.' Patrick eyed her curiously. Was it the way she was dressed, or some wildness in her that he recognised?

'D'you want to wait?' He rubbed the back of his hand across his brow, apparently unaware that he was daubing it with brilliant rust.

Charlotte nodded. She was hardly going to go back to Wales. Her senses were slowly returning. And she felt tired. So, so tired.

He bounded ahead up the stairs. 'This way.'

As if she'd never been here before. 'Were you working? Am I disturbing you?' She'd rather wait for Ellie alone.

'I came to a good stopping point.' He grinned as he opened the door and ushered her inside.

He had a nice grin. Had she misjudged him? First impressions had told her that he'd never give Ellie what she needed. Maybe he hadn't. But he was probably a nice guy. And he'd been betrayed too. She mustn't forget that. It created a bond between them.

'I should have phoned first.' Charlotte caught a glimpse of her face in the hall mirror, and it startled her. She looked wild all right. There were still leaves in her dark, dishevelled hair from when she'd been in the bivouac, her face was flushed and slightly grubby and her hazel eyes had a raw and crazy look about them.

He was watching her. 'You look like something out of *Midsummer Night's Dream*. I should paint you. Are you all right?'

She turned away from his concern. Concern might make her cry and there was no time for tears now. 'I just need some coffee. It's been a long journey.' She had been mistaken before. Not a short journey at all. A lifetime. She wandered into the kitchen. 'How long do you think she'll be?'

Patrick laughed. 'Who can tell? Let's put it this way. Alex is with her, but Alex has a flexible bed-time when Ellie's involved in a song.' He picked up her guitar and started strumming it. Winced as he hit the wrong note. 'That's where she is. Working on some lyrics with a friend of hers.' He looked across at Charlotte. 'I could call her. I'm sure I've got the number somewhere—'

'No.' Charlotte knew her voice was too loud from the way Patrick glanced at her with surprise. My God. A thought occurred to her. Supposing Ellie was with Jeff? Supposing they were doing it right now? The blood rushed to her head and she almost fell. She clutched on to the dresser. They could be. She had no idea where her husband was. She hadn't known that for a long time now.

'Don't bother to phone.' Charlotte forced herself to remain calm. Besides, she wanted to put off the moment. And she wanted to have the weapon of surprise. Something told her that Ellie would guess why she had come.

'She loses track of time,' Patrick said. 'You know what she's like.'

'Do I?' Charlotte filled the kettle. She didn't feel as though she knew her at all any more. What was Ellie had turned out to be someone quite different. The real Ellie must live here, in Manchester city centre. In a flat above a wine bar, with this man. Not at Pencraig as Charlotte had always believed.

'Everything is okay though, isn't it?' Patrick had followed her into the kitchen and was leaning against the wall.

He was still watching her, although she couldn't make out the expression in his cool, clear eyes. 'I mean, you only saw her last weekend.'

Charlotte suddenly felt sorry for him. 'Yes, I did.' She spoke very slowly. She still wasn't sure how much she wanted to hurt. 'But I need to talk to her again.'

He nodded, his eyes understanding. Why had she ever imagined that he disliked her?

'When she turns up I'll do a disappearing act,' he said.

'Thanks, Patrick.' She attempted a smile. He was trying so hard to be nice to her. As if he knew. As if he'd read it in her eyes. She should try to be nice to him too.

'And how's the painting going?' Charlotte wanted to laugh. How could she function like this, here, in Ellie's territory? So normally? As if her world hadn't fallen apart. As if Olivia hadn't come to see her, and as if everything was okay. As if anything could ever be again. Charlotte shivered.

'Pretty well.' His face lit up. 'I've got an exhibition coming up in a fortnight. It's make or break. A real career booster.' He told her the details. 'It means more to me than anything. And I could never have done it without Ellie.'

'Really?' Charlotte poured the coffee. He didn't know the half of it.

'She's encouraged me to think I could do it. That I had it in me. Enough talent. I'm used to drifting, you know? I've hardly ever been in one place long enough to know my way around, let alone get a show like this one.'

'I'm very pleased for you.' Charlotte knew she sounded cool and stilted. But it was hard to share his enthusiasm. Everything that Ellie might have done for him seemed a farce compared with what she'd done to him.

God. If he only knew. From what Olivia had said, it sounded as if Ellie and Jeff had been screwing their way right through Ellie's relationship with Patrick. Charlotte felt sick. But why would Ellie have done that? She had seemed so serious about Patrick, until last weekend. Wasn't she so proud of loyalty?

Charlotte closed her eyes and remembered Ellie's words. Bare feet on wet sand as she and Ellie walked around the bay, searching for shells for Alex.

'I don't know what I want any more, Charlotte. I don't know where we're going, Patrick and I.' Green, slanting eyes trying to hold on, searching for something elusive.

He's losing her. He's losing her.

The words had hissed and murmured in the tide swishing on to the shingle, sucking it back, drawing it away.

Charlotte had been so pleased. It wouldn't be long now.

And yet here she was telling Patrick that she was pleased for him. She was as much of a hypocrite as Ellie.

She sighed deeply, and looked around at Ellie's things. There was little of Patrick's – hardly any evidence that he even lived here, while Ellie and Alex's clutter littered the flat. Ellie had always been untidy. She picked things up and then discarded them again, without noticing where they fell. Without caring where they fell—

Charlotte leaned forward on the drainer. She had to be strong. She must look around and absorb everything of Ellie's that she could. While she had the chance.

That tiny black teapot with the chipped spout that Ellie had always loved and would never throw away. It was on the old pine dresser. Charlotte reached out and touched it gently with her fingertips. Last year's birthday card from Charlotte to Ellie – daisies in a meadow, Ellie's favourite flowers. The pottery bowl with the honey glaze that Ellie had fallen in love with in a junk shop when she was walking around Didsbury village one day with Charlotte.

She rubbed desperately at her eyes. And how many

things were there whose history she didn't know? She looked through the open doorway into the lounge. Who knew the history of the white porcelain cat on the mantelpiece? The dried roses in the basket by the fireplace? Was it Jeff? Did he know all of Ellie's secrets?

And in the end, did any of it matter? So what, if she'd slept with Jeff? Did it really have to destroy what was between Ellie and Charlotte? That was the vital thing, surely? The only thing worth having. But perhaps it meant nothing to Ellie after all. It was beginning to seem that way.

'Come and sit down.' Patrick led the way into the small lounge, draping himself over an old armchair. All legs and elbows, like some gangly teenager. Charlotte sat down opposite him. For a few seconds she closed her eyes. God, she was tired.

'Don't forget your coffee.' His gentle voice came from a distance away as though she'd been dozing. Charlotte opened her eyes.

On the wall directly opposite her was a photograph – an enlargement that had been framed and given pride of place. Alex was looking directly at the camera. There was a certain expression in the dark-blue eyes that tugged at Charlotte's heart and made her think that she was still dreaming.

She stared at the little girl's face with the snub nose, the mass of dark curls, and the kind of grin that made you want to just take her in your arms and love her. And she thought her heart was going to stop beating.

'Oh, no,' she whispered. 'No.'

Patrick stared at her. 'What's wrong?'

'Oh no. Jesus, no.' The hot tears came from nowhere, spilling down her cheeks. 'No!' she screamed.

'Charlotte? What the hell's the matter with you?' He got up and came towards her.

She scrabbled in her bag. 'Jesus Christ.' She pulled out a photograph and threw it on the table in front of him. It was a small, dog-eared snapshot of Jeff. A close-up. The dark curls reached past his shirt collar. He needed a hair cut. He was grinning. That same, very special grin. The likeness was uncanny. How on earth hadn't she seen it before?

It had always been there for her to see. They must have thought her crazy not to realise. It was right in front of her eyes, and she'd chosen not to acknowledge it. The unnamed father. Christ. The two of them must have thought she was a bloody idiot. She was. For trusting either of them. Especially for trusting Ellie.

Patrick was staring at the photograph. His face had grown very pale. 'You don't mean—' He stared up at the picture of Alex. 'I knew there was a family resemblance, but I just thought—'

'Ellie is my sister, Patrick. Jeff is my husband. They're not related.'

She felt a wave of sympathy for him. But she couldn't have kept quiet. Everyone had to be hurt now. Because Ellie had borne Jeff's child. The child that Charlotte would have killed for. It was the end.

Patrick reacted as if in slow motion. Charlotte gazed at him, fascinated and repelled. Confusion, understanding, denial, realisation of the truth. One, two, three, four in about thirty seconds.

'Not Jeff and Ellie? Not Alex—' He said the names with a peculiar emphasis. She knew that he was asking himself as much as he was asking her. Asking himself why. Asking how it could be.

'Is that why you came here?' He stared at her with hatred.

'I didn't know about Alex.' The tears had stopped. She

felt as if she had a remarkable control, one she'd found on a street corner somewhere, knowing it would come in useful one day. Not one belonging to her, that had been fought for.

Patrick wasn't looking at her now. His blond head was buried in his hands. His thin shoulders were shaking under his black T-shirt.

He was crying and Charlotte hated to see a man cry. Although she didn't know him well, she hadn't expected him to cry. He hadn't seemed the type to care enough.

'I bloody knew it,' he muttered in a strange, thin voice that was unknown to her. 'They always screw you up in the end. Why did I come back? Why the hell did I come back?'

'Why did you come back, Patrick?' Charlotte asked softly.

He looked up in surprise as if he'd forgotten she was there. His eyes were red.

'I thought she deserved better. She seemed to give me so much, you know? And I just took it. Gave her nothing in return.' He looked away. 'I thought she was the one. Bloody fool. But I really thought she was different.'

'She is different.' The pain had gone. Charlotte felt so strange. She wasn't sure what was happening to her now. Maybe she was past pain. Or maybe the pain would come later, when she started to feel again.

Patrick shook his head in absolute denial. 'You've got to be joking. She's just the bloody same as all the rest.' He slammed his mug down on the table. 'Or maybe she is different, you know? Maybe she's worse. I mean—' He glanced at Charlotte. 'Screwing her own sister's husband? That's different all right.'

Charlotte winced. He had a right to be angry. Every right.

'How long has it been going on?' he asked her.

'For some years, so my mother informs me.' Her voice was bitter.

'Years?' He shook his head in disbelief. A sudden thought seemed to occur to him. 'And recently?'

Charlotte nodded. 'And recently.' She sighed.

He got up and began pacing around the room. The small lounge didn't seem big enough to contain him. 'The night I left. When we had that row. Alex's birthday. Christ! She couldn't wait five minutes. He was bloody well here in the morning when I walked in. Having breakfast with Alex.'

'Having breakfast with Alex,' Charlotte echoed. Oh, God.

She'd more or less sent him there. She'd phoned Jeff and begged him to go round, take them out, bring a smile to Ellie's face. He'd done that all right. And what else besides?

Ellie had taken the only help Charlotte could offer her, being so far away. Jeff. And thrown that help right back in her face. How could she have done that? Charlotte shook her head. She'd never known her at all.

How many breakfasts had Jeff and Alex had over the years? He'd had all the joys of a child and denied them to Charlotte. No wonder he was never at Pencraig. No wonder Manchester held such a fascination for him. It held Charlotte's darling little sister and his own precious daughter – something that his wife couldn't manage to provide him with. No wonder Alex was so fond of him. Because he was a lot more than Uncle bloody Jeff.

They must have laughed themselves sick.

'I should have known—' Patrick was still muttering to himself.

'How could you?' She took hold of his hands. They were still covered in paint. She wanted to help him somehow. 'How could you have known?'

'Because like I said – women are all the same.' There was an awful blankness in his eyes that frightened her. She let his hands drop.

'I told myself last time that I wasn't going to care again.'

'Last time?'

His laugh was hollow. 'It was a bit like this time. A woman who I fell in love with.' He got to his feet. 'The only difference was that last time she had a kid while we were together. I didn't know he wasn't mine until the day she walked out on me two years later.'

'I see.' She didn't. Not really. It only seemed that everyone had pain. That no one was free from it.

'I'm going to pack.' Patrick moved towards the door.

She stared at him. 'You're leaving?'

'How can I stay?' His eyes were cold. 'After this.'

She shrugged. 'Where will you go?'

'Somewhere. Anywhere. Who bloody cares? I'll move on like I've always moved on.'

Charlotte sighed. It seemed so final. She felt oddly responsible, as though she should say something to stop him. 'Maybe you should talk to her first—' Strange, but she couldn't bring herself to say her name.

'I won't be changing my mind. I'll leave a note.' Patrick left the room.

Charlotte followed him to the doorway. She could hear his voice, and the sound of drawers being opened and slammed shut.

'Commitment stinks,' he said.

She moved to the front door of the flat. She couldn't stay here either. How could she stand the sight of either of them?

She'd get a taxi, find a bed and breakfast. And then tomorrow she'd go back to Pencraig. What else was there?

She turned. 'It doesn't have to be that way, Patrick,' she said softly. Tears were pouring down her cheeks. Silent tears. 'Don't stay bitter for ever.'

He appeared, framed in the bedroom doorway, his face thin and bleak. A rucksack was slung over his shoulders. 'Fast and loose. That's how it's gonna be for me from now on.' He looked past her. 'I bruise too easily. And I'm not cut out for the betrayals of family life.'

Ellie returned home and put Alex to bed before she saw his note. She never even noticed that his things had gone. He had so few of them.

'Charlotte's been here. She knows everything. She doesn't want to see you. And neither do I.'

Everything. Ellie felt sick. She ran to the bedroom, opening drawers at random. Nothing much had been there, but everything had gone.

She sat down. Charlotte knew everything? Charlotte didn't want to see her? She had to hear that for herself.

Stumbling into the kitchen, she grabbed the bottle of vodka that had been sitting there since last Christmas, and took a glass from the shelf. Her hands were shaking, but the hot sweetness of the drink calmed her. Where would Charlotte be now? She wouldn't have gone back to Pencraig at this time of the night.

Her fingers hovered over the dial of the phone. Friends? Of both Jeff and Charlotte? She couldn't even think of any. Leonard? Hardly, with Sarah around.

Jeff? Would she be with Jeff? The bastard. It must have been him who had told her. Told her everything after all this time. Did he hate her so much then? No. Charlotte wouldn't be with Jeff. She'd be holed up in some anonymous hotel somewhere. Hating and hurting and alone.

Ellie dug her knuckles into her eyes. She wanted to cry, but she couldn't even manage that. There was this void. It had been in front of her for a long time, and she'd pranced merrily on, trying to ignore it. Only now had she fallen down. And she'd sunk so low that there would be no hands to help her up. Not this time.

So she got drunk. She poured more and more vodka down her throat, until she stopped feeling. They had trusted her. She'd let everyone down. And now she had none of them. None of the people she'd tried to love.

Would Charlotte forgive her? She had to, didn't she? They at least had too many links in their chain. They couldn't be broken by this.

Eventually Ellie gave up, slipping into a drunken sleep of terror, crammed with dreams that left her sweating and clutching on to the sheets, while her head was splitting into the most awful sense of loneliness that she'd ever known.

The following day she tried phoning Pencraig. But there was no answer. If Charlotte was there – and where else would she be? – then it was obvious she didn't want to talk to Ellie. And who could blame her?

At last she turned her attention to Patrick, phoning the gallery where he was going to be exhibiting. They must have a new address or number for him. Patrick had put everything into his preparation for this show.

'He's cancelled,' the girl told her. 'And let me tell you, it's most inconvenient. How are we supposed to find a replacement in a week? Answer me that.'

Cancelled. Jesus. She'd done that to him. Inconvenient. Ellie gripped the telephone receiver. Yes, it was inconvenient. Losing a lover was very inconvenient, and a replacement never easy to find.

'But what did he say – exactly?'

The girl sighed. 'He said, "I'm pulling out. I'll send an

address for the stuff to be sent on." Then he hung up. Satisfied?'

'When was this?'

'Look.' The girl sighed again. 'I'm too busy to give you the lowdown on your love life. All I can tell you is that he's blown it in this city, and probably anywhere else he cares to go. He phoned an hour ago.'

'I'm sorry.' Ellie's voice was broken. 'I just wondered where he'd gone.'

The girl's voice became more sympathetic. 'Left you in the lurch too, has he? Well, I'm sorry too. But I rather got the impression he was heading abroad.'

'He would be.' Ellie put down the phone.

He'd gone then. There was no turning back now. Patrick had left her – for better, for worse. Blown the exhibition that could have made him an overnight success. Blown his career. And not even given her a chance to explain. And why should he? What could she have told him that would have made a difference?

Ellie sighed. But in a strange way she felt relieved too. It was a horrible way to end it— She shuddered. But she knew it would have ended some time. And with pain, because there was always pain. So perhaps it was better for it to end now while it was still apparently easy for Patrick to take his things and walk.

Ellie cared for Patrick. No other man apart from Jeff had meant as much to her. But she also knew that he'd been a straw to clutch at – a desperate bid for happy families. And happy families was a game that Ellie didn't seem to be very good at.

It would always be Charlotte who mattered most, and yet Charlotte seemed as far out of reach as Patrick. There was still no answer from Pencraig, and although the urge to drive there right away was strong, Ellie forced herself not to. This was her punishment, and it felt almost good to be suffering it, after all these years. Only suffering could ever free her from guilt.

She had to give Charlotte time. She had to wait, but waiting was hard. So she wrote to Charlotte. Long tortured letters, some of which she sent and some of which just gathered dust in a drawer. She wrote and she waited, but months passed, and still she heard nothing in return.

17

For the next few weeks of that summer Charlotte was living in a pit of emptiness, not sure if she would climb out of it, sometimes not wanting even to make a start. Hardly even touching the sides.

Wherever she went she was cut by the painful memories – in the wood, in the bay, in the house itself. But at least Pencraig kept her going. It always had. It gave her the space she needed, to breathe. She could plug herself into the earth at Pencraig. Recharge herself, and maybe even regain some of what she'd lost. Every day she stayed outdoors. And every evening she sat, knees hunched to her chin, in the window-seat of the attic bedroom they'd shared.

Food was a sideline. She ate only cereal and toast whenever hunger pangs interrupted her introspection. As if life was a continual breakfast that couldn't progress any further.

She stopped going in to help in the school, and she saw nobody. Much of the time she kept the phone off the hook. The silence swamped her, but it was preferable to people. And the radio didn't help. Every programme seemed to be discussing adultery, and every song-lyric became charged with deeper meaning. Every chord found an answering chord of significance in her mind.

Jeff sent her money, but she didn't need much and most of it stayed in a drawer. She knew that one day soon she'd have to find a source of income. And that one day soon she wouldn't be accepting his money. But for now she would take it, because he owed her.

Charlotte hoped that this vacuum was the start of a process of forgiveness. But maybe she could only ever forgive herself. Because this was a time when every humiliation, every deceit, every moment when she had not known about Ellie and Jeff, returned to fuel her jealousy, her wild rages, her goading periods of self-blame. Scene after scene collected into a kaleidoscope as she played them over in her mind. Over and over they spun, creating a cocktail of primitive emotions that Charlotte couldn't escape from.

Ellie kept phoning – God knows how often she tried to get through when the phone was off the hook or Charlotte was out. Each time Charlotte slammed the receiver down fast. She mustn't be tempted into listening to her. That would be dangerous. Ellie was more tempting than a siren. She always had been. But there was no going back this time.

Most days a letter appeared. Charlotte would stare at the large, untidy handwriting on the envelope, and the postmark from Manchester. She would carry the letter around with her all day – half-meaning to read it. Maybe. And then she would put it away in a drawer. With the others. Unopened and unread.

After a couple of weeks Jeff turned up unexpectedly. She saw the car and dreaded the sheepish expression on his face, the smooth voice explaining it away into nothing. He shouldn't have come.

She stood there in the doorway like some tall, dark sentinel.

'Hi. How've you been?' He kissed her with tenderness. Walked past her as if nothing had changed.

'The same.' She followed him into the kitchen. Desolate. Meaningless. Why should it matter to him?

He filled the kettle. 'I've been busy. Trying to work things out. Everything's getting out of hand. I'm not sure what's going to happen, Charlotte.'

She watched him. He had been busy. With Ellie perhaps? How many times had she imagined them – always in bed, and always talking about her. The expressions in their eyes. What they were wearing. Nothing presumably. What they were saying— Probably even less.

'What are you talking about? What's getting out of hand?' She saw from his face that he didn't realise she knew. He hadn't seen Ellie, then. Or Ellie hadn't told him.

He turned towards her. 'The business. It's blowing up in my face.' His eyes held a look of desperation.

Charlotte watched him cover them with his hands, and she felt a shaft of satisfaction. She'd never seen Jeff like this. Needing her, like he never had before. The whispers of defeat were in the slant of his shoulders, and in the expression of his eyes. Charlotte was glad. She could feel no pity.

'I don't know what to do.' His voice was lost.

He'd taken everything she treasured, and left her with nothing. Now he thought that he could run to her and she would give him what he wanted. But there was something that Charlotte wanted too—

'Come upstairs,' she murmured.

He stared at her. 'I can't stay long.' He seemed beaten. Ground down.

'Come on.' She took his hand. She wasn't finished with him yet.

One hot day, after two more weeks of solitude, Charlotte was swimming up and down the stretch of water that formed Dragon Bay. She would only stop when her legs were so weak that she'd be in danger of going under.

She kept thinking of Ellie. And especially of that first summer at Pencraig. No summer since that time had lived up to those distant promises.

It wasn't that she didn't want to talk to Ellie. She did want to talk to her. So much. She wanted to sit in the garden with her, side by side on the bench and talk about everything. Reminisce. Crawl into the bivouac with her, lie next to her and sleep. She wanted to run with her. Through the wood, down the cliff path into the bay. Into the sea, hand in hand. Swimming, like she was now, only with Ellie swimming beside her. If Ellie were here, she wouldn't have to keep going until her legs gave up. She'd be able to stop any time.

But betrayal meant rejection. And rejection left gnawing doubts about what she'd always taken for granted, always trusted. Their sisterhood had been her security.

Charlotte closed her eyes and floated on her back. Why? She found that question sitting under everything she lifted, everything she touched, and anything she wanted to take hold of. But she couldn't keep asking why. Somehow she had to launch herself on to a road of acceptance. It was the only way forward.

She turned, to swim on. Her legs were getting tired, each stroke requiring more effort. Her kicking was flailing, her movements no longer smooth and flowing.

It couldn't have been an accident. No one had affairs by accident. And so it made a farce out of everything Charlotte felt to be true. Maybe Charlotte had only imagined their closeness. Maybe for Ellie it hadn't been the same— She had always been so casual. Charlotte could forgive her so much. But she didn't think she could ever forgive her the child.

Gasping for breath, she moved into shallower water. Just in time. She was within her depth. She dragged her body out of the sea. It was hot – every day was so hot. She imagined herself lost in this spiritual desert. With each passing hour the oasis was harder to find. Every day seemed purposeless and couldn't stand alone – it only shifted into the one that followed it.

She walked, heavily, past the sand, up to the pebbles, and on to the rocks high on the beach, never wet from the tide – they just burned under the sun. How she longed for rain. Everything in the bay had become arid in the heat – like her emotions. As dry and parched as her throat, thorny as the spiky thistles on the cliff path, and empty as the never-ending blue sky.

After two more weeks of unbearable heat hanging heavy over Pencraig, Charlotte decided to have the bonfire. She wanted to be purged and rid of it all.

It was the hottest afternoon of the entire summer, so hot that it was an effort to move – and there was a distant rumbling in the air that seemed to settle on her temples until she could barely breathe.

She chose the spot – the clearing in the wood where there had been a bonfire once before, and returned to the house. Slowly she collected all the things from their past – photographs, letters, wedding souvenirs, and her own childhood diary. Bound with red leather, it was. She'd always treasured it.

She put them all in a wheelbarrow and wheeled it through the garden, up the path, into the wood and to the clearing. When she arrived she was sweating – her thin shirt clung to her back, beads of perspiration coated her eyebrows, and her bare legs were wet.

One by one she scrunched up the papers, the photographs, the letters, slowly building a pyramid. Then, when it was ready, she lit the match. It was time to release some emotion at last.

She waited. The flame rested in the heart of the bonfire. Had it caught? Then the first photograph began to toast. Slowly the edges browned. The crisp, black line curled and spread, and so did Charlotte's triumphant smile—

It seemed a long time before the tears and the memories began to push her back into the present.

Slowly she got to her feet. Dust to dust. Ashes to ashes. Was she purged from the past by reliving these beginnings? At least she knew that her wounds could begin to heal.

That night the rain came at last. There was a storm – the thunder woke her and drew her out of the house, through the wood and on to the very edge of the cliff. Charlotte stood there like a madwoman in her nightdress, with a rain-cape slung over her shoulders. Feet in red Wellington boots planted far apart, hair clotted and stuck to her face, her eyes, her stinging cheeks.

She watched the lightning streak a passage over the water, and she screamed. Louder and louder she cried. She screamed out all her hurt into the rain and the wind and the night. With a supreme act of will, she let the hurt go. Screamed it out, then hugged into herself the small tender feeling of release as she ran back to the wood.

She stayed in the bivouac until dawn, eventually sleeping and waking to the early morning wilderness. Some of the answers were making themselves known.

It was a turning point for Charlotte. She'd gone past the point of change, and now her days held the unpredictability of a roller-coaster – surging and diving, always posing a different question. One day she would wallow in the solitude, have her walk and her swim, decide to go into town, decide to phone Ellie. The next day she'd want to die. The grief, lurking around her, felt like the death of a loved one. The loss of a life. She couldn't phone her yet. She didn't know if she ever would.

One day she spotted Joy Pringle standing on the coastal path on the east side of the bay. It was rarely used, although Charlotte had seen an occasional and unwelcome holiday-maker there from time to time. Luckily it was almost impossible to gain access to Dragon Bay or the wood from that path, so she wasn't too concerned.

Charlotte waved. 'Come round to the house,' she called. Some days she would have shrunk from this, but today she felt stronger.

She went back to Pencraig to meet her.

'I didn't mean to pry,' Joy said at once. 'I hope you don't think I was watching—'

'Of course not. I'll make us some tea.' Charlotte led the way into the kitchen.

'Only it's so beautiful. And very hard to resist.'

There was an odd tone in Joy's voice, and Charlotte eyed her curiously.

'The scenery, I mean.' She seemed embarrassed, there was a high flush on her cheeks.

'You come here quite a lot,' Charlotte observed.

The first time she'd seen her was on one of her visits home from university. They'd met on the lane that led to Pencraig and stopped to chat about the wild flowers and the weather. She'd met her again during the following summer, and again when she was with Jeff, the first time she'd brought him home. Her first mistake. The beginning of the end.

'I like walking.' Joy smiled. 'This is one of the few places that's still uninvaded.'

Charlotte nodded. But she wasn't convinced. The lane only led to Pencraig and a few derelict farm buildings. There was nothing else to see.

'Have you always lived around here?' There was another question in Charlotte's voice.

'Oh, yes.' Joy's light-brown eyes misted over with memory. 'I used to come here as a young girl. This was where I grew up.'

'So that's why you love it.' Charlotte's tone was thoughtful.

'Yes.' Joy smiled once more. 'That's why I love it.' She seemed about to elaborate, and then stopped, eyeing Charlotte warily.

'It meant a lot to you?' Charlotte prodded. She wondered if Joy had known Grandfather.

'Yes. It did mean a lot to me. It still does.' Joy took the tea that Charlotte offered her.

'Let's go outside.' Charlotte led the way. 'It's a very special place,' she said.

Joy nodded as if she understood perfectly. 'It always has been. Your sister loved it too, I remember. Although I haven't seen her here for a while.'

'She's busy,' Charlotte turned away before she could betray her thoughts to this woman. She wasn't sure that Pencraig did mean anything to Ellie any more. Perhaps it was just a small piece of the past she'd shrugged off for good. Ellie was different now. She had a new life, a new world that included the city, bars, singing, adultery—

'She was obsessed with this place.' Joy sipped at her tea. 'I rather resented her for having it. She was interesting to teach. Such a dreamy child. I tried— but we never got along.'

Abruptly Charlotte got to her feet and walked to the far edge of the lawn. Her fists were curled tight, her hazel eyes shuttered and cold. She didn't want to talk about Ellie.

Joy watched her. 'Why don't you teach at the school any more? I know it's none of my business, but those children do miss you. Not to mention the staff. Perhaps you should have taken up teaching as a profession.'

Charlotte turned. Her laughter had a hollow ring to it. 'I was hoping to have a child myself. Sometimes it hurts too much to see all those kids.' Why had she told her that?

Joy went to her, and squeezed her arm. 'Don't despair, my dear,' she said softly. 'It's not too late for you.'

Charlotte stared at her.

'Come and see me whenever you like. You know where I am? Perhaps one day we can have a talk.'

Charlotte nodded. 'Maybe I will.' It was true that she felt some sort of bond with this woman – perhaps because of Joy's love for this place. 'And you must feel free to come here too.' She smiled slowly as she looked across at the wood. 'I know all about memories.'

It was six weeks after this conversation that Jeff turned the key and stormed into Olivia's Chiswick home. She was sitting on the Chesterfield, turning the glossy pages of a catalogue with those scarlet talons of hers. Always bloody spending money, that woman. But then she had plenty of it.

'Well, hello.' Olivia's flawlessly painted, poppy-red lips smiled at him as though he were a welcome surprise, and he didn't know whether to smile back or start raving at her.

She had this effect on him – making him feel powerful one minute and dependent the next. She was at once infuriating and then irresistible. Class and money. With those two commodities she could probably accomplish anything.

And she had him right where she wanted him – he knew that. She now owned everything he'd ever owned – including Pencraig. And she'd like to believe she owned him too.

He never wanted to come here, and yet he kept coming. Dancing to every tune she played.

He didn't come here for sex – he could still get better elsewhere, although perhaps not anyone with quite the same touch. Jeff had to admit that Olivia had a certain way with those fingertips of hers. Turned him on more than fifty pairs of big tits. And she was willing to do almost anything to please him.

But he did get a different, unexpected kind of comfort from her, that was almost maternal. Only Olivia could make all his worries go away. Like a mother was supposed to. And perhaps that's why he came.

'Hi.' He sat down in the chair opposite, and stared morosely at the pale-grey carpet he hated. Who was he kidding? Even Olivia couldn't make this worry go away. And she was about as maternal as a Martian.

'What's the matter, darling?' She was all concern. 'Have you had a hard day? Would you like a drink or something? Tea? Beer? Scotch?' She stretched out her legs invitingly.

Very sheer, very nearly black stockings. And very high heels. Jeff felt himself hardening in response. Jesus Christ. He ran his fingers through his dark, unkempt curls. His blue eyes were helpless. Would it never end? He looked away.

'Or something more satisfying?' Slowly, like a prowling lioness, she got to her feet and moved across the room to sit on the arm of his chair.

The top three buttons of the black blouse were undone. The skirt had a slit up to the thigh. He caught a whiff of the hardly discernible, expensive scent that she wore. She put it in her bath and it acted like an instant aphrodisiac on Jeff.

'Scotch and soda,' he growled. He had to look at her again as she moved to the drinks cabinet. Anything a man could want. He knew that, underneath, she'd have on some very sexy underwear that he'd probably never seen before. Upstairs the bed covers would be drawn back for him, and he could sleep or make love or do anything he wanted to. Just as Olivia would do anything he wanted her to. In bed.

She brought his drink. 'What's wrong?'

'Everything.' He slammed a fist down on the delicate, smoky-black coffee table. It shook from the force of the blow, the whisky glass rattled ominously, and Olivia winced.

'She's pregnant.'

'Who?' Her voice was faint.

'Charlotte, of course. Who do you bloody think?' Oh, yes, it was hard to believe, after all this time.

This had been only his second visit in three months. And after last time, he hadn't wanted to go there at all. Last time had been a cry from the heart. He'd gone for help and advice – to reach out to her. After all, she was supposed to be his wife. But instead— He could still see the triumph in her hazel eyes as she'd led him up those stairs. As she'd sat astride him in her other world. Using him. Instead, she had got herself pregnant.

Christ! Jeff put his head in his hands. How he missed Eloise.

'When did you see Charlotte?' Olivia's voice was brittle.

'This morning. She phoned and asked me to go there.'

She'd been waiting for him at the white gate, tall and serene. Looking quite different from the last time. A bit like the Charlotte he fell in love with all that time ago.

'Jeff.' She held out a hand to prevent him from kissing her. 'I asked you to come here, because I've got something to tell you. I'm pregnant.'

'Pregnant? How can you be?' He stared at her. She'd finally lost her senses.

'It only takes the once. Or so you've always told me.'

Snap, snap, snap. The old Charlotte was back. Could this be a chance for him?

'That's great news.' He searched for the enthusiasm, but to his own ears the words sounded hollow and meaningless.

'I'm pleased.' Charlotte smiled at him. She looked so beautiful. He wanted to touch her, but he didn't dare.

'But I don't want to see you again. Ever.'

He blinked. What was she talking about?

'And I don't want you to see the child.'

He moved closer. 'But Charlotte—'

'No buts.' She reached out to touch his cheek.

The warmth shot through him. Was there a glimmer of regret in her eyes?

'Don't make me go into details. Neither of us wants that. I just wanted to say goodbye.'

There was nothing he could do. She was so far away. He knew that it was over.

Jeff drove back to London like a madman. They were finished then. He'd never imagined it would actually happen. And certainly not like this.

'I see.' Olivia got up and walked to the window to hide her anger. Why the hell was he still sleeping with Charlotte? Why should he need anyone else now that he had her? Charlotte was pregnant with Jeff's child. This could ruin everything. Did the girl have no pride?

After Olivia had dropped the bombshell on her elder daughter she had waited for the explosion to come from Jeff. Charlotte was bound to challenge him about it. And she wasn't entirely sure that she could keep him, having told Charlotte everything. Of course she had warned him what would happen when she'd signed that cheque. If he didn't keep his side of the bargain— And when it came to threats, Olivia always kept her promises.

But the explosion never came, and gradually the truth and triumph dawned. Charlotte wasn't going to tell him. She was nothing but a door-mat. And now she'd let herself get pregnant!

'Is Charlotte pleased?' The words grated out from between clenched teeth.

Jeff raised his glass and downed the contents in one go. His eyes were bloodshot. 'You'd think she'd be pleased, wouldn't you?' he said thickly. 'You'd think she'd be over the bloody moon.'

'But she's not.' Olivia took the glass from him and refilled it. She had the feeling that Jeff wanted to get very drunk. And she was happy to oblige.

'Oh, she's pleased.' He grabbed her wrists as she returned with his drink. 'She's bloody pleased to be free of me.'

She was scared of the pent-up violence she sensed in him. 'What do you mean? Why is she free of you?'

Pulling her towards him, he hung on with a frenzied strength. She held her breath. And then she felt him relax, as he buried his head in her breast. 'She's finished with me now.'

Olivia eased herself on to the chair, cradling his dark head. 'It's all right, my darling,' she whispered.

'She's gone so far away from me,' he said. 'I can't even recognise her any more.'

She stroked his neck and tenderly rubbed the tense shoulders. 'She'll come round. Don't worry.'

'No.' His voice was muffled. 'She doesn't need me any more, does she?' He began to sob. Violent, painful sobs that seemed to tear through his entire body. 'I've given her the only bloody thing she ever wanted. Only it's too late for me to have any part of it.'

His shoulders shook. On and on he cried, like a child, into her breast.

Olivia stroked the dark curls, murmuring soft words of comfort. He belonged to her now. She had Jeff and she even had Pencraig. But she would let Charlotte keep Pencraig. For now. She wasn't a heartless woman. The place meant nothing to Olivia, and it would keep Charlotte out of the way.

She looked down. His hair was black next to the whiteness of her slender fingers.

'I'll look after you, my darling.' Olivia's voice was gentle and her touch was gentle too. But the smile that he couldn't see was a smile of bitter satisfaction.

18

It was summer. One of those early summer days still hanging on to a sense of spring. Hopeful. And that was how Ellie wanted to feel on this particular day.

She was drifting in the hammock. Her body was moving very slowly from side to side, and her mind was moving backwards.

In her mind she was drifting back to Pencraig. Back to that first summer. To the lushness of the overgrown summer garden, Ellie and Charlotte lying on the grass, lulled by the heady battle of the scents. Jasmine versus honeysuckle. Daisies scattered like confetti through the grass, the blending mauves of lavender and wisteria soothing her senses. The lemon blossom of the buddleia waving to her in the breeze, stately hollyhocks beckoning.

Summer secrets whispered in the hideaway. Two heads – one dark, one fair. Too many promises. With every summer that passed, the urge got stronger. To go back to Pencraig, and to see Charlotte again.

Ellie closed her eyes and squeezed hard. There was no time for crying now. All the tears had gone. She could hear Alex, Jamie and David in the kitchen. She should get up, go inside and see them. But she was immobilised by the languor and the memories.

She fingered the daisy chain, now wilting on her bare thigh. Alex had made it yesterday. Daisy chains never lasted long enough to be enjoyed. She remembered that all right.

'Queen of the May.' Ellie had taken the chain of small flowers, placing it as a coronet on her daughter's dark head.

'But it's for you, Mum.' The blue eyes were very solemn. Against her will, Ellie thought of Charlotte.

'It's for you.' The words, the daisies, the chain, sometimes almost everything began and ended as an echo of that summer.

'Mum!' Alex was very much in the present. 'Hey, Mum – where are you?'

Ellie sat up, shielding her eyes from the sun. 'Over here. Dossing.'

Alex bent to kiss her and Ellie had to restrain herself from grabbing her daughter and pulling her into a fiercely protective bear-hug. Sometimes she was so afraid of losing her.

'Did you have a good time?' she asked instead, with the studied casualness that children approve of in parents. Ellie remembered these things.

'Okay.' Alex grinned. 'David's a whizz at cricket. Wow! You should see him bat.'

Jeff's grin. Still it cut into her heart. Pain and pleasure just a little too close for comfort. The grin that could melt and mesmerise. Sometimes Ellie just stared at Alex, marvelling at how like her father she was. Down to the confused frown, the expression of vague perplexity, the confident smile. But not his character. No, Alex would never have that.

Alex leaned forward confidingly. 'But I still wish that Jamie was a girl.'

Ellie smiled, wishing that things could have been different. That she could have given Alex a sister, like she'd had a sister. Given her a childhood to treasure and stay in her memory. But maybe Alex treasured different things. Like David being a whizz at cricket. Who could ever say what would give children their biggest excitements? And what would break their hearts?

Jamie, a year older than Alex, and showing no regret at not being female, came into the garden with his father. David was smiling – he was the kind of man who smiled a lot. She liked David. He was only a little taller than Ellie, and had kind brown eyes and a generous smile. He'd been her closest friend since Leonard and Sarah moved to France, and he'd prevented her from going crazy in the last couple of years. Yes, she had a lot to thank David for.

'How did it go?' She got up and they went inside, into the small kitchen of the terraced house in Hayfield that she and Alex had moved into two and a half years ago.

'It was good fun.' David's hair was windblown and his cheeks flushed. He looked like a kid himself.

After what had happened in Manchester, Ellie felt a desire for escape that was so strong she would have uprooted them to a place much further away from the city, if it hadn't been for her friendship with Sarah. Sarah had gladly bought her out, and now the wine bar was sold, and with it the last dregs of Ellie's city life had drained away.

And she'd come to like it here, living next door to David and his son. The two small families had a lot in common – they were like two halves of a whole.

'Coffee?'

Ellie filled the kettle and grabbed two mugs from the cupboard. Lost and incomplete families. She had lost touch with Olivia, and she couldn't pretend to miss her. But she'd never stop missing Charlotte.

'Can I borrow your keys, Dad?' Jamie bounded into the kitchen. 'I forgot to bring my tape. I want Alex to listen to it.'

'Sometimes I think we should just knock a hole in the wall and be done with it.' David handed them over. He pushed his dark-brown hair out of his eyes and glanced at Ellie over Jamie's head. It was a dreamy look that she recognised and avoided like a bikini on a cold, cloudy day.

She turned away to smile. She knew David wasn't just after a hole in the wall. He wanted them to become one family. He wanted a mother for his son and he wanted to be a father to Alex. He'd be good at it too – Alex already adored him.

'Let me help you.' He put mugs on to a tray, his hand brushing lightly against her own. He wanted her. He was a good man – she'd never find a better one. He was kind, reliable and attractive. So what was she waiting for? Something that was lost to her for ever?

'Let's have this outside.' Ellie held the door open for him. He'd never push the point. Oh, yes, Ellie liked David. She even cared for David. But love? Love was not a word in her vocabulary these days.

They sat down on the steps of the small patio, in a companionable silence. She felt the sun, hot on her hair, and she closed her eyes, remembering their first weeks at Hayfield.

This stuttered friendship between herself and David had begun with the odd word of greeting, and smiles over the garden hedge. At Christmas he invited her over for a drink.

'Are you and Alex spending the day alone?' His eyes were incredulous.

She nodded.

'Then spend it with us.'

She hesitated, they both laughed, and went on to cook two very small turkeys side by side in David's oven.

'What happened to your husband?' he asked her after coffee and two brandies.

'I never had one.' She still wouldn't talk about Jeff. She hadn't spoken to him since the morning after their outing to the zoo, and if she never saw him again she wouldn't care.

She looked at David thoughtfully. 'What happened to your wife?'

'She left me.' The brown eyes became bitter.

'And Jamie?' Ellie nodded towards the boy, engrossed in a game of Snakes and Ladders with Alex, on the far side of David's comfortable lounge.

'Her new man didn't like children. She had to make a choice.' He poured himself another brandy. 'Lucky for me, I guess.'

She nodded. 'Lucky for you.' If she hadn't had Alex, what point would there have been? Without Alex she would have had nothing.

With this confirmation of each other's single disillusioned state, and through the growing friendship of their children, their relationship developed. They shared the occasional supper and countless pots of tea. They became friends, but Ellie made sure that's where it stopped. She was alone and she was distrusting – of herself as much as anyone else.

She'd often thought herself a fool. Expected David to give up on her, find some lucky, lonely woman and leave Ellie with even more regrets. She even told him her life story last New Year's Eve after four glasses of champagne. Every sordid detail.

'So you see what I'm like.' She stared at him. 'You can see what I've done to the people I loved.'

David smiled and took her in his arms. Offering comfort – and what else besides?

'I don't care about all that, Ellie. That's the past. We've both been hurt. I'm only interested in the future now.' She'd forgotten that the Davids of this world thrive on disastrous pasts. They never wanted the challenge of a woman expecting paradise.

It would have been so easy to sweep her doubts aside. To let him take her to bed, to relax in his easy companionship, allow him to take over the responsibilities that hung so heavily on her shoulders. But once she'd done that there would be no turning back.

And she couldn't. So she pulled away from him. The past wasn't finished for her. It wasn't just clouding her present, as David imagined. It was still there, still to be finalised, put away in a cupboard, accepted. She wasn't ready for the future. She was waiting. For more punishment, or absolution, or perhaps only for love.

Ellie opened her eyes to see David staring at her. No one could mistake his expression.

'Ellie—' he began.

'No, David.' Her slanting, green eyes begged for time. 'I don't know if I ever can.' It was only a whisper.

'You can't stop me from loving you.' His dark eyes were reaching out to her. All the safety and security in the world was tempting her. He reached out and took her hand in his.

'Dad?' Jamie and Alex appeared. 'What time's dinner? I'm starving.'

David glanced at Ellie, a sad smile on the kind face. He let go of her hand. 'I'd better be off. See you tomorrow.'

Ellie repressed the sigh of relief. Her hand was still warm from his touch. She nodded. 'Tomorrow.'

David was looking after Alex tomorrow, because Ellie was venturing into Manchester – something she rarely did these days. Tom and Peter were setting up their own Italian restaurant in Oxford Street, and she'd been invited to the grand opening – something she just couldn't miss.

David and Jamie walked away.

Ellie watched them go. She couldn't put it off for much longer. She had to make a definite decision. She owed David at least that.

The following afternoon, as the bus whisked Ellie into Manchester city centre once more, Charlotte was in the loft at Pencraig sorting through bagfuls of children's clothes for the local school jumble sale, suitcases full of old, moth-eaten blankets, and boxes stuffed with junk that obviously hadn't seen the light of day for decades.

No use hoping for any old treasures though – this stuff had been put here because it wasn't wanted, and the best thing Charlotte could do was chuck the lot. She was in that sort of mood.

But in a far corner, hidden under a pile of curtain material, she found a black book, coated with thick dust. Charlotte opened it gingerly. A photo album.

She sat back on her heels, swamped by bitter regret. Why had she burned all those precious photographs? All those sweet letters that could never be replaced? Those childish mementoes of their happy times together. The tears pricked at her eyelids. Surely she had destroyed her past for good? And if she had destroyed her past, then what hope did she have for the future?

She turned the pages, peering at the pictures. But their subjects were unrecognisable in the gloom of the attic. And then Sophie, with two-year-old expert timing, awoke from her afternoon nap.

Charlotte threw the photo album into her box of jumble, carried it down the attic ladder with some difficulty, dumped the whole lot in the sitting-room, and only got around to looking at it a couple of hours later.

The photos were black and white, mostly faded into brown and cream. A family – Dad's family, she recognised him as a young man, although it was hard to equate the dark, upright youth of the big smile and soulful eyes with the stooped man he had become.

She touched the photographs, her hazel eyes dreaming the years away. Dad's family on holidays in their far-off summers. She sat up straighter as she squinted at the background cliff and waves. Here, here at Pencraig. Because of course, as she'd always known, Rolf had come here as a boy, stayed in the cottage Grandfather had bought as their country retreat. Grandfather, who had moved here when he retired, and lived here till he died.

Her eyes half-closed. And then when Mother had made life unbearable for Dad in London, he had brought her here – brought them all here – in an effort to begin again. To find the love and happiness he'd always looked for in her. And never really found.

Her fingers flicked over the thick card of the pages. The photos were tucked in the diagonal cuts of the card, some of them labelled in italic scrawl that had faded with time. Not Mother's writing. Rolf's writing. It was Dad who had put these memories together. Dad who had felt he belonged here in Wales. And Dad who had passed that legacy on to Charlotte, even if he hadn't managed to pass it on to the woman he loved.

Charlotte sighed. Poor Rolf. And yet still he'd left Olivia the house, rather than giving it to the daughters who loved it. Still, he worshipped her and wanted to make her love the place that he loved. He'd never allowed himself to know Olivia at all.

At last the photographs came to an end, with a pageful of snaps of two teenagers – one of them Dad, and the other a girl Charlotte couldn't recognise, although something about her was vaguely familiar. They looked happy. But it was the next page that caught Charlotte's eye.

It was a plan – a drawing really, of— She frowned. Surely it was—? Yes. She leaned closer, eagerly, her eyes intent and curious. It was the bivouac. No doubt about it. A rough plan, but with a surprising amount of detail. Definitely the bivouac – she could tell by the shape, the position of the old beech, and the pattern – how the branches had been woven together.

So. Charlotte stared out of the window at Sophie, playing on the lawn outside. Did this mean that Rolf had built the bivouac? Why had he never said?

A ring at the door broke into her reflections, and she reluctantly got to her feet. She didn't want to be brought into the present – she wanted to wallow in this piece of the past, this newly discovered past.

'Oh, come in, Joy.' The distraction remained on her face.

'Have you found me lots of jumble then, dear?' Joy smiled as she followed Charlotte through into the sitting-room. The photo album lay open on the table beside her. She glanced down at it briefly, looked back in utter amazement, and the smile froze on her face.

'What—?' Her hand reached towards it, and she paled and staggered slightly, as if she might fall.

'Joy?' Charlotte helped her to the armchair. 'Sit down for a minute. Whatever's the matter?'

But Joy just stared at the photo album. 'Where did you get this?' Her voice was soft.

Kneeling at her feet, Charlotte reached to hand it to her. She knew that Joy loved this place, but she couldn't imagine why she would be interested in old drawings of the bivouac.

'It's our bivouac,' she whispered. 'Mine and Ellie's. A kind of hideaway. We found it when we first moved here.' In that first summer. She frowned. That first summer.

But Joy wasn't looking at the drawing. She was looking at the photos on the facing page. 'So he kept them all,' she murmured.

Charlotte stared at her. 'They were Dad's,' she said.

But Joy didn't seem to hear her. Her faded-blue eyes were washed with unshed tears as, ever so gently, she prised one of the photos from its place, and held it, close to her breast. 'Rolf,' she said.

Charlotte looked at the teenage girl smiling at the camera. Smiling at the cameraman. A smile of love. And then she looked at Joy. Her face was lined, and her lips were thinner. Her hair had lost its sheen and was curled into a perm rather than hanging to her shoulders. But there was no doubt. She was the girl in the photographs. And Rolf was the man holding the camera.

'You knew Dad. When he came here for the summer.' Charlotte put an arm around her thin shoulders.

Joy smiled. 'Oh, I knew him all right.' Her voice took on a dreamy, lilting quality, in the way that Welsh voices sometimes do. 'We lived in a cottage down this lane, Mother and I. My father died when I was very young. I never knew him.'

'I'm sorry,' Charlotte murmured. But Joy only squeezed her hand, clearly concerned with the story she had to tell.

'It's derelict now, our cottage. But it was a nice little place. We had a bit of a smallholding, chickens and a goat. We managed.' Her voice changed. 'Nobody even knows it was there nowadays. No one visits it.'

'Except you,' Charlotte said. That explained why she'd

often seen Joy walking down the lane, with that odd and remote look on her face.

'Except me.' Joy paused. 'And then there was this cottage.' She smiled at Charlotte. 'Your father's family owned it – but generally they only came here for the summer. Your grandfather had to work in the city, and this was his summer hideaway.' She paused. 'We all need one of those, don't we, dear?'

Charlotte nodded.

'This isn't what you'd call a social hotbed, as you know for yourself, dear.' She sighed. 'So I and your father, well—' Her eyes misted. 'We were friends.'

Charlotte patted her hand in comfort. She could see it all. It was easy to see. Two kids playing in the wood, climbing down to the bay, swimming, collecting shells, making a hideout—

'Did you and Dad build it?' she whispered. 'The bivouac?'

'That thing!' Joy laughed. 'Oh, you bet. We built it all right. Rolf insisted. He made the plans the very first summer he came here. But it was two more summers before he finished it. He was a perfectionist. Build it to last, he said. It'll always remind us, he said.' Her shoulders sagged. 'So you see, he always meant to come back. I always knew this place was in his blood.'

'It has lasted.' Charlotte sat up straighter, staring at Sophie, who was still playing in her sand-pit outside. 'It's still there now.' She looked doubtfully at Joy. This was very hard for her to say. 'Would you like to see it?'

The tears in Joy's eyes spilled over, rolling down her powdered cheeks. 'I never thought it would still be there. He'd be proud.' She glanced at Charlotte as if she understood. 'But I won't come to see it. It's a secret hideaway, isn't it, my dear? It belongs to you and Ellie now.'

Charlotte was silent. How long before Sophie was old enough to want to start exploring? How long before she found the bivouac? Before it passed on to the next generation?

'You cared for Dad?' Charlotte needed the confirmation. It was all slotting into place – Joy's interest in the two sisters, her deep concern when Rolf slipped into the abyss of grief and alcoholism. Her tears at his funeral.

Joy folded her arms and hugged herself. 'Oh, I cared for him all right. The last summer he was here – he was seventeen.' She replaced the photograph carefully in the album. 'That's when he took these.'

'And when you carved your initials in the beech tree.' Charlotte had almost the whole story now. RM L JP.

Joy nodded. 'It meant a lot to me,' she whispered.

'And to him?' Charlotte wanted to hear it all.

'He promised to write.' Her head drooped. 'But he never did.'

'I see.' Charlotte was doing some mental calculations. It was after that summer that he'd met Mother. When his world was turned upside down.

'And that next summer he never came back.' Joy straightened her shoulders. 'I was a fool. It had only been a bit of teasing. A few kisses. And yet I thought it meant so much.'

'I'm sure it did.' Desperately Charlotte wanted to comfort her, this woman who had given her heart, here at Pencraig.

But Joy was hardly listening. 'He had a life apart from me, I suppose. After all, I only saw him once a year. But for me—'

She looked beyond Charlotte as if she was looking back to her past. To the young man from another world, who came into her life, claimed her soul and then threw it away.

'For me, it was all there was. I looked forward to it all year. Those summers.'

Charlotte got up and looked out of the window, beyond the garden, towards the wood. It was made for summer. Made for two people as close as two people could be.

'Then we moved, Mother and I. Into the village. She couldn't manage the smallholding, and I made plans to go to college and become a teacher. I was going to move away, but there was Mother— And I always hoped he'd come back.' She laughed at herself. 'But I was foolish. A silly girl. I was sixteen that last summer. Not such a child any more, you see.'

'And when he came back he brought Mother.' Charlotte's lip curled. 'He must have been crazy.'

'She is your mother, dear.' Joy frowned.

Charlotte's laugh was harsh and devoid of humour. 'You don't know her like I do. He was besotted with her,' she said. 'And she destroyed him like she tries to destroy everything.'

Joy was silent.

'But you had more of him than she ever did.' Charlotte turned from the window, her eyes full of fire. 'You understood how he felt about this place. You and he shared a dream. It's all here.' Striding to the table she picked up the photo album. It was there, Rolf's dream – in the faded photographs and the pencilled drawing. Mother had never known any of it. And Charlotte was glad.

She handed the black album to Joy. 'Keep it,' she said. 'Dad was young. Maybe he didn't realise how much you wanted him to come back to you.' The thought of Ellie pushed itself into her mind, and she blinked it away again.

'Ah, well.' Joy rose to her feet, still clutching the album. 'It's all past now. I was a fool to hang on for so long – I should have built a life for myself like Rolf did. Moved away, married even.'

Charlotte stared at her. 'And after Mother left him? Did you tell him then how you felt?' Surely it wouldn't have been too late for them.

'I couldn't.' Joy frowned, and the frown seemed to stay on her kind face. 'He loved her so much. And I couldn't bring myself to admit the truth to him. I felt a fool.' She shook her head. 'Pride, my dear. A nasty thing. It can keep you from happiness.'

That night Charlotte sat in her rocking-chair and thought about Rolf and Joy. Funny, but after all those years of Mother's indifference it had never occurred to Charlotte that there might be another woman who loved him.

Pride. Like Joy said, it could keep you from happiness. She'd already wasted too much time. She knew what she wanted, and she had to go for it now, while she still had the courage. There was only one person who could ever understand.

From the drawer in the side of her chair, she took Ellie's last letter – the one telling her that she'd moved. It was the only one that Charlotte had ever read. There had been nothing for almost two years. Ellie might even be married by now.

The phone number was on the top of the page. Charlotte knew it by heart. She'd even dialled the first two numbers, but never got to the end of it. It seemed to be too hard to make the first move. Too much had happened – too much pain. But if she left it much longer it would be too late for her as well.

She moved to the phone, and dialled the complete number. The phone rang, and rang. She let it ring for five minutes, unable to believe that Ellie wasn't there. Then she replaced the receiver, not even knowing if she would ever be able to bring herself to do it again.

'Eloise.'

The voice came from behind her. It was as low, husky and inviting as ever, and it sent a shudder of pure fear shooting down Ellie's spine.

She had just left Tom and Peter's party, was still glowing from the unaccustomed sociable atmosphere, and was only twenty paces from the taxi she'd called to take her to the bus station. So it was hard to believe that he should be here, now. The odds were stacked against it. Maybe it was her imagination? Maybe she'd drunk too much champagne.

She twisted around. 'Jeff?' She was unable to disguise the longing and disbelief in her voice.

He stepped out of the shadows of the Midland Hotel. 'Eloise. Where have you been hiding?'

She couldn't make out the expression in his eyes. She stared at him, wanting to see more, unable to speak, absorbing the lines and contours of the face that she'd touched so often. But he looked different.

'It's been a long time.' The familiar male scent of him made her dizzy. He moved closer.

Her first instinct was fear. This man had always had the power to disrupt her life, had always known he had that power, and had never hesitated to use it. Ellie couldn't face any more disruption.

But the second feeling was pleasure. Slowly it washed over her. She stared at him. He didn't know what to say to her. He didn't know how to deal with her. For the first time since she'd known him, she was immune.

No tiny thrills dancing into knots inside her. No chemistry. At last. She was free of him.

'It's been ages.' She smiled. Even looked around her, across the square, towards the classical dome of the huge library. Wonderful buildings. But she didn't miss any of this – not one bit. 'What have you been up to?'

His eyes shifted warily away from her and she wanted to laugh. 'Oh, you know. The usual.'

'Wheeling and dealing?' Ellie felt so much in control that she wanted to scream with delight.

She examined his physical appearance, paring impressions down to the bone. The light was bright enough to see that he was dressed expensively in a maroon waistcoat, a silk shirt and well-fitting trousers. But although the effect was stylish, there was something missing. Ellie frowned. He'd lost the charisma that had made him exciting. And she'd always thought him invincible.

He laughed uncertainly. 'You know me.'

He'd lost weight and it didn't suit him. He looked beaten. His hair was too long and in the glare from the shop windows and street lights she couldn't miss the deep lines that cut into his face. Lines of pain. What the hell had happened to him?

'How's Alex? I suppose she's forgotten me by now?'

'I suppose she has.' Ellie smiled, to soften the blow. But she had to remember that she owed him nothing.

His shoulders drooped a little more. 'Where are you living now? I'd love to see her. It would mean so much to me. Maybe sometime I could—'

'No, Jeff.' Ellie was aware of the taxi waiting. 'That's impossible.' She wouldn't let him screw up Alex's life. She was both parents to Alex. It had to be enough.

'Eloise—' He grabbed her arm. 'I want to see Alex, I need to see my child—'

The fear shot through her. 'No!' She pulled her arm away. 'I've got a good memory, Jeff. You didn't want fatherhood to be an option, remember? Well, it's too late to change your mind now.' She was shaking violently.

'You're right. I'm sorry.' He let go of her arm.

Ellie turned away, hating the look of failure in his eyes, almost feeling responsible for it.

'You and Charlotte—' he muttered.

'How is Charlotte?' She turned back to him. Scared to even think of her but needing to hear. 'Tell me how she is?'

'How the hell would I know?' He stared at her. 'I left over two years ago. She threw me out. Don't pretend you didn't know.'

'But I didn't.' Ellie stared back at him, at the face she'd once loved so much. 'She hasn't seen me since you told her about us.' The anger flooded through her. With Jeff in his bloody silk shirt and with his slicked-back hair. 'Why did you tell her, Jeff? Why the hell did you do that?'

Jeff stared at her with utter incomprehension in his blue eyes. 'I never told her anything.'

Instantly she believed him. 'Then who did?'

He shrugged. But she saw the knowledge on his face. He knew all right.

She sighed. There was only one other person who would have told Charlotte.

'Do you want this lift or not, love?' Ellie's cabbie called out of his window. 'Only time is money.'

'Yes. Just a minute.' Ellie moved closer to Jeff. 'Is Charlotte still at Pencraig?'

He shrugged once more. 'I suppose so. I never see her. She's out of bounds. Since—'

'I see.' Ellie turned and walked towards the taxi-cab. So Charlotte was alone at Pencraig. Or had she found someone else to share it with?

'Eloise—'

She stopped.

'For what it's worth—' He smiled, and the smile lit up the tired features, the dull eyes. 'I still care. And any time—'

'No, Jeff.' Funny how easy it was. She should have said it a long time ago.

She got in, slammed the door shut and wound down the window. She needed some fresh air. 'The bus station,' she told the driver.

The taxi drew away from the kerb. There was a sports car parked in front. A platinum blonde on the wrong side of forty was doing her hair in the mirror. Ellie's taxi stopped beside it, waiting for a gap in the traffic. Ellie looked over as the blonde opened the door and called into the darkness.

'Come on, Jeff, honey. We haven't got much time left.'

He was walking towards the car. All Ellie could think of was Charlotte alone at Pencraig. Not much time left at all.

She couldn't wait any longer. She didn't sleep that night, and in the morning she took Alex and drove – fast, before she could change her mind – along the familiar route into West Wales. But as they got closer she began to panic. What if Charlotte didn't want her? What if she had someone else with her? What if they had nothing to say to each other after all this time apart? What if they were strangers? She wouldn't be able to face that. That would be worse than missing her.

'Oh, Charlotte,' she whispered.

Two hours later, they were there at last. Everything looked the same, only new to her eyes, changed from the familiar fantasy. She drove down the lane, parked outside the white gate, took a deep breath and sat holding the steering wheel with numb fingers as if it could save her.

'Let's get out then, Mum.' Alex was impatient. Ellie knew that she barely remembered Pencraig.

Slowly, inch by inch, Ellie opened the door, swung herself round, pulled herself out of the car, moving cautiously towards the white gate. Alex ran ahead.

A figure came out of the house – tall and dark, awkward and wonderfully familiar. Charlotte had her dark hair tied in a ponytail as if she were fifteen again, and there was a wide smile on her mouth that reached out to touch her hazel eyes. It touched Ellie too.

They said nothing, but moved towards one another, staring into each other's faces. And when they were close enough, Charlotte was the one who took Ellie into her arms, and held her there. For ages, almost for ever. They rocked, side to side, until they were aware of Alex and her look of confusion.

Charlotte let go, knelt, and traced a pattern down Alex's cheek with her forefinger. 'She's still a female version of Jeff. She's beautiful.'

Ellie nodded, they both smiled, tentatively at first, testing the water, and then somehow, with the mention of his name out of the way, the tension between them evaporated. Ellie felt as if they'd last seen one another yesterday. No, they could never be strangers.

Then, as they stood in the porch, a tiny bombshell of humanity exploded out of the door, in the shape of a small child with blonde curls, green eyes and a magical smile.

Ellie gasped. She could have been looking at a young version of herself.

'You didn't know.' Charlotte smiled, held her daughter still, and stroked the fair curls lovingly. 'Sophie, this is your Auntie Ellie.'

Ellie took the little girl's hands, and gazed into her face. She was perfectly lovely. 'I can't believe it.'

'It's true.' Charlotte grinned.

Alex stepped forward. Ellie took her hand and pulled her closer. 'This is Alex. Your cousin.'

'Sister,' Charlotte corrected. She looked at Ellie over her daughter's head. 'They're as close to sisters as they could possibly be. We could almost have planned it.'

She was right. They were sisters.

Laughing, and linking arms, they began to wander around the garden. Ellie sniffed deeply all the familiar scents, and let out a contented sigh. 'God, I've missed all this.'

She glanced at Charlotte. 'I bumped into Jeff last night,' she said. 'In Manchester. I never realised you'd separated. And he never told me you had a daughter.' She gazed at Sophie. No wonder Jeff was bitter. No wonder he looked beaten – with both his daughters denied to him. 'You did it at last, Charlotte!' She squeezed her arm. She couldn't tell Charlotte how pleased she was. And how much it released her from the guilt she still felt.

'How was he?' Charlotte didn't look interested.

'Fed up.' More than fed up, but Charlotte didn't need to know that.

'I can't blame him.' Charlotte sighed. She pushed her dark fringe from her brow, and Ellie wanted to hug her for the familiar gesture. 'He could push for access rights, but he's in no position to push for anything these days.' She bent to pick some lavender. Sniffed it and handed it to Ellie.

'Why not?' It smelt delicious. Why didn't Charlotte even seem surprised to see her?

Charlotte looked mysterious. 'My guess is that he's too busy building Mother's business empire for her. Seeing his daughter wouldn't be included in Mother's plans. And being Mother, business involves a lot more than property dealing.'

Ellie stopped walking. She stared at Charlotte. 'You mean Jeff and Mother are— You don't mean they're lovers?' God, that was disgusting. The woman was sick. He was sick.

Charlotte shrugged. 'It doesn't matter to me. It was over between Jeff and me years ago. Christ, Ellie – you know that it wasn't just you. He ripped me apart.'

'You should have left him before.' Ellie had never understood why she hadn't.

'I needed this.' Charlotte waved to Sophie. 'And I knew I'd get her eventually.'

Ellie shook her head. What faith she had. 'But Jeff and Mother? That's horrid, Charlotte.'

Charlotte shrugged. 'She and I never had anything in common. We never even liked each other. Why should I care? It means nothing to me.'

What did mean something to Charlotte? Ellie realised that she'd changed. She'd have to get to know her all over again.

'Was it she who told you?' It was falling into place for Ellie. Olivia's hand in their lives. Destroying instead of caring. Resenting every happiness.

Charlotte nodded. 'And she enjoyed every minute of it.'

'Oh, God.' Ellie put her hands over her face, but Charlotte gently pulled them away. 'Don't. I haven't seen you for so long. Don't feel bad any more. I don't want you to.'

Ellie looked at her. Had Charlotte really forgiven her? She thought of Jeff. 'Did he leave you when you were pregnant? What a bastard.'

'No.' Charlotte pulled her forward. 'Calm down. You still don't get it, do you? It was my decision. I didn't want him here. Don't you see? Jeff never belonged here.'

'And you do.'

'And I do.' Charlotte seemed about to elaborate, but changed her mind.

'But you must be lonely.' Ellie looked around at all the familiar parts of Pencraig. She glanced towards the wood. She couldn't wait to go there.

Charlotte smiled. 'It's a lonely kind of place. But I could never leave. I love it. I could never live in a town again. Too many bricks, not enough trees.' She was standing very upright, her deeply tanned arms and legs a striking contrast to the white dress she was wearing. She did belong here. She was embedded in the very spirit of the place.

'I can understand that.' Even walking round the garden, Ellie could feel it seeping into her mind again, into her body, the peculiar atmosphere that was Pencraig.

'How do you manage—?' She hesitated. 'For money, I mean.'

Charlotte laughed. 'This and that. There's some hens out back – I sell the eggs. We grow our own vegetables. I do bits of washing and ironing for people in the village, a couple of private French lessons a week. There's nothing to pay on the house – we manage pretty well.'

Ellie nodded. It sounded wonderful.

'And you?' They stopped to sit on the bench, watching the two girls playing on the lawn. Alex was making a daisy chain.

'I'm lucky. The wine bar made a lot of money for me. Sarah invested hers in a café in France, and I can just about live off the interest of what I've got left. And I still write songs.' She didn't feel lucky. She felt sad.

Charlotte nodded. 'And have you found another man to love?'

Ellie hesitated. She thought of David. 'There is a man. I'm fond of him, he's a good friend. But— He's not a man to love. Not for me anyway.'

'Are you lonely too?' Charlotte's words were charged with meaning. And there was a plea in the hazel eyes that Ellie responded to instinctively.

She took her hand. 'Oh, yes. I'm lonely too.'

Charlotte put her arm around Ellie's slim shoulders. The touch was warm, pressing into her. 'I've missed you, Ellie,' she said. 'It's not just shared childhood memories, is it?'

The tears came unexpectedly to Ellie's eyes. 'You know it's not.' She could feel the frustration, the anger, punching away at her ribcage. 'Why didn't you ever contact me?' she cried. 'Why did you make me wait so long, Charlotte?' She pulled away from her. 'Jesus, if I hadn't come here today, I'd still be waiting, wouldn't I?'

'I tried to phone you yesterday.' Charlotte frowned. 'I tried to phone you lots of times.' Her face was sad. 'But pride takes a lot of healing.' Then she brightened. 'It was odd, seeing you at the gate like that, almost as if I was expecting you.'

'Yeah. Sure. You tried really hard.' Ellie rubbed at her eyes. 'I know it was unforgivable. But he'd come between us anyway. I only wanted to be closer to you. That's how it started.'

'First of all I wanted to punish you.' Charlotte spoke as if she were in a dream. 'You and Jeff. And then after that, I wasn't sure. If you could shatter what you and I had so easily, then I wondered if it was worthless to you.'

Ellie sighed. 'Come on, Charlotte. You must have known that wasn't true.' She thought about it. The opposite was true. 'Maybe I held on too tightly. Maybe I made it shatter. But I always loved you. I loved you too much. It was you who broke away from it. It was you who betrayed it.' Ellie took a deep breath. Old resentments that had never quite gone away. 'You even showed Jeff the bivouac.'

Charlotte laughed. Tenderly she lifted a few strands of Ellie's fair hair, glinting like gold in the sun. 'It's grown though, hasn't it?'

Ellie tried to turn away, but Charlotte was touching her cheek with soft fingertips, smoothing her hair from her temples. Easing away the pain. Speaking in an urgent whisper. 'Oh, sure, I tried to break away. But I didn't get very far. You were always there holding me back.' Her tone changed, and she stretched her long brown legs out lazily in front of her.

'I regretted showing him our hideaway. I shouldn't have done that. Maybe I was trying to make it not matter so much. I was involved in my first relationship with a man, don't forget. And you were screwing it up.' She nudged Ellie. 'I couldn't even have an orgasm with Jeff when you were in the house.' Her eyes widened.

They burst into schoolgirl giggles. 'I couldn't either,' Ellie told her. 'I was afraid you might hear me.'

They stared at each other, shocked at what they were saying, conscience-stricken at treating so lightly what had always seemed so important in the past.

'Listen to us,' Charlotte whispered in her ear. 'What do we sound like?'

'We sound wicked. Our parents would be ashamed of us.' Ellie's voice had a mocking ring to it. And she was glad. She could say anything to Charlotte now that Jeff no longer stood between them. Just like she always used to in the past.

'I'm ashamed of them.' Charlotte pulled a face. 'Of Mother, anyway.'

'Will Jeff be happy with Mother?' It seemed impossible for Ellie to believe.

'Of course not. She'll destroy him.' Charlotte's voice was matter-of-fact. She'd always known Olivia much better than Ellie had. Ellie had been a fool to consider that she understood Mother's motives.

'Like she destroyed Dad.' Ellie rested her head on Charlotte's shoulder. It fitted perfectly. This was like coming home.

'You don't know the half of it,' Charlotte murmured. 'She didn't destroy us though.'

'She had a bloody good try.'

There was a strange silence between them.

'Will you come back here to live, Ellie?' The question hung in the air.

Ellie closed her eyes. 'I don't have a choice.' Her voice was soft. 'I belong here. I always did.'

Charlotte smiled, resting her hand on Ellie's arm.

Alex came up to the bench. 'Can I take Sophie into the woods?' she asked. 'Just for a few minutes? I'll look after her.'

Charlotte nodded. 'Fancy a swim?' She smiled at Ellie. 'I think those two are on their way to Dragon Bay.'

Ellie nodded, watching the smooth relaxed movements of Charlotte's tall, brown body as she ran inside the house with an animal grace. Then she turned to watch the two girls scampering down the garden, through the gate, up the path, Alex keeping a very tight hold of Sophie's hand. One dark, one fair. One of them always the leader.

'Wait for us!' she called.

'Do you think they'll find the clearing?' Charlotte reappeared. 'I had a bonfire there myself a while back.'

Ellie eyed her curiously. 'More to the point, will they find the bivouac?'

'Ah, yes.' Charlotte took her arm and they strolled towards the wood. 'They've got plenty of time for that,' she said. 'We haven't finished with it yet. But about the bivouac— You'll never guess who built it.'

'Who?'

Charlotte winked mysteriously.

'Come on. Tell.' Ellie laughed.

'Well. It was like this—' And as they walked through the wood towards Dragon Bay, Charlotte bent her dark head closer to Ellie's fair one, to tell her the sad, romantic story of how hearts had been lost at Pencraig in some other long-lost summer.